Vivian Randall

She grew up in Philadelphia's slums and, as a lady's maid in a wealthy family, learned manners and breeding. Later she'd become a wealthy businesswoman and learn the meaning of self-respect and independence. . . .

Brian Mallory

A big, handsome political boss determined that his new mansion be graced by the beautiful Vivian

Jamie Fitzhugh

An artist, traveling in pursuit of the perfect photograph

Clinton Webb

The attractive young scion of one of Philadelphia's first families

Max Delacey

A self-made millionaire with a string of shops in New York, he appreciates the life Vivian has carved for herself

VIVIAN
OF CAVENDISH SQUARE

KATHRYN DOUGLAS

BALLANTINE BOOKS • **NEW YORK**

Library of Congress Catalog Card Number: 81-22867

ISBN 0-345-28923-4

Printed in Canada

First Edition: August 1982

To D.H.E.

Part I

1

"It suits me," said the girl standing before the pier glass in the flickering gaslight.

"Humpf! Suits you, does it?" responded the woman, not bothering to look up from the hem she was turning, muttering around the pins clamped between her lips.

"Indeed it does. As good as her, I think."

"Well, she's the one to be wearing it."

As though I don't know, thought the girl, suddenly aware of the stifling heat that lay upon the city of Philadelphia on this April evening in the year 1904, of the shabbiness of the little front parlor that housed her mother's dressmaking establishment, of the knife-sharp pain that shot across her narrow young shoulders when, as now, she was very tired.

From her perch on the small fitting platform, she looked down at her mother, who sank back on her heels and said, "There now, Vivvie, turn round a mite and let me be pinning the sides."

Vivian Randall inched around.

The dress was a saffron yellow voile, a tea gown with leg-of-mutton sleeves, the top a wonder of the tiniest pleats and stitches, the waist nipped in smaller than the span of a man's hand, the full, filmy skirt cascading to the floor.

Her mother had cut it to a Butterick pattern, but its inspiration was pure Charles Dana Gibson. It was a Gibson girl dress made in the popular Gibson girl style of the day, and perfection for a willowy young woman with slender neck and a shining mass of red-gold hair. In short, for just such a young woman as Vivian Randall herself.

"I love it," she breathed.

"Yes, it's pretty," said her mother.

"It's beautiful," said the girl yearningly. "I wish you'd make something this pretty for me."

"It's your wedding dress I should be making."

Vivian's heart skipped a beat. "Not yet."

"Not yet, is it? And what would you be waiting for, then?"

What she was waiting for was Jamie Fitzhugh. But he had said more than once that he wouldn't ask her to marry him until he had a little money in hand from the invention he was working on at odd hours in Morrissey's blacksmith shop down the alley.

She didn't tell her mother this, however. "I've time yet to get married," she said.

"Not to a man like Mallory, you haven't. Don't think you can dally with him as you do with others. He's a man, not a boy, and used to having his way."

Vivian didn't doubt this for one moment. A person could tell Brian Mallory was used to having his way just by watching him stride into a room. For one thing, likely as not he would be the tallest man in it. For another, he was bound to be expensively dressed, although he wore his fine clothes so carelessly as to seem unaware of them. On top of this, he possessed the cocky assurance that comes of being petted and admired by all the world or at least that part of it situated in South Philadelphia and bounded by St. Bonaventure's Roman Catholic Church on the north, O'Reilly's Food Market on the south, Muldoon's Funeral Parlor on the east, and the Tipperary Saloon on the west.

The Tipperary Saloon, with its great green shamrock swinging in the breeze above the door, belonged to Brian Mallory. It boasted so good a business, especially on Saturday nights, that its owner had never been known to sully his hands wiping off tables for the ladies or drawing a draft of beer behind the polished mahogany bar.

But Brian Mallory could usually be found on the premises. Handsome, with brilliant blue eyes, a cleft in his chin, and a diamond stickpin in his tie, he was always available, always willing to escort a person into the back room behind the bar and there discuss the need of a job or a loan.

Vivian Randall had never visited this back room, although she had heard many tales of its luxury: the thick Chinese rug on the floor, Mallory's desk that was six feet long, and the wall of fake bookshelves that could swing back at a touch to reveal the safe hidden behind.

But she knew, as did everyone else who lived between Butler and Bryce streets, that no one had ever gone into that back room and come away empty-handed. She knew, too, that once you received a favor from Mallory, you did things his way.

"They say his new house is a wonder," said Mrs. Randall, squinting up at her daughter, taking the pins out of her mouth the better to make herself heard. "Mrs. Duffy was after telling me when I met her on the church steps coming out of the six-thirty only this morning. Her Tom did all the plastering, don't y' know. Scrolls on the ceilings, roses, cupids. Oh, a wonder she says it is."

"Everyone says it's a wonder," observed Vivian. Indeed, since last year when Mallory had begun to build what Vivian privately considered a monstrosity on the corner of Butler and Pierce, people seemed to talk of nothing else.

Once upon a time she, also, would doubtless have considered it a wonder, with its bright yellow brick facade and red-and-white-striped awnings. But for the past three years, from the day, in fact, of her fifteenth birthday, she had been in the service of Dr. C. Alden Webb and his family on Cavendish Square, a circumstance that had changed her in countless ways and altered her perceptions of style and good taste forever.

"It's all wrong, you know," she said now.

"All wrong, is it?" replied her mother indignantly. "And what might be all wrong about it?"

"Why, everything. In the first place, why would anyone build a mansion on Butler Street? It's surely not the proper location for such a thing. And it's so big. What does Brian Mallory want with a house the size of that? Except to show off. And that's it, it is. All just for show, like that diamond stickpin he wears in his tie."

Until this moment Vivian hadn't realized how provoked she was by Brian Mallory's vulgar display of wealth. She didn't pause to consider that he never failed to be the soul of refinement when in her company. If anything, his extravagant courtesy quite got on her nerves for she sometimes surprised a dancing glint in his eyes that made her feel he was secretly mocking her own impeccable deportment, acquired by diligent observation of the way things were done on Cavendish Square.

"And why shouldn't he be building his house wherever it suits him?" demanded her mother. "He's not giving himself airs and thinking Butler Street is no longer good enough for him, like some I know. And you can be sure he's planning to fill it up with fine sons and daughters who will

never want for a thing. They'll wear fine clothes and go to
fine schools. And his wife, whoever she's lucky enough to
be, will have silks and furs and servants, and her own little
runabout."

"Let her!" retorted Vivian feelingly, for since the day
three weeks ago when she had turned eighteen and her
mother had given Brian Mallory permission to come courting, never had Vivian grown so weary of anything as the
ever-growing list of luxuries that awaited his fortunate
wife.

"Let her, is it?" asked her mother, jabbing pins into the
hem of the skirt. "It could be you, if only you'd give him
encouragement. It could be you walking around in the garden and taking your ease on the porch. But he won't hang
around with his hat in his hand forever, waiting for you to
make up your mind."

Vivian's heart dipped. Her mind had been made up from
the moment she had first clapped eyes on Jamie Fitzhugh
when he came to work as Morrissey's backhander two
years ago. But her struggling young life had been lived too
close to the raw edge of poverty to permit her to lightly
regard Brian Mallory's suit.

What could she not do if she became his wife! Her green
eyes with their flecks of gold traveled over the small cluttered room. So much was needed. The stained walls were
hopelessly begrimed with the dust and dirt of decades. Bits
of colored thread were trodden into the worn carpet, and
bins overflowed with odds and ends of fabric. The sewing machine stood open as it had as far back as Vivian
could remember, and under the bright, brave, new flowered coverlet her mother had made, the old mohair sofa
sagged badly.

But the room could look quite pretty if it were freshly
papered with a delicate floral print, perhaps something on
the order of the pattern Irene Webb had chosen to adorn
the morning room in Cavendish Square. In her mind's eye,
Vivian could see a small and elegant divan replacing the
sofa, and a bright new rug on the floor.

Oh, if only one had money, there were so many things
one could do!

She might, for instance, see to it that her sister, Mary
Claire, attended the conservatory as she deserved instead of
playing the piano and selling sheet music in Lawson's Music Store. And ten-year-old Bucky might well go to college

when he grew up. As for Neil. . . . she caught her breath at the thought of this favorite. With just a little financial assistance Neil could become the great writer he was meant to be instead of clerking fourteen hours a day in O'Reilly's grocery store and too frequently drowning his sorrows at the Tipperary Saloon.

A shiver trembled through her. When she thought this way, it sometimes seemed as though she must marry Mallory after all—as though she were doomed. It was perhaps because of this that she said defiantly, "I don't care for him at all."

"That will come," said her mother.

"It won't!" she burst out, infuriated by the placid assurance. "How can I ever feel about him the way I feel about—"

She stopped abruptly, wishing the words back, while at her feet, her mother crouched above the hem of the dress.

"I know who it is you've set your heart on," said Mrs. Randall balefully. "I know it's Jamie Fitzhugh you're after. You're addled by him and his talk of inventions just as I was by your father's grand schemes when I was a girl. Don't think I don't know."

Vivian made no answer. She adored the handsome, eternally optimistic gentleman who was her father, despite the misery endured by his family because of his ill-fated dreams.

Nothing he had ever turned his hand to had met with success. Hopes for promising enterprises, plans to achieve partnerships with the wealthy and famous, proposals to make millions on the ideas that teemed through his busy brain: all came to nothing in the end. Even his present sojourn in the West, where he had gone to investigate what he declared to be "the glorious new cattle industry," had resulted only in a lowly job on a ranch, from which he sent home assurances of future thousands, accompanied by a few dollars every now and again.

But for her mother's skill at dressmaking, heaven only knew what might have become of them all. One of Vivian's earliest memories was of falling asleep at night to the relentless clickety-click of the sewing machine in the cramped little front room.

Jamie Fitzhugh, however, with his dark eyes burning like coals in his angular face, with his grim, determined mouth and jutting jaw, shared nothing whatever that Vivian could see with the improvident Edward Randall.

"Jamie isn't like papa," she ventured now, for she longed for the approval of this fierce, spare woman who had always been the mainstay and bulwark of her life. "He doesn't take chances. He studies things and thinks them through. And he never lets things stand in his way. You wait. You'll see."

"I'll wait and see your best chance slip away, my lady. I'll wait and see Brian Mallory walk up the aisle with some other bride. Miss Dolly Muldoon, like as not. She's always had her cap set for him, sure, everyone knows that. And," added her mother slyly, "she'll look like a flower tomorrow in this pretty dress."

"Who cares how she'll look?" demanded Vivian, for Dolly Muldoon had ever been a cross to bear. All her life Vivian had been made to stand on this wretched platform so that her mother could pin up the clothes that Dolly Muldoon would wear. Oh, the aching hours of fittings, only to see all the pretty things on Dolly's disdainful, ramrod-stiff back! Truly, the *one* real pleasure Vivian could conceive in marrying Brian Mallory would be in cutting this haughty young woman out.

"There now, it's done," said her mother with a final tug at the skirt. "You can be taking it off."

"In a little while."

Her mother frowned. "I'll not have you throwing yourself around in it."

"I'll stand perfectly still."

"You'll be getting it sweaty."

"Not if I stand perfectly still."

She was glad when her mother left the room. It was easier to pretend when she was alone, easier to imagine herself in some such place as the ballroom of the Webb house on Cavendish Square, with hansom cabs drawing up to the lighted front doorway, and violins playing, and perhaps young Clinton Webb inviting her to dance.

Enraptured with the pretty dress, with the pretty girl in the mirror, she began to sway ever so gently. Standing before the pier glass, oblivious to the hot night, to the shabby room, to the pain that streaked across her shoulders; heedless of the ever-present footsteps of pedestrians outside just under the open window, she hummed and swayed and slowly spun around.

"And might I be having the next, or is it promised?" inquired a voice, and her half-closed eyes flew open to discover Brian Mallory at the window.

She had no idea how long he had been watching as she turned dreamily this way and that, but the gleam in his eye told her he had found her behavior amusing, and indignation seized her. "Brian Mallory, you're no gentleman," she told him, unable to think of anything more scathing to say.

"Am I not, then?" he replied unchastened, and before she knew quite what was happening he bounded up the front steps, pushed open the old screen door, and swept her into his arms.

> *"Meet me in St. Louis, Louis,*
> *Meet me at the Fair . . ."*

Like everything else about him, his voice made up in volume what it lacked in quality. But she had no time to make this observation, for he whirled her about the room, barely letting her toes touch the floor, hugging her to him so tightly she could scarce catch a breath. Never had she felt arms so strong nor a lead so sure, and for all she meant to protest, her heart fluttered deliciously.

Dipping and turning, derby hat cocked at a rakish angle, Brian Mallory swung round and round while she clung to him, lips parted, forgetful of the new dress, a strange, surging sweetness surprising her when her legs chanced to brush his.

Then, of a sudden, her heel caught in the hem of the skirt, and there was a sickening rip.

Too overcome with remorse even to speak, Vivian inspected the damage. The dress had ripped from the waist and was torn in a long, jagged line through rows of shirring. How many weary hours had her mother spent on the tiny delicate stitches?

Raising stricken, tear-filled eyes to Brian Mallory, she whispered, "It's ruined."

"Surely not? Surely it can be mended?" Gently, as though it were the most precious thing in all the world, he took the skirt in his hands and frowned down at the rent in it.

"She won't be able to ask full price for it," said Vivian hopelessly. "Not now."

His eyes met hers, and she noticed for the first time how steely blue they were. "It's not yours, then?"

She shook her head. "It's for Dolly. Dolly Muldoon. To wear to your house exhibition tomorrow."

A smile lit his face. "For Miss Muldoon, is it? Well, then, no harm's done at all, for that little lady already has more dresses than she'll ever wear."

"But the money!" cried Vivian distractedly, marveling at how obtuse those could be who had plenty of it.

"Ah, yes," he said quickly. "But of course I mean to pay up. Sure, I'd never let your mom suffer after me causing the accident and being at fault. How much might such a gown cost?"

Vivian could scarcely believe the huge roll of notes that appeared as if by magic from his pocket—nothing less than a five, and most of them twenties and tens. Mesmerized, she stared at them, unable to say a word.

"How much, Miss Randall? Is one hundred enough?"

One hundred! In the honor of God, did the man believe a woman's gown could cost that? Whoever he married would lead him a merry chase if he didn't wise up. "Twenty-five," she told him, pitying such ignorance. "Twenty-five is more than enough."

He frowned. "Are you sure now? I was pricing some gowns from Paris just the other day. They were one hundred and fifty for the least of them."

Jolted once more, she frowned at him. Where in the world had he been pricing Paris gowns? And why? She wasn't quite sure what this surprising information implied, but she didn't approve. "Twenty-five is quite enough," she said stiffly, and with a sharp eye silently counted the bills as he peeled them off and laid them in the pink and white palm of her hand. Then, with a courteous respect due the customer he now had become, she said, "If you'll just take a seat on the sofa, I'll mend it and be wrapping it up."

"I'd as lief you keep it."

"But you've paid for it!" she cried, almost adding a deferential "sir."

"And what would I do with a dress such as that? Besides, it becomes you. The color is better for you than for Miss Muldoon."

A smile tilted her small, full lips, for she thought so, too. Really, he was being very nice.

"Thank you," she said. And, striving to match such commendable behavior, added in her most cultivated tone: "I shall wear it tomorrow to your *soirée*."

"Please do," he replied with a small bow. "And may I have the honor and privilege of escorting you?"

She looked at him keenly then, spying the dancing little smile that tugged at his lips.

Oh, she had been right in the first place. For all his money, he was ignorant and had no idea how real ladies and gentlemen behaved. It gave her pleasure to say, "I'm going with Jamie Fitzhugh."

If she had expected this to dash his spirits, she was mistaken. He merely lifted an eyebrow inquiringly. "Oh? He'll not be on his way by then?"

"On his way?" she faltered, for she knew of no journey.

"Why, he's off to the grand Exposition in St. Louis. He's thinking to sell his invention there."

She knew Jamie was desperate to get to the Louisiana Purchase Exposition, as the St. Louis World's Fair was called. A camera craze had swept the country. Mr. Eastman's boxlike little Kodak let everyone take a picture simply by pressing a button, and with a seemingly insatiable desire to preserve the present for posterity, almost everyone did. Photographic development, however, was still less than perfect, and with a zeal that at times struck Vivian as almost fanatical, Jamie Fitzhugh had set out to test a few theories of his own in the small shack attached to Morrissey's blacksmith shop. Working early in the morning and late into the night, on Sundays, and whenever else he could steal the time, he experimented with emulsion techniques and formulas until at last he showed her a picture he had taken of her.

"I've even entitled it," he said, a rare note of self-approval in his voice. "It's called 'Vivvie in White.' I'll never part with it."

The photograph had been taken beside the giant forsythia bush that burst into bloom and camouflaged, each spring, the privy in the Randalls' narrow backyard. Borrowing some sheer white crêpe de chine that her mother always kept on hand for underthings, Vivian had pinned and drapped the fabric about her in the Grecian style favored by the dancer Isadora Duncan. One smooth, rounded shoulder bare, hair done up in Grecian curls, she posed barefoot by the forsythia, and the play of fragile light, the shadow of her legs through the sheer folds of drapery, and something arching and ardent in the pose combined to form an impression both luminous and hauntingly seductive.

Technically the development of the shot proved a marked advance over other methods of processing, and now Jamie talked of nothing but the St. Louis Exposition, where he might find a chemical firm that would back him, if only he could afford to stay there awhile.

"But he has no money," she told Mallory now, thinking, There it is, money again.

"He has. I've made him a sizable loan."

Her mouth dropped open in surprise. "Why, that was most kind."

"I didn't do it for kindness. I've no doubt he's on to a good thing. He brought his pictures to the Tipperary; showed me the results he's been getting, showed me the one he took of you."

" 'Vivvie in White,' yes. It proves his method perfectly."

"I don't care what it proves," snapped Mallory so vehemently that she started. "He's no call to be showing it around from hand to hand. No man who respected a woman would do that."

His words both astonished and incensed her, for the photograph was merely an experiment in light and shadow, as anyone would know, and had nothing whatever to do with Jamie Fitzhugh's regard. It was Brian Mallory who had read something quite different into it, making her blush to think those compelling ice-blue eyes had rested upon it at all.

But she forgot her displeasure in the thought of the loan—the *sizable* loan—he had made. It was all they had ever needed, Jamie and her. Just a bit of money to give them their start. Now, thanks to Mallory, they had it at last.

No sooner had he departed by the front door than Vivian left by the back, running down the alley with wings on her heels.

2

Morrissey's blacksmith shop loomed large in the soft darkness. Its door was propped open, and from deep within, a flickering light still glowed in the forge.

Hurrying by, Vivian could feel its hot breath on her face and smell the familiar odor of charcoal. How often she had come this way, seeking Jamie. But now everything was changed. The St. Louis Exposition with its lights and fountains and grand possibilities lay before them, no longer just a glittering dream but as real as the railroad tracks that would carry them there, as real as the price of the two tickets they now could afford.

Beyond the blacksmith shop the door to Jamie's quarters stood open, and a light burned there. Breathless, she caught herself up in the doorway, an exotic yellow moth fluttering into the small, hot room.

Jamie looked up in surprise from the box he was packing. "Vivvie!" he cried.

She clasped her hands and laughed softly. "Mallory stopped by."

He smiled. Never had she thought him handsome. He was somehow too unfinished, too rawboned, and there was an unsettling air of tension about him that could put people off. Like a leashed tiger, her brother Neil had once said of him, and it was true that there was something edgy and extreme in his manner, something held under tight control.

But now his dark eyes glowed. "Then you know."

"Oh, Jamie. I'm so happy I could die!"

She ran to him then and he caught her in his arms, sweeping her off her feet, whirling her around. But when, after kissing her soundly, he set her down, she looked up at him shyly, thinking that soon he would be her husband, that there would be more than kisses now.

"How much did he give you?" she asked.

Jamie grinned. "Two thousand."

13

Vivian's heart all but stopped. Two thousand dollars. Why, it would keep them for two years. "So much," she gasped.

He nodded. "Thurman Foy lent me his money belt," he said, and pulled up his white shirt to show her the bulging piece of canvas about his waist. "I can't be taking chances 'til I get to St. Louis and put it in a bank."

"Yes, indeed," she agreed, observing now that he wore his best blue serge trousers, that he had made great inroads into his packing. Orange crates stood about, some filled with the secondhand books that had given him his only education in chemistry, others containing the bottles of emulsifiers and fluids that had once lined the rough wooden shelves of the small room.

Seeing such progress, she felt the need for haste assail her. "When does the train leave?"

He moved to the blue serge vest that hung by a nail on the wall, and consulted his pocket watch. "In exactly one hour and forty-five minutes."

Vivian sucked in her breath. "One hour and forty-five minutes. Dear God!"

Smiling, he came and took both her hands in his. "I was just about on my way up the street to see you. To tell you the luck of it and say good-bye."

"Say good-bye?"

"Thurman Foy and Morrissey will take me to the station. Thurman will be coming along in his milk wagon in about an hour. It all happened so fast, don't y' know? Mallory coming by tonight to give me the loan. My ticket, too. He gave me my ticket, would you believe? Said he knew I'd more than make it up to him. And that I will. That I will and no mistake."

She heard every word he said. Standing before him, she heard and would remember forever every word. But at the moment she didn't take in their meaning.

"Am I not to come with you, then?"

She saw the light leave his eyes. He took a step back, raising both hands. "Not . . . not now. Not right away."

Cold sweat prickled out on her forehead, and a presentiment of disaster seized her. "When, then?"

"I don't know. I'll . . . I'll be in touch. I'll send for you."

"When?"

"I said I don't know!"

He ran a hand through his dark hair. "Look, Vivvie
. . . please try to understand. I'll have so much to do when
I get out there, so many people to see. And I don't rightly
know how to go about things. I don't know anything about
St. Louis; where to live . . . anything at all."

Her brow cleared and a trembling smile broke upon her
lips. She had forgotten his cautious nature. Naturally he
would have qualms. But life was full of practical problems,
and she was used to facing them.

"I'll help you!" she cried. "Oh yes, Jamie, I can help
you. You needn't concern yourself at all with such things.
Believe me," she assured him, "I can find a little place for
us, fix it up. Oh, you've no idea all the things I can do. I
won't be a burden, not at all. Quite the contrary." she paused
and, with all the fervor and love in her heart, stated the
one thing in the world she most wanted to do. "I'll make
things nice for you."

With a surge of joy she saw her last words draw a smile.
Raising a hand, he brushed back a lock of her hair. "Vivvie," he murmured. "I think I know how nice you could
make things for me, for any man. But wouldn't it be better
to wait a while? Let me come back and be married here?
Will you really want to be giving up a wedding at St. Bonaventure's?" He paused and then added, "Think of your
mom. What will your mom say?"

"I can't think of her," she replied swiftly, for something
deep within her, something beyond reason, knew that when
Jamie left he wouldn't come back to be married at St. Bonaventure's. No, nor send for her, either. He would hesitate
and waver and end up not marrying her at all.

"She doesn't like me," he said darkly.

"She doesn't know you. She doesn't know how clever you
are. But Mallory does. That's why he gave you all that
money. And someday she'll know, too. The whole world
will know."

He laughed aloud. She had always been able to raise his
spirits, jolly him along. She laughed, too, unaware of her
high-spirited, infectious self-confidence, of how goldenly
beautiful she was.

Shaking his head, Jamie said, "You won't even have a
wedding gown."

She knew she had won, then, and that there wasn't a

moment to lose. She would, she told him hurriedly, be back at Morrissey's in less than an hour. Neil would be home. He would help with her bags.

Jamie readily agreed, both of them understanding it would be best if he didn't come by the house for her, both of them knowing Mamie Randall was there.

They were all in the kitchen when Vivian flung open the back screen door and burst in upon them: Neil home from O'Reilly's Food Market, Bucky in from play, Mary Claire just back from choir practice.

The kitchen smelled of lemons and her mother stood at the sink stirring a pitcher of lemonade. Neil sat at the oilcloth-covered table, chair tipped back; Bucky sucked on a chip of ice. They would have a glass of lemonade and a doughnut or two and then go to bed, the same as any other night.

But this wasn't the same, and Vivian gazed at them, drinking in small details: the square set of Bucky's shoulders, the pale, poetic cast to Neil's face, Mary Claire's cloud of raven-black hair.

They looked back at her in surprise, sensing something different about her, taking in the feverishly bright green eyes, the heaving bosom, the beautiful dress.

Mamie Randall recovered first. "What!" she cried. "You've gone running about in that dress?" Her eyes widened in disbelief, and letting her spoon fall with a clatter, she swept across the room. "And you've torn it!" she gasped, taking up the skirt. "Yes, torn it you have."

"It doesn't matter," Vivian assured her, astonishing herself, astonishing them all by a frivolous giggle.

"And you laugh?"

With effort Vivian forced down the urge to hysteria that bubbled to her lips. "Mallory paid for it," she managed.

"What!"

"Mallory paid for the dress, mama. He was dancing with me and I stepped on it and so he paid for it. But that doesn't matter. I'm getting married."

The mistaken happiness that flooded her mother's face swept all inclination to hysteria aside. "Not to Mallory, mama," she said quickly. "To Jamie Fitzhugh. Mallory lent him two thousand dollars to sell his invention at the Fair. He's leaving on the train for St. Louis in an hour. I'm going with him, mama. We'll be married there."

Her mother stared at her in stunned disbelief and then shook her head. "No," she whispered.

"Yes, mama! Yes!" cried Vivian. "You can't stop me, nobody can. I'm going to St. Louis with Jamie. I only came home to get my things. To say good-bye to . . . to all of you."

She looked around appealingly at the startled faces, but her brothers, her sister spoke not a word. Nor did she expect them to. She was the only one who had ever stood up to their mother. She was the favorite. This they all knew.

She turned back to her mother. "Please give me your blessing, mama. Please wish me well."

"How can I wish you well when I know you're ruining your life going off with that man?"

"I'm not ruining my life. I love him. You don't understand."

"I understand well enough. I understand you're throwing yourself at him, going off this way. Why else would you be doing it? Why wouldn't you be waiting a bit and having a proper wedding here at St. Bonnie's? Why so fast? Just answer me that, my lady. Why so fast?"

Vivian made no reply. With uncanny accuracy her mother had put her finger all too near the mark. But it wasn't really like that. Jamie loved her, oh, he did! He was merely hesitant, cautious, as became a scientific man.

Someday her mother would understand.

Neil beside her, carrying her quickly gathered belongings in a battered old trunk, Vivian hastened back down the alley to Morrissey's.

Her mother hadn't said good-bye. Bucky and Mary Claire had kissed her, shyly, self-consciously, for they weren't a family who kissed. But her mother was nowhere to be found. When, at the bottom of the scraggly yard, Vivian turned to look back for a last time, only Bucky and Mary Claire stood silhouetted at the door.

She almost weakened then. She almost thought it might be better to wait a bit and get married in St. Bonaventure's as she had always dreamed, with Father Shields at the altar, and candles glowing and bouquets of flowers tied with white ribbon at the end of the pews. But not for nothing had she been born under the sign of the ram, and with all the stubborn optimism of her Aries nature she clung to her decision, certain the time for Jamie and her was now.

It was this conviction that urged her footsteps forward
while Neil loped stolidly behind. And it was this conviction
of the rightness of what she was doing, of the fitness of
things, that made her look searchingly around the shack
when they reached it even after Morrissey said, "He ain't
here. He's gone."

"Gone?" she repeated.

Seated on an upturned orange crate, Morrissey smiled at
her bewilderment. He was a huge man, fat but strong, with
a thick neck and powerful arms. More than once Vivian
had watched with awe as he brought hammer down on an-
vil, sending sparks out of the red hot iron. But for all his
size and power, his eyes were small. Thurman took him off
in his milk wagon."

"I'm late, then?" The anguished, incredulous cry beat
against the walls.

"No, I wouldn't say you was late," said Morrissey. "I'd
say it was more like Jamie changed his mind."

3

"The bastard!" said Neil. *"The scurrilous cad!"*

"Hush, Neil," she told him. "It doesn't matter."

And incomprehensible though she would have found this
statement only moments before, it was now absolutely true.

Marching back down the alley, cheeks stinging with the
shame of it, she vowed silently she wouldn't marry Jamie
Fitzhugh if he were the last man on earth. Nor did it occur
to her that there was some humor in such a belated decision.

All the qualities she had previously viewed through the
tinted glasses of her infatuation appeared now in a different light. She saw that Jamie had never been appropriately
cautious, only timid; never single-minded, only selfish; less
reserved, than unfeeling and cold.

Had she desired proof, she need only hark back to the
cowardly, sneaking way he had departed, hurrying off in

Thurman Foy's milk wagon, leaving her to mortification at
Morrissey's hands. Stamped indelibly and forever behind
her eyelids was the smirk on Morrissey's face. She hadn't
the least doubt that by the last mass at St. Bonaventure's
tomorrow morning, all Butler Street would have learned of
her disgrace.

Oh, they would! Morrissey had always thought she gave
herself airs just because she tried to speak nicely and make
something of herself. As for that runty little Thurman Foy,
he had hated her from the moment two years ago when she
refused to dance with him at the Hibernian Fire Company's New Year's ball.

How they would love to spread this tale about her now!
Why, it was as bad as being left waiting at the altar. Worse,
she thought, fresh shame overwhelming her. Oh, much
worse, for, just as her mother said, hadn't she thrown herself at him?

"I'm not going in," she declared upon reaching the gate
in the Randall picket fence.

"Now, Vivvie," began Neil disapprovingly, but she flung
back her head and her eyes blazed up at him.

"No, I am not!" she repeated.

He looked at her helplessly. "Where will you go?"

"I'm not sure."

"What will I tell mom?"

At the pity in his eyes, fury welled up in her. She hated
everyone: Neil, with his sad eyes; her mother, with her
canny ones; Morrissey and Thurman Foy. But most of all,
she hated herself—Vivian Randall, who everyone knew
could have any beau on Butler Street, even Brian Mallory,
and who had been jilted by Jamie Fitzhugh.

"You may tell her I'm going for a walk," she said imperiously and, brushing past him, moved on down the alleyway.

In hot weather people on Butler Street didn't go to bed
until all hours, especially on Saturday nights. The brick
row houses with windows only in the front and the back
could be insufferable when heat and humidity clamped down
upon the city. In such weather, man, woman, and child
moved outside to sit on the cool marble front steps, hopeful
that a breath of air might stir the dusty leaves of the buttonwood trees that clung, here and there, to the edge of the
uneven brick sidewalks. Hopeful, too, of a bit of gossip as

they fanned themselves and drank pitchers of cold beer fetched up by a child sent running off to the Tip, as it was called.

It was to avoid the interested glances of neighbors that Vivian kept to the alleyway for all she hated it, with its broken-down picket fences, its foul-smelling privies, and, now and then, a rat or two. But she couldn't bear to meet people now, any more than she could bear to brave the look she was sure to spy in her mother's black eyes. *I told you so,* that look would say even if her mother uttered not a word. *I told you so. Throwing yourself at him. Making yourself small.*

Were it a bit earlier, she might have slipped into St. Bonaventure's. Confessions were heard until nine o'clock on Saturday nights. Nothing would be thought amiss if a young woman of the parish stepped inside to sit in the cool dark shadows with only the banks of votive candles blazing before statues of St. Bonaventure and Our Lady, and whispers coming from the confessionals at the back.

But the great carved wooden doors would be closed now and Father Shields back in his rectory. God himself, it seemed, had turned from her, knowing as He did her inmost thoughts: her vanity, her inordinate love of pretty things, her preference of elegant Cavendish Square to Butler Street, and the way she gave herself airs. Perhaps Jamie Fitzhugh had been sent of a purpose to humble her.

But the moment she thought this, she cast it aside. She had loved Jamie, oh, she had! And proved it, too; posing for pictures, listening for hours on end to chemical theories she couldn't understand, everlastingly praising and encouraging and jollying him along.

And he had repaid her by publicly deserting her, humiliating her so she could never hold up her head again. Oh, such a man deserved hellfire, and she fervently hoped he would see it! The pleasure she took in this prospect was brief, however, as it in no way diminished her own misery.

Added to this was the bitter stroke, having reached the end of the alley, of coming out on Butler and Bryce streets face to face with Dolly Muldoon.

"Why, it's Vivian Randall!" cried Dolly in surprise.

She stood under a street lamp in conversation with Thomas O'Reilly, at her back the cast-iron railing that protected the Muldoon Funeral Parlor and residence from contact with the world.

Until Mallory built his mansion, Muldoon's had been far and away the most imposing establishment in the neighborhood; even grief became circumspect when entering its front door. Fashioned of massive dark red square-cut stone, it was a source of local pride rather than envy, as was the Muldoon way of life.

Neither Mrs. Muldoon nor Dolly was expected by anyone to do a lick of work. Mrs. Muldoon devoted much of her time to the church, being president of the sodality, a member of the altar guild, and chairman of the annual spring bazaar. A markedly unattractive woman with bulbous nose and sallow complexion, she had produced a fairy tale creature in her only child, a confection of dimples, blue eyes, and curly blond hair whom she and her husband regarded in devoted awe.

Thus adored, Dolly had acquired everything in life that money could buy. But since this was not nearly all she wanted, there was a dissatisfied pout to her rosebud mouth and often a petulant frown between the blue eyes.

Under the light from the streetlamp these eyes now rested upon Vivian in amazed displeasure. "You're wearing my new dress!"

Having long since forgotten what she was wearing, Vivian looked down at herself in dismay.

"And very fetching it is, if I may say," said Thomas O'Reilly.

"Fetching!" cried Dolly. "Why, it's all bedraggled and dirty. Just look at the hem of the skirt. And it's torn! Torn!"

"Can't it be fixed?" asked Thomas.

Vivian gave him a grateful glance. She had always liked Thomas O'Reilly. At one time, before Jamie Fitzhugh, she had entertained a crush on him. It had been mutual, she knew. Indeed, from the way he was looking at her, it seemed he still retained a lively interest. It was a look she inspired in many a young man, and for all its rather silly, calflike expression, she could tell it was making Dolly Muldoon cross.

At one time Vivian would have guiltily relished this state of affairs. But all she could think of now was what Thomas O'Reilly would think—above all, what Dolly Muldoon would think if they knew about Jamie Fitzhugh. And by tomorrow, they *would* know. *Everyone* would know and be laughing at her. It was too much to bear, and two tears slid down her cheeks.

"Look, now, Dolly," said Thomas O'Reilly. "You're making her cry."

"And well she should, for she's spoiled my dress!" exclaimed Dolly, incensed by this reproof. "And if you think I'm going to pay for spoiled merchandise, Vivian Randall, you'd best think again. I'll not be giving your mother one cent, no matter how much you cry."

Instantly the tears vanished.

"Nor need you!" replied Vivian tartly. "It's already paid for, it is."

"Paid for! By whom?"

"By Brian Mallory, that's who. As a gift to me, since I'm to become his wife."

The words were out, shimmering and triumphant in the soft night air. They echoed in Vivian's ears, spun round her brain, while Dolly Muldoon and Thomas O'Reilly stared at her, dumbstruck, and over and over she thought: What have I done? Oh, what have I done?

Thomas broke the spell. Understanding dawned on his plain, open face, and he said, "Ah, ha! It's to be announced tomorrow, is it?"

"What?" asked Vivian numbly.

"Your engagement. It's to be announced tomorrow at Mallory's open house."

She made no reply, and taking her silence for coy assent, he turned to Dolly. "Well now, isn't it grand? Isn't it fine? Dolly, don't you be wishing your friend well?"

Watching tears fill the blue eyes, Vivian was overcome by remorse, and she stretched out a hand, knowing she must own up to the wicked lie. "Dolly," she began.

But Dolly flung the hand aside. "Don't touch me!" she cried. "You've seen that big house he's built and you want to live there, that's what it is. You don't love him. You don't care for him at all. You're just marrying him for his money, Vivian Randall. Just for his money, that's all."

"Dolly!" said Thomas O'Reilly sternly. "I refuse to stand here while you insult Vivian—"

"Ooooh!" wailed Dolly, turning on him. "Ooooh!" she cried again and, raising a hand, slapped him full across the mouth.

"Gol' darn, I sure don't know what's got into her," said Thomas as, hand to face, he watched Dolly hammer her feet up the wooden steps to her house and, as a final gesture, slam the front door.

"I hope," he continued, looking apologetically down at Vivian, "you won't let this mar your happiness."

Since he insisted upon it, saying it was getting late, Vivian let Thomas O'Reilly accompany her along Bryce Street.

She would have much preferred to be alone for, though she struggled like a mouse in a knothole with the dilemma into which she had plunged herself, it was impossible to really concentrate with Thomas going on and on.

He had been to Mallory's mansion only that afternoon, he told her, to deliver a grocery order for the grand spread there would be at the open house. He had only been in the kitchen, but what a vision it was! Bigger than any kitchen he had ever seen in his life, bigger, in fact, than most people's first floors, and with every modern convenience man could contrive.

"No doubt you'll find it a pleasure, Vivvie. No doubt at all. Though I guess you'll seldom see it, what with all the servants you'll have. How many do you mean to employ?"

"How many what?" replied Vivian distractedly.

"Servants. How many servants do you mean to employ?"

"I'm sure I don't know!"

Thomas nodded understandingly at this display of impatience. "Naturally you wouldn't, as yet. But isn't it luck you've worked at Cavendish Square and know how these things are done!"

"Yes," she said with real satisfaction, for in this Thomas O'Reilly was right. She did indeed know just how a fine house should be run. She had fallen in love with the Webb residence the moment she set foot in the door, and had paid the closest attention to every detail.

"A cook and a butler and a housekeeper," she said now. "They're the most important ones. And then an upstairs maid and a downstairs maid, and a lady's maid, of course . . ."

Her voice trailed off. At present she was a lady's maid, but married to Mallory she'd have one for herself! It was precisely what her mother had been saying these past weeks, but until this moment Vivian hadn't seriously considered such possibilities; no, not once.

Thomas glanced down at her. "I guess you'll go off on a fine wedding jaunt. Atlantic City, I would suppose?"

Atlantic City! What fun that would be! Her heart skipped a beat, and she choked.

"Forgive me!" cried Thomas. "I hope you'll overlook such an impertinent question as that. Wherever you go, I'm sure you'll be treated like the beautiful young lady you are."

There was respect, almost reverence, in his voice, and, when she looked up at him under her lashes, the most flattering admiration in his face.

How different from Morrissey's smirking little eyes! And with the comparison, her way became crystal clear. Marrying Mallory would solve everything! Oh, how she would love to see Morrissey when he learned she was to be Mallory's wife! Thurman Foy, too! And Jamie Fitzhugh, when he heard of it. Yes, Jamie Fitzhugh most of all. He had thought to make a laughingstock of her. But now, oh, now it was her turn!

A thrill rippled through her, and for the first time in her life, she tasted the heady sweetness of revenge.

"I must get to the Tipperary saloon," she said suddenly.

"Ah ha!" said Thomas. "A lovers' tryst?"

She made no answer but hurried on over the uneven brick sidewalk, clutching up her skirts in her hands, heedless of carriages and trolleys, of people on their front steps and Thomas O'Reilly at her side.

Sweat bathed her, standing on her forehead, making her clothes stick to her back, her legs. Having no handkerchief, she raised an arm and wiped off her flushed face with the sleeve of the saffron yellow dress. Her breath came in short gasps and her heart beat so rapidly she thought she must faint. What if Mallory didn't want to marry her? But he did, he did! He had asked her mother for permission to court her and had presented himself, together with flowers, fruit, or candy, whenever she was permitted home from Cavendish Square. Since this wasn't often, she hadn't spent much time in his company nor, now she thought of it, had she been especially nice to him, but this hadn't seemed to alter his determination that she should be his wife.

Clinging to this knowledge, she arrived ashen-faced and breathless at the Tipperary's swinging doors. From inside came the smell of beer and the din typical of Saturday night.

Even as a little girl, when Brian Mallory's father owned it, she had considered the Tipperary an abomination. She had seen men stumble out of its doors to fall down in the street as if dead. She had heard the drunken shouts and curses and the women's pleading tears and, worse, screams of pain, that frequently rang out from open windows on Saturday nights. And she had seen the ill-concealed bruises at mass on Sunday mornings and had known from whence they came.

"If it wasn't the Tip, it would be some other place," her mother once had said. "It's not the saloon that's to blame."

"But if it weren't so easy to come by, things might be better," Vivian had retorted. "That's what Mallory does. He makes it easy to get. He makes his money by making it easy."

Thomas O'Reilly held open the swinging door. "Are you not going in?"

"Yes," Vivian said.

Mallory's mother sat behind a table placed upon a platform just by the door. Except for Tuesday nights, when she went to St. Bonaventure's to make the novena, it was where she always sat, where she always *had* sat every night for the past twenty-five years.

Short, stocky, with coarse black hair pulled back into a large bun, she had worn only black bombazine since her husband died years ago. "Ma" Mallory she was called, although she was not in the least motherly, looking out over the crowd from her aerie with sharp gray eyes that never missed how many drinks the piano player had or which gentleman was becoming too obstreperous to keep around.

A flick of her eye to Solly, the bartender, and her will as if by magic was done.

Now Vivian stood before her, and something within her recoiled under the cold, keen gaze.

"Good evening," she all but whispered. "Could I speak to Mallory, please?"

Ma Mallory merely nodded and raised a plump index finger as her eyes shot over the heads of the crowd.

Seconds later, a waiter appeared.

"A visitor for my son."

"This way, Miss," he said.

* * *

Whether it was the errand she had come upon or her unfamiliar surroundings, Vivian couldn't have said, but as he rose from behind a huge desk to greet her, Brian Mallory looked somehow different to her. Her green eyes opened wide and she sucked in her breath in something like awe.

For his part, an interested amusement lit eyes that could change from cold blue steel to the sunniest of smiles. Tall, broad shouldered, and with a penchant for expensive clothes, he wore a brown-checked flannel sack suit whose style and pattern would have overcome a lesser man. A heavy gold chain from watch to fob pocket crossed the checked vest, gold cuff links winked from the sleeves of a high-collared green shirt, and a green silk four-in-hand tie was held in place by a diamond stickpin. Because of her sojourn on Cavendish Square Vivian knew the checks in the suit were so large as to be outlandish, and the green shirt and tie all wrong, but withal there was a sense of confident power about the man who wore them that the men of Cavendish Square didn't quite possess.

"Have a seat," said Mallory, and motioned to a large upright chair covered in leopard skin.

Vivian sank back upon the soft fur and grasped the carved mahogany arms with both hands.

Mallory studied her, his dark head cocked inquiringly to one side. Then: "You wanted to see me?"

"Yes," Vivian managed.

"About . . . ?"

She swallowed. So intent was she on reaching her destination that she had given little thought to what she might say once arrived, and consternation seized her. True, he had asked permission to come courting, but how in the world was she to get him to propose? And *tonight!*

"About . . ." she began. "About your open house tomorrow."

"Ah, yes," said Mallory, nodding his head encouragingly.

"I'm . . . I'm pleased to tell you I'll be happy to accept your kind offer to accompany me."

"But I thought you were going with Jamie Fitzhugh."

She took a deep breath. "Mr. Fitzhugh and I are no longer friends. I wish to have nothing further to do with that gentleman. The truth of the matter is . . ." She took another breath. Oh, hail Mary, full of grace! "The truth of the matter is, I prefer you."

"To Jamie Fitzhugh?"

"To . . . to all gentlemen."

She had made this confession staring at the tips of her scuffed and muddy shoes, but the silence that greeted it lasted so long that her eyes flew up to meet his.

"Why are you saying these things?" he demanded.

"Because . . ." she faltered weakly. "Because they're true."

"They are not true!"

Slamming both hands on his desk, he lunged toward her, sparks seeming to fly from his eyes. "You don't really know me, so how can you prefer me? Until this moment, you've scarce given me the time of day."

She couldn't deny this, nor could she think of a single word in self-defense. Her position was worse now than ever. Throwing herself first at Jamie Fitzhugh and now at Mallory. Oh, what would her mother say? And being abused and unfairly dealt with by both of them into the bargain!

At this thought, fire lit her eyes and she said scornfully, "You gave my mother to believe you wished to marry me!"

"And by heaven, so I do! But not this way."

"What way, then?" she cried out.

"In honesty and truth."

Honesty and truth. Dear God, what did the man mean? Did he mean she must love him first? But she never could. She would be his wife, run his house, even . . . yes, she must bear him children, she supposed. But love him? How could she? How could she ever again love any man?

"I don't love you," she said bluntly.

"That's more like it."

"More like it?" she repeated, thoroughly confused.

"I know you don't love me. I don't even believe you prefer me to other men; certainly not to Jamie Fitzhugh. I believe you still love Mr. Fitzhugh, but Mr. Fitzhugh loves only one thing—his inventions. I thought it was time you knew."

A chill settled over her. "What do you mean?"

"I mean my house is finished and I need a wife. I want you to be my wife because you're the best I can get, the top of the line, just like my house. But Jamie Fitzhugh stood in my way. Not because he loved you, but because you thought he did. I had to prove otherwise."

"That's why . . . that's why you gave him the loan?"

"And two tickets to St. Louis."

"Two?"

"One for you if he cared to take you."

Of a sudden the room swam, and Mallory seemed to waver back and forth before her eyes.

The next moment he was forcing a glass to her lips. "Drink," he said.

She murmured a protest, but he placed a firm hand on her brow and tilted her head. "Drink," he urged more gently, and she swallowed some brandy.

It burned going down but it revived her, and she looked up to meet his compelling eyes.

"I had to do it," he told her. "I had to make you see the way things were. That's as close to an apology as I'll ever come. And now I'd like to ask you to do me the honor of becoming my wife."

4

She stared at him.

It was what she wanted, what she had hoped for, hurrying along through the heat and the dust of Bryce Street with Thomas O'Reilly by her side. But she hadn't really expected it to happen, couldn't quite believe it even now.

"You want me to be your wife," she said.

"I do."

She hesitated, and in that moment, searing and sharp, came the recollection of the smirk in Morrissey's eyes. "Then I will," she said firmly, and held out her hand.

It didn't appear strange to her that they should shake hands. Certainly she never for one moment considered that such arrangements were usually sealed with a kiss. Indeed, it seemed quite appropriate that Mallory should return to his desk, seat himself, and draw toward him a pad of paper.

"Your full name?" he inquired.

"Vivian Mary Randall," she told him.

"Date of birth?"

"April the second, eighteen eighty-six."

"I would like us to be married as soon as possible, if that is agreeable. Three weeks to announce the banns. Say, the middle of May?"

"The middle of May will be fine."

"That's all for now," he said pleasantly, drawing a line across the paper. "Tomorrow morning I'll look in on your mom and ask for your hand. Then I'll drive you to church. After mass we'll have a word with Father Shields." He glanced up, fixing her with riveting blue eyes. "Might you be having any questions?"

Vivian shook her head wordlessly.

"Good enough, then. I'll just step outside and tell Bunty O'Hare I want him to see you home."

A young woman less favored with masculine attention, less accustomed to being sought out and fought over for just such a privilege as that of escorting her home, might have found nothing annoying in this arrangement. Being used to quite different treatment, Vivian rose and said chillingly, "I am quite capable of walking home alone."

There was a gleam in his eye. "Ah, but I won't hear of it," he protested with elaborate courtesy. "You are my fiancée and we must keep you safe and sound."

He went to the door, opened it, and, like Ma Mallory, raised a finger. Then he turned to her. "Come along, Miss Randall," he said, and off she went with Bunty O'Hare.

Though it was late, her mother was waiting up for her. Vivian had known she would be, but finding her tired-eyed and wearily waiting seemed only to increase the ill humor that had beset Vivian in Mallory's office and followed her home.

"I'm going to marry Mallory," she announced tersely, coming in the front door.

An old blue wrapper over her nightdress, Mamie Randall sat in a rocking chair and rocked back and forth. Under the chair a floorboard creaked in time to the tick of the clock on the wall. Two gas jets on either side of the pier glass had been turned low, obscuring the dingy flowered wallpaper, but despite the dim light the room was depressingly shabby, and stifling hot.

"That's good," Mamie Randall said.

At the placid response all the pain and frustration of the evening welled up in Vivian, and helpless tears stung her eyes. She felt trapped—by the wretched little room, by her mother's tiredness, above all, by the mystifying chain of events that had led her to accept Mallory. Beside herself, she burst out accusingly, "I hope you're happy. I just hope you're happy."

"Hush, now, girl. They're asleep upstairs." The voice was stern, used to authority, and the dark eyes in the thin, worn face fastened severely upon Vivian. "I'm happy if my children are happy."

A lifetime of dedication had proved this true, but at the burdensome reminder fury surged through Vivian. "Well, I'm not happy," she flung out almost triumphantly. "I'm not happy at all. I've never been more miserable in my life."

"Why are you marrying the man, then?"

"Because you want me to."

Her mother stopped rocking. "And that's a lie."

"It's not," cried Vivian, writhing in the vise of her unhappiness, longing to lay blame. "You've been after me and after me. It's just what you want me to do."

"But that's not why you are doing it. Don't tell me different. I know what goes on and I know the saints in heaven are after answering my prayers, for if Fitzhugh would have had you, why, you'd have gone off with that dreamer and ruined your life. As it is, you're the luckiest girl in the world."

Fresh pain struck Vivian's heart. That such pitiless desertion as Jamie's should have made her the luckiest girl in the world and that, into the bargain, it should be brought about by the saints in heaven in response to her mother's prayers, was such treachery on all sides that she was left speechless.

Into the silence her mother said, "Now listen, girl, and hear me out. You've gone and got yourself promised to a man who will take good care of you for the rest of your days. No one made you do this. You've done it of your own free will.

"I happen to think you're a lucky young woman and it's thanking the good Lord that I am. But what I think is neither here nor there. It's what you think that counts. It's the face you decide to put on it. And if you aren't ready to be a good wife to him, if you aren't willing to turn your thoughts and your heart his way, then you've no right to promise yourself at all."

In the dark of the hot, tiny bedroom, Vivian peeled off the mussed and muddy saffron yellow gown and gingerly, so as not to disturb a sleeping Mary Claire, slipped into the lumpy bed.

Could people, as her mother seemed to believe, turn their hearts simply by making up their minds to do so? Far from trying to love Mallory, she wasn't sure she could even come to like him. If truth were told, she was somewhat afraid of him. A shiver ran through her when she thought of the way he had slammed down his fists on his desk, making the silver inkwell leap and the pens quiver. It had taken every ounce of pride and all her willpower to gaze steadily back into those keen blue eyes. That he was to be her husband, that they were to share the same house—moreover, the same bed—took her breath away.

Tormented by second thoughts, she fell into fitful sleep only to awaken panic-stricken when a shaft of early morning sunlight struck her eyelids. Was it wrong to marry a man one didn't love? As in every dilemma of her life her thoughts turned to the Church, and with swift conviction she knew she must speak to Father Shields.

Behind St. Bonaventure's was a small, ancient apple orchard enclosed by a high wall, and it was here, after the six-thirty—the first mass of the day—that Vivian sat on a weathered old stone bench, eyes cast down, the sun making a red-gold glory of her hair.

She couldn't quite believe what she was saying: that Jamie Fitzhugh had gone off and left her, that she was promised to become Brian Mallory's wife. "Though I don't love him, Father," she added.

She had expected this admission to evoke at least a frown, but Father Shields merely nodded and said, "Like a princess of ancient times." From his round, pink face lively eyes regarded her with a candor that seemed to see into the nooks and crannies of her soul. "Yes, a princess of ancient times. They, too, rarely knew the luxury of marrying for love. Alliances were needed to patch up differences between countries, seal a peace, avert a war."

What, thought Vivian, did sealing a peace or averting a war have to do with her marriage to Brian Mallory? But Father Shields was clearly taken with the notion.

"Such marriages prevented bitter suffering," he continued. "Saved countless lives, did enormous good. It was the age of romantic love—the troubadors, the knights wearing milady's colors—but not of romantic marriage. Ah, no. Marry for love? That's quite a new idea altogether, one that until recently wouldn't have been taken into consideration for a minute."

Unhappiness welled up in Vivian, and it was all she could do to swallow the aching lump in her throat. How could she feel sorry for the princesses of ancient times with her own heart freshly broken? How consider dusty centuries when the woeful present overwhelmed her?

Was there no one to understand or feel for her blighted hopes of happiness? Not her mother nor Father Shields, clearly. They were old and burdened. Once, long ago, her mother might have known what it was to feel the heart leap, the pulse quicken. But no more. As for Father Shields, he had never known such pleasures. Why had she come to him? What advice had she expected? She listened with only half an ear as he took on about the rewards of self-sacrifice.

"And he needs you," the priest was saying. "You're just the one to help him."

Roused out of herself, Vivian said: "Needs me? *Mallory* needs me?" For surely no man of her acquaintance appeared less in need of anyone than Brian Mallory.

But Father Shields nodded. "Only think for a moment of his power."

Vivian thought instantly of his strong arms as he had whirled her around her mother's parlor, lifting her off the floor; thought, too, with a blush, of his legs brushing hers. But it wasn't this, of course, that Father Shields had in mind.

"Some say he inherited from his father," said the priest. "True enough, say I. True enough. I'm not the one to be disparaging Matthew Mallory, nor all he taught the boy. But mind you, I say, mind you, that Matthew Mallory was only a ward leader. Whereas Brian, now, has it all."

"You . . . you mean the saloon?" asked Vivian uncertainly.

Father Shields cocked his head to one side. "Surely,

child, you know your intended is the finance chairman of the Amity Club? Sure and you know whosoever holds the purse strings of Amity controls the political machine that governs this fair city?"

She didn't know. She had never given so much as a thought to politics. The Amity Club on Pierce Street existed, for all she knew, only to treat the neighborhood to Fourth of July picnics, to sponsor summer outings in Willow Grove Park, and, each winter, to join with the other Amity Clubs thoughout the city for a gala dance in the Grand Ballroom of the Bellevue Stratford Hotel.

But the mention of purse strings had riveted her attention and prompted her to whisper shamelessly, "It's really true, then? He's very rich?"

A finger flew to Father Shields's lips. "Hush, child, that's not talked about. And does it matter, after all, if he skims a bit from the top? The thing of it is, will he put up a fight against the interests? The railroads and the public service companies and the like that grab all the land and pay next to nothing in taxes?"

He shook his head sadly. "So much needs to be done in this city. You've seen for yourself, no doubt. All the vice, and the police corrupt. Ah, that's the pity of it. The very upholders of the law, the very defenders of the populace in the pay of every bookmaker and madam who peddle their infamous services in our streets.

"Brian Mallory can put a stop to all this. He's the boss now and things can go his way if only he'll put his mind to it. But he may not become the man it's in him to be. It may be he's too like to fritter away his great talents of leadership, too like to have a good time."

His eyes sought hers. "That's why it's a blessing he's to marry. Marriage has a salubrious effect on a man. Not," he added hastily, "that Brian Mallory will be an easy man to harness to virtue. But there's that in him that can be most rewarding if a woman has the mettle for it."

Vivian's head was in a whirl. She herself liked nothing better than to have a good time, nor had she any idea what the old priest meant by harnessing Brian Mallory to virtue, much less any confidence in her ability to do so.

"As to love," Father Shields was concluding, "like as not that will come after you've been together."

She thanked him but placed no faith in the prediction. Only one thought comforted her as she walked home in the

April sunshine: Brian Mallory must indeed be a very rich man.

Any least doubt she might have retained on that score was banished later that morning when she opened the front door to a firm knock and found him standing on the stoop, derby hat cocked at its usual angle and a great bunch of long-stemmed red roses in hand.

"Good morning," he said. "I've come for a word with your mom."

Beyond him, drawn up to the curb in the Sunday quiet, sparkled the most elegant machine she had ever laid eyes on.

"What *is* it?"

"My new Overland," he replied offhandedly, smiling as though something about her amused him. And without doubt the spectacle of the Overland parked in glittering splendor in front of the house, in full view of all the neighbors, had inspired in her such gratification that she gawked at it in covetous delight.

What fun to ride off to church in it, waving to passersby! What satisfaction to draw up before St. Bonaventure's, especially if that Morrissey or Thurman Foy happened along! How green with envy every young woman in the parish would be! But it irked her that somehow Mallory seemed to understand all this, to have spied out these not-quite-ladylike thoughts and found them entertaining. Grudgingly, she held wide the door.

He bowed extravagantly and entered, treading carefully, as though the small, untidy room with its open sewing machine and bits of colored threads matted permanently into the worn rug might be too fragile to withstand him.

"Please be seated. I'll fetch my mother," said Vivian, but now her eyes were on the roses. Hothouse, they were. From Joseph Grady, the florist, and done up in green waxed paper, tied with red satin ribbon. Pleasure rippled through her. Such delicious extravagance!

"For your mother," said Mallory, following her gaze. "Though by rights it's your father I should speak to, if only he was handy."

His eyes gripped hers, and the import of the occasion swept away all frivolity. He was going to ask for her hand. Feeling light-headed, she went in search of her mother.

"Mallory's in the parlor wanting a word with you," she said.

Her mother looked up from the pan full of cornmeal mush she was frying. "Mallory, you say?"

"He's come to ask for my hand."

"And what am I to say to him?"

Vivian looked at her in surprise. "Why, that you'll be pleased and happy for him to have it."

"And you wishing it was Jamie Fitzhugh?"

Vivian thought of the shiny Overland. "That's all in the past."

With his customary urbanity, Brian Mallory had arranged to escort Vivian through his new residence well in advance of the hour set for the open house. And so it was that, a vision in saffron yellow—with the mud sponged off, and the dress freshly mended and pressed by her mother—she moved sedately from room to room, her hand resting lightly in the crook of Mallory's arm.

"What you'll do with the inside is up to you," he had said as he ushered her in the front door.

She had turned to him in surprise. "I am to decorate it, then?"

"Most certainly. It is, after all, to be your home."

In hushed awe she inspected the first and second parlors with their windows trimmed in stained glass and their twin fireplaces faced in glowing cherry wood. But when the heavy golden oak doors to the dining room were parted, she was hard put to remember her manners and stifle a gasp.

It was twice as large as the Webb dining room on Cavendish Square. Sunlight streamed in from six floor-to-ceiling etched-glass windows that looked out over the broad veranda to what would be a side garden. A fireplace framed in carved and reeded golden oak and faced with tiles of turquoise blue occupied one wall. Except for this touch of color, the room awaited her ministrations. A surge of delight coursed through her.

"Oh, Mallory!" she cried with more warmth and feeling than she had ever addressed him. "Could we have a figured carpet with some turquoise blue in it? And do you think . . ." Rushing to the center of the room and striking a finger to her lips, she glanced about her. "Do you think the furnishings—the table and chairs and sideboard—do you think they could be in golden oak?"

"I don't see why not."

"Oh, Mallory!" she repeated, quite transported by the prospect. "It will be heavenly!"

"You think you'll be liking it here, then?"

He waited, and for a moment there was a look in his eyes, something quickening and hopeful, then he said brusquely, "Too soon to tell, of course. Too soon to tell."

Why, she thought with a twinge as they moved out of the room, hadn't she replied that for sure she would like it? Only a heart of stone could fail to appreciate its possibilities, or the generosity of this strange, various man who had so kindly left the decorating to her. Her small hand clasped his arm more firmly as they proceeded up the broad staircase to the first landing, upon which, she saw in an instant, was the perfect spot to set a grandfather clock.

She could never love Mallory. He was too flamboyant and show-offish, and he had tricked her into marrying him, oh, yes, he had. Nonetheless, she began to think Father Shields might be right. There was much in him that could be most rewarding if a woman possessed the mettle for it. And mettle was one thing Vivian Randall knew she had.

Thurman Foy sidled up and pressed the envelope into her hand as she stood beside Mallory receiving guests. Without so much as a glance Vivian had known it was a message from Jamie, and she quickly tucked it up into the sleeve of her gown.

Now, hours later, with the open house long since over and everyone home and in bed, she sat barefoot in her nightdress at the oilcloth-covered table in the Randall kitchen and held the unopened letter in her hands.

She had waited, sleepless, for this little moment of privacy in the small quiet hours, aching to know and dreading to learn what the letter might contain. So long as it remained unopened she could continue to hope, although for what, she scarcely knew. And so she was in no hurry as she studied it under the light that spread down in a pool from the lamp above the table and turned her hair to burnished gold.

At length, with fingers that trembled, she slit open the envelope and took out a single sheet of paper torn, she knew, from one of the copybooks in which Jamie kept his chemical notes.

> *"Dear Vivvie,"* she read.
>
> *By the time this reaches you I shall be far away and commencing upon the greatest adventure of my life.*
>
> *I am too full of too many emotions to say what is in my heart. But I must tell you that you mean the world to me and someday when I sell my formula—which I am absolutely sure I will do—someday I will come back for you.*
>
> *Meantime I want you to know that I will never, never forget you, and that it's better this way.*
>
> *As ever,*
Hastily,
Jamie

She read it over three times. By the third time it was written indelibly upon her heart. Then she rose from the table, placed the letter in the stove, and put a match to it.

5

Had fate dealt a different hand, had Vivian Randall been society belle rather than lady's maid, Clinton Webb might well have courted her, or so Vivian in her romantic young heart liked to believe.

Moreover, she believed Clinton Webb suspected this, for all his circumspection and stiff ways. There was, had been from the beginning, something just under the surface of their impeccably correct relationship, something that didn't know its place and leapt out, as now, in the swift disapproving frown between his eyes as he said, "You are to marry *Mallory?* Brian Mallory?"

He had, it appeared, just received this information from

his mother, to whom Vivian had given notice bright and early only that morning, and now he stood in the drawing room between the two long, narrow front windows that looked out upon Cavendish Square. Behind him an elaborately carved gilt Empire mirror reflected the resplendent length of him: tan worsted English walking suit, black calf shoes, tan spats, and, in his lapel, the grape hyacinth his sister Nancy had fixed there at breakfast. Tall, erect, dark mustache meticulously trimmed, each strand of wavy dark hair slicked uncompromisingly back, he was every inch the son and heir of the cultivated and aristocratic Dr. and Mrs. C. Alden Webb and, in his own right, full partner with his uncle in the Webb Woolen Mills just up the Delaware River.

But his usual composure was marred by a scowl as Vivian said, "Brian Mallory, yes, sir. You know him, sir?"

"Everyone in this city knows him, everyone in this state."

"He is famous, then?"

"Infamous is more like it. Notorious, some would say."

"And why should they be saying that, sir?"

She stood before him ramrod straight, her head in its red-gold glory far too imperiously set for a lady's maid, her green eyes flashing, her lithe young figure elegant in the black broadcloth uniform she wore, a ruching of muslin at collar and cuffs gleaming stark white against the rosy, glowing skin.

She was too fine a prize to be won by a boor like Brian Mallory. The very thought of such a union incensed Clinton Webb.

"You love him?" he demanded in disbelief.

But for her conversation with Father Shields, Vivian would have been hard put to answer. Thus primed, however, she replied, "Not everyone marries for love. In ancient times many a princess married to avert a war, seal a peace."

"And pray what war are you averting? Who filled your head with such claptrap?"

"Why, it's not claptrap, sir. Father Shields said it's true. Mallory needs me."

"Did Father Shields say that, also?"

"Indeed he did. He said Mallory can put a stop to all sorts of things: vice, corrupt police—"

"What?" cried Clinton Webb.

At such obvious incredulity, Vivian hesitated. Had she got it wrong? But no, she distinctly recalled the part about corrupt police, and the bookmakers and the madams. "Yes, indeed," she assured him, adding: "And the *interests*, the railroads and the like that grab all the land and pay no taxes."

"Ah, that, too, eh? Father Shields knows all about that, does he? And Brian Mallory is the man to fight them?"

"If he doesn't fritter away his great talents for leadership."

Clinton Webb laughed harshly. "He's talented, I'll give you that. There's not a contract let out of City Hall, nor a job either, that doesn't pay dues to the Amity Club. As for the police, every last one of them kicks back to the Mallory machine. But what has this to do with you? Surely you aren't about to make a ridiculous marriage simply because of the jabbering of a foolish old priest?"

She had been doing her best to make sense of the bitter words, but now there swept through her a fierce new loyalty to the man she would marry. "It's not in the least ridiculous," she said and, seeking to prove this by proclaiming the one attribute that in her eyes could not fail to recommend him, added proudly, "It so happens that Brian Mallory is a very rich man."

"Ah ha!" cried Clinton Webb, pouncing. "So that's the reason! And you would sell yourself?"

It wasn't the reason, but she could never tell him this; no, never would she admit to him or to anyone that she was marrying Brian Mallory because Jamie Fitzhugh had cast her aside. Better, far better, to let the world think she was marrying for money. "And what's wrong with that?" she demanded harshly. "What's wrong with that if all my life I've wanted the chance to better myself, and now it's come to me? What's wrong with that if I want to live in a fine house like this one with servants to run up and down stairs and plenty to put in my belly?"

With a gasp, she stopped abruptly. *Belly*. To have uttered such a word in such surroundings—a word never mentioned, as she had long ago learned, in polite society; a word she was certain had never passed the lips of Irene Webb.

Consternation claimed her. To have lost her temper with Mr. Clinton, scion of the house! To have so far forgotten herself! "I'm very sorry, sir," she whispered humbly.

Clinton Webb also appeared to recall himself. "It is I who must apologize," he said stiffly. "I wish you every happiness."

Vivian remained in the drawing room after Clinton Webb walked briskly past her and out the front door. The little tiff was upsetting. In three years of service, never before had she talked back. Nor had there been occasion since, though exacting, Dr. Webb and his family were unfailingly kind. She had loved working in this serene and gracious home with its many social affairs and polite good times.

It was here that she first had learned what chamber music was; first discovered the difference between oil paintings and pastels from the examples that hung in ornate gilt frames upon the walls. It was here she had marveled that people could talk passionately and for hours about things that took place only within the covers of a book. Though she herself much preferred a bit of gossip about real persons and events, still, she had come to look upon reading with profound respect. Oh, a hundred things she had learned here, some by earnest observation, others taught her by Irene Webb: how to set a table, how to use a fish knife, how to correct a servant, how to greet a friend, how to enter a room, sit in repose, speak in a cultivated tone of voice.

Eagerness to please and skill with needle, thread, and curling iron had led her quickly from kitchen girl to the position of lady's maid, while a lively curiosity soaked up like a sponge all manner of things she had never known existed before. The Square, the imposing brownstone houses around it, and the people who lived in them were far from the bruising realities of Butler Street. Nor did she count it a hardship when she was forced to leave school to augment the family income, for she had entered a world of utter enchantment.

From the beginning she took like duck to water to its elegant ways. It was the manner in which she meant to live one day, she and Jamie, when he finished his invention and struck it rich, and so she studied and copied each nuance and gesture, for all that the people on Butler Street said she gave herself airs. She had set out to make herself into a lady. It was this that appalled her now, for she had railed at Clinton Webb like a fishwife, in a house where people behaved properly and voices were never raised.

Even as she fretted, a voice behind her said; "Now, now, Vivvie, it wasn't your fault, you know," and she turned to find Irene Webb in the doorway.

"I overheard the whole thing," the woman continued, "and my son was entirely to blame. He had no call to take on so. I do believe he's a bit jealous. He's always rather fancied you, you know."

Vivian couldn't have said which surprised her more, the confirmation of her own idle romantic notions or the knowledge that her employer had been aware of certain inclinations all along.

The suggestion of a smile touched Irene Webb's finely etched lips. "I can admit now to a few anxious moments when I first engaged you. But my son is a man of principle, and you turned out to be a good sensible girl of practical aspirations, so there was nothing to fear." She held out a hand. "Now come along. The girls are all ready for you to do their hair."

Vivian followed her up the stairs, imitating out of habit the effortless carriage, the way Irene Webb had of seeming to float. It didn't occur to either woman that the little speech had been patronizing. Vivian took it as a compliment that as a lady's maid she had known her place, and indeed, it had been intended as such.

The room in which Nancy Webb and her friends waited was on the second floor at the back of the house. Once upon a time, long years ago, it had served as a nursery. Sunny and pleasant, it was still something of a playroom, a place where girlfriends frequently gathered, equipped with gramophone, upright piano, window seats filled with ruffled and embroidered pillows, and, tacked upon the walls and overflowing every available surface, framed photographs and mementos of all manner of festive occasions, including an open Chinese parasol depending from the ceiling, and a large American flag.

There was also, somewhat surprisingly, a dry sink, for it was in this room that Vivian washed and dressed the hair of those Cavendish Square ladies fortunate enough to be close friends of Irene and Nancy Webb, and hence invited to avail themselves of Vivian's services.

That Vivian Randall had a way with hairdressing was
readily conceded by all, and her skill in arranging the com-
plicated pompadours of the day had been enhanced by
none other than Dr. Webb himself, who, as it turned out,
had certain theories concerning the care and grooming of
the hair. Taking Vivian aside one day, he had given her
careful instructions. First, the hair must be absolutely
clean, and to achieve this she must use a secret soapy solution, a fresh jug of which she mixed each week. After the
hair was washed and thoroughly rinsed, it must be gently
brushed until dry. Only then was it ready to be piled into
the intricate and singularly shining creations that other lady's maids were at a loss to achieve.

This morning, there awaited Vivian four young women
in charming deshabille, shirtwaists doffed and kimonos
flung loosely over dainty camisoles, unpinned hair tumbling down to slender waists.

"But now who will do for us?" someone wailed.

"Here she is," sang out Irene Webb. "Here's our sly old
Vivvie. You must ask her."

A cry went up, and like bright birds they surrounded
her, except for Nancy Webb, who hung back and stood
apart.

Exactly Vivian's age, the two girls were far less maid
and mistress than close friends. Nancy knew all about Jamie Fitzhugh, had met him, had listened countless times to
all the bright hopes and dreams. Now Vivian found herself
avoiding her friend's puzzled dark eyes.

"You are to marry Brian Mallory?" exclaimed Camilla
Cavendish.

It was precisely the question Clinton Webb had asked.
Did all the world know Mallory, then? "Yes, ma'am," replied Vivian.

Camilla Cavendish was a handsome young woman with
snapping black eyes, wife of State Senator Roscoe Cavendish, whose grandfather had given his name to the Square.
Everyone, even Irene Webb, deferred to her, and so the
little group regarded Vivian with quickened interest when
Mrs. Cavendish said, "Oh, my dear, what a catch you've
made."

Irene Webb clasped her hands in surprise. "A catch! Is
he really?"

"One of the most powerful men in the city," declared
Camilla Cavendish. "Wealthy, too."

"But who *is* he?" demanded Thea Allenby querulously. "I've never heard of him."

"Nor are you likely to," responded Camilla Cavendish. "Not in the places you frequent. Try a visit to Butler Street sometime. He's just built himself a mansion down there."

"A mansion on Butler Street? But how preposterous!"

Although precisely the sentiments Vivian herself once had owned, she now took bristly offense at this opinion and was pleased to hear Mrs. Cavendish say, "Not preposterous at all, my dear Thea. Butler Street is Brian Mallory's constituency. All South Philadelphia is."

What in the world, wondered Vivian, was a constituency? Whatever it was, it belonged to Mallory. Her greedy little heart thumped happily as she tied on a long starched white apron and rolled up her sleeves.

On hairdressing days Effie, the kitchen girl, was kept busy running with buckets of hot water to replenish the large flowered china washbowl that sat in the dry sink. Meanwhile, Vivian soaped and soothed to such effect that nerves grew calm and headaches disappeared.

The deeply sensuous nature she was yet to discover in herself led her to believe that having one's hair dressed should be a gratifying, a voluptuous experience. A woman should emerge from it, she held, feeling rejuvenated and looking as relaxed and beautiful as it was possible for her to look, and to this end she bent all her efforts.

It didn't bother her that during these ministrations the ladies poured out their troubles and triumphs to her. She was adept at savoring life secondhand, and no detail escaped her attention, since it was of such stuff that dreams could be made. In the small hours of the morning, waiting to help the Webb ladies undress after concert, dinner, or ball, she would sit in her bedroom at the back of the house and gaze into the hissing gas fire. Feet tucked up on the fender, green eyes remote, she would stare into the flickering blue and golden flames and fancy herself in attendance at the glittering affair. Nor, in these dreams, was she ever found wanting, so ladylike were her manners, so refined her speech, so perfect her demeanor in every way. Oh, she longed, she ached to be a part of this infinitely desirable world that beckoned and teased with its glimpses. To her bedazzled eyes even its troubles seemed worth enduring, so acceptable were the palliatives: trips abroad to mend broken hearts, heirlooms and legacies following closely upon bereavement.

In such aspirations she was no different from hundreds, thousands, of other little servant girls who hovered starry-eyed in the wings as the well born, or the merely wealthy, twirled in the spotlight of society. For this was the *belle époque*, the heady turn of the century when champagne was drunk from satin slippers, parties lasted into pearly dawns, mansions were built to rival the palaces of kings, and one's name in the social register was the prize sought by all.

Today, as she combed and curled, Vivian Randall had to all but pinch herself to realize that this world was about to become hers, for the talk was of Brian Mallory, and she hung giddily upon every word.

He had, she learned to her amazement, recently dined at Cavendish House. At Cavendish House, think of that! And this because, according to Mrs. Cavendish, Brian Mallory was a major reason why the distinguished Senator Cavendish retained his seat in the statehouse year after year.

"People may rail all they like about the Mallory machine," declared Camilla Cavendish, "but it can be counted upon to get out the vote. As to dear Brian, he's the most handsome and charming Irishman I've ever known. I'm only relieved he's about to marry our Vivvie instead of one of those silly little chorus girls he forever brings to the house."

Vivian gulped. Was there no end to the things she was discovering about this astonishing man? Everyone seemed to hold the strongest opinions about him: Father Shields, Mrs. Cavendish, Clinton Webb. Saint or devil, which was he? She would soon be finding out. For good or ill, she would soon bear his name, live in his house, sleep in his bed.

A double bed, she had been given to understand. The rest of the furnishings might be left up to her but, escorting her into the high-ceilinged, airy master bedroom only yesterday, he had said quite definitely, "In this room I want a large double bed."

"Um," she had managed.

Now misgivings shook her. She knew next to nothing about the man. Only one fact stuck like a burr. Hearing Mrs. Cavendish's allusion to chorus girls, Vivian no longer doubted Brian Mallory knew the price of Paris gowns.

* * *

Shining hair drawn up to dip beguilingly over smooth foreheads, the ladies left the Webb residence in a happy little flurry of self-satisfaction, with the exception of Thea Allenby, who loudly complained that she didn't look at all the way she would like to look.

"Pay no attention, Vivvie," advised Nancy Webb, helping, as always, to collect the damp towels left strewn about the deserted room. "Thea never knows what she wants. Unless," she added, "it's to be Mrs. Clinton Webb."

For the first time that day Vivian was drawn from her own concerns.

She knew, of course, as she knew all sorts of things about the Webbs and their friends, that the attractive and much sought after Clinton was the sometime escort of Thea Allenby. But Nancy implied the possibility of a new and more lasting relationship.

And a pity that would be, thought Vivian feelingly, for of all the ladies whose hair she dressed, Miss Allenby was the one she couldn't abide. At times it vexed her that the silky blond tresses looped above the pale, autocratic features should turn out so well. Not that Miss Allenby was ever happy with the result. Despite beauty, wealth, and social position, she seemed to be permanently out of sorts with herself and the rest of the world. Tales of her hot temper and imperious ways had traveled nimbly around the Square through kitchen doors, and Vivian knew that more than one lady's maid had had her hair pulled and her arms pinched when things didn't go just to Miss Allenby's liking.

That Clinton Webb could be seriously interested in such a person irked Vivian. He deserved better, she fumed, forgetting that he apparently took a similar view of the alliance that she herself was about to make. "And will he have her, do you suppose?" she asked.

Nancy sighed. "Oh, I expect so. Though I wish he wouldn't. I don't much care for her. Sometimes I don't believe Clinton does either."

"Why marry, then?"

Nancy shrugged. "Clint's not like me. He does what's expected of him, and ever since he and Thea were children, the Allenbys and mama and papa have expected this."

"But that's no reason to marry."

"Oh, there are lots of reasons to marry." Her candid dark eyes fixed on Vivian. "Why are you marrying Brian Mallory instead of Jamie Fitzhugh?"

The question swept past Vivian's careful defenses. Surprised by the sob that shook her, she dropped her face in her hands. "Because Jamie has left me, that's why."

"Oh, my dear," cried Nancy softly, her pretty heart-shaped face stricken. "Left you? Really left you?"

Snatching up a towel and dabbing at her eyes, Vivian drew a quivering sigh. No point whatever in trying to dissemble with Nancy, who, after all, knew all about Jamie Fitzhugh. "He's gone off to St. Louis to sell his invention at the Fair."

"But surely he'll return?"

Vivian shook her head. "No."

"But why not?"

"He doesn't want to marry me."

"He said this?"

"No. But he wouldn't take me with him."

"Perhaps he couldn't afford to take you."

"Oh yes he could!" At the memory of what had happened, how it had been, a shamed flush welled swiftly up into her face. "He had two thousand dollars that Mallory gave him."

"Mallory gave him two thousand dollars?"

"As an investment. So Jamie could go to St. Louis and sell his invention. Two train tickets he gave him, too."

"Two?"

"One for me."

One for you if he cared to take you, Mallory had said. But he hadn't.

She swallowed hard. She hadn't meant to tell all this to Nancy, but now she was glad she had spoken. It was good to have said it aloud, to remind herself how he had humiliated her. Too frequently in the past few hours she had caught stray thoughts slipping off to Jamie Fitzhugh—traitorous, treacherous little curls of hope, pipe dreams, castles in the air.

"So it's over, you see," she said bluntly.

"But why Brian Mallory?"

"I mean to marry him, that's all."

"But you don't love him!"

"Nor does he love me."

"Then why are you doing this?"

"He has his reasons. I have mine."

"And what does your mother say?"

It often struck Vivian as strange that Nancy seemed to regard Mamie Randall with the devoted admiration that Vivian, for all she adored her mother, deemed appropriate only to creatures such as the beautiful and elegant Irene Webb.

The crowded, noisy life of Butler Street seemed to hold endless fascination for this delicately reared girl. She never tired of the tales about the Randalls that Vivian brought back to Cavendish Square, and often begged to accompany Vivian on her occasional visits home, where even the withdrawn and moody Neil welcomed her as though she were a fairy princess dropped into their midst. How truly unfortunate, Vivian sometimes thought, that life in its perversity had set her down on Butler Street and Nancy Webb on Cavendish Square when clearly each would have much preferred just the opposite.

"My mother," she now said with signal understatement, "likes Mallory very well."

"And Neil?"

"Neil?" exclaimed Vivian in surprise. "Why, what should Neil care?"

Nancy's dark eyes glowed. "Oh, but he will. Your brother is such a fine, high-minded person. And he admires and loves you so. I can't believe Neil would want to see you marry except for love."

Love, thought Vivian. She had loved Jamie Fitzhugh with all her heart, and what but grief had it brought her? Married to Mallory she would at least have everything she ever wanted; everything she craved. "Oh, let's not talk about love," she said impatiently. "Let's talk about my wedding. I'm going to have the most beautiful wedding in the world."

"Why, of course you are," agreed Nancy, warmheartedly. "And will I receive an invitation, dear?"

Vivian's mouth dropped open in dismay. "Oh, no, Miss. It wouldn't be right."

"And why not, I'd like to know. Don't you want me to come?"

"Sure and I do. But——"

"It's settled then," declared Nancy firmly and, glancing beyond Vivian to the doorway, exclaimed, "Mama, we've been discussing Vivvie's wedding, and I'm to be a guest."

Vivian turned just in time to see the horrified little frown that crossed the placid countenance.

"How nice," said Irene Webb smoothly. And then, "Vivvie, Somerby tells me you have a visitor waiting to see you downstairs. Mrs. Mallory."

6

Foreboding gripped Vivian as she descended the back stairs. Mrs. Mallory come to see her here? At the Webb residence? Mother of God, what could such a visit mean?

Heart pounding with nameless apprehension, she moved stiffly past Effie, who was now dusting the morning room, and on to the second flight of stairs. When she reached the kitchen Lady Burns glanced up at her with a keen look from the pie crust she was rolling, and Somerby left the silver he was polishing to jerk his head toward the servants' sitting room. The door stood open. Vivian entered, closed it carefully, and turned to face Ma Mallory.

Dressed in the inevitable black bombazine, the woman sat on a straight-back chair. So upright and still did she hold herself, clutching a great black leather purse in both hands, that she might have been one of the large waxwork dolls that eerily grace the Hall of Fame in an amusement park.

Nothing of Mallory's buoyant good humor and ingratiating charm appeared in the flat gray gaze, but there was no denying the woman was handsome. Despite a plumpness veering perilously toward obesity, the strong, clean-cut features, deep-set eyes, and thick, gray-streaked jet black hair drawn up under a black straw hat gave ample evidence of the beauty she must once have been, and she carried Mallory's air of command.

"I was after wanting to keep our little chat private," said the woman by way of explaining so unexpected an appearance. "That's why I've come here. I hope you'll do me the kindness to hear me out."

"But of course," replied Vivian.

"Thank you for that," she said, a lilt in her voice despite its brusqueness. And then, "Mallory tells me it's himself you're to marry. But he knows and I know your heart's set on Jamie Fitzhugh."

Instantly Vivian forgot her diffidence. "Not anymore," she declared.

"Not anymore, is it? Well, that's neither here nor there. Sure, it's no business of mine which other you marry, so long as it isn't my son."

Vivian sucked in her breath as though slapped. Like all very pretty girls, she was used to people liking her. From childhood her vivid beauty had won indulgence from utter strangers, and she had blossomed into womanhood expecting smiling approval. Never once in her life had she been summarily rejected.

"But *why* don't you want me to marry him?" she asked, with an incredulity some might have found appealing.

Unmoved, Ma Mallory replied, "Because you don't give a snap for him. You've no thought for him at all, but only yourself and the life he can give you."

"I mean to make him a good wife."

"I don't doubt that, but it's not in you to do it. Butler Street won't hold you, for all it's where my son belongs. It's where his people are—the ones who know and trust and support him."

"And it's where we're going to live, in the house he's built there."

"For how long? Answer me that. For how long before you'll be putting ideas into his head, making him restless, coaxing and cajoling him to forget where he came from and move away. And he'll do it, too. He'll do it, for he's got a taste for fancy living, which is why he's needing a wife who will keep his feet on the ground."

"A wife such as Dolly Muldoon?"

"Think what you please, she'd be a fine choice for him, and he'd choose her, too, if it wasn't for you; all but promised, they were 'til he took it into his head to start courting you."

Vivian didn't doubt how dear to Ma Mallory's heart such a union would be. Dolly was her godchild, and there was no secret of the bond between the two. There were those who said it was the Muldoons and Ma Mallory who had fostered the notion that Mallory would one day marry the girl.

But these considerations flew from her head as she watched Ma Mallory open the black leather handbag she held in her ample lap and extract from it a long white envelope.

"There's no call to talk further," said the woman. "I could talk myself to my grave and not be after changing either him or yourself. That's why I'm wanting to make you an offer. This," she said, holding out the envelope, "is for you."

Vivian froze. "What is it?"

Ma Mallory's chin thrust forward and she shook the envelope as though seized by an ague. "Take it. Take it and see."

Contempt swept through Vivian. "No."

"Don't be a fool, girl." Ripping open the envelope, the woman snatched from it a thin stack of bills secured by a rubber band. Holding them aloft, she whispered, "Ten one-thousand-dollar bills. Ten thousand dollars. All for yourself if you'll but leave this city and not come back again."

Dismayed by the awesome amount, Vivian said, "It means so much to you?"

"Sure and it does."

"But why?"

"Haven't I told you? You're not the wife for my son."

"But you don't know me."

"I know well enough. I know your kind."

"What kind?"

"The kind that will marry to set themselves up in a grand style. Sure and it's what everybody's been saying since Mallory's announcement yesterday. Not a soul but knows it's no love match he's making, not a soul but knows about you and Jamie Fitzhugh. Why, it's a laughingstock you've made of him. A laughingstock, with everyone whispering and talking."

"Who's whispering and talking?" said Vivian, anger mounting hotly within her.

"Why, everyone who's heard of it, that's who. And it's only the truth they're saying."

"What are they saying?"

"Why, just what's what: that you always had grand ideas and now you've seen your chance."

"And you listened to them?" cried Vivian, white with fury. "You believed them?"

"Tell me it's not true."

In the silence the woman drew a sigh and sat back. "There now, you can't deny it, and it's not blaming you that I am. What other way does a young woman such as yourself have to better her lot in this world? Looks soon fade, and what then? But I'm offering you a tidy sum for a nest egg. Put at interest it will grow, and you free as the birds in the air to enjoy it, with no one to make demands or say you nay. Marriage is no bed of roses for a woman. No, it's not. Marriage without love is a devil's bargain, and that's the truth."

A shiver passed through Vivian at the dire words. They were like a malediction, for she shared the belief that those who married without love had the devil to pay, and she felt herself begin to weaken. Almost, she weakened. She could see this expectation in the sudden wary hopefulness that surged in Ma Mallory's calculating eyes, in the raising, once again, of the money-filled fist. And what might people say then? How would tongues wag and heads nod then, with the betrothed fled and Mallory left as she had been left by Jamie Fitzhugh?

"No, and I'll not do that," she murmured.

"How's that?" asked Ma Mallory sharply.

"I mean to marry Mallory," she said.

But the unpleasant little visit proved upsetting.

"Don't give it a thought," advised her mother. "The old woman is just a mite jealous of her son's love."

"Love!" exclaimed Vivian.

Mamie Randall nodded her head. "He loves you," she said matter-of-factly. "Why else do you think he's marrying you?"

"Why, because of what he said. That . . . well, that I was the best he could get."

"And do you think the likes of a man such as Mallory can't get almost any woman he has a mind to? Go along with you, girl. He's head over heels in love. Anyone who couldn't see that would have to be blind."

Far from being heartened, Vivian found this explanation unnerving. She thought of her love for Jamie, the way her heart would pound at the sight of him and her breath come in light fits and starts. Was Mallory similarly affected at sight of her? Did he think of her always? Was she ever a part of him, ever on his mind, no matter where he went, what he did?

She couldn't believe this and, in fact, preferred to think otherwise. She didn't want him to be in love with her for, despite what she had told Ma Mallory, deep in her heart lurked the thought that she might not marry him after all.

Yes, although each day preparations went forward for the wedding, the banns announced by Father Shields from the altar, the date set, all manner of plans made, still, still, in her heart of hearts, was the thought that she might hear from Jamie. Another letter would arrive, or a telegram, or perhaps of a sudden she would open the front door to a knock and find him standing there, smiling at her in that way he had. For though she told herself this would never happen, she remembered every word of his letter and wondered, despite herself, if she hadn't acted too hastily. He had, after all, said that someday he would come back for her. There was still time.

But not much of it! No, and what remained seemed to be flying by. Already the last of April had given over to the balmy days of May. Fragrance of lilac and flowering chestnut trees filled the air, making bowers and gardens of the narrow backyards that looked so bare and mean all winter, sending drifts of perfume through open windows and doors.

And the nights. Were there, thought Vivian, ever such nights, soft as velvet, white with moonlight, filled with stars. Filled, too, with parties and all manner of celebration, for everyone in the city knew Brian Mallory, or so it appeared.

"Lucky you!" sighed Mary Claire, observing the mountain of wedding gifts with artless envy. "You're so lucky, Viv."

"You're the lucky one. Just wait and see," Vivian promised, for already she had plans in mind. One of the first things she meant to do, once securely married, was to persuade Mallory that Mary Claire should complete her education. And she knew precisely the school Mary Claire must attend: the select Villa Maria Academy, just outside the city.

Mary Claire, however, was less than enthusiastic. "More school," she said scornfully, a mutinous frown between provocative, almond-shaped gray eyes. "I tell you I *like* playing the piano at Lawson's. I don't *want* to go back to school."

"Well, you must, so that's settled," declared Vivian, quite used to bossing this younger sister. "Anyway, it's not like Saint Bonnie's. It's a great gray mansion that looks like a castle, with acres and acres of ground about it. And tennis courts and riding stables and a music room with two grand pianos."

Her voice trailed off wistfully, for suddenly she longed to be fifteen and about to be enrolled in Villa Maria Academy instead of engaged to marry a man she didn't love.

But if she didn't love him, she never failed to find his company exciting. She was used to her brother Neil and beaus like Thomas O'Reilly and Jamie Fitzhugh, but it was an altogether different experience to be squired about by this man who knew not only her own two worlds of Butler Street and Cavendish Square, but the glittering thoroughfares in between. The shops, the theaters, the restaurants whose facades she had once gazed upon from a streetcar with such passionate curiosity now opened welcoming doors to her as, on Mallory's arm, she floated through a world filled with foods she had never heard of, wines she had never tasted, sights she had never seen.

Money was the secret. Always deeply respectful of it, now she watched it work miracles as all over the city cabinetmakers and upholsterers and shopkeepers of every description labored frantically to furnish Mallory's house in duplication of the pages in the shiny new women's magazines that Vivian found of such enormous assistance.

Poring avidly over them she discovered, illustrated with helpful examples, the very latest in good taste as well as those pitfalls to be at all costs avoided. "The design of this couch," cautioned the *Ladies' Home Journal*, for instance, "is not particularly objectionable, but the fringe at the base is bad and unsanitary." Or again, "This modern Louis XV bed seems unsound in construction, overornamented and generally weak and insipid throughout. Such furniture should have no place in any sane American home. . . ."

In a perfect fever that nothing in Mallory's house—*her* house—should be in the least insipid, unsanitary, or objectionable, Vivian spent every spare moment at the oilcloth-covered table in the Randall kitchen surrounded by lists, pictures torn from magazines, and swatches of material. To her consternation, except for his demand for a large bed in the master bedroom, Mallory kept to his promise that she should have full say.

"But suppose I spend too much money?" she said worriedly.

"You won't," Mallory assured her. "I've made up a budget for each room. Just keep within that."

And so saying, he presented her with a little red morocco notebook on the first page of which she read: "Front Parlor—$1,000."

"One thousand dollars!" she cried. "Mother of God, Mallory, do you mean for the front parlor, or for the whole house?"

"The front parlor. Done properly, it's none too much."

She frowned and caught her full lower lip in her teeth, and he said, "What's the matter, Puss?"

She had got used to this pet name he had for her, although not to the way he said it: easily, almost lazily, but as though she belonged to him.

"I'm afraid I won't do it properly," she confessed.

"Sure and you will."

"How do you know?"

They sat on the lumpy sofa in the parlor while Mamie Randall sat in the kitchen under the gas lamp, every once in a while giving the newspaper she was reading a cautionary rattle to remind them that she was still awake and alert.

"I know," said Mallory, "by the way you dress and the way you talk and everything about you. I always meant to marry a lady, and that's what you are."

Perversely, since all her life she had striven to be exactly this, she now felt dissatisfied with the achievement. The truth was, although she might readily admit he wasn't her type at all, she very much wanted him to marry her not because she was a lady but because he was in love with her.

She was used to men being in love with her. Ever since she had received her first valentine they had been declaring their predilection. But the trouble with Mallory, for all he called her Puss and seemed to feel he owned her, was that he had ice water in his veins and no sentiment whatever.

She looked at him on the sofa beside her, handsome despite the awful plaid suit he was wearing, and so powerful that he weighed down his end of the sofa, making it necessary for her to press herself back against her end else she would tumble down into his lap. "And why in the world," she demanded irritably, "is your heart so set on a lady?"

"A lady goes with what I have in mind."

"Which is?"

"Oh, I don't know. To live in a certain way. Yes, that's it. To live in a certain way, don't y' know?"

She nodded for she did know, indeed she did. He had expressed her own dearest dreams. Were he only Jamie Fitzhugh, how heavenly it all would be!

Something of this wish may have shown in the tender longing that flickered so briefly in the green eyes, for he looked at her sharply and said, "What is it?"

Startled and guilty, she caught her breath. "What do you mean?"

He lunged toward her to grasp her wrist, and in doing so forced her to topple forward into his shoulder.

"What's the matter?" he demanded.

She looked up, frightened, into his blazing blue eyes, unable to right herself for he held her, his grip on her arm like a vise. "Nothing. Nothing is the matter," she whispered.

"There is. Tell me. I want to know."

She had never been so close to him. She had danced with him, he had handed her into and out of vehicles and, at appropriate times, offered her his arm. But she had never been pressed helpless against him, his shaving lotion stinging her nostrils, his face, with the clean, firm line of the lips, the sharp, straight, broad nose, and the thick, curly black hair, mere inches from her.

Nor had she ever been betrayed and overpowered by her own body, so shaken and impelled by the strange heavy sweetness that surged up through her that she no longer felt in command of herself. Heretofore those mysterious animal urges against which the good nuns of St. Bonaventure's so sternly warned had, in her experience, reposed in the pleasant little sensations she enjoyed when young men held her hand or slipped a timid arm about her waist. Even with Jamie, kisses had been full-hearted but circumspect, for it went without saying that she was a nice girl and a decent fellow must respect this.

But Mallory seemed to pay no heed to such conventions if, in fact, he had ever been aware of them. His strong muscular arms tightened about her like bands of steel. "You still want him, don't you?" he said, grinding out the words between even white teeth. "You still want that two-for-a-nickel little inventor who left you in the lurch."

"No," breathed Vivian.

"Yes, you do. And by God I should let you have him. I should let you rot waiting for him to come back to you."

"No, no. I want you!"

His face reddened with fury. "Don't lie to me."

She shook her head and tears of frustration stood in her eyes at his stupidity. "I mean, I want you . . . to kiss me. I want—"

She didn't finish the sentence because, like rain on a parched field, his lips sank upon hers.

A subtle change seemed to have developed in their relationship after this particular evening, much as Vivian tried to ignore it.

For one thing, frequently now she surprised a glint of she couldn't say quite what—impertinence? uncalled-for amusement?—in Mallory's eyes when he looked at her. For another, she couldn't forget that she had mortified herself by asking, no, *begging* him to kiss her.

Oh, if only she hadn't done that! If only she could snatch back those words! It was the man who begged and pleaded for favors, the woman who remained cool and calm, and bestowed or withheld. She couldn't imagine what had gotten into her. Such appalling behavior shook her to her toes, and she tried to push the memory from her. But at odd moments it returned, vividly intruding, making her stop what she was doing and look up from her work, hands slack, eyes wide and unseeing, lips parted in recollection of the wave of feeling that had swept over her.

If a difference had crept between herself and Mallory, there was also a distressing change in her mother's attitude. With money no longer a problem, with, moreover, shopkeepers all but begging her to merely sign her name, Vivian found herself thwarted at every turn.

"I'll not see you charge so much as a thimble to Brian Mallory 'til you're decently married to him," said Mamie Randall over protestations that Mallory had encouraged the use of his accounts for personal needs. "It's not the way of a young woman such as yourself," she would answer to Vivian's pleas. "Now, that other kind, yes. Let the likes of them charge whatever to whoever. But as for you, no. If I can't run up what you need, then you'll do without."

The truth was that the dresses Mamie "ran up" on her sewing machine were no longer suitable to her daughter's engagements. Simple, girlish frocks like the saffron yellow gown were all very well, but almost every evening now Mallory alighted from the Overland, or more likely from his two-wheeled hansom carriage with Bunty O'Hare in livery and seated in the driver's seat up on top. Resplendent in evening dress, a cape flung over his broad shoulders, opera hat in hand, he presented himself at the front door, ready to sweep his fiancée off to the fanciest of parties and balls.

Fancy was the only way Vivian could describe these affairs, for the world into which Brian Mallory introduced her had none of the quiet elegance of Cavendish Square, nor did she ever meet there any of the people who frequented the Webbs'. Yet clearly Mallory's friends were wealthy. Although she wouldn't have believed such a thing possible, they appeared to be even wealthier than families like the Webbs and the Cavendishes. Their homes, stretching north from City Hall on Broad Street or out City Line Avenue, were enormous—far larger than houses on the Square. And while Vivian sometimes discovered in them furnishings that the *Ladies' Home Journal* would severely deplore, there could be no doubt as to the expense lavished upon them.

It was, in fact, just this aura of money, of vast expenditures, that assailed the senses and dazzled the eye even as, thinking of the poverty of Butler Street, Vivian found herself appalled. Such considerations, however, didn't trouble her for long, since there were more pressing demands on her attention: the furnishing of Mallory's house, her approaching wedding, and, always these days, unpleasant little tiffs with Mamie as to what she would wear.

It was Gert Barkin, one of her newly acquired friends, who solved this last dilemma.

"Borrow anything you like, dearie," Gert urged, flinging open the door to her dressing room. "Hell, I don't care."

Vivian blanched at the casual profanity and then looked quickly to Gert to see if the young woman had noticed so parochial a reaction. In Gert's circle—Vivian's also now, she supposed—several of the women swore as readily as the men. Others, according to Gert, knew how to swear like sailors but they were too "nasty nice" to let on, pretending to such delicate breeding that they grew faint if rough language were used in their presence.

"Which gives me a real pain in the ass," Gert told Vivian. the direct hazel eyes flashing in the small, pert face. "If there's one thing I can't stand it's people putting on the dog and acting like they never heard tell of where they come from.

"Harry and me now, we come from a little old town in Indiana where the train didn't even blow its whistle, and we're proud of it. Hell, my old man used to get soused on Saturday nights and beat us all up proper. Never done us no harm, neither. And Harry's folks was just plain dirt farmers.

"But Harry could always sweet-talk people out of a little money, and once he got his granary started, he even sweet-talked the railroad into stopping their trains right beside it. And from then on, it's been this way."

She winked and waved small, bejeweled hands to include a bedroom the like of which Vivian had never encountered. Cupids were everywhere: peeping from white clouds painted on the sky blue ceiling, perched in gold leaf upon marble pedestals. White lace draperies filtered the sunlight that streamed into the huge room. More white lace was drawn up over a pink satin coverlet on the bed, which, adorned with myriad heart-shaped pillows, was made, Gert proudly informed her, of solid bronze. "One thing Harry hates is a squeaky bed, if you know what I mean."

Vivian tried to respond to the wink and the grin, but Gert wasn't fooled by the stiff little smile. "There now," she said quickly, "I shouldn't have said that. I'll bet you don't even know what it's all about yet. Don't pay me one speck of attention. Just pick out something to wear to the party tonight."

Overwhelmed with embarrassment, Vivian entered the dressing room and moved dazedly along the rows of gowns. Sometimes she liked Gert so much, with her generosity and forthright ways, but at others she was repelled by the woman's brash crudeness, her vulgarity. Something warned her not to get into Gert Barkin's debt, yet here she was looking rapturously at a flame-colored silk Gert had pulled from its hanger.

"Here it is!" said Gert triumphantly. "This is it. This is you."

The gown was shot through with hundreds of tiny red glass bugle beads that gathered themselves to form a sunburst effect from the hips to a bodice trimmed in a boa of dark red ostrich feathers. Holding it against herself, gazing into Gert's large gilt cupid-festooned mirror, Vivian's pulse quickened. There was something exciting about the dress, something mature, sophisticated. She loved the color, although she had never worn red before.

"But do you think," she said uncertainly, "with my red hair . . ."

"Old-fashioned nonsense!" cried Gert. "It's perfect for you. What were you planning to wear?"

"My blue. My blue voile."

"Oh, that one," said Gert, nodding, and it was this that decided Vivian. She wouldn't be seen in blue voile tonight. No, nor her pink and white dimity nor her flowered organdy either.

"Oh, Gert, I'd love to borrow it," she murmured gratefully. "I'll take ever such good care of it and have it back first thing tomorrow morning."

"Keep it as long as you like," said Gert airily. " 'Til after you're married, why don't you. Then you'll have lots of duds of your own."

Gert had sent her own victoria down to Butler Street to fetch Vivian for their little visit, and now it was returning her home. Drawn by Harry Barkin's matched pair of dappled grays, two grooms in livery and top hats perched on top, it bowled smartly down Broad Street in the late afternoon sunshine, and many were the eyes that sought a second look at its remarkably pretty occupant.

Oblivious to the little stir she created, Vivian sat perfectly straight, a large if rather worn leghorn afternoon hat, once the property of Nancy Webb and freshened now by a large white organdy bow, tilted beguilingly over her red-gold hair. Above her she held the dainty white ruffled parasol that Gert, at the last moment, had pressed upon her for fear she would ruin her complexion. By her side was a valise containing not only the red silk gown but a mauve velvet evening wrap to wear over it, a gilt-edged fan, and almost new elbow-length white kid gloves, for Gert's eagle eye had noted the mended and shabby pair long since flung aside by Irene Webb.

Considering her borrowed finery, Vivian breathed a

happy little sigh. She could scarcely believe the good fortune that seemed to have fallen upon her out of the very air. But a short time ago she had scurried along these very streets, a little lady's maid intent on errands for the Webbs, looking enviously at those young ladies who rode at such ease in passing carriages, wondering what it might be like to be part of such a world. And now, here she was. Here she was!

But as the victoria lurched over the uneven cobblestones of Butler Street and drew up to the Randall front door, her high spirits faded somewhat and her chin rose stubbornly. She knew in her bones that her mother would take issue with the red gown. Gert Barkin's generosity notwithstanding, the party dresses of unmarried young women were always pastel.

7.

Vivian was not to be proved wrong in her expectations.
Heart fluttering apprehensively, she stood on a chair before the battered old bureau she shared with her sister and strove to see the lower half of herself in the small mirror that hung above it.

Since the room boasted no full-length mirror, both girls had become adept at inspecting themselves in sections, first the top half, from the waist up, and then, nimbly mounting a chair, from the waist down. Little agility was possible, however, in the red silk creation Vivian was presently wearing, for the waist was so tight she could scarce draw a breath and the décolletage so low that only by remembering to thrust back her shoulders and hold herself ramrod straight was she saved from daring exposure.

From the kitchen below came the rich aroma of warm brown bread and baked beans, and she could hear the voices and bustle that meant the family had gathered round the table for Saturday night supper. Dare she go down and face them? No one left the house upon any occasion of importance without first meeting Mamie's merciless inspection. Might it not be wise to call Mary Claire, whose eyes, as she struggled to hook Vivian into the dress, had grown round as saucers, and ask her to come back upstairs and help her into the blue voile?

But even as she considered this she recalled Gert Barkin's raised eyebrows and her "Oh, that one." After all Gert's time and efforts, and the loan not only of gown but cloak and gloves as well, how could she now appear in something else? Besides, she was no longer a girl going off to little neighborhood parties. On her fourth finger was a diamond ring, far larger than she would have chosen but, despite its embarrassing ostentation, proclaiming to all the world that she was a woman grown. Her mother must be made to understand this. Teetering off the chair, she scooped up Gert's cloak.

Neil was the first to see her as she appeared in the shadow of the kitchen doorway, and his mouth dropped open. Seeing this, the others turned to look at her.

Bathed in the warm golden light of the gas lamp above their heads, they appeared welded together, a unit, complete, gathered about the table as they would be all the days after she had left them. Already her chair, like her father's, was set back against the wall.

Beside the range, freshly blackened since it was Saturday, the clock ticked loudly. The smell of freshly made coffee filled the air, and suddenly, looking at them, such love for them filled her heart, such nostalgia for the place she had occupied among them, that it was all she could do to keep tears from her eyes.

"Well, step in, then, where we can see you," said her mother.

She moved into the light and submitted to her mother's eyes, all their eyes, traveling over her, noting the flaming color, the tight stretch of silk over hips and stomach, the low dip of the neckline against which the high young breasts pressed, the slender glistening shoulders that rose vulnerable and naked out of the dark red feathers.

"So you're going to wear that," said Mamie.

"Yes," answered Vivian firmly.

"I see."

Turning back to her food, she picked up her fork. The others, Neil, Mary Claire, Bucky, did the same.

Nonplussed, Vivian stood rooted to the spot. She had been prepared for opposition and had her arguments all ready: her age, her right to some independence, the fact that she was engaged. But she was to be permitted no self-justification, and just as a moment before she had all but melted with love for them, so now she hated them, for she could feel their disapproval, silent but strong. Ill-judged and angry, she swept from the room.

Having begun on the wrong foot, the evening contrived to continue so.

One look at Mallory's face as Vivian opened the front door to him and she knew that he, too, wasn't taken with her appearance, although without a word he placed about her shoulders the mauve velvet cloak with its scrolls of gold passementerie. Even Bunty O'Hare looked askance from his perch on top of the carriage.

Settling herself back on the pearl gray cushions, she stared disconsolately above the sleek chestnut haunches before her as, with a little slap of the reins from Bunty, the horse clip-clopped lightly and energetically forward.

It was a lovely evening, beckoning and balmy. It should have been such fun to be all dressed up and setting forth to a party. Never, she knew, had she looked so alluring despite the frowns she had received all around—including, she reminded herself, from the man who was shortly to become her husband. *Especially* from him, in fact, for never before had he failed to compliment her when she made her appearance dressed in those childish voiles and organdies.

"These clothes were lent me by Gert Barkin," she said, glancing up at him defiantly.

"I wouldn't have thought you bought them."

"Why not?"

"They aren't the type I would think you'd choose."

"And what type would I choose, may I ask?"

"I'm not sure now, but something more becoming, I would imagine."

Stunned, she caught her breath. She wasn't used to masculine criticism. The young men she knew would have declared her beautiful whatever she wore. And she had spent hours preparing for the evening, traipsing all the way up to Gert's house and back, taking special pains with her hair, even, after she left the kitchen, rebelliously crayoning a small, round, black beauty patch on her cheek, something she never before had done in her life.

"You think I look unattractive?" she demanded challengingly.

"I think you're spoiling for a fight."

"Not at all," she cried, piqued by his accuracy, by the look he gave her, patronizing, a trifle bored, as though she were a quarrelsome child. "Not at all," she repeated, longing to bait him. "I'm just interested that you think you know how ladies dress."

He swung his head to her. "I'm not sure how ladies dress, my dear. But I'm an expert on tarts."

Scandalized, she stared at him. Everyone got the better of her—her mother, her sister, her brothers. And now to be talked to in this way! Blind fury shook her, and she raised a small white-gloved hand to strike him. Deftly he caught her arm. "Don't you ever," he said through his teeth, bending above her, eyes piercing hers. "Don't you dare. Not now, not ever."

"You're hurting me," she breathed.

"I want to hurt you. I want you to know people always get hurt if they raise a hand to me. I want you to remember it. Will you? Will you remember?"

She closed her lips, biting them against the pain.

"Answer me. Will you?"

"Yes," she snapped, fearing her arm might break.

Instantly he released her, but she forbore to nurse the sting. With every ounce of dignity she could muster, she said, "I wish to return to my home. Kindly tell O'Hare to turn the carriage."

"Certainly not."

"What!" she cried, outraged.

For answer, Mallory's laughter, full-hearted and explosive, greeted her offended ears. Turning to look at her, he appeared to find something still so humorous that he sailed off into more loud gales, leaning against her and all but crushing her as he reached into his pocket and took out a fine linen handkerchief to wipe his eyes.

"You sound like England's queen," he said at last, still gasping. "As to turning the carriage, sure now, I'd like to oblige, but we can't be disappointing Paddy. He's my best friend in all the world and he'd take it ill, don't y' know. We'd be hurting his feelings if we didn't appear. No, now, and we'll not do that."

Snatching up her hand, he held it firmly against his knee, and they rode the rest of the way with Mallory going on and on about the scrapes he'd gotten into with his best friend, Paddy Doyle.

Vivian paid scant heed. Mallory, it appeared, was careful enough of Mr. Doyle's feelings but seemed not to care one whit about hurting hers. Resentment smoldered within her. She began to look forward to the party. She had no doubt of her powers of seduction. It would serve Mallory right and teach him not to criticize her if she was the most sought-after woman there.

The Doyles occupied a massive red brick residence off Spring Garden Street, just across a broad lawn from a similar brick residence belonging to Mr. and Mrs. Otto Ritter, Augusta Doyle's parents.

Not far away in Brewery Town was the Ritter brewery house, bottling plant, beer storage house, and cooper shop. Years ago, when old Mr. Ritter arrived from Germany with little more than a recipe for beer in his pocket, he and his family had lived in Brewery Town. But he had long since situated himself and, as they married, his three sons and his only daughter, Augusta, in mansions in Spring Garden where the other beer barons lived.

It was, Vivian learned, a great leg up in the world for Paddy Doyle when he married Augusta Ritter.

"Not that he went to her empty-handed," Mallory added as they traveled up Broad Street in the carriage. "He was in a position to bring with him exclusive rights to the city docks should Mr. Ritter care to expand his business by establishing an ice company. The which he decided to do, I'm happy to say."

Wrapped in her own schemes, this information drifted right over Vivian's red-gold curls. It didn't occur to her to wonder who might be powerful enough to give Paddy Doyle's father-in-law exclusive rights to unload ice onto city docks. Excited anticipation raced in her veins, and as they followed the line of carriages that turned smartly into a sweeping crescent drive and wheeled up to stop under a porte cochere, her breath came light and quick and her green eyes sparkled.

It would, she could tell, be just the sort of party she adored. Into the soft evening, heavy with the fragrance of honeysuckle, golden light spilled from the open windows and doors of the huge house. Japanese lanterns festooned broad porches, while from inside came the surge of violins and the strains of a waltz, and it was clear, from the shadowy figures dipping and gliding past the windows that the Doyles had a ballroom. A ballroom! And to think she had directed Mallory to take her back home, when she loved to dance better than anything in the world.

She didn't, however, much care for the Doyles. Dazzling in a large, blond, Teutonic way, Gussie Doyle seemed never able to remember Vivian's name when they chanced to meet and more than once had pointedly snubbed her. Paddy, on the other hand, was overly friendly, taking advantage of Vivian's desire to be sociable and pleasant by placing his fat, damp little hands upon her at every opportunity.

But tonight no aversions prompted her to temper the radiant smile she turned upon the pair as, on Mallory's arm, she swept to the top of the steps leading down into the sunken ballroom. Never had she felt so sure of her own beauty, so aware of the picture she made in the shimmering red silk gown.

The orchestra had just finished a set. The dancers turned to inspect the newcomers as, red-faced and perspiring, eyes popping, Paddy Doyle breathed, "Christ, Mallory, what have you done to deserve her?"

Despite the thundercloud that darkened Gussie's features, Vivian took a mischievous little satisfaction in the remark. Let Mallory remember his friend's accolade when next he was tempted to censure the clothes she wore. A smug little smile curving her lips, she deigned to let herself be led down to the dance floor.

Never had she felt so fleet-footed and light. Whirling in Mallory's strong clasp as the orchestra swung into "The Blue Danube," her feet skimmed over the waxed floor. Above her head swayed great ropes of greenery studded with live purple orchids, while from the center of the room depended a giant crystal chandelier, its loops and pendants of cut glass bursting into a thousand prisms of light. Everything, everyone, was beautiful—the men in white tie and tails, the women in their colored dresses, the tables that rimmed the room glistening with white linen cloths and bedecked with candelabra and bouquets of roses, the great gilt-framed mirrors set between the open windows and reflecting, enhancing, the twirling dancers. And on every side, admiring glances—frank masculine ones; covert feminine ones—directed at her.

Surely this could not be lost upon Mallory. Surely it must already be borne in upon him how faulty his judgment of her had been. But he seemed quite unaware of the little flurry she occasioned, and at the end of the set escorted her to their table, thanked her, fetched her an iced lemonade, and immediately fell into conversation with the gentlemen seated there.

Like the other ladies, Vivian smiled, docilely sipped her lemonade, and affected an attentive air. Not that she cared one bit about the trolleys and traction lines and rights-of-way that the men apparently found so absorbing. She was very glad she wasn't a man and didn't have to bother her head about such things. But it pleased her mightily to be seated at table with a judge, a banker, and a state legislator.

Only weeks ago she would have deferentially addressed such gentlemen, had she occasion to address them at all, as "sir." As to their wives, such a night as this at Cavendish Square would have found her running her legs off to fetch and carry cloaks and shawls, sew up ripped hems, and provide comb or smelling salts or whatever else was requested, just like the little maid who, with a shy "Thank you, ma'am," tonight had taken her own—or rather, Gert Barkin's—velvet cloak at the door. Did the Doyles, she wondered idly, see to it, as did the Webbs, that the servants got their bit of salad and iced cakes after the party was over? Some houses did, some didn't, as she very well knew. The Allenbys, kitchen gossip had it, never did.

But she was far too intrigued by the glittering present to waste much thought upon that drab past when the prospect of a bit of chicken gallantine and a slice of Black Forest cake could light up her life. Opening her fan, she turned a polite ear to the gentleman beside her who was saying, "If the city is going to go ahead with it, my bank would like to hold the mortgage, I can assure you."

Mallory swirled beer around in a cut-glass beer mug. "What rate?" he asked.

"Three percent."

"Penn National offered two and one-half."

The banker looked around the table, and Vivian observed the judge and the state legislator give almost imperceptible nods.

He cleared his throat. "Well, now," he said, "we could go that, too. But the board was figuring that if the city pays us three, then that extra little one-half of one percent might make a nice little contribution to the Amity Club." He smiled affably. "Bert, here, will be coming up for re-election. We'd like to help him win."

If Mallory found this information useful, took it into consideration, he gave no sign, and Vivian was suddenly aware of the expectant hush that had fallen upon the table. The ladies had stopped sipping their lemonade, and all eyes were fixed upon Mallory. Without quite knowing why, Vivian found her own gaze riveted upon him, also.

He possessed, she had noticed, this ability to become the center of attention. Unlike anyone she had ever known, Brian Mallory combined a casual ease with an indefinable air of command that seemed to dwarf men such as the ones who presently shared the table. It wasn't merely his size or the suggestion of great physical power just under the impeccably tailored clothes he wore. It wasn't even the remarkably incisive features—the deep cleft in the chin, the firm, full lips, the prominent nose, the electric blue eyes that could change so swiftly from laughter to steely reserve. These attributes could account for a kind of matinee-idol appeal. But there was something more, something special about him that, although she didn't trouble herself to try to define it, seemed to be recognized by all.

Continuing to swirl beer in the mug he held cradled in both his hands, he said, "We'll have to condemn some land." He glanced at Judge Wickersham's plump, pink face. "Kenyon, did you ever get around to buying up that land I told you about?"

Judge Wickersham eagerly assured Mallory he had. He looked pleased, indeed delighted, as did the banker who wanted the mortgage and the state legislator who would need funds. As did Mallory himself, although what he was getting out of it Vivian couldn't have said.

Naive and unschooled as she was in such matters, it was nonetheless clear to her that a deal had just been made. Above the gilt-edged fan, green eyes that were less flirtatious than curious studied legislator, banker, and judge. All three gentlemen looked the same: confident, impressive, above all, possessed of a wealth that showed itself in subtle ways. More than in the fine fabric and cut of the clothes they wore, more than in the glint of gold cuff links and watch chains, it resided in the telltale care of their persons: the professionally clipped moustache, the pink, scrubbed scalp, the buffed and polished fingernails. To Vivian's observant eye, such perfection of personal hygiene was the very hallmark of the rich. The poor, on the whole, were clean only upon occasion.

But what struck her more than this new acquaintance with what Father Shields would surely call "the interests" was the fact that Mallory was obviously in thick with them. Clinton Webb had hinted at certain alliances, but she hadn't known what he was talking about. She still didn't have a glimmer of the particulars, but of one thing she was certain: contrary to Father Shields's rosy expectations, Brian Mallory was already in with the greedy, grasping "interests" hand and glove.

Rather coolly she refused his invitation to dance, saying she must go across the room and visit with Gert Barkin.

8

Her reception at the Barkins' table was satisfactorily flattering. Except for Gussie Doyle, everyone appeared to be delighted to make room for her. She only hoped this was noted by Mallory, who had escorted her to the table and, with a little bow, left her there.

If he failed to observe the appreciative glances bestowed upon her by Harry Barkin and by Gussie Doyle's brother, Heinz Ritter, certainly he couldn't help but hear Paddy Doyle's booming, "Here she is! The most beautiful belle at the ball!"

Vivian greeted this remark with a light flirtatious laugh directed at Brian Mallory's receding back. Nor did Gussie Doyle's low, sullen, "Shut up, Paddy," diminish by a jot her enjoyment of the little triumph. A giddiness had seized her, a feverish gaiety that led her to flutter her eyelids over the rim of her fan, toss her head coquettishly, laugh trillingly. This performance was intensified when, out of the corner of her eye, she spied Mallory dancing past without so much as casting an eye in her direction.

At the sight of him her vision blurred, refusing to mark whether the partner at whom he was smiling was old or young, beautiful or ugly. How like him, she thought, seething, quite forgetting she had just repulsed him, how like him to affect nonchalance, to pretend he didn't know she was holding sway at the table, that it was the gayest party in the room, that others looked her way with envy.

Gussie Doyle didn't join in the hilarity, nor did Heinz Ritter's wife. But Vivian didn't think twice of these ladies. Truth to tell, she gave scant attention to the gentlemen. The little arts and graces of seduction were second nature to her, and with half a mind she teased and parried, laughing merrily at the men's labored sallies, pretending rebuke in the same moment she enticed, working her fan rapidly back and forth, revealing and concealing the high young bosom, red lips smilingly parted over small glistening teeth, green eyes flashing.

But it was of Mallory she thought, Mallory whom she desired to best, to bring to heel as she could so easily do with other men. But he eluded her always; more, he seemed ever to have the upper hand, as he did tonight, waltzing by without so much as a glance at her. Oh, how she would love to make him jealous, change that half mocking, half amused, sometimes bored look he frequently turned upon her to one of abject supplication.

So caught up was she in this fantasy that she didn't notice the conversation had taken an ugly turn until Paddy Doyle glowered at his wife and said, "What's the matter? The hell she's not the most beautiful. I'll take a vote. Gert, what do you say?"

"She's beautiful, Paddy," said Gert.

"*Most* beautiful," Paddy insisted belligerently.

"Okay, *most* beautiful," Gert agreed all too readily, and Vivian realized that not only was she herself the subject of discussion but that, except for Gert and perhaps Mrs. Ritter, these people had been drinking too much—Harry Barkin, Gussie and Paddy, Heinz Ritter, all of them.

"Harry, you're next," Paddy continued thickly. "What do you think of our little Vivvie here? Look at those eyes. Ever see the like of them, Harry? And those lips, those—"

"Whoa there, Paddy," trumpeted Harry Barkin as Vivian blushed furiously. "Whoa, there. Don't go too far."

"What d'ya mean, too far? I ain't even begun."

"Shut up, I said," commanded Gussie.

Viciously Paddy turned on her. "What do you mean, shut up? Where do you get off telling me to shut up? Just because I work for your old man, you think you can say anything to me? I'm your husband, damn it. I want a little respect. If it wasn't for Paddy Doyle, you'd still be hanging on the vine. Just where do you get off?"

"Come on now, Paddy," put in Gert cajolingly. "Gussie didn't mean anything. She's right. You're embarrassing Vivian."

"What!" cried Paddy, turning to Vivian in surprise. "Am I, now?" he inquired, peering down at her. "Sure, and I'd never want to do that. Come on, doll. You and I will have a little dance."

"No, thank you," murmured Vivian uncomfortably.

"Why not? Come on, I want to make things up to you with a little dance."

Swaying unsteadily, he rose to his feet.

"Damn it, Doyle, she said *no*," Gussie burst out wrathfully.

On the dance floor and at nearby tables people turned as, rounding on his wife, Paddy shouted, "You keep out of this. No little broad tells Paddy Doyle she won't give him a dance."

Lurching back to Vivian, he slammed his hand down on the back of her chair, pulled it away from the table, and, grasping her arm, jerked her to her feet.

"No!" she cried indignantly, battling him.

As if by magic, Paddy was lifted away from her, spun around, clipped on the chin, and sent sprawling back upon the table amid a crash of splintering glassware. Somewhere a woman screamed; the orchestra stopped playing, and in the silence that followed, Paddy raised himself on an elbow. Gingerly he moved his jaw, then his bloodshot eyes rested balefully on Mallory standing over him, fist again cocked. "I won't forget this to you," he said.

"Nor," replied Mallory coldly, "will I."

Sunk in gloom in her corner of the swaying carriage, Vivian stared bleakly out into the night as Bunty O'Hare drove them smartly back down the gas-lit drive up which they had so recently traveled.

She would be happy again someday, she tried to tell her-

self. But she was just eighteen, and with the dire certainty
that informs such tender years, she doubted she would ever
again know the lightheartedness that had been hers before
Mallory punched Paddy Doyle.

In his corner Mallory sat upright and unspeaking, massive in the shadows, thinking, no doubt, about his friend.
Erstwhile friend, Vivian reminded herself unsparingly, recalling Paddy lying among the roses and the candelabra
while everyone looked on in dismay.

Oh, what must they think of such behavior, that Judge
Wickersham, and the banker, and the state legislator? And
it was all her fault. All her fault, indeed it was. But for her
vanity, her false pride, her vengeful desire to teach Mallory
a lesson, he and Paddy would still be the best of friends.
Oh, if only she hadn't gone to the party. Or, having gone,
if only she hadn't led Paddy on. Or, having teased and
flirted, if only she hadn't refused to dance with him.

Peeking up at Mallory, she gave a polite little cough and
said, "I led him on, Mallory. I led him on, and that's the
truth."

"You behaved like a flighty girl and no mistake," he
agreed, making her cheeks sting with his candor. "But he
was bullyragging you."

"He was drunk."

"Don't I know it?"

"He didn't know what he was doing."

"And that's just an excuse; a means of doing whatever
you please without having to face the consequences. I've
seen many a man drunk, and women, too, for that matter,
and good or bad, I've not doubted but I was seeing the true
person."

"But, Mallory—"

"Now I'll hear no more of this," he cut in bluntly.
"You're mine, not his, and I'll wipe up the streets with him
or any man that dares lay a finger on you."

The vehemence of the statement startled her, although
the little tingle that went shooting down her spine was delicious. Suddenly she longed for him to sweep her into his
arms as he had done only once before, that astonishing evening on the sofa in the parlor. The memory of the rough
possession he had taken of her, his arms like bands of steel
and his lips crushing hers, seemed to Vivian to tremble between them whenever they were together, to crackle in the
very air.

Surely, she fumed to herself, surely he felt this, too, knew her willingness, nay, eagerness to repeat the occasion. But he had never again touched her except in the most perfunctory manner, though several times she had gone so far as to rather invite an advance.

How, then, she wondered now, could her mother surmise that he loved her? He had wished to make a point, that was all. Her ardent response to his lovemaking doubtless set him to secretly crowing. Offended by the very thought of such a possibility, she pushed farther back into her corner and elaborately gathered her skirts away from him. But if he was aware of this indication of her displeasure, he gave no sign.

The truth was, it seemed not to matter to anyone whether she was pleased or displeased, happy or not, and to her mother least of all. With a single-mindedness that Vivian found almost unseemly, Mamie Randall appeared to be intent upon only one thing, namely, the getting of her older daughter married to a wealthy man.

Their relationship was no longer as it once had been. Gone were the old close, easy days when Vivian had basked in the knowledge that, of all Mamie's children, it was she upon whom her mother doted and relied. Now it seemed everything she did invited censure. Little tiffs about the wedding, about clothes, about new friends like the Barkins, left feelings bruised and tempers short. Moreover, the entire household appeared to be in disarray. With the wedding in the offing everyone was run ragged, what with answering doorbells, carting mountains of gifts up to Mallory's new house, and helping sew up wedding finery.

Even the neighbors had been pressed into service for this last, and while, each evening, Vivian departed on Mallory's arm to yet another prenuptial celebration, Mamie's sewing machine worked like fury. The others—Bucky, Neil, Mary Claire, together with whatever neighbor ladies looked in to lend a hand—kept busy at the kitchen table sewing on snaps and buttons, laces and ribbons, hooks and eyes. On the kitchen range crimping irons were kept heated, and in the parlor, hanging on a clothesline strung the length of the cramped little room, were the bridesmaids' frocks in various stages of completion, together with Vivian's wedding gown.

Mallory had insisted that Mamie let him provide for the

large and elaborate wedding reception he wanted, nor was she in a position to refuse. But even with money no problem, and with caterers engaged to set out the wedding feast in a tent to be erected behind the Hibernian Firehouse, there was still much to do, and Vivian felt more and more guilty about all the work and fuss.

Caught in the demanding social whirl of a bride-to-be, she had little time to help out at home, and the shadows she saw deepening under the eyes of the indefatigable Mamie troubled her. The very last thing she wished was yet another quarrel, but this appeared unavoidable when, two days after the Doyles' disastrous party, she received a note from Gert Barkin: "Must see you. Come at once."

Outside, in a torrential downpour, waited the Barkin carriage sent to fetch her.

"And does this mean," demanded Mamie, "that you must drop everything and run off to her?"

"But why shouldn't I go?" responded Vivian.

"Because it's raining cats and dogs, for one thing."

Vivian had been down on hands and knees in the midst of scrubbing up the kitchen floor when the little note arrived via the Barkins' coachman. Now, forbearing to dispute her mother, she opened the back door and flung the sudsy water into the streaming yard.

"For another," Mamie persisted, "why do you feel you must do everything that woman says?"

Vivian was well aware of her mother's low regard for Gert Barkin. According to Mamie, Gert was nothing but a flashy upstart, a baggage, a bold piece, and nothing Vivian glowingly reported about the Barkins' big house and many servants could induce Mamie to alter this opinion. Moreover, Mamie felt, and repeatedly stated, that her daughter paid far too much heed to this wealthy new friend, and there was just enough truth in the observation to irk Vivian.

"Mama," she said tartly, "I don't feel I must do everything she says. But she's my friend and she wishes to see me."

"Fine friend, to get you in trouble."

"She didn't get me in trouble."

"She lent you that dress. That's what did it. That was the cause of it. Nothing at all would have happened had you but worn the blue voile."

Vivian disdained comment and energetically wiped her reddened hands on the old towel hanging on a roller on the back door. She wished she hadn't breathed a word about that awful party! Her distress at the outcome, and a long habit of confiding in her mother, had gotten the story from her, but the succor she usually received wasn't forthcoming. Her embarrassing entanglement, pronounced her mother, was just what she deserved for making a display of herself in such fashion, adding that men only took liberties where they were invited.

Gert Barkin, on the other hand, was sure to offer sympathy and understanding. It was a relief to be out of the hot, stuffy little house and riding through the rain up Broad Street in the luxury of the Barkins' carriage.

Respite was brief, however, for no sooner had she been shown into Gert's boudoir than Gert presented her with a news clipping from a gossip column in *The Item*.

"*Bash Becomes Brawl*," she read.

What great mahatma of the political arena all but K O'd his best friend and chief lieutenant in fisticuffs over the former's beautiful titian-haired fiancée at a posh soirée in Spring Garden on Saturday night? Down at the docks rumor has it that this friendship is now on ice.

"Isn't it rich?" cried Gert gleefully.

Clad in pink satin negligee trimmed with yards of white maribou, she lay back among the heart-shaped pillows that graced her pink velvet chaise longue.

Vivian raised stricken eyes. "I'm really sorry for what happened."

"Don't worry about it! Look, that story would never have reached the newspapers if Gussie hadn't paid a reporter from *The Item* to cover her precious ball. Isn't that just like Gussie—paying to get her name in the society columns? Serves her right, that's what I think. I told her so, too, when she came crying to me."

"She was crying?" inquired Vivian, finding it difficult to imagine the stony-eyed Gussie in tears.

Gert nodded, causing the nest of curls tied atop her head with a pink velvet ribbon to bounce vigorously. "This morning. Oh, it was rich, I tell you. Old Gussie blubbering about how Heinz and the boys are furious with Paddy, to say nothing of old Papa Ritter himself. Because of their ice company, y'know. Mallory won't let them use the city docks anymore."

"How can he stop them?"

"Come again?"

Determined to understand at least something of Mallory and his doings, Vivian pressed on. "How can he stop them? I mean," she added with a deprecating little laugh, "he doesn't own the city docks, does he?"

The awkward attempt at levity was lost upon Gert, who stared at her open-mouthed. "Great gawd awmighty!" she exclaimed softly. "You mean you don't know Mallory holds all South Philly in the palm of his hand?"

Patting the pink velvet chaise longue, she said, "Sit down. Mama's going to tell you a story."

Brian Mallory's father, Vivian learned, had given a politician named Big Bill Brady his start in the Third Ward.

"The way I hear it, Brady was a legend in his time," said Gert, settling into the tale with obvious relish. "A two-fisted fighter who would take on the devil himself. Like Mallory, I guess. People who knew Brady say the two are a lot alike, except that Mallory is smarter." Gert giggled. "Sexier, too, I bet.

"Anyway, Mallory was just a little shaver when his daddy was a precinct captain in the Third Ward. A guy named O'Donnell was the ward boss back then, and him and Matt Mallory had a falling out. The way the story goes is that Matt Mallory felt his precinct wasn't getting a big enough piece of pie."

"Pie?" repeated Vivian, refusing to let embarrassment at her own ignorance stand in her way.

"Patronage," explained Gert. "Jobs on the city payroll to pass around to the faithful when your party wins an election. There are hundreds of 'em—the Water Board, public works, stuff like that. Come election day, a ward leader like Matt Mallory encourages a lot of people to go to the polls and vote the way he says. And when his party wins, he likes to be able to reward his friends by passing a few favors around. So when Matt Mallory had his falling-out with O'Donnell, he encouraged his friends to vote for Big Bill Brady. And Brady won: first committeeman; then councilman, and then"—Gert's voice turned reverent—"treasurer of the Amity Club."

The treasurer of the Amity Club, according to Gert,

kept no books, made no report, answered to no one. But every contractor who wanted to work for the city, every lawyer who needed special consideration for his client, every banker who hoped for a mortgage on city property, made a contribution to the club. From these funds the treasurer of the Amity Club was able to finance the election to City Council, to the state legislature, to the municipal courts of gentlemen who, in turn, would help him grant favors to those who had been so generous.

Vivian's thoughts winged back to Judge Wickersham and the moment at the Doyles' party when she had known that a deal was being made. She was beginning to understand. Thanks to Big Bill Brady, Mallory was now treasurer of this club and held the power to bequeath or to withhold. Brady had been grateful to Mallory's father for giving him his start, and when Matt Mallory died, he had taken an interest in the boy.

Gert grinned. "In Ma Mallory, too, so I hear tell—even though Brady was a family man."

There could be no doubt of the type of interest Gert implied, and Vivian caught her breath. "Ma Mallory?"

Gert's eyes twinkled. "So the story goes. At any rate, Brady brought Mallory right along—taught him how to fight, how to win elections; made him his right-hand man. They say Mallory and his Butlerites were regular terrors around the polls on election day—beat up the opposition proper while the cops just stood by. Cripes, why should the cops interfere? Brady was letting them twist arms just like Mallory does today."

Twisting arms, Vivian discovered, meant extortion, petty bribery, graft, the very practices Father Shields had so vigorously assailed. Appalled, she said, "I'm sure Mallory doesn't countenance such things."

Gert's eyes seemed to start out of her head. "Doesn't countenance them? Why, kiddo, there isn't a numbers game or a prostitute in all of South Philly that doesn't pay off some cop. Are you trying to tell me Mallory doesn't know this?"

"Maybe he knows it," she faltered, for there seemed no possibility that Gert would be wrong. "But I'm sure he doesn't, well . . . approve."

"Oh, he doesn't, eh? And how do you think he gets his? How do you think he's paying for that fancy palace you're about to move into?"

Vivian felt her face grow hot. Why had she listened to all these unsavory tales? Why had she cared? She had never been interested in such matters. But now she had to know more—knew she *must* know more. "I don't know how he's paying for it," she said quietly. "If you know, I want you to tell me."

Gert's eyes skidded away. "Forget it, kiddo."

"Gert, I mean it. I want to know. I've got to know."

"Ask Mallory."

"He won't tell me."

It was only after she said this that she knew it was true. She thought of Mallory now as an iceberg—the glittering tip sparkled in the sunlight, but underneath, in the icy, black depths where strange fish swam, lurked the vast bulk that she would never fathom. "Please, Gert," she said. "Don't make me beg."

"Cripes, why don't I keep my trap shut?"

"I'm glad you haven't. If you were in my place, you'd want to know."

"But I don't know anything. Or leastways, not much. Just what Paddy Doyle says when he gets tanked up and shoots off his mouth."

"How does Paddy happen to know so much?"

Gert held up two fingers pressed together. "Like this, Mallory and him. Before the party Saturday night, that is."

Vivian brushed aside the twinge she felt. "What does Paddy say?" she continued relentlessly, surprised at her own persistence, at how firm her voice was. "You must tell me. What does Paddy say?"

Gert shrugged a pink satin shoulder. "Mallory gets his rake-offs, that's all," she said, pouting, her voice an injured whine. "Oh, not," she added quickly, "from the cops. Mallory won't touch anything like that, Paddy says. I mean, nothing from prostitutes, or anything. But nobody knows how deep he dips into the Amity Club. And he gets a lot of tips when he does a favor—what stocks to buy, when to sell 'em, stuff like that."

Relief overwhelmed Vivian. Would she have moved into Mallory's house if Gert had said it was built on petty graft? It was a decision she didn't have to make. Somehow, dipping into the treasury of the Amity Club and tips about the purchase or sale of stocks didn't seem so bad.

"Thank you, Gert," she said.

"Listen, don't never breathe that I spilt the beans. I

mean it. Harry would kill me if he knew. He wants to stay on Mallory's good side."

"I'll never tell."

"Is that a promise?"

"It's a promise."

"Geez, the way I open my big mouth! On the other hand, a girl has a right to know what she's getting into when she marries a man." Suddenly she smiled. "Which brings me to the reason I sent for you today." With a wink she reached under a pillow and withdrew a long, flat box covered in thick black velvet. "Something old, something new, something borrowed, something blue," she crooned. "This is something new. From me and Harry. You're to wear it on your wedding day."

Vivian unfastened the small metal clasp, opened the box, and caught her breath. Resting on a white satin pillow lay a necklace of matched pearls—lustrous, pink-tinged, exquisite.

"Gert!" she breathed.

"Like it?" asked Gert offhandedly.

"They're beautiful! But . . . well, I can't accept them."

"Why not?"

"It's too much. They're too expensive. It's too much for you to do."

"Phooey!" responded Gert. "We've got the money. Harry's made of it. And after all, me and you are best friends, aren't we, kiddo?"

How, wondered Vivian, could the question be answered without hurting Gert's feelings? Warmhearted and generous to a fault, the young woman was nonetheless very different from lifelong friends like Rita Celano, Iris Ferguson, and the Wade girls, with whom Vivian had gone to St. Bonaventure's school. For all she was fond of her and grateful in a dozen ways, she would always be put off by the crudeness, the downright vulgarity that Gert seemed to flaunt with a brassy pride, and not for the first time did she have the feeling of being put on the spot by Gert, of being asked for more than she could give.

"It's very kind of you," she began, "but—"

"But me no buts," said Gert. "They're yours, strung up for you special. Harry ordered them from a friend in New York. You're just mean if you don't take them." Once more she winked in the way she had, screwing up one side of the small, pert, monkeylike little face. "Besides," she added, "who knows? Maybe you can do a little something for me and Harry sometime."

9

Vivian could only wonder what "little something" she would ever be able to do for Gert and Harry Barkin, but with her wedding day fast approaching, she had little time to dwell on such puzzles.

She had long since given up all hope of hearing from Jamie. Not one word had come from St. Louis, and the feverish eagerness with which, day after day, she waited for the postman, contriving never to leave the house on Butler Street until after the mail's arrival, had given way little by little to the cold certainty that she would never hear from him again.

That he could have left her so, abandoned her, served only to prove how right Mallory had been about him and how little he had cared for her. But this did nothing to assuage the qualms she had begun to have about her present circumstances.

"It's only natural you should feel a mite nervous," Mamie told her. "Most brides do."

Most brides marry the man they love, Vivian silently amended, and then felt churlish, for surely no man could be more generous in every way than Mallory had proved himself to be. But then, he didn't love her, either. They had their own reasons for marrying. She took comfort in this thought as, modeling her wedding gown, she slowly turned around on the fitting platform before her mother's critical gaze.

"Ah, there now, Vivvie, it's that beautiful you are," sighed Mamie at last, sinking back on her heels from where she knelt at the platform, the final inspection over and done. " 'Prepared as a bride adorned for her husband,' " she added with biblical fervor and, taking up the edge of her faded old gray-striped apron, dabbed at her eyes.

"Mama, please don't cry."

"And why should I not, if I've a mind to? Lord knows, I've worked that hard for it and there's no prettier gown in all the world."

"Wurrld," the word came out in her mother's soft brogue, and Vivian could only agree. In the cramped little room, its shabbiness helplessly exposed by the bright morning sunshine, her slender body, encased in dazzling cream-colored satin, seemed to float up out of the yards of white tulle.

Seed pearls encrusted the hem of the satin train and banded the low bust line where it gave way to a deep yoke of silk Chantilly lace terminating in a high wired collar and long, tight lace sleeves. From the tips of her white satin slippers to the glory of flaming red-gold hair veiled in mists of tulle above the green eyes, she presented a picture.

"And him not troubling himself to come home and give you away," said Mamie.

The bitter words were like a shadow across the sun.

"Mama, he can't."

"Can't he, now? Me working my fingers to the bone to give you the wedding you should have, and him not taking the interest to walk you down the aisle?"

Vivian forced back the sudden aching lump in her throat, not wanting to show the keenness of her own disappointment and hurt and thus heap more coals of fire upon her father's head. On her wedding day he would be commencing the first leg of his journey to, of all places, the Klondike to hunt for gold. Only that morning a letter containing this surprising information had arrived.

I can never tell you how grieved I am, and will ever be, to be forced to miss my baby's wedding. But we've got our transportation and must be on our way. Fortune has smiled upon me and I am lucky to be included in this group of fine gentlemen, but I must leave with them or lose my chance and stay behind.

The gentlemen in this group are superior types who do things scientifically. They aren't going off hit or miss. Two of them have been up to the Yukon and staked a claim, so we know just where we must dig.

By rights we should be there now since it's past the spring thaw, but our scientific way of doing things will make up for lost time. And when we strike pay dirt you may be sure I'll make it up to you with the biggest and best wedding present you ever saw, plus lots of things for your ma and your sister and brothers for there will be no more hardship and worry since at last my fortune will be made.

Mr. Mallory is the luckiest of men to have won the heart and hand of my dear little girl. You have always been my ideal of the best daughter a father could wish. Along with my beloved wife and my other wonderful children, you will be an inspiration on this arduous but lucrative journey.

And now I must close, but be sure your papa will be thinking of his little daughter on her wedding day, with a tear in his eye and love in his heart.

On a separate but similar sheet of cheap ruled paper carefully torn from a copybook were enclosed a few lines of poetry:

There is a tide in the affairs of men,
Which, taken at the flood, leads on to fortune;
Omitted, all the voyage of their life
Is bound in shallows and in miseries.

Wm. Shakespeare

Long ago Vivian had asked her father why he so often quoted poetry.

"Because," he replied with thrilling sonority, "poetry is the wine of the soul."

It was, she knew, with poetry that he had won her mother. Poetry and his schemes—his heady, impossible dreams.

"He's never been here when he was needed," Mamie grumbled reproachfully. "No, never once. When Neil had his appendix and the doctor said I must get him right away to the hospital and him near dying, where was your father then, I ask you? Where was he then?"

Vivian had heard endless times where he was: out in Dakota Territory working on a plan to build a chain of icehouses to the Columbia River in Oregon so that fresh Columbia River salmon could be swiftly rushed to New York restaurants in the new refrigerated trains.

"And when Mary Claire was walking along that picket fence out back and slipped and fell and a picket near poked her eye out, and me pregnant with Bucky at the time, where was he then? Off with that Frenchman," continued her mother. "Off with that Frenchman on some wild notion to plant fifty thousand cabbages in the Little Missouri Valley, wherever that may be, and feed them with fertilizer made from offal. Offal, would you believe! And who in the honor of God would be wanting to eat cabbages grown in that?"

No one, it seemed. The offal-fertilized cabbages were just one more pipe dream joining myriad others. But Vivian never failed to thrill to her father's tales of the wealthy and dashing Frenchman, Antoine Amedée Marie Vincent, Marquis de Morès, who, with his beautiful young French wife, had settled out in Dakota Territory and owned a hotel there, and a slaughterhouse and railroad cars, and who, when her father was invited to dinner, had served iced champagne. Nor was she likely to forget his stories of the Badlands, and of Theodore Roosevelt, now President of the United States.

"If I had but one honor granted to me in my life," he more than once had told her, "I could not but choose the privilege of having been in the company of that brave and brilliant man. 'Old Four-Eyes,' we called him. But only at first, mind you, and on account of his spectacles, don't y' know. But when we took the measure of the man—his strength and his courage and his intelligence—why, we'd have followed him into hell. And some of us did—up San Juan Hill to free the Cubans from the heel of the Spanish."

Her father, a friend of the President! But he hadn't gone off to join Roosevelt's Rough Riders in the war with Spain as, Vivian had come to know, he so desperately wanted to do. Her mother had been pregnant with Sean, and he had stayed at home.

In the long litany of his offenses down through the years, her mother seemed never to remember how wonderful he had been at that time, making her stay in bed, carrying her meals to her on a tray with always a little something special on it—a funny drawing to make her laugh, a flower.

Once Vivian had reminded her of his concern for, being twelve years old, she had noticed.

"And must I be forever grateful?" her mother had demanded fiercely. "And him knowing I should have no more babies at all? Someday you'll learn why it was he owed me the kindness."

In the face of such wrath, such mystery, Vivian shrank back, her fragile attempt to champion her father defeated.

The baby boy was born dead. Her father took her to Muldoon's funeral parlor to see him, the first time in her life she had looked upon the newborn, or the dead. How perfect he appeared to be in the small white casket, dressed in the christening robe her mother had made for him, the beautifully formed little head covered with pitch-black down, the tiny fingers of his hand delicate and starlike. Looking up at her father, she had seen tears streaming silently from his eyes.

Remembering, she felt tears prickle behind her own eyelids, and a cold clammy sweat broke over her, at strange variance with the mid-morning sun blazing into the stifling room.

"The truth is," said Mamie, up off her knees now, her fingers slowly traveling down Vivian's spine unfastening each small, cleverly concealed hook and eye, "the truth is, your father never took the interest in his family that other men do. He never cared."

Vivian felt herself stiffen. He did care, oh, he did! She knew he did! She hated it when her mother talked this way. It was all she could do to stand there while the fingers moved with little tugs down her back, the light breath chilling her skin as the gown parted.

"And where did he get the money to go to Klondike?" Mamie demanded, warming to her subject. "Would you be telling me that? Not sending one penny home all this month, but taking himself off in fine style. Pawned his watch, that's what. Pawned that watch again, so his sisters will redeem it. The Lord knows, that's all he's got."

Her mother seemed perversely pleased by this lack of capital, and she was almost certainly right. The gold watch that once had belonged to Edward Randall, Sr., was the only thing of any value her father had ever possessed. How many times he had pawned it and his sisters, the Randall girls, had redeemed it, Vivian couldn't guess. She knew only that sometimes it appeared, linked across his trim, muscular belly by its gold chain, and at others it was gone again.

"They've spoiled him and that's the truth, those two girls," Mamie persisted relentlessly. "Spoiled him and laid the blame to me for being a Catholic and raising his children in the Faith. Always felt he married beneath himself, they did. Hated the sight of me from the beginning."

With a pang Vivian recalled the oft-told story of that day when, a new bride, her mother had invited the Randall girls to tea. Afterwards they had described to their brother how Mamie had poured her tea into her saucer and drunk from it, how she had eaten a piece of cake with her fingers and caught up a drop of cream from the cream pitcher with her thumb. The young groom had tried to instruct his bride in polite behavior and was astonished when she burst into tears; was even more astonished when she declared that from that day forward the Randall girls would never enter her home again.

A deep pity abided in Vivian's heart for that long-ago young woman with her one good tablecloth brought with her from Ireland and spread over four orange crates lashed together with chicken wire, and her china begged special for the occasion from the rectory of St. Bonaventure's. Had the Randall girls, her own Aunt Sarah and Aunt Opal, known the effort and anxiety that went into that ill-fated little tea party, would they have responded differently?

Vivian doubted it. Nothing her mother might have done would have made the marriage acceptable to the two spinster sisters living in their snug little home off Chestnut Street, with their membership in the Philadelphia Cultural Society and their high school diplomas hanging in frames on the living room wall. Nothing would ever induce them to believe that Mamie Brogan was good enough to be their brother's wife, for Mamie had proved she was no lady, and Edward Randall, despite his lack of worldly success, was a gentleman down to his toes.

"There now," said her mother, lips pursed, jaw thrust forward, "best get out of that gown and run over to your aunts with that letter. No point letting them think they'll be seeing their brother anytime soon."

Released from the hot, uncomfortable dress, from the tightly laced corset that so effectively achieved a stylish wasp waist, Vivian in vest and knee-length underdrawers hurried up the steep wooden stairs and into everyday clothes only a bit less confining: long dark blue broadcloth skirt, white shirtwaist with ascot, and, on her head, a cheap dark blue straw boater.

From under the handkerchief case in her bureau drawer she took her father's letter and placed it in her reticule, but no sooner was she out the front door than she bethought herself of someone other than the aunts who should know that no father could be expected to accompany her down the aisle on her wedding day.

Changing direction, she proceeded to the Tipperary Saloon.

10

Coming from out of the noonday glare and bustle of Butler Street with its hurrying pedestrians and its carts and carriages lurching over cobblestones and flinging up swirling clouds of dust in every direction, Vivian was surprised at how pleasant the Tipperary Saloon was.

From the ceiling of its dim, cool interior, three large fans rotated slowly. Only a handful of men stood over their beer at the long mahogany bar. They peered round at her with interest when she entered, unaccompanied young ladies rarely being seen in such places, and from behind the bar Solly set down the glass he was polishing and hurried protectively to her side.

"You want to see the boss?"

"If I may."

Mallory looked up quizzically from the ledger lying open upon his huge desk as Solly stepped aside and motioned her through the doorway.

"I don't mean to intrude," she murmured.

"But you're not," said Mallory, rising instantly and putting on a checked jacket over the bright yellow silk shirt he was wearing. "You must always feel free to stop in anytime you've a mind to. I shall always be delighted to see you."

Grateful for such gracious assurance, she took the chair

he offered. "I've just received word from my father that he is unable to attend our wedding. But perhaps it's best if you read his letter yourself."

In the quiet room with its high ceiling and thick rugs, the noise from the street was distant, muted, and sunshine filtered in through the striped green awnings with a cool, bosky light. On the dark brown pressed-metal wall, ornamented with chrysanthemums in low relief, a large clock ticked loudly in the stillness as Mallory bent his attention upon the letter.

What a sorry bargain he was making! thought Vivian of a sudden, forced into unaccustomed objectivity by the sight of those two flimsy sheets of cheap copybook paper in the strong, square, well-cared-for hands, a garnet winking from a heavy gold setting upon one finger.

She was struck afresh with how truly handsome he was: shoulders powerful and broad under the checked jacket; the wavy hair, one lock falling a bit forward, thick and dark and springy; the cleft in the firm chin; the broad, sharp nose; the thick, black eyebrows, pointed rather than curved, in a manner that at times gave his face a diabolic air. Nor was he handsome only, she reminded herself, but in command of wealth, power, success beyond her father's wildest dreams.

And whom was he marrying? A young woman as poor as her own mother had been when she stepped off the boat from Ireland. Poorer, for, unlike her mother, she possessed not even a tablecloth by way of dowry. A young woman uncommonly pretty, perhaps, but with looks that would soon enough fade, as Ma Mallory had duly noted. An uneducated servant girl who hadn't gone past the tenth grade, who had spent her days scrubbing heads and running to fetch and carry, who wore hand-me-down hats and shoes and dresses—a young woman, in short, with nothing to offer at all, bringing with her to this marriage not even a heart full of love.

Appalled by such discrepancy, she said impulsively, "If you don't want to go forward with it, I will quite understand."

Mallory's head shot up. "What are you saying?"

"I mean," she persisted, "it is possible you may not wish to marry a person such as myself, with things not done proper and no father to give me away."

"You're thinking this means so much to me?"

"Does it not?"

"Only for you."

"For me?"

"Surely you wanted your father to be at your wedding. Surely you wanted him beside you, as most girls do. Surely you wanted to feel his support and love at such a time, did you not?"

At the kindness in his voice, at the perfect truth of his statements, the tears that all morning had pressed insistently behind her eyelids now welled up in twin pools and she surprised herself by exclaiming brokenly, "Oh, Mallory, I wanted it so much."

Overwhelmed by a grief so deep and hidden that, until this moment, she had been unaware of its very existence, she dropped her face in her hands, the hot tears slipping through her fingers while words as bitter as any her mother had ever uttered were torn from her lips.

"He's never been where I needed him," she sobbed raggedly, powerless to stem the surging anguish in her heart. "No, never once; never once could I count on him. That time when I was May queen . . . yes, that time when all the other fathers were there . . ."

Forgetful of Mallory silently listening, forgetful of everything, she was riveted upon the memory of that never-to-be-forgotten day: the May procession, the church filled with lighted candles, the odor of incense, the children dressed in white. Before she mounted the steps to place the crown of bridal wreath upon the brow of the statue of the Virgin, she had sung a solo: "Bring flowers to the Fairest, Bring flowers to the Rarest. . . ."

"I had the best part, you see," she continued doggedly, choking on the words. "And he said he would be there like all the other fathers. But he wasn't. He hadn't come."

Later he had explained that a very important business matter had intervened; she long since had forgotten the particular excuse.

"But that wasn't the only time he failed me. There were lots of others; oh, lots of them . . . But with my wedding . . ."

She gulped and stopped abruptly. To have made such a spectacle of herself! To have spoken so of the father she adored, to have said he had failed her! Shaking her head, she rose from her chair and, tears coursing down her cheeks, dashed blindly to the door.

Her hand was on the doorknob when Mallory reached her, swinging her into his arms, pressing her to him so tightly that she could hear the powerful pounding of his heart.

"Hush, hush," he crooned, his chin hard against her forehead, rocking her as though she were a child. "It's all right now. Everything will be all right, my brave darling. Everything will be fine, for I will never fail you. No, Vivvie. Never will I fail you, no matter what."

The unexpected outcome of her visit to the Tipperary left Vivian thoroughly bemused.

She walked home almost in a trance, the memory of Mallory's arms about her, the gentleness in his voice, more vivid than the uneven slate sidewalk or the long line of red brick row houses that she passed. From windows flung open upon the street came scolding voices, a baby's disconsolate wails, a burst of laughter, snatch of song, but she was as oblivious to these as to the screech of streetcars and clatter of carriages and wagons.

Had her mother been right all along, and did Mallory love her, then, for all he had never said so? More incredible, did she love him? Or, since she was so unused to masculine succor, was it gratitude only that filled her heart? Whatever the reason, there was no doubt but that he now occupied the very center of her world.

Were proof needed, she might readily have found it upon opening her own front door, for none other than Clinton Webb rose to greet her.

"Why, Mister Clinton!" she gasped in surprise, but with no trace of the romantic flutterings that heretofore had accompanied the sight of him.

"Your mother said she expected you shortly. She kindly invited me to wait."

"Of course." Drawing up for herself the stool that stood before the sewing machine, she motioned him back to the lumpy sofa. "Please sit down."

Despite the heat of the day, not a wrinkle marred the pale gray linen sack suit he was wearing. Dark mustache neatly clipped, wavy hair slicked meticulously down, he crossed long, slender legs and easily balanced a straw boater on his knee. But there was a grim line to his finely etched mouth, a reserve that was almost belligerence in the dark eyes that fastened themselves upon her. "Have you seen my sister?" he asked peremptorily.

"Miss Nancy? Why, no, sir, not since I left service."

"Do you know her whereabouts?"

Alarm swept through Vivian. "Her whereabouts! Isn't she at home?"

"She left the house sometime last evening. She hasn't been seen or heard from since."

Stunned, Vivian learned the particulars. Miss Anthea Allenby had been the sole guest at a family dinner in the Webb residence last evening. Thinking only to amuse, she had recounted a bit of gossip from a recent issue of *The Item.*

Vivian's cheeks grew hot. She could well imagine the elegant, candlelit dinner table and Anthea Allenby repeating with little trills of laughter the mortifying account of that disastrous party at the Doyles'. *My dears, too funny! A regular brawl! Fisticuffs over your former lady's maid! Can you believe it?*

Clearly Clinton Webb could not. "It baffles me, Vivvie," he said severely, "absolutely baffles me how you can contemplate a lifetime in association with such people. I admit to being unable to understand it, unable to fathom it at all." For a moment he regarded her in fury and then, abruptly clearing his throat, added, "But that is your affair. My concern is for my sister."

Anthea Allenby's tale had led, Vivian discovered to her horror, to a row between Nancy Webb and her father.

"It wasn't in the least Miss Allenby's fault," Clinton Webb continued. "Naturally she had no idea how the Governor would react, what with Nan insisting upon going to your wedding and all."

How unwise it had been, thought Vivian, to accede to Nancy's wishes and mail that invitation!

"Where do you think your sister is, sir?" she asked.

Clinton sighed and spread his hands, his manner softening. "To tell the truth, Vivvie, I had placed all my hopes on finding her here."

"Here? But surely she would be more comfortable with a friend."

"She considers you a friend." He nodded gloomily. "Yes, Vivvie. I think you don't realize the unusual ideas my sister cultivates in regard to the lower classes. They haven't exactly endeared her to her chums, I can tell you. Last night she had the temerity to tell the Governor to his face that she counted you no different from her other acquaintances; in fact, a sight better than most. I swear I thought the poor old Guv would pop!"

In the honor of God, thought Vivian, what could have gotten into the girl? It would be one thing when marriage into such wealth as Mallory possessed conferred upon his wife an elevated position in society. Then, of course, it would be fitting and proper that they should become friendly. She already had planned to give an elaborate tea at the Bellevue Stratford Hotel upon her return from her honeymoon. The list was drawn up and included Senator and Mrs. Cavendish, Judge and Mrs. Wickersham, several bankers and their wives, possibly Miss Anthea Allenby, and most certainly the Webbs.

But this was *after* she became Mrs. Brian Mallory. For the moment she was still a mere servant girl and must keep to her place. Why didn't Nancy Webb understand this? Not that there was any help for it now. The worrisome thing was where the young lady could have got to. And with a sudden lurch of her heart, Vivian said firmly to herself: Neil knows.

Hurrying Clinton Webb out the front door by pleading an engagement, scarcely waiting to watch him out of sight, she set off in the opposite direction in search of her brother.

O'Reilly's Market, when she reached it, was all but deserted in the heat of the day. In the window hung dressed chickens, rabbits, smoked hams, and a side of beef, while from out the screen door sailed a heady blend of aromas: fresh ground coffee, pickling spices, cheese.

"You'll find him just out back," Tom O'Reilly obligingly told her. "It's plucking chickens he is."

Making her way through the storeroom, she moved down a narrow aisle between unopened wooden crates and boxes of groceries to a battered screen door. This opened upon a scraggly yard containing still more crates and boxes, albeit empty and tossed into a heap.

Here she found Neil. Wearing a long, stained white apron, he sat on an upturned crate methodically plucking chickens. Sunlight struck his red hair and full beard, encircling his head in a bronze glow.

Like Mamie he was all skin and bones, but without her air of wiry endurance. His white shirt, wet with sweat, clung to his thin shoulders, and so absorbed was he—although not, Vivian would have wagered, by the chickens—that he was unaware of her presence until she spoke.

"Vivvie!" he exclaimed, his head jerking up.

"Mr. Clinton has been to see me," she said without preamble. "Miss Nancy left home last evening and can't be found."

Confirming her suspicions, Neil looked guiltily down.

"Where is she, Neil?" she demanded, green eyes snapping.

His own, when he shot them back up at her, were equally truculent. "She doesn't want them to know. They don't give a snap for her. They're to blame for all this. That father of hers gave her a right smart tongue-lashing last night. He all but told her to leave his house, and neither her mother nor her brother stepped forward to say a word in her favor or lift a finger to help her."

"They're frantic now."

"And well they may be," replied Neil with satisfaction. "Well they may be. Sure, it serves them right for all the heartaches they've caused her, keeping her a prisoner."

"A prisoner!"

"Oh yes! Telling her she can't go to your wedding. That's what did it, I regret to inform you. That's what put the fat in the fire. And who are they, so high and mighty and full of themselves as to look down their noses at others? Who are they to tell an enlightened young woman where she may go and what books she may read and what lectures to attend?"

It was clear Nancy Webb had confided in Neil quite a lot, but Vivian said only, "Why, of course they must tell her! They're her parents!"

"And does that give them the right to ruin her life?"

"Ruin her life! Why, she has everything in the world!"

"Except her freedom. Parents! Fine parents indeed! A gentleman who calls himself a doctor but treats only the rich for the highest of fees. A lady who spends all her time and money on clothes and parties. Deny it. Deny it, if you can."

He paused, chin thrust forward, awaiting her response, but as always she was no match for the torrent of words that poured from him.

"As for that brother," he continued scathingly, "what care has he but for his woolen mills, with no thought at all to the little children who labor for him from dawn to dusk. What care has he for anything but lining his pockets?"

"That's not true!" countered Vivian loyally.

"It is, by God. And someday I'll take you up the river to one of those mills and prove it."

"I don't mean about the children," she retorted, for of course she knew that children worked. Hadn't she worked since she turned fifteen? And what was wrong with it? "I don't mean about that."

"What do you mean, then?" Neil demanded.

She didn't know. She was never a deep thinker; intimations and half-thoughts whirled through her head but she could grasp none of them. Only one thing was clear. She should have known better than to let herself get sidetracked into words with this brother who all his life had bested her in any argument.

"I haven't time to stand here all day, Neil Randall," she said fiercely, adding, "You just tell me where Nancy Webb is or I'm going straight home and tell mama."

It struck neither of them as childish that this tactic should prove successful. Only in shocking, exceptional circumstances, such as Nancy Webb's predicament, did one defy one's parents. For the most part, the young of whatever age deferred to their elders, knowing it was right and proper to do so and that one day their turn would come.

"I just want to speak to her," continued Vivian more gently, aware that she had prevailed. "I won't tell her family where she is. Not if she doesn't want me to. But I must see her, talk to her, so I can go and tell them she's safe and sound."

11

When Neil sullenly, reluctantly, revealed that Nancy Webb was staying with Aunt Lizzie Tole in her home on Henry Street, Vivian wondered why she hadn't thought of this herself.

Who but Aunt Lizzie, in no way related to the many who, over the years, had turned to her for help, would leave her bed at all hours to lend a hand with the birth of a child? Who but Aunt Lizzie would open her door to a woman afraid to stay the night with a man who had drunk too much? Who but Aunt Lizzie could be counted upon to take in Nancy Webb?

Making her way to Henry Street, Vivian dwelt less on this than on Neil's parting words: "Make sure you go round to the back door when you get to Canvendish Square."

The bitterness in his voice left no doubt about his contempt for the ways of the Square. Such a black hatred there was in him for those who were well off! Where had it come from? Everyone else seemed to realize quite matter-of-factly that people with money were smarter than other people, or worked harder—in short, deserved it. If they inherited it, then those who went before had earned it in some way. How wrongheaded, spiteful, really, to claim as Neil did that it was only the result of luck or, worse, chicanery. To be sure, there might be some who enjoyed ill-gotten gains. But Vivian had no doubt such persons were paid back with misfortune and unhappiness.

Neil, however, refused to see this, quoting from those books of his, talking about dividing up the wealth, about taking money from the rich and giving it to the poor. The very idea! Once she got her hands on a little, just let someone come along and try to take it from her!

But it wasn't this prospect that weighed heavily upon her as she turned down Henry Street. From the moment when with sinking heart she had thought to herself, Neil knows, a vague unease had gripped her. It wouldn't be shaken even as she determined to do all in her power to urge Nancy Webb to return to Cavendish Square.

"But I won't go back, Vivvie," declared this young woman. "No, I won't, and you mustn't harry me. It was hard enough the first time. I won't have it all to do over again."

They sat together on a horsehair-covered sofa in Aunt Lizzie's dark, cluttered little front parlor, a lowered awning outside the room's single window effectively cutting off all hope of a breath of air. In one corner a votive candle flickered before a small plaster statue of the Virgin Mary, and from behind a framed daguerreotype of Mr. William Tole, Aunt Lizzie's late husband, there sprouted a long, ungainly palm leaf, brittle and dusty memento of a Palm Sunday long since past.

In such surroundings, thought Vivian, how out of place Nancy Webb appeared. She wore a long white linen skirt and lawn shirtwaist that bore the unmistakable small details of expensive finery. A ruching of lace banded her delicate wrists and encircled the slender neck, from about which fell a small round chased gold locket on black grosgrain ribbon. The wealth of shining brown hair was done up in a thick chestnut mass that looked almost too heavy for the small head that must bear it. Altogether she seemed fragile beyond words and certainly not capable of fending for herself, but the dark eyes in the heart-shaped face were, for all their gentleness, not without determination.

"I'm sure things will be different now, Miss. I'm sure things will go better if only you'll return," said Vivian, floundering, for how could a life such as Nancy Webb's possibly be improved upon?

But Nancy raised both hands. "Please, Vivvie, no more 'Miss' or I shall have to ask you to leave. I'm here precisely because I wish to have done with all that. I believe in equality. You are no more my servant than I am yours." She added in gentle reproof, "It's high time you overcame that servant mentality, dear."

Vivian had every intention of overcoming it the moment she became Mrs. Brian Mallory and had servants of her own to command. And was everything to be changed now? Were there to be no more maids and mistresses just as she

was in reach of a position to tell others what to do and boss
them around? But she would never put up with such fool-
ishness. Nor, she was sure, would the rest of the world.
Who would want such a state of affairs, except perhaps . . .

"When you talk this way, Miss," she said tartly, "you
sound just like our Neil."

"Oh, Neil is far more eloquent than I!" cried Nancy, her
face turning bright pink. "I could never begin to expound
the cause of the common man as Neil can."

Vivian's heart gave a great thump as the vague unease
that had troubled her took specific shape and form. It was
suddenly clear as day that Nancy Webb had a crush on
Neil Randall. All too likely it was returned and, oh, the
folly of it! A young lady nurtured and reared like Miss
Webb and a young man, brilliant though he might be, no
more than a lowly grocery clerk with not a penny to his
name.

"Oh, Miss," said Vivian fervently, "you must go home.
You must forget these ideas and go back where you belong."

"No, Vivvie," replied the girl quietly. "Never."

"But what will you do? What's to become of you?"

"For the present I shall continue to rent my little room
from Mrs. Tole. Fortunately I have a small nest egg left
me by my maternal grandparents. If I'm careful I can
manage very well while I hunt up some employment."

"You mean it is your intention to work for pay?"

Nancy gave a light little laugh. "Dear Vivvie! Working
for pay isn't the worst thing in the world!"

"I know all about working for pay, Miss," replied
Vivian, stung by such presumption. "And better than you
do."

Instantly Nancy was contrite. "Dear, please don't be angry," she begged. "I meant only that it can't be worse than
being treated like a little doll as my mother is, with nothing
to do but go to parties and dances for the rest of my life."

Stunned, Vivian stared at the young woman, a dozen im-
ages racing through her brain: Nancy Webb's dresses, her
pretty bedroom; the cold mornings when she chose to remain in bed, a cozy fire lit for her in the grate and her
breakfast carried up on a tray; the hot summer afternoons
when she reclined at her ease on a wicker couch in the
garden, reading and sipping lemonade; the latest sheet mu-

sic she bought, a dozen airs at a time with never a thought
for the cost; the fur tippet she had needed to mention but
once. And more than this—oh, far more!—the doting smiles
in the eyes of Dr. and Mrs. Webb when they rested upon
her.

"They've given you everything!" she burst out accusingly
from her own sore needs and aching wants. "Everything!"

Nancy sighed. "I think I know how I must seem to you,
how spoiled, ungrateful, unfeeling I must sound." She
smiled. "Dear fierce, loyal, loving Vivvie. I believe I know
you much better than you know me. I believe I know my
parents, too. They love me, but only if I behave in a certain
way, if I live as they want me to. Clinton is willing to do
this.

"But I'm not like Clinton, although I've tried to be. Believe me, Vivvie, for years I've tried to lead that silly, shallow life. But now I can't anymore, because I want something that my parents will never understand or approve. I
can't tell you what it is yet, dear. But someday you'll know
and be happy for me."

Vivian's slim young shoulders sagged and she shook her
head silently, ruefully, fearful that she already knew.

Cavendish Square always seemed cool, even on the hot-
test days. Big, old trees shaded broad paths that criss-
crossed the neatly clipped grass and a fountain threw jets
of water into the sunny air, sending a fine iridescent spray
above the children who launched toy boats in its stone
basin. Seated upon iron benches, nannies chatted amiably
together beside English prams while keeping an eye to their
charges, fashionably turned-out little boys in knee pants
and the Russian tunics that had become so popular since
the start of the Russo-Japanese war, little girls with sashes
to their dresses, a froth of petticoat peeping out below. In
the waning afternoon, ladies whose skirts just skimmed the
pavement held parasols above fetching wide-brimmed "picture" hats festooned with feathers, flowers, and veils, while
gentlemen raised straw boaters in salute to those they
passed, for few were strangers.

This reassuring familiarity included not only pedestrians
but vehicles as well. Service carts and wagons used the al-
leyways behind the grand stone mansions that looked down
upon this sociable scene, and it was only such conveyances
as properly belonged—victorias, hansoms, and the like—

that entered the stylish thoroughfare surrounding the Square.

Caught in a nagging dilemma, Vivian approached the Webb residence. Should she or should she not knock on that imposing front door? Never once in three years of service had she used it save in the capacity of her employment— helping Somerby hand out young ladies under umbrellas in inclement weather, perhaps, or running out to a waiting carriage with a forgotten fan or glove.

But Neil's challenge had raised a point of propriety, and all the way up Market Street in the swaying clangorous streetcar she had twisted the question this way and that. On the one hand, she was no longer staff, this was clear. On the other, she was not yet a lady. Nor, as she knew in some discomfort, did she look like one, flushed as she was by the exertions of the day, her old blue poplin skirt wrinkled and dirty, her cheap dark blue straw clapped precariously to her head.

That there were gentlemen, and ladies also, who glanced her way more than once as she hurried across the square, noting less the wrinkled skirt and misshapen hat than the tiny waist and remarkable green eyes, was lost upon her. Despite the disquieting interviews, first with Clinton Webb, then with Neil, and finally with Nancy, it was Brian Mallory who was uppermost in her thoughts, as though his embrace that morning had wrapped her in a magic spell, and it was this that decided her. She wore his ring upon her finger. Was the betrothed of such a man as Brian Mallory to knock on back doors?

Somerby, it appeared, thought so. Answering the bell, he looked down upon her in horrified disbelief.

"I've news of Miss Nancy," she told him.

His pale eyes flashed angrily. "And you may take your news around to the back and wait in the kitchen."

"That's a thing of the past, Mr. Somerby," she replied promptly, well prepared for this offensive. "I'm no longer a servant, and I'll take my news home before I'll go to the back door."

She turned to retrace her steps but Somerby said, "Just wait now. Just wait now a moment." And then, seeing the lift of her chin, the glint in her eye, "Step in, then. Step inside."

Resolutely clutching her reticule, she stood just inside the front door, heart hammering against her ribs, for what

if the Webbs should make similar objection? But Irene
Webb came hurrying down the stairs gathering a mauve
silk dressing gown about her and crying, "Vivvie, Vivvie,
news of Nancy? Do come into the library, dear!"

She was followed by her husband and her son, and now
all three ranged themselves expectantly before Vivian, Dr.
and Mrs. Webb on the tufted emerald green velvet love
seat that graced one side of the fireplace, Clinton, tall and
thin, by the marble mantel, hands clasped behind his back.

Confronting them, she felt the self-confidence with
which she had faced down the irate Somerby ebb away,
and scarcely above a whisper, she said, "I've come to tell
you I've just spoken to Miss Nancy. She's safe and well."

"Where is she?" snapped Dr. Webb.

In Vivian's eyes Dr. C. Alden Webb had always been the
very picture of the learned physician. He was a bit short,
perhaps, and a mite heavy; nonetheless, the thatch of thick
white hair, the pink and glowingly healthy complexion, the
neatly trimmed vandyke, above all, the small lively eyes,
gave assurance of intelligence and brisk competence, albeit
mixed with a certain quick-tempered hauteur. All the servants stood in awe of him, as did, it was rumored, certain
of his patients, especially the ladies. Vivian could well believe
it. She had seen even Somerby quail before him. He insisted
upon a high degree of efficiency from others; this, he
sometimes explained, was because he demanded the highest
standards of himself. Since no one was in a position to contest this observation, everyone agreed it must be so and did
their best to please him.

Vivian had little hope, however, that the present conversation would bring him satisfaction. "Sir," she said reluctantly, "I can't tell you her whereabouts. I've been sworn to
secrecy."

Dr. Webb's face reddened. "Sworn to secrecy! By
whom?"

"By Miss Nancy herself, sir."

"What sort of tomfoolery is this? Young woman, I command you to tell me where you have hidden my daughter."

Vivian threw an appealing look to Clinton Webb and his
mother, but their eyes were held fixedly downcast and she
couldn't but wonder if this was the same response with
which, last evening, poor Nancy had met.

"Miss Nancy is safe and sound," she repeated doggedly.
"That's all I'm permitted to say."

An aguelike spell seized Dr. Webb, and his eyes seemed to start forward. "Well then," he said, voice quivering with rage and frustration, "I give you permission to return to my daughter, wherever she may be, and tell her she has forfeited all privilege as my child, all claim to inheritance, and all right to enter this house."

"Alden!" cried Irene Webb, her head jerking up, tears filling her eyes.

Dr. Webb swung round upon her. "Irene, I'll thank you to stay out of this!"

"But, Alden!"

"Not another word, I say!" he shouted. "She doesn't deserve my least consideration. She has shown contempt for my values, disdain for my position in society, and no regard for the duties of a daughter to a father. Let her go then, I say! Let her go! She's dead to me. You are never to mention her name again."

As Vivian watched, Irene Webb seemed to crumple and sink into herself so that even the space she took up on the sofa appeared somehow diminished. In a day full of surprises, nothing could have been more astonishing. Were there, then, no quarrels in the Webb residence because Irene Webb never disagreed with her husband? Was this what Nancy meant when she said she refused to be a doll like her mother?

Not any of this did Vivian sort out until later. At the moment she had all she could do to complete her mission. "Miss Nancy," she continued, "has asked me to pack up her belongings and see to their removal."

This request seemed to constitute the final outrage.

Red-faced with fury, Dr. Webb propelled himself from the sofa. "Her belongings!" he cried. "She has no belongings. Her belongings belong to me, since I paid for 'em. And now, Miss, I suggest you depart."

So saying, he gave the bellpull such a jerk it was a blessing it didn't come loose from its moorings. Somerby appeared on the instant; Irene Webb fled weeping from the room, followed by her son, white-faced and tight-lipped, and in a twinkling Vivian found herself out upon the front doorstep.

Shaken, she proceeded across the square toward Market Street, so unaware of her surroundings that she didn't hear footsteps until she looked up to see Clinton Webb beside her.

"I must speak to you," he said, his hand at her elbow. "Please, Vivvie, spare me a moment," he pleaded and, turning her off the path, led her to a bench.

One look at his anguished face somewhat dispelled the animosity she had felt upon seeing him.

"First, allow me to thank you for coming to the house as you did," he said. "It can't have been easy, and I very much appreciate it. I owe you a debt of gratitude I shall never forget."

She met his eyes coldly and nodded.

Perhaps he had hoped for a more fulsome response, for he looked at her searchingly, then sighed and said, "You are angry with me, aren't you? Please don't be, Vivvie. I admire and respect you so much."

"You might have helped out a bit," she answered tersely. "You might have spoken up."

"It would only have made things worse."

"And how could they be worse than they are?"

"Oh, in any number of ways, I assure you. That's why I must beg you to take a message to my sister, if you'll be so kind. Tell her I must see her, ask if I may visit her."

"And won't your father object to that?"

"Of course he's not to know, Vivvie."

"I see," she replied, not concealing her contempt for such weak-kneed stratagems.

Color rose in the handsome, somewhat arrogant face. "No, I don't think you do. I don't believe you have any idea of what this escapade of my sister's has cost my parents and me in worry and sorrow, nor the embarrassment to our name once the story is out. This is why I want to see her, why I must see her: to urge her to come home now, before it's too late."

"But it's already too late. Dr. Webb has said she is never to enter the house again."

"He was angry. He didn't know what he was saying. Believe me, Vivvie, I can assure you he will much prefer having my sister quietly back at home to all the gossip and scandal her departure will invite."

"And is this why she is to return?" demanded Vivian hotly, heedlessly. "To save the family from scandal?"

He looked stung, truly wounded. "I believe many would find that sufficient reason," he replied, and it struck her that at one time she would have wholeheartedly agreed. Wasn't it, after all, to avoid scandal that she had sought to marry Brian Mallory? But now the memory of Irene Webb's piteous weeping lingered, and things were no longer so clear.

"I might add," Clinton was saying, "that if my sister returns to her home she will be saved from a life of poverty and struggle for which she is ill prepared."

There could be no doubt as to the probability of this, and tightly, grudgingly, Vivian nodded. "I'll ask her to see you," she said.

12

Nancy Webb, however, remained adamant in her determination to keep her whereabouts secret. She would, she informed Vivian, write her brother a letter declaring her intention to maintain her independence.

"Clinton may as well save his breath," she said. "Nothing can induce me to return to that life again."

Vivian had little time to spare for the misgivings she felt at this decision. Mere days now separated her from her wedding, and the hours seemed to fly by.

Behind the Hibernian Firehouse a huge green-and-white-striped tent had been erected and outfitted with dance floor, bandstand, and a dais upon which the wedding party would sit. In case of rain the two fire wagons would be pulled out of the firehouse and the reception held within, but with the number of novenas being offered up for clear weather, no one expected a cloud in the sky.

The ladies of the Hibernian Fire Brigade Auxiliary were festooning the tent with white crepe paper streamers while the St. Bonaventure Altar Guild planned to bedeck the church with pink and white apple blossoms and mock orange. Additional folding chairs for the large reception would be provided by Muldoon's Funeral Parlor, delivered compliments of O'Reilly's Food Market; flowers for the bridal party would be supplied, gratuitously, by Joseph Grady of Grady's Flower Shoppe; beer would be on its way, gratis, from certain beer barons of Brewery Town, purveyors to the Tipperary Saloon; while chicken à la King, new peas, parsley potatoes, and wedding cake would be served up, free of charge, Mallory told Vivian with a wink, by caterers favored in the past by the Amity Club.

"Don't you pay for anything?" Vivian asked.

The smile left his eyes. "Everyone pays for everything, Puss. That's a lesson you'll have to learn."

It had frightened her the way he said it, as though there were something she might not like that he would be holding her to. Icebergs, again. When she thought of him like this she shivered and longed to run away. But since that moment in his office when he had taken her in his arms, holding her so tightly that for the first time in her life she had felt truly safe, the frightened feeling hadn't come so often, and when it had she was able to chase it away.

Except for today, she thought, panic-stricken.

Trembling like a leaf, she stood ashen-faced at her mirror, arrayed in her bridal gown. Just under the window in the busy street below, and attracting considerable attention from all who passed by, waited two shiny black landaus, tops down and drawn by docile horses, compliments, once again, of Muldoon's Funeral Parlor.

In them, chattering excitedly and pretty as flowers, sat the young ladies of her wedding party: Rita Celano, Iris Ferguson, the Wade girls, and her sister, Mary Claire. It was a rainbow motif that Mamie Randall had settled upon for their costumes, each attendant in a different pastel, and the blending of the pale blue, lime green, lemon yellow, rosy pink, and soft violet gowns, together with broad-brimmed picture hats of ruffled organdy, achieved this effect to perfection.

Only Vivian was missing from the assemblage, and peeping down upon the scene from behind a wispy curtain, she saw Neil, awkward and uncomfortable in rented morning coat, top hat, and striped cashmere trousers, glance impatiently up at her window for a glimpse of the bride he was soon to give away.

But oh, how reluctant a bride! How icy cold her trembling hands, how violent the fluttering of her heart, how queasy her stomach—how, in short, impossible the journey down St. Bonaventure's long aisle!

"Well, come along, girl."

Mamie stood in the doorway, regal as a queen in pearl

gray soi-de-chine, the bodice boned from waist to the tip of her high lace collar. On her head sat a large hat covered in gray lace, its underside bearing a spray of pink silk roses. Beneath this creation a small firm chin was thrust forward and black eyes shone with a resolve and determination appropriate to the demands of the day. A fierce frown was now added as she said sharply, "What ails you?"

Vivian drew a quivering breath. "I'm ill."

"Ill!"

The total unacceptability of such a predicament at such a time was manifest in every fiber of Mamie's being. Crossing the room, she grasped Vivian's cold hands in her own.

"Now listen to me, daughter," she said ferociously. "There's not a bride in the world that doesn't feel as you do on her way to the church. There's not one but has last-minute qualms. This will pass, like as not, when you see your intended waiting for you at the altar. But even if it don't," she added, "it's too late to turn back now."

So implacable was this pronouncement that Vivian, no less queasy, found herself meekly descending the stairs and moving out to the waiting carriage.

Upon her appearance, sighs and a patter of applause went up from the little gathering of onlookers. Later she was to learn that she had been the most radiant of brides, poised as a princess, gracious as a queen, a vision of loveliness not to be believed.

She could only be grateful for this opinion, since she moved through the proceedings in a daze. Far from being reassured by the sight of her intended waiting for her at the altar rail, she approached him, clutching Neil's arm, with the benumbed tread of the sleepwalker, as though he were a handsome but utter stranger she had never before set eyes upon.

The pervasive sense of unreality was heightened by the dazzling interior of St. Bonaventure's itself. Incandescent, it seemed, ablaze with light, shimmering with candles, with apple blossoms. Ranged behind the stranger who was the bridegroom were other strangers for, in honor of Brian Mallory, six priests graced the altar, two of them monsignors. In vain Vivian searched for Father Shields and ever afterwards could scarcely believe he was present, though it was he who stepped forward to marry them.

Throughout the ceremony—the giving and taking and

plighting of troth—one phrase rang in her ears, holding her steady, stiffening her spine: *Too late to turn back. Too late to turn back.* Like an incantation, it seemed to cast a spell, raising, without her volition, her icy hand to receive the ring that the stranger slipped upon her finger, tilting back her head to accept his light kiss, guiding her through the ritual of the solemn high mass that followed, with the organ swelling and the choir singing and incense ancient and heavy on the air. *Too late to turn back. Too late to turn back.*

Standing in the reception line beside the stranger, Vivian smiled at all who spoke to her. *Too late to turn back. Too late to turn back.*

"You're going to find out what it's all about now, aren't you, kiddo?" Gert Barkin whispered, giggling, in her ear.

"Does a fella get to kiss the bride?" asked Tom O'Reilly.

"It was a very pretty wedding," said Mrs. Muldoon, nodding somberly, accusingly. "Very nice, indeed."

"I wish you happiness, I'm sure," sniffed Dolly.

"You look like an angel, dear," said Nancy Webb. There were tears in her eyes.

"He's your husband, but never forget he's my son." Ma Mallory winked up at the stranger and he roared with laughter, but had the quip been only in jest? *Too late to turn back . . .*

Champagne corks popped, the band struck up, dancing commenced, she and the stranger first, waltzing alone under the striped tent while people smiled and nodded and clapped their hands.

And then: "It's time to go," said the stranger.

"To go?" She looked up at him, politely askance, and he drew a large, flat gold watch from his waistcoat pocket. "The ferry leaves at four. We'd best be off."

How elaborately secretive the plans for their departure, exciting as a children's game. She made her escape giggling nervously, drifting off as prearranged from the tent to the firehouse, her arms about Rita Celano and Mary Claire.

There, on the second floor, in a room reserved to the use of the Ladies' Auxiliary, her jade green linen going-away suit hung waiting on a clothes tree. On a wooden chair beside it, neatly arranged in advance by her mother, was her underwear: batiste chemillette, scalloped and feather stitched; blue silk hose with embroidered clocks; blue changeable taffeta petticoat richly trimmed on its under-side with heavily ruffled rosettes to assist in kicking out the skirt while walking. On a second chair lay her hat, a cloud of jade green tulle and silk bird-of-paradise flowers.

They whispered, Rita and Mary Claire, modestly avert-ing their eyes as she was helped from bridal gown and un-derpinnings. Despite three small open windows, the room was hot as an oven, just under the roof as it was. It smelled of the stable next door, and of dust and mouse droppings between the creaking wooden floorboards. The sound of music and laughter floated to them from the tent, but within the room were only their muted giggles and whis-pers, and a bumblebee droning away.

"Why are we whispering?" asked Vivian, and in answer all three girls giggled softly, nervously, and whispered again.

Mamie came up the wooden stairs just as Vivian fin-ished dressing, just as she pinned on the remarkable jade green hat.

Mamie didn't whisper. "Well, now," she said, looking Vivian over from top to toe. "You've got yourself ready, then?"

Vivian nodded. It seemed she had lost the power of speech, swept away by this appalling thing she was doing, by this journey with the stranger that lay ahead.

"Well, then," said Mamie. Her lips snapped shut, and whether she swayed slightly or whether this was only imag-ined, Vivian couldn't have said. "Well, then," she repeated, "go along now. Best you be on your way."

The incessant splashing of the waves on the beach sounded like wind rustling through treetops, or, thought Vivian, like a water spigot that hadn't been turned off. Yes, that was it, more like a spigot carelessly left running, running. The sound made her nervous. Lying in bed in the bridal suite of the Hotel Rudolf, she kept listening to it and wishing it would stop.

The Rudolf was the best hotel, the most expensive, in Atlantic City, Mallory had said. She had never lain in such a bed, so vast. And the sheets, smooth as silk. There was the bed she had shared all her life with Mary Claire, al-ways having to hold herself back from rolling down into the gully in the center, and her narrow cot at Cavendish

Square. But this bed was fit for a queen, and she felt she must look like one, all dressed in her bridal set with her hair fanning out over the pillows.

When she had first crept into this bed she had lain back and folded her hands across her breasts rather in the manner of a corpse in Muldoon's Funeral Parlor. But this certainly wasn't the way she wished to look when Mallory returned from the solitary little late-evening stroll on the boardwalk that he had said he was in the mood for taking. And so she had gotten out of bed, brushed her hair again, climbed back under the light sheet, and spread her hair out over the pillows. Her arms were held stiff and straight at her sides, having been tried first outside of and then under the cover. For the life of her she couldn't remember what she had used to do with them.

But these problems were as nothing compared to the quandary that, as she stared up at the high, garlanded ceiling in the softly lit room, now occupied her mind. Should she or should she not be in bed? Was bed where Mallory, when he returned, would expect to find her? What was the right thing to do at such a time?

With all the talk about the wedding, she had never sought to discuss this aspect of things with her mother. Or, better still, with Gert Barkin. Gert, she was sure, could have told her precisely what to do. But she had been too shy to mention such matters to Gert; and her mother, she somehow knew, was too shy to talk about them. With the result that now she lay rigid as a statue dressed in her fine white embroidered nainsook bridal set of night robe, chemise, and underdrawers, straining her ears past the sound of the waves for Mallory's key in the lock.

When she heard it, her heart leapt to her throat. Mother of God! But he strode in with just a glance at her and said matter-of-factly: "It's a beautiful night."

"Is it?" she croaked.

"Indeed it is. Come have a look."

He stepped out onto the balcony, and it was only his averted gaze and the promise of darkness beyond the French doors that gave her courage, scantily clad as she was, to slip out of bed and join him.

For his part, he appeared to be far too absorbed by the view to take note of her wispy apparel. "See the path the moon makes on the water?" he asked, looking out at the polished black swells. "When I was a kid and mom and pop brought me to the seashore I used to wish I could walk on it. When I told this to pop he looked at my mom and said, 'This kid we got, he wants to be Jesus Christ.' "

A giggle escaped her. "Oh, Mallory, blasphemy, hush!" she said. But for the first time in hours she felt like herself, and she said, "Tell me some more about your folks."

"Tell you some more? Well, let's see now. Would you take it amiss if I smoked?"

The light from his match flared up over his strong features. When he extinguished it, the tip of his cigar glowed cozily in the dark while below them, all the way up the curve of the shoreline, lights glittered like a strand of multicolored gems flung upon the black velvet of the night.

"Let's see now," he said again. "Of course, my pop, he didn't have a penny to bless himself with when he landed here. From Clonmel, he came. Which is the county seat of Tipperary, if you might wonder how the Tip got the name.

"But my mom, now, with her it was different, for she had a bit of a dowry. You see the thing of it was, her father was a doctor at Lifford in County Donegal, and she was his only one. Her mom died giving birth to her, and him a doctor and not able to save his own wife.

"My grandfather, he held it against my mom. He was a bitter man. But he drilled her on her studies and made her an educated girl, too keen for any of the young men in Lifford. She'd have none of them, or it may be they'd have none of her, for all her being a great beauty and so smart. And she was on her way to keeping house for her father and being an old maid, when all of a sudden he ups and dies.

"Well, with no one to stop her, she takes the bit of money he left her and sets sail for the New World. And who does she meet the minute she steps off the boat but Matthew Mallory, standing on the pier."

Mallory broke off his tale to send his cigar over the railing in a wide arc. "You're cold, Puss," he said absently. Taking off his jacket, he draped it, warm from his body, about her shoulders, and somehow, she could never have said quite how, he was sitting in one of the wicker lounge chairs on the balcony, and she was perched on his knee.

"Well, as I was saying," he continued, as though this state of affairs were the most ordinary thing in the world, "as I was saying, there was Matthew Mallory, big, tall, and strong as a bull, looking out over the heads of the crowd of men on the dock who were waiting for the brides to come in."

"Brides?" managed Vivian, despite his arm lightly around her; despite her pounding heart.

Mallory nodded. "You see, there was this enterprising gentleman in mercantile shipping. He figured there was many a man sorely in need of a wife and helpmate, and not enough females to go around in this big land. So he places advertisements in the newspapers of Ireland, England, and Scotland, inviting unmarried young ladies to embark upon the sea of matrimony by booking passage on his boat. He guarantees that honorable men will be waiting to make them their wives as soon as they set foot on the shore, or he will give them free passage back home."

Never had Vivian found herself so mesmerized by a tale; and when Mallory gently pressed her head down upon his broad shoulder, she sank against him compliantly.

"So mom steps off the boat, and there is pop standing on the pier," said Mallory. "Only there to have a look, as he tells it, with not a thought to marry. But he spots mom among all those beauties, and he's smitten entirely.

" 'What's your name?' says he.

" 'Morna Malone,' she answers.

" 'You're mine,' says he. 'You're taken.'

" 'I'm nothing of the kind,' she snaps back, for remember she has money of her own and can afford to be choosy. But pop says, 'You're mine, whether or not you know it. And you won't even have to change your initials to take my name.'

"Well," continued Mallory, "it took a bit of effort on his part, but it was just such cheek that won her, for she was never spoke up to before and she liked it so well they were married six weeks later in St. Bonnie's—if maybe not so grandly as we were married today."

His voice went on, talking, talking, but Vivian had ceased to listen for as he talked he had gently removed his jacket from her shoulders and was untying the three white satin ribbons that secured the front of her gown. When he parted it, it slid from her shoulders, and in the sudden silence, for he had stopped talking now, she could feel his eyes upon her, feel the hard strength of his thighs under the thin nainsook cloth of her bridal set.

"Lovely," he murmured, surveying her in the light that spilled from the French door. "Lovely, lovely." And then, "It's too chilly for you out here."

As though she weighed nothing, he gathered her to him, arose from his chair, and moved into the bedroom. Placing her upon the bed, he stood above her, looking down at her, his eyes moving slowly over her.

Her white chemise had tiny snaps hidden among the embroidery. When he sat down beside her and sought them, they readily parted, yielding to the pressure of her high, firm young breasts as his fingers moved slowly downward, leaving her upper body naked under his gaze.

His blue eyes, now almost black in their intensity, held hers, and she felt herself grow weak, possessed by the languid sweetness she remembered from once before, and she felt she must die if he didn't touch her.

But this was not as yet to be, not until he had drawn down her drawers, sliding them slowly over hips, thighs, knees, ankles. Again his eyes moved over her. Only then, when she felt she must perish for want of him, did his lips sink down upon hers.

13

She awakened the next morning almost surprised to hear the waves still restlessly breaking upon the shore, to look up and find the garlanded ceiling still above her and the room unchanged except for the dazzling sunlight that filled it. How could this be, when she knew herself changed utterly, so different from the fearful young woman of only hours ago?

Turning her head, she gazed at Mallory, still deeply asleep beside her.

Last night when they entered the dining room the maitre d'hotel had come hurrying forward. "Mr. Mallory," he had said. Others, too, knew him by name: waiters, wine steward, even the violinist who led the small three-piece orchestra and who came to their table to serenade her. It had been the same upon their arrival at the hotel, with the manager coming from behind his desk to shake hands. In

the sitting room of their suite a great basket of white roses
awaited them, compliments of the management, and a silver tray bearing two cut-glass goblets and a bucket of iced
champagne.

It had surprised her that he was well known so far from
Philadelphia. But even those who didn't know him took
note of him. When he passed, heads turned.

Small wonder, thought Vivian, studying as if for the first
time the handsome face on the pillow beside her, so masculine in its appeal. And then she remembered how patient
had been his deft seduction of her last evening, how considerate the ploys that had made her his, and if once upon a
time she had paid him scant heed, esteemed him but
lightly, considered him not at all except in terms of his
wealth, now she felt like a child who has carelessly pock-
eted a copper penny only to discover, however belatedly,
pure gold.

Desire rippled through her, surprising, compelling her,
and raising up on an elbow she put her lips to his ear.
"Mallory," she whispered. "Wake up."

"I want to buy you a present," he said.

They were being propelled down the boardwalk in a rolling chair. Sunlight glinted on the ocean and Mallory held
her hand in his.

"A present, Mallory? But you've already given me so
much." She thought of the rings on her fingers—
engagement diamond, narrow gold wedding band—of his
wedding gift, an emerald brooch she wore at her throat.

"But I chose them. Now you must choose for yourself
and I'll pay like a proper husband. Tell me, what would
you like?"

"Violets," she said suddenly.

"Violets?"

"Yes, a bunch of violets to wear on my coat."

In the florist shop Rudolf Mallory took out his wallet
and paid for the bunch of violets he pinned on her green
linen suit. Then, taking her firmly by the arm, he steered
her into a salon called La Modiste right next door.

"She has nothing," he told the woman who came forward.

The woman's black eyes widened. "Nothing, monsieur?"

"Except what she has on her back. You must supply her
with everything she needs."

The woman's eyes rolled heavenward. "Everything? *Mon Dieu!*" Then she smiled dazzlingly. "With pleasure, monsieur."

It wasn't quite true, of course, that Vivian had nothing. But the splendid wardrobe trunk with hardwood slats and brass trimmings that the aunts, the Randall girls, had presented to her as their wedding gift, with its sliding hanger rod and its drawers for underwear, hats, and shoes, was sparsely filled—a state of affairs that was clearly about to be remedied.

With energy remarkable in one so petite, Madame Modiste slid aside case after mirrored case to whisk out, with Gallic flourish, a series of gowns for Vivian's inspection. Or was it Mallory's opinion the woman sought? Certainly with every presentation the dark eyes rolled archly toward him, seated silent and attentive at Vivian's side.

Ready-to-wear fashions were now in vogue even for the most discriminating, and elegant little shops such as La Modiste had quickly arisen to cater to the trend. In their perfumed, gray-carpeted interiors no sign of merchandise met the eye, no vulgar racks of dresses. Instead, paneled walls upholstered in pale pink silk, a marble-top commode offering purple iris in a Chinese porcelain jar, gilt chairs, elegantly uncomfortable, and, behind the mirrored cases, creations enticingly hidden until summoned forth by Madame.

Used all her life to the tedious process of dressmaking—choosing pattern, choosing fabric, cutting, stitching, fitting—Vivian relished the luxury of deciding among such ravishing finished products.

A heliotrope tea gown in changeable silk, shading from palest violet to deep plum, was chosen, together with a morning frock of sprigged muslin, green on white. But the costume that won her heart was a dress of pink chiffon with wide boned waistband above short pleated overskirt, the bodice cut low and cunningly made to expose neck and shoulders rising out of a froth of white chiffon.

"With this Madame must wear a shawl," declared Madame Modiste, and unfurled a shimmering length of deeply fringed heavy cream-colored silk, hand painted with roses. "*N'est-ce pas?*" said Madame, bright eyes darting from one to the other of them. "*N'est-ce pas?*"

Mallory took out his wallet. "How much?"

The bill came to five times Vivian's yearly wages on Cavendish Square.

She could scarcely believe her ears. A fine sweat broke upon her forehead, the palms of her hands grew moist, and her face paled. One dress would have been sufficient— indeed, at such prices, far too much. But she had gone on and on, unable to stop herself, smiling hotly and greedily whispering yes! yes! not only to gowns but to ribbed pink silk stockings with lace inserts, to a boa of white ostrich feathers, to a parasol, so darling, of white eyelet-embroidered linen.

"Oh, Mallory!" she moaned in remorse the minute they reached their rooms. "Oh, Mallory!" she repeated and dropped her face into her hands.

"What's the matter?"

At the alarm in his voice she raised her head to find his face drained of color, chalk white as her own.

Seeing the fright she had given him, she said quickly, "Only the money you've spent."

"Money?" he repeated uncomprehendingly.

"The money for all my clothes. It's too much."

He was upon her so quickly that she gasped, his hands gripping her tightly, bruisingly. "You are never to do that again," he said harshly. "I thought something had happened to you. I thought . . . I don't know what I thought." His eyes blazed down at her and she felt his hands tremble on her arms. "I love you, damn it," he said furiously. "And you're never to do that to me again."

Mallory's stunning admission of his love took Vivian's breath away. It spun round in her brain, over and over again, startling her afresh with its awesome revelation. At times she believed she might have dreamed it, especially as, during the days and nights of passionate lovemaking that followed, he never once alluded to the subject again.

True, Mamie Randall had insisted Brian Mallory was in love with her daughter, but Vivian had credited this opinion to no more than the expression of a mother's fond vanity. That it might be an accurate assessment hadn't for one moment occurred to her. Moreover, had she believed this to be so, she would never have married Mallory, knowing full well how unable she was to meet love with love, how bereft of those feelings of enchantment, of devotion and fervor that she had so wantonly squandered on Jamie Fitz-hugh.

Naive though she was, she didn't mistake for love that wild sweet ecstasy to which Mallory could rouse her. She knew only too well, and most especially just after their passion was spent and a deep secret sadness sometimes stole over her, that it was her body, not her heart, that found such delight in his arms.

Nonetheless, perversely, the knowledge of his love for her sang in her blood. Wonderingly, over and over, she would say to herself, He loves me! He loves me! Far from home, she now perceived him through the eyes of others and found herself bedazzled, as they clearly were, by his charm, his striking good looks, his way with people. Everyone seemed to adore him. He had, it appeared, the knack of turning the most ordinary affair into a celebration. And such a lot of people he knew! Invitations poured in to beach picnics, teas, dances, boat trips.

Dressed in her fashionable new gowns, leaning ever so lightly upon his arm, she managed these occasions with aplomb. Long observation had taught her the refinements of behavior, but it was the heady knowledge of Mallory's love, his hand firm at her elbow, his eyes upon her from across a room, that fostered the self-confidence indispensable to success in society. They were a golden pair, handsome, rich, and petted. Vivian had always known she would adore such a life and now she had proof of her conviction, for nowhere could pleasure be pursued more singlemindedly than in the city that impudently called itself The Playground of the World.

Brash, exciting, with everything in it for sale, it contrived to satisfy every taste. Brighton Punch at the Brighton Hotel (so potent a mixture that ladies were permitted no more than two glasses per day), *thé dansants* at the Traymore, dinner at the Marlborough-Blenheim, supper at the Shelburne. These glittering hostelries neither took notice of nor competed with the gaudy little shops clamoring for the attention of the strolling crowds on the boardwalk.

Vivian loved all of it.

"Put this in your purse," said Mallory, and handed her twenty five-dollar bills.

"One hundred dollars!" she exclaimed.

"Do you require more?" he asked quite seriously.

Vivian blanched. More! Mother of God! "What will I need this much for?"

"Why, just to have in your purse, of course. You can't go about without money. You may find something you'd like to buy. When you spend it, just be sure you ask me for more."

How easily he said it. And how lovely to have twenty crisp new five-dollar bills to tuck into her reticule—more than she'd ever possessed at one time in her life. The moment she was alone she counted them out, lining them up one after the other on the white marble top of her bureau. So much! She met her eyes in the mirror, wide with wonder, shining like stars.

Resolving not to take undue advantage of Mallory's generosity, she determined to hoard this little cache. But she had reckoned without the orgy of spending that overtook her. Everything appeared irresistible. Money jingling in her purse, she swept into store after store along the boardwalk, purchasing an opal brooch and a lacquered fan for Mary Claire, a complete set of imported bone china dinnerware for her mother, a lap desk fashioned of silvery driftwood for Neil, and, on impulse, a banjo for Bucky. Fringed silk scarves for the aunts and ornate handtooled leather writing kits for her bridesmaids joined the growing pile of presents stacked in one corner of their hotel room.

Cheap, totally useless things appealed to her also, and she snapped them up: a piece of coral, a packet of seashells, Japanese fern seeds. Possessing, for the first time in her life, the means to gratify her least wish, she bought in a frenzy. Far from discouraging her, Mallory fostered every whim, and often she caught his eyes upon her, smiling, indulgent.

"What will you buy for mom?" he asked one morning as, fortified with a breakfast of lamb chops and sausages, they took their daily constitutional on the boardwalk.

For Vivian, her hand nestled in the crook of his arm, these brisk early morning walks were a favorite time of the day—not, of course, to be compared with evenings full of people and gaiety, but bearing their own fresh charm. At this hour few vacationers had left the big hotels or the rooming houses that were beginning to line side streets like Baltic, Mississippi, Mediterranean. Except for a lone bather now and again, the beach stretched white and deserted down to the dark, wet sand at the water's edge where terns hurried before each pursuing ruffle of wave. In the sunlight the ocean sparkled as though caught in a mesh of diamonds, while sea gulls wheeled and dipped above it, uttering their strange cry.

Turning her eyes from the scene, Vivian said, "I can't think what to buy her. What would she like?"

"Oh, I don't suppose it's so much the gift itself as the fact that you've thought of her. She's that fond of you, don't y' know."

"She is?"

Mallory looked down at her in surprise. "Why, sure you must know it!"

"But she wanted you to marry Dolly Muldoon."

"Now who filled your head with such nonsense? Dolly's her godchild and the Muldoons have always been grand friends, but the last thing anyone would dream is that I'd marry a little flibbertigibbet like that one."

Vivian said no more. Had she spoken she would have had to assure Mallory that all Butler Street had been certain of it.

The gift for Ma Mallory proved troublesome. With all manner of things to choose from, Vivian seemed unable to find an appropriate remembrance. No sooner had she made a decision than she would change her mind, pouncing upon first this, then that, trying Mallory's patience with consultation, buying something one day and returning it the next.

Until Mallory had mentioned it, she hadn't given a thought to a gift for his mother, but now her walks on the boardwalk became an anxious quest for the perfect present, whatever that might be.

"It isn't all that important," Mallory told her kindly. "You make too much of it."

"I want it to be just right."

"But, Puss, she'll treasure whatever it is because it comes from you."

It surprised Vivian how much she wanted to believe this. Mallory's devotion to his mother was legendary. Because of the untimely death of his father, he had tried in what ways he could to step into Matthew Mallory's shoes. Not only had the two of them managed the Tipperary Saloon together and shared the same small house, but from childhood the seven o'clock mass each Sunday morning, together with every wedding and every funeral in the parish, had found him at her side. Far from poking fun or calling him a mama's boy, people admired this solicitude. Men thought the better of him for it, while women held him up as an example to their own sons.

Fully aware of this relationship, Vivian longed to find favor in Ma Mallory's eyes. Nothing, she knew, would please Mallory better, and she now greatly desired to please him in what ways she could. His kindness, his thoughtfulness, his generosity to her appeared to know no bounds. And as to the world of sensual pleasures . . .

She had been totally unprepared for the tides of passion he could cause to sweep through her, a virgin with no experience whatever. The delicious little thrills she had known with Jamie's kisses were as nothing compared to the trembling eagerness she felt when naked in Mallory's arms. With skill and tenderness he had awakened to quivering ecstasy her dormant passion, and in doing so had completely enthralled her. Nothing she could do in return seemed too much.

But what he appeared most to want was simply to be near her. His eyes seemed always upon her, and often he invented quite transparent little ruses to remain at her side, studying with apparently the utmost fascination every lift of her hand, each turn of her head.

"Why do you stare at me?" she once asked, thinking there must be something amiss in her appearance or behavior.

"Because I am obsessed by you," he said.

He spoke the words harshly, as though he suffered a weakness, an illness he wished to be shed of. Even as she turned from him, piqued by such response to so innocent a question, Vivian felt a pang of sympathy. She was no stranger to such torment. Wasn't this, after all, the way she had felt about Jamie Fitzhugh?

But usually he was gallantry itself, showering attentions upon her, taking interest in everything she did: how she fixed her hair, how well or ill she slept at night, what she might like to eat; choosing for her the most enticing delicacies—stuffed flounder, crab imperial, charlotte russe. If they dined at the Rudolf he saw to it that the string ensemble gave renditions of her favorite tunes during dinner. Flowers from the hotel florist shop—roses, orchids, lilies of the valley—his card tucked among them, were delivered to her each day. Always at hand were baskets of fancy fruit and boxes of the delicious new saltwater taffy that was all the rage. In the fashionable gambling casinos, disguised, since gambling in Atlantic City was forbidden, as elegant restaurants or as exclusive rod-and-reel clubs, he introduced her to everyone, taking immense pleasure in what he called the "splash" she made.

And it did appear that his friends liked her. The women, coiffured, glittering with jewelry, wearing the latest styles, seemed to take to her instantly, calling her "honey" and "dearie" and drawing her into their circle, although it was difficult at times to understand their innuendos and follow the quick, bright chatter punctuated by loud, hooting laughter. They reminded her of Gert Barkin, just as the men resembled Mallory's political friends back home.

With the Republican convention just over and the Democrats about to meet, politics absorbed these men who stood about gaming tables in the luxuriously appointed back rooms, their pockets bulging with money but looking somehow ill-at-ease in the expensively tailored clothes they wore.

They talked about San Juan Hill and Theodore Roosevelt and Cuba. They talked about fighting the Spaniards and winning Guam, Puerto Rico, the Philippines. They talked about the new United States naval base at a place called Pearl Harbor, and about all the sugar Hawaii grew and Queen Liliuokalani not wanting the United States to take over her country but the United States doing it anyway.

They quoted William McKinley saying, "We must keep all we get when the war is over, we must keep what we want." And they agreed the country wanted it all and meant to keep it.

They talked about President McKinley being assassinated by an anarchist and Theodore Roosevelt taking office. They shook their heads in awed admiration about the way Roosevelt dissolved the giant Northern Securities Company and ended the coal strike and fought rebates to The Interests. Above all, they talked about how popular the new young Republican president was, and how difficult it would be for any Democrat to beat him.

It was while listening to such talk one evening that, quite by chance, Vivian discovered Mallory meant her to accompany him to the Democratic convention that, in this summer of 1904, would be held in, of all places, St. Louis.

"Vivvie and I will be staying at the Hotel Southern out there," he said casually.

At his words her lips parted in a gasp so keen and sharp she might have been stabbed. A panicky weakness overcame her and her heart fluttered wildly.

St. Louis. Jamie.

The notion of their meeting again simply had never occurred to her, but instantly now a score of possibilities presented themselves. Would she pass him on a street? Walk into a hotel lobby and come upon him? Turn a corner to find herself looking into those eyes?

More shaken than she would have thought possible, she waited until the men turned back to their roulette and then slipped up thickly carpeted stairs to the ladies' lounge.

Once there, she sat down before a long cretonne-skirted vanity table that spanned one wall and clasped her hands, trying to quiet the trembling that seized and shook her. She had no desire ever to lay eyes on Jamie Fitzhugh again. It was the last thing in the world she wanted. From the mirror her eyes stared back at her, appalled, and under the décolletage of white chiffon her bosom rose and fell quickly.

Go to St. Louis? Why, in heaven's name? Why do such a thing? Was Mallory aware of the circumstances that chance might engender? Not, she assured herself, that there was any reason she and Jamie *shouldn't* meet. Not at all. But why risk a situation that could only prove—well, awkward and embarrassing?

And how unnecessary! After all, there wasn't any reason for her to go to St. Louis. On the contrary, she had no interest whatever in who the Democrats might choose to nominate for president. She would only be a nuisance, in the way. Far better that she remain at home and let Mallory go about his business with a free mind.

Convinced he must see the merit in such a proposal, she grew calm and was about to rejoin the party downstairs when one of the young women she had met earlier in the evening entered the room, sat beside her at the table, dumped an assortment of cosmetics from her purse, and began talking immediately.

"Geez, kiddo!" She looked at Vivian with a shake of her somewhat frowzy blond head. "You sure got that guy going."

Preoccupied with St. Louis, Vivian politely turned to the girl. "What do you mean?"

"Gaga," the girl replied, rolling eyes and head dizzily. "I mean you got him gaga. Geez, I never seen him like this before. I wouldn't of thought it could happen to Brian Mallory."

"Do you know him well?" Vivian asked absently.

"Not the way you mean. He brought his from Philly." With total absorption the girl began energetically applying powder to all exposed areas: face, neck, scarcely concealed milk-white young breasts. "About once a month he'd come down here with somebody. Sometimes more often. It would depend on what shows were playing Philly. Fleurette, now. He always saw a lot of her when she was in town. She's with the Florodora Girls. You know Fleurette?"

"No," managed Vivian, so stunned by the girl's breezy intimations she could scarcely speak.

Having finished with the powder, the girl opened a tin of Ruby Salve and began lightly creaming it into her cheeks. "Yes," she continued affably, "he always brought Fleurette down here when she was in town. And then, Dimples Dolloway. She has an act with that horse. What's the name of that horse?"

"I don't know," Vivian breathed.

"You've never seen that horse act? Geez, that horse is the smartest animal I ever seen. Smarter than a lot of humans. That horse can count, add, subtract. Geez! And Dimples always rides in like she's Lady Godiva. On the horse, y' know what I mean? With just this long blond wavy hair, and her birthday suit. Of course, she's really got on some kind of mesh thing." She laughed and began applying Ruby Salve to her lips. "But that fool horse was a royal pain in the ass when Mallory wanted to have a little fun. Like once he said, 'I don't mind paying for a bed for Dimples, but having to hunt up a place to bed down her horse is . . .' "

Almost with a will of its own, Vivian's hand shot forward. "Stop!" she cried, digging her fingers into the girl's arm.

"Hey, cut it out!" exclaimed the girl, Ruby Salve flying. "Whatcha think you're . . ." Then, with a keen look at Vivian, "Geez, whatsa matter? You sick or . . . Geez, honey! Y' mean you didn't know? About the way Mallory played around?"

Vivian took a deep breath. "Certainly I knew. I just got a bit light-headed there for a moment. I just . . ." Reeling slightly, she looked about the small mirrored room, seeking the exit. "If you'll excuse me, I'll just go outside and get a breath . . ."

"No, wait!" cried the girl. "You don't understand. What I started to say is, this with you is different. I've never seen him like this before. When he looks at you, he . . . Geez, I can't even describe it. It's not like with those others . . . It's . . ."

But Vivian had fled, stumbling on legs that trembled down the thickly carpeted stairs, pushing her way through the crowded rooms, jammed with people, blue with cigar smoke, an inferno of heat and music and noise. Women called out as she passed them, men put out hands to detain her. She eluded them all, brushing through the swinging doors and bursting out upon the empty, late-night city pavement.

At the curb the Negro doorman, resplendent in red and black coachman costume, said, surprise in his soft voice, "A carriage, Mrs. Mallory?"

But she shook her head and, gathering her billowing silk skirts in both hands, hurried up the wooden ramp to the boardwalk, the fashionably narrow heels of her pink satin beaded slippers catching on the cracks between the boards, tripping her, delaying her.

She had no idea where she was going, what she meant to do, and was stopped cold in her headlong flight only by the protective railing that ran along the far end of the deserted boardwalk. Before her, under jagged moonlit clouds, stretched the broad beach, a vast inky blackness, while beyond, waves pounded and plunged, crashing over the huge glistening boulders that served as jetties, throwing a ghostly spume into the night.

Minutes after she reached the railing she felt, rather than heard, Mallory behind her.

"What happened?" he said.

"Nothing happened," she replied, not turning to him, not looking at him.

"Come now, Puss," he persisted patiently. "Don't be that way. I saw you go flying by like the devil was after you."

"Nothing happened!" she repeated. "Nothing I shouldn't have known, mightn't have guessed. But why couldn't you have told me?"

"Told you what?" he said with maddening amiability.

"About your Fleurette, your Dimples. About the bother of finding a bed for a horse. Or was it finding a bed for Dimples?" She caught her breath in a sob. "Oh, no, it was the horse that was the problem, wasn't it?"

He was silent a moment, then, "Stop it," he said quietly.

His poised calm served only to further infuriate her. "I won't stop. I want to know."

"Know what?"

"Everything."

"I doubt that," he said, and Vivian gulped. She couldn't imagine what "everything" might possibly be, but from the tone of his reply, she knew she would rather die than hear about it.

"Anyway," he continued mildly, "that's all in the past and doesn't concern you."

"And if the shoe were on the other foot?" she flung out, longing to upset that unruffled countenance. "If Jamie Fitzhugh and I, for instance . . ."

"Fitzhugh didn't do more than kiss you. Chaste little pecks at that, I'll warrant."

"And how would you know?" she demanded, goaded and galled by such accuracy.

He grinned. "Oh, I've no doubt he wanted to. But I just figure you aren't the kind of girl who would let a man take liberties with her. Even a man you were so mistakenly sweet on as Jamie Fitzhugh."

Though she refused to so much as look at him, she could feel his eyes upon her and knew the mocking, teasing light that rode in them.

"However," he continued pleasantly, "I'm always willing to learn. Did you let him? Do more than kiss you, I mean."

"You know very well I did *not!*"

"Ah," he said, nodding.

At this response, fury seized her. Who better than he knew her timidity, her awkwardness, her inexperience. Outraged tears stung her eyes. "How you must be laughing at me!" she spat out scathingly. "What fun you must have comparing me with your Dimples and Fleurette!"

Instantly the bantering little smile left his face and the glittering eyes that gripped hers were strange, cold, and frightening. "Is that what you're thinking?"

"What else am I to think?" she faltered.

"I'll tell you precisely what you're to think," he said

harshly. "You're to think you are lovelier, more passionate, more desirable than any woman I have ever known. You are to think I would rather look at you fully clothed across a crowded room than be in bed with Fleurette, Dimples, or a host of other women I could name.

"You are to remember that on the day of our marriage I pledged to you my eternal devotion, and that naked women could be served to me on platters and I would have no inclination to lay a hand on them. You are to understand that no thought of another ever enters my mind, that I am as true to you in my heart, in my brain, as in my bed. Finally, you are never to forget that I love you more than my life and that I pray God every night to make me worthy of you."

He stopped and stood panting before her as though he had run a race. "Now," he added savagely, "I want you to answer one question. Do you believe what I've just told you?"

Slowly she nodded. "Yes," she said.

Part II

14

*Mallory's wild, angry declaration of love left Vivian dis-*concerted and sobered.

She had never known such a man. At times he could be the most devoted of husbands, indulging her least wish, regaling her with tales of Big Bill Brady and the Butlerites, displaying in their lovemaking a tenderness, a consideration that could bring a rush of tears to her eyes.

At others, as when he had stood on the boardwalk under the cloud-ridden skies, eyes aglitter and a kind of rage upon him, he became once more the stranger. There was so much she didn't know about him, but one thing was crystal clear: he meant to keep her by his side.

"What, Puss?" he said sharply when she suggested he attend the Democratic Convention alone. "Have you forgotten the World's Fair? Why, people are coming to St. Louis from the ends of the earth. Why would you not be wanting to go?"

"I'll only be a bother, a nuisance."

"Indeed not! All the delegates will have their wives there. You ladies will go off every day and have a grand time. Besides," he added, "I want to show off my beautiful wife."

But she persisted in her campaign to remain at home, pleading the new house and all there was to do in it. And at length, indulgent of her to a fault, he agreed. He would go off alone when the time came several weeks hence, and she would remain happily busy on Butler Street. With relief Vivian pushed Jamie Fitzhugh, if not quite from her thoughts, at least from her daily concerns, for there were more felicitous matters to distract and claim her attention.

For all she enjoyed the luxury of the bridal suite at the Rudolf, it had been the keenest of pleasures to draw up to the front door of Mallory's new house and know it was now also hers. Alighting on his arm from the hansom cab that brought them from the station, she quite forgot she had ever considered the place a monstrosity with its red and white striped awnings and yellow brick facade.

Bits and pieces were still missing from every room—a rug here, draperies there, a chest, a divan, a table. The wicker porch furniture had been delivered, but the mahogany pier glass and the armoire for the master bedroom had yet to arrive. Enough of an idea could be gleaned, however, to assure Vivian that the close attention she had paid to the furnishings of the Webb mansion, together with the hours spent poring over magazines and swatches of fabrics, hadn't been in vain.

From the damp, cool cellar already stocked with bottles of wine, its empty bins and shelves awaiting the fruits of summer, to the attic with its gables and dormers and, tucked under the eaves, a little eyebrow window at which one must lie on one's stomach to see out, the house offered interest and delight at every turn. For Vivian, each room held a favorite aspect: in the hallway the sweep of the staircase up to the handsome grandfather clock on the landing, and then up yet another flight to the wide upstairs hall; in the double parlors, the way the sunlight struck through the stained glass that bordered the windows to lay red and blue lozenges on the floor.

True to his promise, Mallory had let her choose a carpet for the dining room that included in its rich design a bit of turquoise blue to match the tiles of the fireplace, and following her wishes, the massive sideboard, the chairs and the dining room table were all carved in golden oak. But what a lot of inventions and devices he had thought to provide as well!

It occurred to Vivian that chores would no longer include the trimming of wicks and the washing of sooty lamp chimneys just when she had acquired a houseful of servants to perform such disagreeable tasks for her, but this didn't diminish by a jot the marvel of seeing a room spring instantly alight with the flick of a switch.

Nor did she underrate the possession of a bathroom. Never again to have to take one's tub in the kitchen, adding a pail of hot to the water left by others. Never again to visit the public baths. Instead, a fine, big room with luxurious fixtures, snow-white towels, and her own toilet chest filled with perfumed soaps and oils and powders. Oh, the bliss of it! Taught by the nuns to desire heaven, she found herself guiltily hoping for a long sojourn upon earth in which to savor such pleasure.

The ring of the telephone could send a delicious thrill coursing through her, although it seldom rang, friends like the Barkins, who owned telephones, being out of town for the summer. The Beckwith Special upright piano in the front parlor, Sears, Roebuck's finest at one hundred and ninety-five dollars, was a special pride, nor did it disturb her that she couldn't play a note.

But oh, the pleasures of the gramophone, its lily-shaped horn filling the house with the latest two-step, or the voices of Patti, of Caruso! Oh, the stereoscope with photographic views of Europe, of Yellowstone Park, of ancient Egypt and Greece! As to the kitchen, with its fancy big stove embossed in nickel plate, its ice box and ice cream freezer and bread toaster and coffee grinder and, yes, a cherry stoner that would stone cherries for a pie as fast as ever the handle turned—as to this bastion of efficiency, Vivian could only regret that her position as lady of the house banished her from its reaches. The truth was, there was no need for her to lift a finger, for Mallory had personally selected a competent staff.

"But I can engage the servants we'll require," she had protested. "I know just what's needed, and I've many a good friend to choose from."

"You don't want to hire friends, Puss," he told her. "You want servants who will understand that you are mistress here. I'll see to that."

Annoyed at first, she quickly came round to his thinking. Halls, the butler, and his wife, Clarissa, the cook, soft-spoken, dignified colored folk, were surely the perfect foundation for a household staff, and she was won over the moment she set eyes on them. Mrs. Doughty, the housekeeper, came from St. John the Baptist in Manayunk, and brought with her her two nieces, Maureen and Peg, for upstairs and downstairs maids. Cassie, the little kitchen girl, Timothy Kerns, the gardener, and Hattie Flanagan, lady's maid, were all Irish and Catholic, but not one was from St. Bonaventure's, nor had Vivian ever met them before in her life. She was grateful for this when she found them all lined up in the front hall to greet her. It flustered her, she discovered, to be deferred to and called madame.

"They kept watching me," she later confided nervously to Mallory.

"Now you're seeing how the shoe fits the other foot," he said. "Just remember you hold the power to hire and fire. The way you look is important to them, if you smile, if you frown. Servants are quick to read a mood, as you surely know. But I could see they liked you."

She wouldn't have thought a mistress cared two pins that servants liked her, but she found herself saying eagerly, "Could you really, Mallory? You musn't say that just to bolster me."

"Why, Puss, you were gracious and smiling and you made a proper speech."

She had said precisely what she had heard Irene Webb say many times to a new servant: "I'm sure you'll do very nicely once you get on to my ways. I hope you'll be happy here." Her voice, she felt, had been a bit skittish, unlike the mellifluous tones of Irene Webb that were a delight to the ear. But perhaps she hadn't done too badly. One thing for certain, she hadn't come so far only to be thrown into confusion by a servant's glance.

With considerably less aplomb did she happen upon a note from Camilla Cavendish among the pile of correspondence awaiting the return of Mr. and Mrs. Brian Mallory.

"Vivvie, dear," Mrs. Cavendish had written in a flourishing hand, "We are having friends visit us for a weekend at Kimberly, and do hope you and Brian will be able to join us . . ."

Vivian raised her head from the expensively heavy notepaper and a tremor quivered through her. Over how many cups of tea with Nonnie, the Cavendish cook, had she not heard about the lavish weekend house parties at Kimberly, the Cavendish summer house just north of Philadelphia? A great fieldstone farmhouse it was, a gentleman's country estate set among acres of farmland and forest, with a pond stocked with trout for those who liked fishing, and croquet set out on a lawn like green velvet, and swimming and horseback riding and, in the evenings, music for listening and for dancing provided by musicians hired up from Philadelphia just for the purpose. The glittering guest list included not only the cream of Philadelphia and New York society but titled foreigners as well: dukes, duchesses, and such like from abroad.

To be invited to such an affair!

Vivian swallowed and choked. Thank heaven for Madame Modiste and the heliotrope gown! The pink chiffon as well. But she must have a long white tennis skirt and middy blouse. No matter that she didn't know how to play this rather silly game; smartly dressed, she would simply wander about as she had seen so many young ladies do upon the occasions when she had accompanied the Webbs on weekend visits.

Closing her eyes, she offered up three Hail Marys in thanksgiving that her employment together with her own alert observation had prepared her to take her place in society without fear or embarrassment. The moment was at hand that, hidden like a jewel in the future, she had always known was there, always hoped might come to her. The fairy wand had been waved, and Cinderella was to go to the ball at last.

"Mallory," she said, scarcely breathing, "We've an invitation from Mrs. Cavendish to go to Kimberly for the weekend."

He had come in the front door, home from the Tipperary for their midday meal together just as the angelus struck twelve noon from the steeple of St. Bonaventure's church.

Clutching the note, Vivian had been watching for him from the bay window in the front parlor, and as soon as she saw him turn in the walk, derby hat cocked above one eye, plaid garters hitching up the sleeves of his pink shirt, checked coat hooked by a thumb and slung over his shoulder, she sped to the screen door to fling it open.

"Give me a kiss, Puss," he said, one arm swinging her to him.

Raising on tiptoe she absently complied. "Mallory, an invitation to Kimberly," she repeated. "Oh, Mallory, I've always longed to go there. I've heard such stories. Oh, Mallory, do say we can go!"

He studied the invitation she had thrust into his hand, and a frown struck between his eyes. "It's the weekend of the carnival," he said.

"Carnival?"

"The Firehouse carnival."

Of course! How could she have forgotten? The three-day carnival put on as a fund raiser by the Hibernian Fire Company was the biggest event of the summer, unmatched even by the Amity Club picnic held every Labor Day. She was well aware that Mallory always played the role of auc-

tioneer at the white elephant booth, whipping up prices
with such wit and skill that, to the delight of all concerned,
the auction each night was a featured attraction.

"Too bad," he sighed, looking down at the invitation in
his hand and shaking his head.

I mustn't cry, thought Vivian, biting her lip, yet so keen
was her disappointment that this was precisely her inclination. Quite calmly, however, she said, "The carnival, yes.
How silly of me not to have remembered. I'll send Mrs.
Cavendish our regrets."

"Regrets? But surely we're going?"

Vivian stared at him in surprise. "How can we when it's
the carnival?"

"There's many a man they can get in my place."

"But you've always been auctioneer!"

"Then it's time someone else had the chance."

"But they're counting on you, like as not."

"Then they must count on some other. Now don't say
me nay, Puss, and pull a long face. All my life I've wanted
an invitation to Kimberly and I'll not be done out of the
honor now it's come to me." Suddenly his dark frown was
replaced by the sunniest of smiles. "It's what marriage to
you has done for me. Yes, by God, marriage to you has
done it. The Senator owes me the kindness for sure, but
Millie Cavendish would never give house room to those
others."

Had anyone told Vivian she would be accepting an invitation to a weekend house party at Kimberly with some
reluctance, she would have been hard put to believe it. But
such were her sentiments when, after lunch, following Mallory's instructions, she went immediately into the library,
seated herself at the big table in the unfamiliar room, set
out writing materials, and, with such care as caused perspiration to stand out on her forehead, penned in large,
round, childlike script an acceptance.

Finished, she gave a little sigh of relief, drew the tip of
her tongue back into her mouth, reread the note, and pronounced it perfect, borrowing as it did the precise phrases
she had more than once overheard Irene Webb dictate to
her social secretary. Very likely she should employ a social
secretary to come in now and then, she thought absently.
But this didn't account for the pensive tilt of her head
as, with the letter sealed and ready to be posted, she re-

mained at the table. In her heart she knew the Hibernians were counting on Mallory. Despite what he said, there simply wasn't anyone who could take his place. The white elephant auction had become the biggest fund raiser of the entire affair, thanks to Mallory and his remarkable memory that could put a name to every face in the crowd, to his quick wit that called forth both laughter and dollar bills. Once upon a time, drawn along with everyone else to stand gaping up at him on the high, lantern-lit platform, she had considered him too handsome, too clever by half. But even then she had been beguiled by him, won despite herself. No, the Hibernians wouldn't do nearly so well without him.

From the kitchen came the faint clatter and clink of dishes being washed to the accompaniment of lowered voices and soft laughter, and a sudden nostalgia for the carefree camaraderie of service swept over her. But how abruptly gossip would cease and faces arrange themselves if, seeking company, she should make an appearance.

On the landing the grandfather clock intoned the half hour, sending a single stroke into the heavy silence of the room. How long the hours that stretched between now and Mallory's return for supper. Small wonder ladies were forced into reading novels, doing fancy needlework. She had envied such leisure as she hurried about her own never-ending tasks, but now the idea that she spend the next four or five hours quietly sewing or reading a book appalled her.

Giving the bellpull several quick tugs, she announced to Halls that she was going off to visit her mother, and clapping a shiny green straw skimmer upon her head, she left the house.

In her purse was the note to Mrs. Cavendish, but she passed the post box on the corner without stopping. She might, she decided, just speak to Mallory again before mailing it. But seated in the Randall kitchen over a cup of tea, she heard news from her mother that drove all thought of the Hibernians out of her head.

"You can't mean Neil wants to marry her!" she exclaimed, yet knowing in her heart it was so.

Mamie nodded grimly. "Taking instructions from Father Shields she is."

"To enter the Church?"

"What else?"

Vivian sank back against the kitchen chair, her sprigged muslin sticking to its wooden splat. In the silence a fly droned, lighting first upon the cracked and worn oilcloth that covered the table, then on the oft-mended square of grimy cheesecloth tacked up at the window to serve as a screen. Nancy Webb becoming a Roman Catholic? Marrying the penniless Neil? "Oh, mama, you must stop them."

"Stop them! And haven't I near talked myself sick trying to do just that? Haven't I offered up communion every day?"

"But what is Neil thinking of? He has no money. Where will they go?"

"They'll come here, where else? They'll have your old room. Mary Claire will come in with me."

How definite it sounded, so many plans made. Vivian's head spun with a dozen memories: Irene Webb sobbing on the sofa; Clinton hurrying across Cavendish Square in the late afternoon; Dr. Webb, red-faced and apoplectic, railing against ingratitude. How infuriated he would be now. His daughter a Roman Catholic, married to a grocery clerk. No, never would he forgive that. And Nancy and Neil, from two different worlds. What chance could such a marriage have?

"Mama, it's wrong. Oh, it's wrong, wrong, wrong."

"Don't I know it? But there's no telling your brother. Full of answers, he is. Thinks he's as good as the Webbs, and that's the truth. Thinks he's better, and him with nothing and them so grand. But the pity with your brother is that he won't take note of his place."

"And who's to say what his place is?"

The loyal response earned from Mamie a look of supreme contempt. "Now don't you be starting that, too," she said. "I've heard just enough about that. We all have our place in this world, and them that knows it live happy and content with their lot. But them that think themselves better must prove it."

"And so will Neil someday."

"No, never. That's not the way of your brother. He'll not look to change his lot. He wants the world changed to suit him. He wants to pull the world down and make another."

Confusion filled Vivian. She agreed that privilege must be earned. Hadn't she striven for just this? Wasn't it due her now? It irked her to hear Neil take on about sharing wealth and taking from the rich to give to the poor. But having met Mallory's wealthy friends and finding many of them no wiser, no smarter, no different from the struggling inhabitants of Butler Street in any way other than extreme good fortune, she occasionally found herself in grudging agreement with some of the wild, passionate things he said.

Not inclined to trouble herself with such speculations, she paid scant heed to this philosophical dilemma. The matter of the moment was Nancy and Neil, and with a lift of her heart she saw what might be done. Mallory's house was so big, far larger than was needed for just the two of them. After Neil and Nancy were married, why couldn't they come to live there?

Hurrying home in the late afternoon, she suddenly bethought herself of the Kimberly house party, and dropped the note of acceptance into the next post box without a second thought. There were, after all, far more important matters than firehouse carnivals.

15

So used was Vivian to her husband's indulgence that she fully expected assent when, over dinner that evening, after recounting the dreary tale told by her mother, she added, "We have so much room, Mallory. Couldn't we invite Neil and Nancy to make their home with us?"

Mallory's fork paused above the helping of chicken pot pie that Halls had set before him. "We've room and to spare, Puss. But I doubt I'd get on with your brother. He doesn't like me."

"Neil! Doesn't like you?"

"I'm the scourge of the working class, to hear him tell it. I'm in cahoots with the oppressors of the poor and downtrodden."

"Pshaw, Mallory, for sure you've got it wrong. Why, everyone knows that whoever is in trouble has only to turn to you."

"And that's just the nub of it, Puss. Your brother says if

it wasn't for the likes of me keeping the poor content with their lot, they might throw off their shackles. At least that's what he says in those speeches he's forever making. You know that for yourself."

She didn't know for, not fancying political subjects, she had never gone to hear one of Neil's speeches. She felt constrained, nonetheless, to say placatingly, "I'm sure whatever Neil said, he wasn't speaking of you."

"And who else is boss of the Amity Club? No, Puss, it's none other than myself he's after when he blames Amity for the ills of the world. But who, I'm asking, helps a man find a job when he's down on his luck? Who sends round baskets of food to the back door? Who has a word with the judge when a young hooligan gets himself into trouble and his mom comes with tears in her eyes? But your brother sees none of the good that's done and spreads only the lies told by such as are jealous of my power."

She nodded bleakly, not so much in agreement as in understanding that surely one household could never contain the two men.

"There now, Puss, don't lose heart," said Mallory, softening. "Here's what we'll do. Your sister shall come to us and have that pretty room at the front of the house."

"Mary Claire?"

"And is there some other sister you're after having? It will lighten the load on your mom, what with that brother of yours moving his wife in upon her. What's more, I'm thinking of that fancy school you've set your heart on. The scholars doubtless will come from fine houses. It won't be amiss if your sister comes from a fine house, too."

Disappointed though Vivian was at being unable to offer suitable living quarters to her brother and the carefully nurtured young lady he had so imprudently determined to marry, still, the more she thought about Mallory's generous suggestion, the better she liked it. After the shabby, poky little hole Mary Claire was used to, how pleasant the big, airy front room with its brass bed and bay windows! As for the myriad advantages accruing to a young woman by virtue of the proper background and setting, why, anyone knew that appearances were everything. What with Mallory's big house and Mary Claire's vivid young beauty, her talent for the piano, and the ways and manners that the Villa Maria Academy would soon teach her, surely some promising chap would come along who, just like Mallory, would love and protect her forever.

Just like Mallory. In Vivian's view no man could possibly be kinder. Never before had there been anyone she felt she could rely upon. Even as a little girl she had sensed that her father's schemes would come to nothing, and his frequent absences left only her mother to cope. What would happen to all of them should anything happen to her? The frightening question had hovered like a shadow over the sunniest days of childhood and at night invaded her dreams. But with Mallory's arms tight around her, with the deliciously masculine and reassuring smell of his shaving soap and cigars in her nostrils, with her ear against the strong rhythmic beat of his heart, she felt safe at last, and gratitude filled her.

It was because she wished to express her appreciation that she acquiesced to the proposal that Ma Mallory spend Sundays with them.

"It's a long day for the old girl, don't y' know," Mallory had said, and Vivian promptly agreed.

Due to Pennsylvania's "blue laws," saloons and bars were closed on Sunday, accomplishing little other than assuring that private establishments like the Amity Club would do a rush business. Men worked hard for twelve hours a day, six days a week, tending looms in the deafening clatter of the textile factories, unloading hundred-pound bags of sugar onto the docks, slaughtering animals in the stench of the abattoir, swinging pick and shovel in bitter cold or blazing heat on the railroad lines stretching out like greedy fingers everywhere. At night along cobblestone streets where garbage lay in gutters and children chased rats between buildings, they went wearily home to an exhausted wife and ailing babies in quarters too crowded, too noisy, too poorly ventilated, too dark, too dirty, too hopeless. For skilled workers—the tile setters, roofers, glaziers, painters—the hours were equally long but the pay was better, enabling them to eschew the crowded tenement in favor of brick row houses such as marched side by side down Butler Street. But for everyone life was harsh and uncertain. Work was hard, pleasures few, and strange maladies and afflictions soon enough overtook a man, striking at him from he knew not where—although later decades would point to the mercury used in hat making, to the dyes in textiles, to poverty, poor nutrition, inadequate housing, filth.

But the weekend always came, and with it payday and Saturday night and the blessed release of a beer and a little sing-song at the Tip or some place like it, and on Sunday more of the same, at the Amity Club, of course.

So it was that the Tipperary Saloon was shut up tight of a Sunday, with the doors bolted and the green window shades drawn down. So it was that Ma Mallory, living alone now in the small house attached to it, was left with a long day on her hands. And so it was that on this first Sunday morning after their return from their honeymoon, Mallory and Vivian set off in the Overland to pick her up, escort her to church, and bring her home with them for the day.

Not, however, without some apprehension on Vivian's part. Three times she had changed the menu for Sunday dinner, favoring roast beef, then roast chicken, then baked ham, all the while imploring Mallory to suggest an appropriate dessert. Brow anxiously furrowed, she moved worriedly through the house, drawing an exploratory finger over table and windowsill in search of nonexistent dust, plumping pillows that needed no plumping, straightening pictures that didn't need straightening, and all in all working herself into what Mallory called, in mystification, a "state."

"Ma doesn't care what she eats," he assured her. "She doesn't care how a place looks."

"Well, I care," retorted Vivian, turning a deeply fringed velvet lampshade to better advantage. "I care a lot."

She knew she was being excessive, and couldn't help herself. Never would she forget that humiliating day at the Webbs' when, thinking to buy off the wedding, Ma Mallory had shaken a fist full of money in her face. Now here was the chance to show her mother-in-law that, in marrying Vivian Randall, Brian Mallory had made a fine choice.

And surely many might think so, seeing her seated beside him in the Overland on Sunday morning, ramrod straight and regal as a young queen. Over the becomingly shaded violet silk of her heliotrope gown she wore a pongee duster, its bertha of three tiered collars forming a capelet over her shoulders. On the shining red hair sat a white straw "automobile bonnet" with yards of white chiffon drawn down over a stiff broad brim to tie beguilingly under a small and rather imperiously tilted chin. Long chamois gloves, a purse, and a parasol completed this ensemble.

But despite all her efforts and preparations, the day seemed destined not to go well. From the very beginning it got off to an unpromising start.

"Hmph! A parasol, is it?" said Ma Mallory by way of greeting, taking in the confection of white eyelet ruffles and velvet ribbons as her black bombazine girth was being helped, or rather hoisted, into the back of the Overland by her son. "A parasol, and not a glimmer of sun in the sky."

Vivian smiled determinedly past the gratuitous little comment while Mallory, linen duster flapping, rounded the Overland and climbed into the front seat.

"Vivvie has brought you a grand present," he said, grinning back at his mother, voice warm with husbandly approval.

"A present, is it?" said Ma. "Sure, I can't think what she'd find to bring me, and me not after needing or wanting a thing."

"She found something you'll like just the same."

"Did she then? And why would she go wasting good money on the likes of me?"

"She gave more thought to you than to anyone."

"And why should she do that?"

Vivian almost felt she wasn't present. She retained no hope now that her mother-in-law would like the gold pencil that waited at home in a box done up in white tissue paper tied with pink satin ribbon. She had been so pleased at finding it, pouncing upon it in one of the jewelry stores on the boardwalk and declaring it to be, at last, the perfect gift. Ma could thread it with black ribbon and wear it about her neck, handy for all the figuring and bookkeeping she did at the Tipperary.

But Ma, Vivian began to believe, was not to be won by presents, nor by Sunday dinners, no, nor by her daughter-in-law, however stylishly turned out.

This opinion was reinforced somewhat later when, from the candlelit altar of St. Bonaventure's, Father Shields pulled from out the sleeve of his surplice, like a rabbit out of a hat, a large limp white handkerchief, mopped his red face with it, and said: "The banns of matrimony are announced for the first time between Henrietta Virginia Muldoon and Thomas Aloysius O'Reilly, both of this parish."

In the stifling heat that lay like a weight upon the congregation, Ma Mallory stopped fanning herself. The fan was large and made of cardboard. On one side it bore a brightly colored representation of the Resurrection of Christ and on the other the compliments of Muldoon's Funeral Parlor.

Ma gave a sad, heavy sigh and plucked Vivian's sleeve. "I knew this was coming. Regina Muldoon was after telling me only this week." She settled back, then roused herself. "Pass it along."

Dutifully Vivian turned to Mallory. "Ma says she knew this was coming," she whispered. "Mrs. Muldoon told her only this week."

Ma plucked her sleeve again. "What did he say?"

Vivian turned back to her. "He didn't say anything, Ma. He just nodded his head."

This response seemed to produce in Ma a dark disapproval that settled itself upon her and was not to be lifted by the end of the long hot service, nor the greetings of friends on the church steps, nor even by the smooth, round, beaming face that Halls presented as, turned out in black pants and short white linen steward's jacket, he stood above the steep flight of steps on the porch of Mallory's house and held the screen door wide open for this, Mallory's mother and their first guest.

"Let all the flies in, he will," Ma observed as, with Mallory on one side and Vivian on the other, they made their way in slow procession up the broad slate walk.

"He means well," said Vivian defensively, remembering her own servant days.

"Needs training," Ma sniffed, unimpressed.

The house fared no better.

Mallory conducted the tour himself, quick to point out his wife's skill in arranging furniture, her taste in choosing fabrics.

If only he wouldn't! thought Vivian helplessly. A man shouldn't praise his wife to his mother. Leastaways, not this man to this mother.

"Hmph!" said Ma, planting herself in a doorway and casting a dour eye upon the matched parlor chairs and divan tufted and upholstered in figured gold-on-gold satin. Hmph, again, to the second parlor with the upright piano, Aubusson rug, and the girandole done in gilt gesso and bearing candle holders on either side of its polished mirror.

A click of the tongue and a shake of the head to the pair of Remington bronzes, two horses rearing, that graced the massive marble-topped console in the vestibule.

"And I take it the Webbs have such folderol in their hallway?"

Vivian was spared the necessity of answering by Mallory's enthusiastic reply that it was the latest thing.

Trailing behind mother and son, Vivian tasked herself with trying to see all these possessions through Ma Mallory's eyes. Such a scandalous lot there was! Not only furnishings, but wedding gifts. An enormous sterling silver tea kettle set upon a silver salver from Senator and Mrs. Cavendish; a cloisonné jardiniere, tall as a young child, from Judge and Mrs. Wickersham; in the library, a Persian rug, gift of the president of the Keystone Bank. And sterling silver candlesticks, cake baskets, sauce boats, beakers; crystal compotes, hand-painted china, pressed glass platters, and goblets of every size and description.

Most of the gifts, of course, were neither costly nor elegant. The *Ladies' Home Journal* would have scorned them, running as they did to overly ornamented pillows and hand-crocheted or hand-embroidered articles of bedding, toweling, and antimacassars without number. Moved by the sentiment behind these homemade efforts, Vivian had overcome her qualms as to good taste and strewed them about the house, contriving to find space for as many as possible.

It was before these items that Ma paused, nodding her head in approval. But as to the rest—the handsome grandfather clock on the landing with its little painted lunar disk; the second floor with its bathroom, which Mallory demonstrated by proudly flushing the toilet; the sewing room under an arch off the hallway in its own little alcove; the master bedroom with its enormous carved mahogany bed and, winking from the vanity table, Vivian's silver-backed hairbrush and hand mirror, each ornately festooned with a large *M*—to this, to everything, hmph! And hmph again.

Not until they sat down at the dining room table did Ma brighten. Nor was this surprising since, striving to please with their first company dinner, Halls and his wife Clarissa had prepared a feast.

On the heavy white damask cloth graced with a low silver bowl of roses and laid with pink and gold Minton china, there rested a platter of ham, its delicate pink slices glazed with brown sugar and studded with cloves. Whipped potatoes, new peas, raisin sauce, and freshly baked beaten biscuits completed the menu and invaded the air with such a mingling of spicy and buttery and yeasty aromas as to soothe the most ill-tempered spirit.

"And so," said Ma Mallory, picking up knife and fork and suddenly becoming sociable, "we now have the wedding of Dolly Muldoon."

Mallory dressed a biscuit with butter. "And a fine lad she's getting."

"That remains to be seen," replied Ma. "The Muldoons don't think he has much get-up-and-go to him."

Mallory laughed. "Sure, Dolly has enough for both."

"Don't be making light. A girl like Dolly Muldoon can do wonders for a man."

"Or drive him clean out of his mind."

"No, no. She'll be the making of him. Too many young O'Reillys growing up and looking to that market to keep them. But the Muldoons, now. What a fine business they're doing, and Dolly their only one."

"You're thinking Tom will fancy dressing corpses to dressing lamb?"

Ma ignored the twinkle in her son's eye. "Dolly will see to that," she said with a nod.

The twinkle deepened. "Ah, he's that kind, then, is he? To be led by the nose?"

"No, not by the nose, not a bit of it!" declared Ma, indignant at last. "He just wants to be shown what's to his advantage."

"And who's to show him?"

"Why, Dolly, of course. She's got a good sensible head on her shoulders. Sharp as a tack, that one. And won't be put off."

Mallory had put her off, thought Vivian. Everyone had expected him to marry Dolly. Everyone except Mallory himself.

People now wondered if they had been mistaken in this. Standing on the church steps that morning, they agreed that Dolly had got herself engaged to as pleasant and likeable a young man as one could wish. And what with him going into her family's undertaking establishment, she wasn't doing badly for herself at all.

Vivian gave no credence to such opinions. She felt Dolly

had speedily accepted Thomas O'Reilly for precisely the same reason she herself had become engaged to Mallory: to save face. Though never overly fond of the young woman, Vivian admired such plucky bravado quite as much as she felt guilty at being the cause of it. She only hoped Dolly's marriage would turn out as happily as her own.

"While we're on the subject of the Muldoons," Ma was saying, "Regina tells me you can have that old sealskin coat of hers for your carnival auction."

Mallory wiped his mouth with his napkin. "I'll not be at the carnival."

"What's this?" said Ma sharply.

"I'll not be running the auction this year. Vivvie and I have accepted an invitation to Kimberly."

"Kimberly." Dumbfounded, Ma repeated the word.

"The Cavendish summer estate outside the city," Mallory told her. "We've been invited for the weekend."

"The weekend of the carnival?"

"That's right."

"And you accepted?"

"Right."

A dark flush rode up into Ma's face. "And who's to run the auction?"

"They'll find someone else."

"Someone else, is it? And what will be thought of that, with you running it all these years, and your father before you?"

"They may think as they please." He shot her a look. "I'll hear no more of this, Ma. We're going to Kimberly and that's the end of it."

A stony silence settled over the table, broken only by the spooning up of the tart and lovely lemon pudding Halls had placed before them.

Never had Vivian heard Mallory speak a harsh word to his mother. Despite a sometimes peremptory manner with others, he had a fond, easy way with her that conveyed the deepest regard and affection. Vivian would have wagered that in any contest between the two Ma would gain the upper hand. Clearly this was not the case.

Dinner over, Mallory left the room frowning darkly.

"Would you like to sit on the porch, Ma?" Vivian suggested rather timorously.

"I don't care where I sit."

"Let's try the porch, then. The house is an oven."

The porch proved little better, although Halls had lowered the awnings all around. On its broad, shaded expanse were rocking chairs, and the set of glistening white wicker furniture had arrived, fan-shaped lounge chairs and settees covered in flowered cretonne. At one end was a porch swing, and suspended by chains above the balustrade and set into wicker baskets were pots of ferns, their feathery fronds suggesting cool green glades.

Beyond the porch the heat of early afternoon lay shimmering above the young grass of the front lawn, where stood two cast-iron reindeer in the center of geranium beds planted in diamond shapes on either side of the walk. Nothing moved. The narrow streets that but an hour or two ago had rung with church bells and the clatter of carriages were now deserted. Somnolent and heavy, the Sunday quiet lay upon the air. Not a leaf stirred.

Ma rocked back and forth in a rocker. Creak, creak. Creak, creak.

How uncomfortable she looked, thought Vivian, laced into the heavy black bombazine. Under the thick pile of graying pitch-black hair, her handsome face was red, whether from pique or overindulgence at the dinner table, Vivian couldn't have said.

Pique, most likely, for after several minutes of baleful silence, she said, "My son is a fool."

Annoyance flared in Vivian. In this heat it was difficult enough to remain gracious and courteous when what she really longed to do was slip upstairs, ring for Hattie Flanagan, and be helped out of heliotrope gown, petticoat, corset cover, and corset. With the window shades drawn and the room dim, what luxury to stretch out on the bed in nothing but chemise and drawers. Unable to thus indulge herself, she at least was resolved not to be drawn into a conversation critical of her husband, and behind his back.

"I think you may not understand how few are invited to Kimberly," she explained politely. "Nor how highly Mallory prizes the invitation."

Ma rocked forward so violently it appeared she might be catapulted out of her chair. Planting her feet forcibly on the porch floor, she leaned into Vivian's face, fixing upon her such a look of wrathful exasperation that Vivian caught her breath. "Do I not, then?" she asked fiercely. "Let me tell you about my son."

Never for a moment shifting her implacable gaze, she said, "He's my father all over again. Oh, he looks like my late husband, God rest his soul. Matt Mallory will never be dead while his son is alive. But it was my father who played the dandy. Never stepped out his front door without top hat and cane. Ebony, that cane was, with a gold lion's head on the top. I'll not forget it. Always wanting fine ladies and gentlemen about; going off to the theater in Dublin with them and giving a great swirl to his cape. Not like my Matt, who would down a beer with any man.

"Why," she continued, warming to the tale, "when the Tip was opened, that room in the back was a storeroom, don't y' know. My Matt had no call for a grand private office with a fine rug on the floor, nor a bartender like Solly, either. Drew beer himself; wiped up the floors with a mop in his own two hands and lived on the premises. But that's not the way of my son."

Saints be praised! thought Vivian, and gave thanks for that dashing grandfather with his gold-topped cane and swirling cape who had bequeathed a taste for fine living to his grandson. What could be wrong with this? "Don't you want your son to better himself?" she asked in perplexity.

"I want my son to hold on to the power he's been given," said Ma, biting off each word. "I want him to know what he is and what he's not. I want him to know who his friend is and who isn't. I want him to have a care for those that have given him his wealth and his power, and that can just as easy take it away."

Alarm quivered through Vivian. Take it away? Could this really happen? Could it all disappear? The fine house and the Overland and most of all the money? To be poor again! Mother of God, could the money disappear?

"But the Cavendishes are his friends," she pointed out faintly.

Ma shook her head. "They are not! The Cavendishes are in his debt, that's all. Yes, my girl. With all their money and la-dee-da ways, they're in debt to my son. When Senator Cavendish wants to be reelected, it's Mallory who gets out the vote. Mallory's friends, that is. The Hibernians and Butlerites and Amity men, for all you may look down your nose at them."

"I don't look down my nose."

"Go along with you, girl. Butler Street won't hold you. I said this in the beginning, and now here's the proof."

Surprise parted Vivian's lips, followed by sudden comprehension. "But I think we should go to the carnival," she cried, misjudged and indignant.

"You're asking me to believe you don't want to go off to Kimberly?"

"Why sure and I want to go, who wouldn't. But he's always been auctioneer."

Ma gave her a keen, hard look. Have I wronged you? the look said. Are you not the flighty girl I thought? "If that's the way you feel," she said cautiously, "then why don't you see to it?"

"How can I see to it?"

Ma winked. "Oh, there's many a way a woman has of getting around a man. Especially a beautiful new bride like yourself." Ignoring the painful blush that enflamed Vivian's face, she pressed on. "Tell him the Hibernians are counting on him and he's to be auctioneer or go off to his fine friends alone. I'll wager he'll not do that."

Vivian knew her mother-in-law had cannily hit upon the right conclusion. Mallory wouldn't be welcome at Kimberly without a wife; indeed, he had received the invitation precisely because he had acquired one.

"Well?" demanded Ma.

"I've mailed off our acceptance."

"Go along, that's easily got around." A smile lit the gray eyes, conspiratorial, warming, wonderful, offering the ancient bond: We women know these men. Such children! But there are ways to make them behave.

How enticing the proferred friendship! But she shook her head. "I'll not do that."

Ma's lips clamped together and her eyes went cold. "Because you want to go yourself," she said accusingly.

"Because it's up to him."

"Up to him, is it? Then he's lost."

16

Ma's prediction haunted Vivian. Surely the woman didn't believe that her son's failure to appear at the Hibernian Firehouse carnival would result in such dire retribution, did she?

But Vivian knew it was more than this that Ma had in mind. It had to do with Mallory's preference for such places as Kimberly; it had to do with wearing a jacket to the dinner table instead of shirt sleeves and galluses or, in this heat, his underwear, as the other men in the neighborhood were wont to do. It had to do with that Dublin grandfather swirling his cape and swinging his gold-topped cane.

It was, in fact, the very things about Mallory that Vivian found most to her liking that Ma seemed most to deplore. Including, she told herself with a blush the next day, making love in broad daylight smack dab in the middle of the afternoon—if Ma but knew.

Vivian herself had been shocked and dismayed when somehow, she could never say quite how, she and Mallory had slipped into the practice. But now the hour or two spent together after their midday meal was part of the pattern of their days. Nor would she have it otherwise. To be sure, Mallory came home each evening for a quick supper, but since he returned to the Tipperary until it closed for the night, frequently at an hour that found Vivian in bed and asleep, this little siesta time together was doubly precious.

This afternoon, moving slowly up the staircase after luncheon, his arm tight about her waist, bodies pressed thigh to thigh, Vivian felt her heartbeat quicken, as always, in anticipation of the moments to come. From Butler Street drifted the clamor of the city, distant, muted, as the house settled into the drowsy summer afternoon. The servants, free for a while to pursue their own affairs, had done up the dishes and vanished, leaving no one about, not a soul.

In the master bedroom Halls, as usual, had lowered the awnings, the noonday sun driving through their red canvas stripes to tint the room a dim, pearly pink. At the open windows fine white muslin curtains billowed and fell in a breeze gentle as a sigh, and young Hattie Flanagan had turned back the pale green silk bedspread upon an expanse of cool, smooth white linen.

In the evening it was Hattie who prepared Vivian for bed, helping her from the voluminous skirts and petticoats in the pretty dressing room next to the master bedroom. But in the afternoon Mallory himself assisted her, and how different the ritual! Hattie with her gossip and chatter and quick efficient way with buttons, with hook and eye; Mallory, so much more deft despite his big square hands, and not a sound from him. Not a sound anywhere except, far off, the din of the city and, in the quiet room, the soft whoosh of a petticoat let fall.

In the pink and pearly room she at last stood naked before him and felt his eyes move slowly up over her until they fastened upon her own, dark green slits now, glittering, feral. Not relinquishing his gaze, he stepped toward her and folded her against him so that she felt the buttons of his coat press into her breasts, felt the buckle of his belt prod her and the rough fabric of his trousers scratch her bare legs.

Tilting back her head, she looked up at him, heart pounding, seared by his eyes, blue black now and looking into hers as though they would plumb the depths of her soul. With a little gasp she felt his hands slip over her buttocks, and he lifted her off the floor so that she dangled helplessly against him, clinging to his broad shoulders while a slow, inexorable surge of desire swept up through her and she thought she must faint with expectation and delight.

Moving to the bed with her, he laid her upon the smooth linen sheet. She closed her eyes, every fiber of her quiveringly alive and waiting, waiting, until at last she felt the bed give under his weight and she opened her eyes and turned to him, reaching for him, running her trembling hand up over the smooth, hard muscles of thigh and flank to be lost in the curling black hair of his chest. Raising himself on an elbow, he looked down upon her. Then, with a cry, she felt his fingers reach that most secret of places and he brought his lips down upon hers.

* * *

Afterward, they sipped the fine chilled Chablis left them, together with two cut-glass goblets upon a silver tray, by Halls. This was the lovely, languid afterglow that Vivian especially prized, filled as it was with idle talk, with soft, lazy laughter.

Today, however, Mallory had Kimberly on his mind. "You must tell me how to act at a fancy house party, Puss," he said. "You must tell me what's what."

Clad in a blue linen dressing gown that intensified the blue of his eyes under the jet-black eyebrows, he sat on the end of her chaise longue, huge, powerful, handsome.

Vivian had discovered she could be utterly frank with him without any danger whatever of his taking offense. In fact, his very determination to learn the ways of society, his eagerness to behave properly and "cut a fine figure," as he said, sometimes gave her pause. You could want things too badly, she reminded herself, and her thoughts winged to Jamie Fitzhugh.

"First off, Mallory," she said firmly, pushing back the long full butterfly sleeves of her lace wrapper, "you must not unpack your own luggage as you would at a hotel. The valet will tend to that. He'll put your toilet articles on your dressing table, your folded things in drawers, and he'll hang up your suits. Then he will ask if he may draw you a bath and you must nod and say please."

"Just please, is it?"

"No more is necessary," she assured him, adding, "It's always best to be standoffish with servants. This earns respect."

"And so does a bit of loose change, I'm thinking," said Mallory with a grin.

But Vivian frowned. "Not until we leave. Then it is proper to give one dollar to the valet and two to the butler. Not any more than this, mind now. Those who tip grandly are looked down upon."

"And what a pity that is. Sure if I were to buttle, I'd jolly well give the best service to him who paid most. Why would a man not be wanting to make a bit more, I wonder!"

"Because valets and butlers have their positions to consider. They are not in trade. They are gentlemen's gentlemen and give the best service at all times, without regard to pay. The bit of money you give them is only by way of a thank-you and must be quietly pressed into their hands without making a fuss."

"And for only a dollar or two there's no fuss worth making, I'm thinking."

"Be that as it may, Mallory, this is the way things are done."

"Then that's the way I'll do 'em. Now tell me what else I must do."

"Well, in the morning," continued Vivian, "you will go downstairs and take breakfast with the gentlemen. Like as not this will be in the morning room and served from the sideboard. I shall have breakfast on a tray in my room."

"And why should it be that the gentlemen and ladies eat separate?"

"I'm sure I don't know the reasons for things, Mallory, but I can tell you that many's the tray I've carried upstairs."

"And then what?"

"Well then, it depends. Certain of the gentlemen will no doubt play tennis or ride horses. Others will fish and some will play croquet, although mostly they'll wait for the ladies for this. Others will go into the library and read newspapers or books."

"And I'm thinking I'll wait for you to come down and we'll play croquet."

"No, Mallory, not with your wife. That's not done. At a house party husbands and wives don't stick to each other as if they're at a hotel on holiday."

"Then how will I get me a partner for croquet?"

"Why, simply step up to a lady and say, 'Would you care to join me in a game?' "

"What! Without an introduction?"

"Sure, Mallory, you've never been shy before."

"I've never been asked to a grand house party afore."

"Not *a*fore, Mallory. *Be*fore. And at house parties everyone speaks whether introduced or not," she continued, sounding precisely like Irene Webb, "since all may rest assured that everyone present is socially acceptable."

"Socially acceptable," repeated Mallory, staring off. He turned a hard, clear gaze upon her and said almost grimly, "It's what I always wanted, Puss. What I made up my mind to be. Anyone can make money today. Look at Harry Barkin. Look at Heinz Ritter and his old man. But I'm not like them. No, nor like Thurman Foy and Morrissey, content to drink beer all their days and get nowhere. There's more to life than that. And it's not just the money. That's only part of it. The Ritters and the Barkins wouldn't be invited to Kimberly if they had all the money in the world. They wouldn't be like you said, 'socially acceptable.' "

He grinned suddenly. "I know I'm just squeaking in under the wire, so to speak. Just getting my toe in the door due to my political empire. But that's all that's needed, for I mean to do things just right. Time will take care of the rest."

Looking into his face, so confident, so handsome, Vivian felt a vague apprehension, and Ma Mallory's baleful words returned to shake her. "Your mom thinks we shouldn't go," she said.

Instantly Mallory's face darkened. "Don't I know it?" he asked shortly. "Don't I know there be those that will share her opinion? Don't I know there be those that begrudge me my fine house and my motor car; yes, and the fine dressy wife I've got me? Don't I know there be those that think I should stay here in the muck of Butler Street and be happy to wallow away my life in this pigsty?"

Rising, he strode across the room and then turned to confront her as though she were a stranger, an adversary, as though the world itself defied him. "Well, I'll not do it!" he flung out. "No, I'll not do it! I'm tired of the poor. I'm tired of the poor with their filth and their smell and their troubles. By God, I'll not be tied here forever!"

Vivian remained among the silken pillows of the chaise longue for some time after Mallory got himself dressed and, his usual good humor restored like sunshine after rain, kissed her good-bye and went off to the Tipperary.

Truth to tell, she had been dismayed by his outburst. What did he mean, she wondered, when he said he wouldn't be tied here forever? Where would they go? How would they live? By now she was well aware of the meaning of *constituency*. Politically, it was simply another word for home. And *constituents* were simply voters who lived in your district, your neighbors, your friends. How could Mallory leave them without losing all he possessed?

Her eyes swept the lovely bedroom. On either side of the fireplace, its dark mahogany inlaid with rosewood, stood a slipper chair, deeply tufted in green velvet, a trim of heavy gold fringe grazing the richly patterned rug aglow with varicolored chains of flowers. Above the fireplace, on the mantel, were two large ivory fans displaying intricate open-work, together with two decorative bronze urns, a family of six ivory elephants carefully arranged according to size, and, in the center, a handsome clock, its facade an imitation of an ancient Greek temple and worked in black Italian marble, onyx, and ornamental gilt. In one corner stood Mallory's immense mahogany wardrobe, giving the room extra dimension by virtue of the huge, crystal-clear, full-length mirror adorning its front. At the foot of the bed stood a table graced by a chinoiserie vase filled with pea-cock feathers, and in the recess formed by three bay windows, another table, round, and skirted first in a cream-colored brocade, then in panniers of red taffeta, and finally in a short, dark green velvet cloth fringed in gold.

The windows, seven in all, counting the bay, were swathed in four layers of cloth following the style of the period: pale green watered silk draperies, their valences ball-fringed in gold, then white lace curtains, then linen blinds, and, next to the window frames, white muslin curtains.

Heretofore, Vivian had viewed this luxurious setting with unalloyed pleasure, but now the knowledge that there were those who begrudged it, who resented the house, the motor car, the invitation to Kimberly, cast a shadow upon her pleasure and filled her with unease.

Yet why, she asked herself, should this be so? Surely Mallory worked unbelievably hard for such rewards as were accorded him. At times it seemed that, but for his intervention, the very world would come to an end. And for more than one poor unfortunate, this was literally true.

That convulsive thrust of history that, like a giant tidal wave, spewed forth humanity upon these shores, also swept up men like Brian Mallory, adept at riding the crest. Tough, tireless, uneducated but street smart, they ruled the cities that teemed like giant rabbit warrens with proliferating human life, demanding unquestioning allegiance but never failing to reward the faithful—with a job, with food, with a place to live or a hospital bed or bail money or a pardon from the judge, with a fine christening or an equally fine funeral, and all manner of assistance and entertainment in between.

Never too busy to listen, never loath to "put in a good word," the political boss ruled ward and precinct like the king of a country under siege, enlisting new recruits with every boat that docked. To the frightened, bewildered newcomer, his lieutenants offered, first, a friendly hand on the shoulder and a place to live, never mind how dirty and airless and dark. First, in this terrifying new world, a place to lay down one's head among one's own kind.

Then, a job—not on a small farm such as that from which one had come, not practicing the skilled craft brought from home, but a job, nonetheless, in the clamorous factories, mills, mines whose beckoning broadsides, posted in the "old country," had promised so much.

And after the job, the language—help to learn the strange new words, and then help to become naturalized, and, finally, help with how to vote. And if the bosses, with their hierarchy of precinct captain, ward leader, committeeman; with their carefully kept lists, including, at times, the names of some already peacefully laid to rest in the graveyard; with their influence reaching into high places and their bursting treasuries reaching everywhere, if these bosses and their machines were roundly denounced in certain quarters, this, nonetheless, was how hundreds of thousands of immigrants were turned into citizens. There was no one else to do the job.

To Vivian, unused to looking beneath the surface of things, Mallory's beneficence appeared nothing short of sublime. How little she had known him! she more than once thought guiltily, recalling the days when she had considered him "full of himself," when, watching him arrive amid shouts and applause at some outing or other, she had privately surmised how he must enjoy the adoring throng.

Now she knew he often went off to such affairs with a resigned groan. But aside from such mild protest, he seemed to think nothing whatever of the long hours he put in, not only in the back room of the Tipperary, trying to solve the troubles of the world, but junketing all over the city to attend funerals, weddings, even bar mitzvahs.

Surely such dedication entitled him to a few pleasures, did it not? she asked herself, drawing her knees up on the chaise longue and resting her chin upon them, green eyes in fiery contrast to the soft lacy ecru negligee she wore. But there were, she reflected, always those quick to criticize, as she herself knew very well. Always those quick to look black upon anyone with the gumption to raise a head above the crowd.

One simply couldn't pay attention to such persons. If one did, one would never better one's lot in life or amount to anything. And for every one who might point a finger at Mallory to find fault, there were a dozen others who gloried in his success. This she knew for true. It stood in their eyes, this pride they took in one of their own, in his big house and his motor car, and everything else about him. There were those who admired her, too, indeed there were. Young girls who took heart at the lady she had become, who marveled at her elegance, aped her clothes and her ways.

The cold fear that had chilled Vivian at the thought of losing all she had so lately won vanished in the rosy reassurance of these considerations. In their separate ways they had worked hard and come far, she and Mallory. She felt in her bones they were destined to go even farther.

As though in confirmation, there was a tap at her bedroom door and she learned, to her surprise and pleasure, that Mr. Clinton Webb had come to call and waited downstairs to see her.

17

Quickly helped by Hattie Flanagan into a becomingly feminine shirtwaist gown of white lingerie, its long flounced skirt affording a four-yard sweep, Vivian cautioned herself to descend the broad staircase with ladylike composure, although her heart was aflutter.

Clinton Webb come to call in this grand new house of hers! Waiting, not for her to run quick to fetch and carry, but to greet her among the gold-on-gold furnishings, the cream-colored satin draperies, the Aubusson rug and gilt girandole of her own parlor.

Oh, I shall pop with pride! she told herself nervously. But as he arose from the divan, the warmest of smiles on his face, she coolly extended a small, perfectly manicured hand to have it enveloped in both his own.

"Vivvie!" he cried softly. "How grand you are, and doesn't it become you!"

Vivian had last seen Clinton Webb just before her wedding, when he had come hurrying after her through Cavendish Square. Since then, Mallory had introduced her to dozens of gentlemen, many of them attractive. But none had possessed that blend of breeding and reserve together with genuine warmth that was the cachet of Clinton Webb. Looking at him now, tall and lean in the lightweight gray frock suit he wore properly buttoned despite the heat of the day, his black mustache a fine neat line above the clearly etched lips, curly black hair mercilessly slicked down, Vivian decided once again that he was the most elegant gentleman she had ever known.

"I'm very happy to see you," he was saying.

"Thank you," she replied with the polite reserve with which she had resolved to conduct herself. "Do sit down."

He returned to the divan and she sat carefully on the chair opposite him, her soft full skirt spread out, hands lightly clasped in her lap. She wished him to take notice of this splendid room and its furnishings. He, however, seemed intent only upon her, shaking his head and regarding her smilingly.

"I can't get over you," he said. "I hope you'll permit me to say you're lovelier than ever. And . . . well, the funniest thing. Sitting there that way, you remind me strongly of my mother. Now why should that be?"

Vivian flushed with pleasure. No compliment could be more welcome than this flattering comparison with the gracious and cultivated woman who had, all unknowing, been the pattern, the exemplar for everything Vivian had ever hoped to become. She would always love and revere the beautiful Irene. She forgot all attempts at sangfroid, and her voice rang with feeling as she said, "How is your mother?"

Clinton's face clouded. "Not well, I'm afraid. And hasn't been, not since my sister wrote to us of her impending marriage." He paused and added, "I say this, Vivvie, knowing you will realize it is not your brother *per se*, to whom we take objection, but the unpromising nature of any marriage outside one's class."

Without the least pique, Vivian nodded. "At first I shared your sentiments," she admitted, choosing her words with ladylike circumspection. "If I do so no longer, it's because I've had opportunity to observe your sister and Neil together. Although their lives have been so different, they think alike in all important matters and love one another deeply. Neil is a dear, fine person. Good, generous, and of a high intelligence. A great reader. A writer, also. And filled with concern for his fellow man."

As she spoke, a flood of tenderness welled up within her for the stubborn, idealistic young man who was her brother. Dispensing with decorum, she left her chair to move swiftly to the divan and drop down beside Clinton Webb, placing an impulsive hand upon his arm. Green eyes glowing, her voice throaty with emotion, she said, "Oh, I do believe you and your parents would be quite taken with him if only you would grant your sister's dearest wish and agree to meet him."

He stared at her. She felt he hadn't heard a word she had uttered, yet there was in the dark eyes riveted upon her face a look of such total absorption, such intense concentration that she was overcome with self-consciousness. Bethinking herself, she quickly removed her hand from his arm and shrank back from him.

The gesture seemed to recall him from some far reverie. A frown flew between his eyes, he shook his head slightly and pressed the tips of long, slender fingers against his forehead. "I do apologize, Vivvie. You were saying?"

Vivian's shoulders sagged but she repeated spiritedly, "Only that you might at least meet him."

Clinton cleared his throat. "It's the Governor who's the one there. He'll not permit it."

"Then of course your mother can't," she agreed, for few women dared go against a husband's wishes. "But what of you? Surely you don't need your father's permission?"

She was fully conscious of the light tinge of scorn her voice carried and quite pitilessly watched him bear up under it.

"Not his permission, certainly not," he replied, reddening. "But I've no wish to court further displeasure. It's bad enough as it is. I tell you, Vivvie, the house is like a bloody morgue these days. I hate to quit work and go back to it. I swear I'd far rather stay at the mill.

"Mother is always in tears and the Governor always in high dudgeon. My sister's room has been cleared out and is now a kind of sitting room, but the door is kept closed and no one sits there. All her furnishings, all her clothes and belongings have been got rid of, given to charity. Neither mother nor I dare speak her name except in private. Not even our closest friends dare ask of her. It's worse than a death. It's as though my sister never existed. Every trace of her is gone, expunged like a . . . like a stain on the floor."

Pity filled Vivian, removing every last vestige of the resentment she had felt. "How awful!" she breathed. "Oh, I'm so sorry for you."

"It's far worse for mother," he responded grimly. "She's aged ten years. Remember how happy and gay she used to be, her voice always light and lilting? And her footsteps, so lively and quick? All that is gone now. She accepts no invitations, goes nowhere. It's as though my sister had robbed her of everything that made life worth living." His jaw hardened. "This is why I'll never forgive Nan."

"Don't say that! Oh, sure and you mustn't," cried Vivian, in her distress lapsing back into the Irish cadence of Butler Street. "Please try to understand, to help your parents understand, that your sister loves all of you, that the last thing in the world she wants is to hurt you."

The corners of Clinton's lips drew sharply downward. "You speak as though she had no choice in the matter, as though she were forced to treat her family, her background, her heritage in this shameful way."

"No, not forced!" put in Vivian quickly. "But hasn't she a right to happiness?"

"What has happiness to do with anything?" cried Clinton, leaping from the divan. "Did you marry for happiness?" He shook his head violently. "No! You told me yourself you did not. You married for money! Money, you said. Money!"

Vivian caught her breath in sharp surprise, as though a firearm leveled at another had suddenly been turned against herself.

"And you were right!" continued Clinton. "Wise and right to advance yourself in the only way a woman can, and your children will bless you for it! As for me! Should I have abandoned all the values and standards of my class as my sister has?" he demanded hotly. "Should I have forgotten all my responsibilities to the past and to the future, and considered only what my own narrow preference might be? My own personal inclinations? Damn it, Vivvie, when I'd have given my soul to—"

Abruptly, like the slam of a door, his astonishing tirade ended. In the awkward silence that filled the room he tilted back his finely shaped head, lifting his chin high, stretching his neck as though his collar hurt. Then, in the rather dry, detached way she had always known, he said, "I apologize for my unforgivable behavior. I'm afraid this talk of happiness has made me forget myself, and I'm deeply sorry. Giving offense to you is the last thing I would wish. Not only because of the esteem in which I hold you, but because I must ask your good offices on behalf of my mother."

Calmly, as though conversation of only the most trivial nature had transpired between them, he put a hand inside his frock coat, withdrew an envelope, and brought it to where she sat on the divan.

"This envelope," he said, "contains money. Cash. My mother asks that you be good enough to give it to my sister for her needs. She asks that you allow me to visit you from time to time to deliver additional funds and to learn how my sister fares. She also would like to know when my sister plans to be married, and where."

Vivian accepted the unmarked envelope, feeling its thickness, running a thumb over the fine, spidery engraving on the back that, she knew without looking, bore the proud address of Cavendish Square.

"You are welcome to come as often as you wish," she said. "And your sister will be married to Neil on Saturday, six weeks hence, at eleven o'clock in the morning, in the church of St. Bonaventure, just down the street."

Clinton Webb's face went ashen. Although he did not move, he seemed to recoil from her, sheer horror dawning in his eyes. "In the church!" he said, choking on the words. "But I thought . . . Forgive me, I'm not clear about the custom. I thought only Roman Catholics were permitted to be married inside their church."

"Your sister is becoming a Roman Catholic," said Vivian quietly. "She's being baptized in St. Bonaventure's on her wedding day."

Vivian was no stranger to the repugnance for the Roman Catholic Church that Clinton Webb had displayed. At the turn of the century antipathy toward this religion was widespread. But perhaps because her aunts, the Randall girls, were not Roman Catholics and, more especially, because her father had turned Catholic only in order to please her mother, she tried to take a lenient view of this cast of mind.

Still, it was hard. And to be both Roman Catholic and Irish was to be doubly accursed, for to the spectacle of worshiping statues, of whispering in the confessional and taking orders from a foreigner in Rome, were added the ignorance, dirt, and disease in which the Irish were known to wallow like Paddy's pig. Unskilled and uneducated, they filled the lowest jobs at the lowest pay for the longest hours at the hardest work—stevedores, pick-and-shovel men on the railroads, day laborers, menials and servants of all kinds. It was thought they brought disease with them, particularly the rampant tuberculosis, although this illness was actually fostered by their overcrowded living conditions and by their work in the bone-penetrating chill of the textile mills, where the air was kept damp so the thread wouldn't break. Certainly they evinced an inordinate love of alcohol, gambling, crime, and gang violence of every kind. Many of their daughters who became neither nuns nor servants became whores, it being Irish girls who were predominant among prostitutes, in Philadelphia at least. They were anti-English at a time when stylish Edward was on the English throne and every American who knew anything knew that things were done the English way. Along with all this, these Irish seemed not to understand that they were inherently inferior, congenitally stupid, utterly incapable of appreciating the finer things. Clearly they thought themselves as good as anyone else. This, together with their priests and popish masses, was the most unpardonable effrontery. Any alliance with them—above all, marriage—was unthinkable.

Clinton Webb had made Vivian freshly aware of this. His extraordinary diatribe made abundantly clear that all expectations of patching things up between Nancy and her family must be abandoned, if indeed such hopes had ever been seriously entertained. Vivian quite understood.

Nonetheless, just remembering Clinton's horrified countenance riled her Irish temper as, made late by his unexpected visit, she approached the sedate limestone house that belonged to the Randall girls.

"It's open for you," sang out her Aunt Opal as Vivian tapped on the screen door. "Come along in, child."

Vivian stepped in and Opal said, "I've just fixed your

Aunt Sarah a pitcher of lemonade, and we're having it out under the pear tree."

Vivian followed the birdlike little woman through the tidy rooms with a trace of the awe that, as a child, she had always brought in such measure to this house. No matter that by now she had seen far better in the way of furnishings and decor—in fact, possessed far better in her own luxurious home. No matter that she knew, had known for some years, that "the aunts," much less being enormously wealthy as she once had supposed, were in reality just comfortable.

Still, for her, the intimation of substance, of refinement, of breeding would ever invest these rooms. It resided in the upright piano in the front parlor, its fringed brown velvet scarf bedecked with myriad curios and small objets d'art from all over the world. It manifested itself in the collection of books that stood, together with assorted bric-a-brac, in the glass-enclosed bookcase; in the etchings of faraway ruins and misty mountains that hung in their dark frames against the flowered wallpaper; in the mahogany dining room suite with the Meissen porcelain from the German side of the family and the silver candlesticks from the English Randalls on the sideboard. This house that her Randall grandfather had built, that belonged to her aunts, that her father had grown up in, never failed to fill her with pride—and with an uneasy sense of disloyalty, since her mother had never set foot in it.

"You're late," observed Sarah crisply from a bench placed under the pear tree. Behind rimless spectacles her lively eyes darted up to meet Vivian's. "It's after three o'clock."

"Only a little late, Sarah," said Opal placatingly.

"Late is late," declared Sarah.

Unlike her sister, indeed unlike most women of her time, Sarah had, of necessity, "gone out to business" in her younger days, a constraint in which she took pride and which had fostered a professional respect for the clock not shared by Opal, who had remained at home.

"I know I'm late," Vivian apologized, dropping a kiss on Sarah's forehead. "I'll get started right away."

Nearby, set up and ready for business, was a picnic table upon which waited a large blue and white enamelware basin together with an assortment of combs, brushes, towels, and other accoutrements of hairdressing, including the "rats" that helped turn the aunts' thinning gray locks into the full, shimmering masterpieces Vivian appeared to be so uniquely able to achieve.

Setting down a jug of the mixture she had brought along with her, and that was partly responsible for these agreeable results, Vivian quickly donned a bib apron. It occurred to none of them that, in view of her vastly altered circumstances, her continuance as their hairdresser was in any way bizarre. The only noticeable change in the arrangement was the tacit agreement that she no longer be paid.

"I was held up by a visitor," she explained now, carefully adding a bit of cold water to the hot she had carried in a pail from the kitchen stove.

"A visitor?" cried Opal eagerly, interest sparkling in her eyes. "What visitor?"

"Vivian may not care to tell us who her visitor was, Opal," said her sister reprovingly.

"But of course I do!" said Vivian, not for a moment wishing to disappoint her Aunt Opal's keen love of any news whatever. "It was Clinton Webb. He came to see me about his sister."

"Came to see you about his sister!" exclaimed Opal, clasping her hands. "Oh, Vivvie, I just knew you'd tell us something interesting today. You always do."

"Vivvie may not wish to reveal the nature of his visit, Opal," admonished Sarah, frowning.

But Vivian knew very well that both ladies would be crushed if, having tossed out this enticing tidbit, she failed to continue.

"Old busybodies," her mother called the aunts. "Sticking their noses into other people's affairs. Haven't enough to do."

But their lives, in fact, had always been active. Early on, Opal had devoted herself to nursing "Pa," whose several strokes had at length forced him to turn over the management of Randall's Imports on Market Street to the capable Sarah. Along with caring for Pa and the store, they had applied themselves to the rearing of Vivian's father, their darling Eddie, some nine or more years their junior.

With Eddie grown, the store sold, and a bit of money invested, their lives now revolved around an organization called the Loyal Neighbors of America, to which they both belonged. At its meetings the Loyal Neighbors raised satin banners embroidered with such exhortations as Courage,

Faith, Unselfishness. Opal bore the banner of Modesty, Sarah held aloft Endurance.

But while they were busy enough, their world offered little in the way of color or excitement. Which was why they looked forward to the visits of this favorite who never scrupled to regale them with a little of both as she soaped and washed.

"Mrs. Webb would agree to a meeting with Neil, I feel sure," Vivian told them, having explained the sorry state of affairs. "It's Dr. Webb who'll not permit it."

"Not permit it!" snapped Sarah. "And why not, I'd like to know?"

"I'm afraid he feels his daughter is marrying beneath her, Aunt Sarah."

"And since when has marrying a Randall been regarded as a step down in the world?" demanded Sarah, a certain irony in this situation lost upon her. "But you do understand at last, don't you, Vivvie? Not that there was ever anything Opal and I could do about it, because the knot had been tied. But we've been criticized to you children by a certain party for being against a certain marriage. Yet this is what comes of such things. Visiting the iniquity of the fathers upon the children unto the third and fourth generation, just as the Bible says."

Vivian felt the discomfort she always endured when the aunts discussed what they considered her parents' unsuitable marriage.

"Now, now, Sarah," said Opal, coming to the rescue. "Vivvie doesn't want to hear any more about that, do you, child? That's all water over the dam."

"But it's *not,* Opal," persisted Sarah tartly. "That's just the way with you, always wanting to brush things under the rug. It's *not* over, and here is the proof."

Forced to agree, Opal nodded sadly. "It was never that we had anything against your mother, Vivvie dear," she said. "It was just that we know about life."

Vivian considered few human beings less versed in this subject. But although constrained to repress a smile, she would never deny that there existed low class and high class and all manner of classes in between, and that in marrying the uneducated, penniless Mamie, Edward Randall had taken a step down in the world.

Even as a child she had known this, for everything proclaimed it. Walking beside her father, her small hand tucked into his on their frequent Sunday visits to the aunts, she could observe the streets becoming cleaner, the sidewalks widening out, the houses growing taller the farther they traveled from Butler Street. There was no question as to the desirability of this neighborhood that her father had been born into, and with a disloyalty that still could bring a hot rush of shame to her cheeks, she more than once had wished fervently that she, too, had been born here.

She would listen to the precise diction of the aunts, watch the way they laid a table with a "real" cloth instead of oilcloth, note their carefully trimmed fingernails showing delicate pink moons, their emphasis on soap and water, their high school diplomas hanging in frames on the wall. She would smell the odor of sachet that came from their closets, the fragrance of violet water wafting faintly from their persons, and pronounce them indeed superior to the hard-working, frequently sweat-drenched Mamie.

That she suffered the most cruel remorse for this opinion, shed bitter, guilty tears, didn't cause her to change it. Far from it, for it was just these visits to the aunts that first kindled the burning desire to be a lady herself someday.

"Have you heard from papa?" she asked, wishing to change the subject.

"We've had a letter, yes!" exclaimed Opal, ever eager to talk about this brother who seemed so nearly a son. "I have it right here to read to you," she said, and, reaching into her pocket, took out the sheaf of cheap lined paper Vivian had come to recognize.

Her father wrote as vividly as he spoke. He loved to make a good story better, and in doing so sometimes altered the true state of things. What was to be made now of the picture he painted of the bustling town of Grand Forks on the Bonanza and Eldorado creeks, of the promising claim he and his gentleman friends had staked out, of the thousands of stampeders pouring into the Klondike, of the fortune certain to be made?

Perhaps more accurate was the scrap of poetry he had enclosed. Written, he said, about a Klondiker by a gentleman named Ambrose Bierce, it read: "Nothing will come of him. He is a word in the wind, a brother to the fog. At the scene of his activity no memory of him will remain."

When Opal read these words, her voice faltered and tears leapt glistening into all three pairs of eyes. The observation seemed to fit no one so well as Edward Randall. So far nothing had come of any of his efforts or dreams. And nothing was likely to, they feared, although none of them said this as they wiped their eyes.

"Remember us to your mother. Yes, remember us to your mother," the aunts had said as Vivian waved them good-bye. They always said this, and Vivian always relayed the message, just as Mamie Randall's thin lips always clamped shut tight upon receipt of it. Mamie never asked to be remembered to the aunts. It was a black hate she had.

Mulling these thoughts, Vivian was making her way home when, on a day that had brought its share of surprises, she was presented with yet one more. Passing a dry goods emporium on Fifth Street, whom should she meet turning out the door but Thomas O'Reilly and Dolly Muldoon.

"Well, if it isn't Vivian Mallory!" cried Dolly, stopping in her tracks, and both girls shifted their parasols, Dolly's of white India linen and Vivian's of modish pongee silk, to exchange a polite kiss.

"You'll never guess what happened!" caroled Dolly. "You'll just never guess."

"Oh, shoot now, Dolly," said Thomas, growing red to the roots of his hair. "Don't go making a fuss."

"I certainly will make a fuss, Thomas O'Reilly," declared Dolly. "I want the whole world to know how proud I am of you."

Thomas grinned in pleased embarrassment as he towered over his diminutive fiancée and shifted the large parcel he carried in his arms.

How nice he is, thought Vivian, and looked smilingly up at him from under her parasol. "What have you done, Tom?"

"It's not what he's done, it's what he's going to do," interposed Dolly. "Tell her, Thomas."

"Oh, shoot, Dolly."

"Well, all right, if you won't, I will." She turned her china blue eyes full upon Vivian. "Thomas is going to be auctioneer at the white elephant booth at the Hibernian carnival. He's taking Mallory's place."

Even years later Vivian was to remember the glint of triumph deep within those blue eyes, and to recall it was precisely at this moment that she had clearly, unmistakably, felt the first faint tug of a turning tide.

18

The unease Vivian experienced upon learning that Thomas O'Reilly was to be auctioneer at the white elephant booth followed her home. That night over supper she said, "O'Reilly is to take your place at the Hibernian carnival."

"So I hear tell," responded Mallory amiably.

It was a lovely summer evening. The bank of six tall, narrow dining room windows that gave upon the broad side porch had been opened to the dusk, and a fragrance of roses from the rose garden swept in on a breeze so gentle as to cause scarcely a flicker in the lighted candles that, in heavy silver candelabra, graced table and sideboard. Having changed from street clothes into a pale mauve voile, Vivian sat close by her husband, at his end of the long table, as was her custom when they dined alone.

"I met Dolly and Tom outside the dry goods," she continued. "They had been buying red, white, and blue bunting to decorate the auction stand."

"Leave it to Dolly to gussy things up," replied Mallory with a grin. He sliced a piece of cold roast beef and dipped it in horseradish sauce. "They say it was herself that got the job for him after pestering the life out of Thurman Foy."

"Thurman Foy!" exclaimed Vivian scathingly, jarred by this revelation.

"He's chairman this year," said Mallory offhandedly. But at her contemptuous cry, two little flames of interest leapt into his eyes. His knife and fork remained poised above his plate, and from narrowed eyelids he watched her like a cat ready to pounce.

Smarter by far than those of his cronies who had scrambled to power only by using their fists, Mallory knew that success in politics depended upon nothing so much as the manipulation of the loves, hates, and fears that lurk in the far reaches of the human heart. To this end he had cultivated the habit of careful observation. It was now second nature to him, augmented in the present instance by the liveliest curiosity concerning anyone who could arouse such ire in his beautiful young wife.

"What have you got against Thurman?" he inquired.

"Mr. Foy," responded Vivian heedlessly, "is nothing but a sneaking, weasel-faced, little banty rooster who hates me!"

"Oh?" said Mallory. "Why should he hate you?"

"Because I once refused him a dance at the Hibernians' New Year's Ball."

At this reply Vivian was forced to watch her husband's flattering attention alter somewhat, and his lips twitch in an effort to restrain ungentlemanly mirth. "Why, Puss," he said, eyes dancing, "sure and the man must have been crushed altogether, but I have my doubts it drove him to hate you for life."

Fully aware of what a vain, silly creature she must sound, Vivian ignored his comment. "Dolly has also purchased a book of jokes," she said pointedly.

"How's that?"

"Yes, indeed, Mallory. She told me so this afternoon. She's purchased a book of jokes, and each night she has Tom rehearse them so he'll have something humorous to entertain the crowd. She means him to be funnier than you, I just know."

Far from giving Mallory pause, as intended, this information appeared to breach the bulwark of gallantry entirely, and engendered such a burst of hilarity that Vivian was on the verge of rising from the table and leaving the room.

Mallory, however, stretched forth a hand to detain her, his touch sending, to her annoyance, a little shiver of pleasure through her despite the exasperation she felt.

"Ah, Puss!" he cried, so handsome and smiling that her heart all but turned over, "I don't know when I've had such a good laugh. Just wait 'til I get back to the Tip and tell the boys! Why, it's a spectacle he's letting her make of him. But the truth is, she's that pretty and sweet it's no wonder."

At such obstinate wrongheadedness, Vivian's patience fled. "Dolly Muldoon may well be pretty," she declared hotly, and quite beside herself. "But sweet she surely is not! She wants only one thing, and that's revenge!"

Mallory's dark eyebrows knit together. "Revenge? Why should that be?"

"Because you didn't marry her, that's why!"

"But she never had an eye for me."

"Oh, Mallory, she did!"

"Then will you be telling me," he demanded, "why, right away, she got herself engaged to Tom O'Reilly?"

"She's marrying Tom out of pique because she couldn't get you!"

For a long moment her voice hung high in the air. Then Mallory said, "The way you married me."

His words were like the swift, surprising stab of a knife. "Mallory, don't!" she gasped.

"Don't what?" he said, and she could hear the sudden fury in his voice. "Everyone I see, everyone I meet, knows you wish you were married to Jamie Fitzhugh!"

"No, Mallory! They're wrong, I swear it!"

"What about St. Louis?"

"St. Louis?" she choked in bewilderment.

"Don't pretend, damn it!"

Rising and flinging aside his chair so that it fell to the floor with a crash, he took her head in both his hands, forcing her to meet his enraged eyes. "Do you think I don't know what goes on in that transparent little head of yours? Do you think I don't know why you've refused to go to St. Louis? Do you think I don't know you're afraid you might meet Jamie Fitzhugh?"

"I'm not afraid," she protested falteringly.

"Prove it!"

"How can I prove it?"

"Come to St. Louis with me."

She drew a breath. "All right then," she flung out defiantly. "And I will!"

The abrupt end to the pitched battle, for such it surely was, left Vivian alone at the table, breast heaving and green eyes afire, as she listened to Mallory's footsteps move through the hallway and then, following the bang of the screen door, pound over the porch and die away.

Growing calmer, she attempted to piece together how it

all had started. They had been talking quite placidly and then, suddenly, they were at each other's throats, shouting one another down. And finally—oh, mother of God!—finally she had been so thoughtless, so foolhardy, as to agree to go to St. Louis!

A sickening dread filled her, as though somehow an unpromising outcome to this ill-considered trip was already decided, as though she had been swept into the swirling vortex of a future she was helpless to either command or evade.

So abstracted was she by this notion that she scarcely heard Halls enter the dining room until, at her elbow, he said, "Will madam care for coffee now?"

Startled, she turned to him.

Like the perfect servant he was, his smooth, round face and dignified bearing betrayed not the least awareness of the vulgar shouting match that had all but raised the roof, every word of it surely overheard not only by Halls but by his wife Clarissa and, Vivian must suppose, the rest of the household staff.

She was no lady and Mallory was no gentleman, as they had both just made abundantly clear. They might sit at a table set with silver and cut glass, they might wear fine clothes and drive a fine auto, but they had behaved like ignorant, ill-bred, bad-mannered shanty Irish.

A sense of defeat engulfed her as she elected to forgo coffee and moved out to sit on the porch swing, grateful for the sheltering dark.

Things weren't going as she had expected; no, not in the least. Even the prospective visit to Kimberly no longer seemed so enticing now that the time of their departure was growing alarmingly near. Although she hadn't breathed a word to Mallory, Vivian was increasingly beset by qualms as to how they would fare with the sophisticated Cavendish crowd, and with wearying indecision daily changed her mind about the clothes she meant to take with her, the way she would dress her hair. Added to this was the somehow upsetting news that Thomas O'Reilly was to take Mallory's place at the carnival.

When Vivian considered the extent of Mallory's awesome power, which, she had come to understand, meant absolute control of the huge, sprawling Amity political machine that governed the entire city of Philadelphia, she realized how absurd she was being. Still, doubtless thanks to Ma Mallory's bad-tempered intimations, a nebulous sense of foreboding had settled upon her regarding the affair.

And then there was Thurman Foy . . .

In the warm dark of the porch, under trailing tendrils of Boston fern, a shiver ran down Vivian's spine. Mallory might smile all he liked, but she knew very well that Thurman Foy had hated her from the moment, two years ago, when she had refused to dance with him at the New Year's ball.

She could still remember the way his small, sharp-nosed face had reddened in affronted surprise when, as politely as she could, she had refused him. She could remember the unvarnished hatred that had flickered in his tiny colorless eyes before he turned and marched away. Oh, he hated her with a black Irish hate and meant her ill, no matter what Mallory might say.

But this wasn't the worst of it, she told herself, staring out onto the lawn from whence drifts of fireflies rose into the soft night. No, the worst was Mallory, knowing all along she didn't want to go to St. Louis, knowing she had made excuses, had lied. But when he had goaded her into the trip, her heart had leapt with a wild willful joy of its own, and a heady eagerness seized her, quivered within her even now.

Engrossed in these thoughts, she heard the sound of footsteps and named them as Mallory's even before she saw him turn up the front walk.

He carried himself easily, completely at home in the world, and the moonlight touched his hair and the broad shoulders of the white linen sack suit he wore. Unable to discern his features, she could see the jaunty, racy attraction about him, the strength and grace that marked him.

He mounted the porch steps and instantly saw her, curled up upon the swing among the shadows.

"So it's here you are," he said.

Coming over, he sat beside her and picked up her hand to hold in both his own. For a moment he looked down at it, studying it almost as though he had never seen such a thing before. Then he said, "I had to come back. Couldn't leave you that way."

He placed her hand back in her lap. "What I want to say is that I knew when you married me you didn't love me.

You never made any bones about that. Also, I don't give a damn what people around here think. As for St. Louis, you don't have to go."

"I'm going, Mallory," she told him, for nothing would stop her now.

It had been their first quarrel, and hence was followed by that special tenderness that accompanies a first reconciliation. Mallory outdid himself.

Women never had been merely ornaments or possessions to him. They fascinated him. He studied them, intrigued by their different ways—different from the ways of men, from one another. He had speculated on what it might be like to be a woman and concluded it would be fun. He thought it might be pleasant to be encouraged to devote oneself to books, to art, to music, as was the fashion for ladies of the day, to be engaged in arranging parties and flowers and love affairs, instead of being constrained to spend a lifetime in the humdrum workaday world. He found women infinitely more interesting than men, more various, more surprising. He paid close attention to feminine styles and finery, and could spend hours selecting those baubles, perfumes, lingerie, and the like that would most perfectly enhance the woman he had in mind. He knew how he would behave if he were a woman, and how he would like to be treated. And he treated every woman this way.

Turning these talents to beguiling his wife, he charmed and bedazzled her with a thoughtfulness that expressed itself in attentions of all sorts, including an abundance of gifts. One day he drew from his pocket an opal-studded brooch; another, a charming handpainted porcelain pin box; and yet another, a kitten whose haughty ways persuaded Vivian to christen her Miss Prim.

But it was his remorse over the quarrel that caught at Vivian's heart, since nothing she said could convince him he wasn't the thoroughgoing out-and-outer he claimed to be.

"I might have harmed you!" he exclaimed, pacing the floor of their bedroom, raking a hand through his hair. And one night he cried out in his sleep.

"It's only a dream," whispered Vivian, waking him.

But a wry smile pulled his lips. "Or a memory," he said. "I'm not quite the fellow you think me. Someday you'll find that out. And I say to myself, what then?"

A need to know more prompted her. "Have you ever killed anyone?" she asked.

"No," he replied. "But I've hurt 'em real bad."

She had settled down into the warm curve of his arm, his answer ringing in her ears.

But the little tiff resulted in a new closeness, with each more careful lest feelings be hurt. As Clinton Webb had observed, Vivian was lovelier than ever. Nor could this be attributed only to closets filled with lots of fetching new clothes. Her figure had subtly changed, the nipped-in waist that was the fashion of the day contrasting all the more sharply with a becomingly fuller bosom. A new and sensual awareness informed the startling green depths of her eyes.

Clinton was not the only one to notice this change. His sister Nancy remarked upon it also.

"Vivvie, you look so happy, dear," she said.

Nancy had come to try on Vivian's wedding gown, of which she would have the loan, and, having donned it, stood regarding Vivian in the little boudoir off the master bedroom. "How wrong I was to feel you should have married Mr. Fitzhugh."

"But I think of him still!" Vivian burst out. She saw the surprise in Nancy's startled face at this passionate announcement but, once begun, seemed powerless to stem the tide of further confession. "Yes," she cried, clasping her hands in anguish, "I think of him all the time, even though he treated me so shamefully. And I'm afraid I'll meet him out in St. Louis, afraid I'll see him again."

"And might not that be the very best thing?"

Vivian stared at her friend in horror. "No, never! It's the last thing I want!"

"Why is that, Vivvie?"

Impossible to dissemble before that calm, candid gaze. "I'm afraid . . ." she whispered. "I'm afraid to discover I love him still, in spite of the way he has used me."

"But you may discover just the opposite, dear, have you thought of that? You're not the girl you once were. You're a woman now, married to a man who cherishes you. You may meet Mr. Fitzhugh again only to realize he's but a dream from the past, and that you're in love with your husband."

"I wish I were!" breathed Vivian. "Oh, truly I wish I were! Mallory is so good to me, so kind. But—" She stopped abruptly. For all his attentiveness and captivating ways, he wasn't Jamie Fitzhugh. It was as simple as that, and as inexplicable. At a loss to understand this herself, how could she explain it to Nancy?

"I'm sure you'll be happy with Neil," she said, turning the conversation.

Too polite to pursue an uncomfortable topic, Nancy nodded readily. "I hope so," she replied, a shadow crossing the grave, heart-shaped face. "But in order to be happy I suppose we need our parents' approval of what we do, no matter how old we grow. Or," she added with a rueful smile, "how righteous our cause."

Such a woebegone little bride she looked! thought Vivian, suddenly torn from her own concerns. The very idea of Nancy Webb dressed in hand-me-downs was appalling. And the dress just didn't suit somehow. A very different style was called for, simpler, more subdued—such a gown as surely would have been hers under other circumstances. Nonetheless, Vivian said encouragingly, "I believe you would have your parents' approval if only they knew Neil."

"Knew him!" cried Nancy. "But that's just the point! They're incapable of knowing him. Neil could be the greatest genius in the world and they wouldn't look twice at him, because he doesn't come from the right family."

She shook her head adamantly. "No, Vivvie. They've got prejudices a foot thick that would stand in the way. The closest my parents and Clinton can come to appreciating what they call the lower classes is as servants. Then they are prepared to show them as much interest and affection as they would display towards a pet dog. Surely you know this!" She sighed. "It's not their fault, of course. It's the way they were raised: to think themselves superior."

"But you were raised that way, too."

"Somehow it just never took, thank heavens. Poppycock. That's what I always thought it was, all the fuss about ancestors and family. It's the person that matters, that *should* matter, at any rate. What kind of person one is." She looked at Vivian and added, "Did I tell you Clinton has become engaged to Anthea Allenby?"

Oh, no! thought Vivian, recalling that self-centered, waspish young lady.

"That was in the letter from mother," Nancy was saying. "They're to be married in Holy Trinity on the Square. It's to be a large wedding. I'm given to understand I'll not be invited."

Wrath at such heartlessness surged through Vivian, and leaping from her chair, she folded the forlorn little bride in her arms. "Oh, Nancy!" she cried. "Try not to let it hurt you!"

"I do try, Vivvie," confessed Nancy through her tears. "I understand very well how it is that they can't . . . why my father won't . . ." She broke off to wipe her eyes, and Vivian noted with a wrench that the fine linen handkerchief was frayed. "Mother wrote that I have dealt my father a blow to the heart," she continued. "That he can never forgive me."

"Does your mother . . . well, *forgive* you?" asked Vivian, stumbling on the offensive word.

Nancy drew a trembling breath. "She doesn't say how she feels."

Vivian felt her own eyes pricking with tears at the thought of Irene Webb. *Worse than a death,* was the way Clinton had described the bereft Webb household. "She loves you, Nancy," she assured the girl almost fiercely. "She thinks of you and has concern for you. That's why she sent Clinton to see me; why she sent the money."

At the mention of money, Nancy's head shot up. "I don't want the money!" Snatching up her purse, she withdrew from it a packet of neatly folded bills secured by a rubber band. "The next time Clinton comes to see you, I beg you to return this to him."

Consternation seized Vivian. "Nancy, do listen to me!" she implored. "Our Neil is a bright young man. I'm certain he has it in him to advance in life. But at the moment he hasn't a penny to his name, and . . ." Despairing at the set of the small, round chin, she cried out, "Oh, Nancy, it's so awful to be poor! Ask Neil. He'll tell you."

"But Neil agrees with me. He says the money is tainted."

"Tainted!"

"Why, yes. Scrounged from the poor and helpless."

Since the patients who visited Dr. Webb failed to even remotely answer to such description, Vivian found this reply so baffling as to preclude further discussion. But she remained in a pensive mood long after Nancy departed, carrying off her ill-suited wedding gown.

The young woman's sentiments were so fine, so noble. But that's not the way life is, thought Vivian, shaking her head. And for the first time, she felt resentment against her brother. Money must never be treated lightly, as Neil should very well know.

19

*The little roll of bills rested in a locked drawer in Vivi-*an's writing table awaiting the next visit from Clinton Webb, whenever that should be. When Vivian thought of what she could only consider the rash and foolish pride that had prompted its refusal, irritation seized her. But she didn't dwell upon this, for she had more pressing concerns, the matter of greatest moment being the weekend at Kimberly.

"Saints preserve us, you're taking all this!" exclaimed Ma Mallory the morning of their departure. She stood just inside the front door and surveyed the mountain of shiny new luggage piled in the hallway. "They'll think you've come for a month!"

A fine perspiration broke out upon Vivian's forehead, making her itch under the three yards of pale blue chiffon that secured her Leghorn motoring bonnet. Although it was still early, the day was hot and muggy. Added to the oppressive atmosphere was the night she had spent tossing and turning, beset with just such misgivings as Ma Mallory had, with uncanny accuracy, instantly hit upon.

Were they taking too much? Would they be laughed at? Frowned upon? Despite tireless efforts at self-improvement, how daunting, after all, to be arriving at a great house as guest instead of lady's maid.

"One never knows what one will need for a country weekend," she offered unconvincingly.

Ma Mallory was not fooled. "Well, whatever is needed, it's certain you'll have it with you," responded the woman, a gleam in her eye. Moving over to the pile for a closer inspection, she cried, "Tennis, is it? And you're telling me my son knows how to play that?"

"The racket is mine."

"So you're the tennis player, are you?"

Vivian was spared the necessity of a reply, for something else had caught the woman's attention. "And what's this?" she demanded. "A fishing rod, is it?"

"The Cavendishes stock their pond with trout."

"*Do* they! Sure, that's bad luck for the trout now, isn't it? And is it you or my son who's to be doing the fishing?"

"Mallory may want to fish."

"Oh, may he! May he indeed!"

Vivian bit her tongue at the mocking response. She had long since given up all thought of becoming friends with her mother-in-law. For Mallory's sake she strove for civility, but even this was often hard to achieve. Trapped in the hallway, she glanced covertly at the small gold watch pinned to her pongee duster and privately hoped Mallory would be quick in bringing the Overland around.

It was perhaps this interest in the hour, this indication that her daughter-in-law desired nothing so much as escape, that prompted Ma Mallory to say more softly, "Ah, girl, now, don't mind my blunt ways. I've come with a word of advice, the which of it is: don't be fretting or thinking there's aught that you're lacking among such grand company, nor be you abashed by their uppity airs. Only recall that, but for Mallory, the Senator would be nowhere at all, at all. Mallory's the lad that sent him to Harrisburg and he's the lad that keeps him there.

"My son will be fine, for sure, he thinks he's the lord of creation. It's you I'm talking about. You're a beautiful young woman with dainty ways, and a pleasure to look upon. No doubt you'll make a grand splash if only you remember one thing: you're a Mallory now."

The toot of a horn announced the Overland. Halls appeared to see to the luggage and Vivian followed him down the walk in something of a daze. Nothing, it seemed to her, that might happen this weekend could possibly be more surprising than the little speech Ma Mallory had just made. Her spirits soared.

As though by magic, even the sun appeared, breaking hotly through the haze to twinkle and wink in the polished hood of the Overland as they started smartly off. Turning in her seat, Vivian lifted a small, lace-gloved hand in farewell, and was further affected to see Ma blow her a kiss.

In the summertime people of means left the city. Many traveled far afield, to Europe, Newport, and the like. But there were those who preferred the beautiful countryside that surrounded Philadelphia. There, among wheat fields that girdled great red barns, among somnolent little villages with white church spires, among covered bridges and low hills and woodlands, they purchased farmhouses or built mansions set upon parklike grounds.

Vivian was well aware of what Kimberly looked like, having seen photographs of it and heard tales told by Nonnie in the kitchen at Cavendish House. Nonetheless, she caught her breath at the charm of the big old fieldstone homestead spreading itself out in the sunshine at the end of the long lane of beech trees. In the shimmering noonday heat several autos already stood glistening on the raked gravel turnaround that curved past the front door, and servants were busily unloading suitcases from them while their owners, still in goggles and dusters, stood chatting with Senator and Mrs. Cavendish on the lawn.

Mother of God! prayed Vivian silently, and her heart sank to her toes.

But Mallory leapt from his seat, rounded the Overland to help her down, and in no time at all Camilla Cavendish was saying, "Vivian, my dear! I'm so happy to see you! Won't you come meet our guests?"

For one awful moment Vivian realized she had been about to reply "yes, ma'am." Jolted, and remembering she was now a Mallory, she murmured, "I'd like that."

Irene Webb could have done no better.

But this auspicious beginning was destined to be short-lived, and by that evening Vivian wondered in despair how she could ever have believed it might have gone differently.

Clad in petticoat and camisole, she sat at a vanity table in the pretty guest bedroom dressing her hair in preparation for dinner. A Degas, a Renoir would surely have delighted to paint such a scene: the young woman alone at her toilette, golden light from the setting sun gilding the rounded young arms, burnishing to a sheen the rich red-gold hair that was being looped above green eyes.

Mallory was still on the terrace. So was everyone else. In the soft evening, bright bursts of gaiety floated up to her through the open window, together with a fragrance of honeysuckle. She had come up to change for dinner much too early. But the truth was that, except for the warm but busily preoccupied Camilla Cavendish, she had been thoroughly snubbed by the ladies downstairs.

She had attended St. Bonaventure's? they had inquired, frowning faintly. St. Bonaventure's, ah! A private academy? No? Ah! But what year had she come out? She *hadn't?* How funny! And imagine living in South Philadelphia! They had never—no, they had never before met anyone who actually *lived* there.

It wasn't enough, Vivian now reflected mournfully, to have lots of money—more money, she would wager from the look of some rather dowdy costumes, than several of the women she had met. It wasn't enough to act like a lady and use the proper fork. How silly of her to have thought so! One must have lived one's life in a certain way. Yes, that was the nub of it. One must have lived in a certain way, and it was best if one's mother and one's grandmothers and great-grandmothers had lived that way, too.

Now although to Vivian this seemed heartless and unfair, for their part the Kimberly ladies were waging a fight to the finish, albeit one they would lose, against the onslaught of the *nouveau riche* of which Vivian was a part. These ladies feared and despised what they considered the *parvenus* who held no standards but money, possessed no qualifications or background, shared no values, and desired nothing so much as to force their way where they weren't wanted and didn't belong. It was the Doyles and Barkins, yes, and the Mallorys, who must at all cost be kept out of their houses, their clubs, their schools—in short, out of their world.

Neither the ladies nor Vivian could know that she was but one infinitesimally small cog in that turning wheel of fortune that later generations would call the Industrial Revolution. And so she sat before her mirror remembering the unfriendly slights with pain in her heart, and there it was that Mallory found her.

"So it's here you are!" he cried, bursting in upon her. "It's high and low I've searched for you. I've made a particular friend, and I want you to meet him."

Striding across the room to her, in the suit whose muted

yellow check had at home seemed exactly right for the occasion but which, Vivian now privately owned, looked a shade too new, he beamed down upon her. "My friend's name," he said, "is Lord Robert St. George Wesley, Baron of Chittendon." He nodded. "Yes, a baron he is, think of that! His ancestral home is in England."

"I've met his sister," said Vivian.

"Ah, yes! The Lady Tanis Langhorne."

"She doesn't much care for me."

Mallory stared at her, thunderstruck. "And why shouldn't she care for you?"

Vivian sighed. "None of the ladies do."

At the stricken look on his face, Vivian regretted unburdening her woes and added, with a light little shrug, "It doesn't matter. It's not important."

"Doesn't matter!" he cried.

Vivian regarded him in surprise. "Well, why should it? We'll never see these people again."

"And would you be telling me why not? Most of them are from Philadelphia. They'll entertain us, we'll entertain them."

Was it possible, wondered Vivian, that he had received no hint of the cleavage that was so obvious to her? "Mallory," she said gently, "we don't fit in."

She watched the buoyancy leave him and his powerful shoulders sag. "What did I do wrong?" he asked.

"Nothing!" she cried staunchly.

He frowned. "Then what do you mean?"

"We don't belong. We didn't go to the proper schools, do the proper things. We haven't . . . We aren't . . ." Unable to explain, she stopped helplessly, and a deep red flush crept up Mallory's neck and over his face.

"Who says this?" he demanded.

"Oh, Mallory, nobody says it! Nobody has to. I just know it. I feel it. It's in the air!"

For a long moment he regarded her darkly. Then his brow cleared and a smiling warmth invaded the cold depths of his eyes. "They're jealous, Puss!" he cried in soft glee. "It's jealous of your beauty they are, don't I know it? Why, at lunch didn't Mister Thomas Eakins himself ask to paint your portrait? And did I not see the eyes of the ladies fly one to the other? But they'll not turn down our invitations. I'll see to that."

Vivian, too, had been aware of envious glances as well as

haughty ones. Moreover, such was her husband's power that he might very well be able to coerce their guests. But this was not the whole of it, for all he refused to see. And as they went down to dinner, she couldn't help but wish he didn't care quite so much about such things.

She had never, however, known him to be so elated. Beneath the superb cut of his blue dinner suit, with its broad shoulders and blue satin lapels, his strong, supple body seemed to vibrate with energy. A kind of triumph glowed in his eyes, and there was an electric intensity to his voice, his ringing laughter, although he laughed too loudly, talked too long.

"I believe I haven't had the pleasure yet," said a cool British voice at Vivian's side, and in the glow of the Japanese lanterns strung above the terrace in the soft summer night, she turned to find a gentleman who must surely be Robert St. George Wesley, Baron of Chittendon.

"Lord Wesley, isn't it?" she responded diffidently. "Brian Mallory is my husband. He has spoken of you."

The young man bowed. "And to me of you," he replied as, with a frankness that verged upon the unseemly, his heavily lidded, dreamy gray eyes slid over her, taking in, she felt, everything about her, from the tips of her green satin slippers to the boa of green and white feathers that graced the deep décolletage of the pale green silk mull that she wore.

A smile touched his full lips. "He failed to do you justice, I must say. No wonder *le maître* desires to paint your portrait! I quite approve. *Je crois me connaître en peinture*, eh?"

Not having a clue as to the meaning of this last, Vivian hoped a smile might suffice. And in fact the young man seemed suddenly quite uninterested in any response of hers, his eyes leaping across the crowded, shadowy terrace to a lighted doorway.

"Tanis!" he cried softly, and in the spellbound hush cast by this single utterance, Vivian turned to look at a woman who, together with the other ladies, had contrived to make her afternoon so miserable.

As fair as her brother, but a good five or six years older—in her late twenties, Vivian would suppose—the Lady Langhorne stood in the doorway. The harsh white overhead light fell on her pompadour of thick, pale hair, making of it a nimbus of gold. She was not tall, but held herself so imperially as to seem so, and this impression of nobility, of royalty, was enhanced by her costume. It was fashioned of black lace over silk so pale as might be mistaken for flesh; tiny rhinestones winked here and there in the sweeping skirt and in the ruching out of which her rounded shoulders emerged, bare and vulnerable looking. Her slender neck bore a choker of gems, and more gems sparkled in her ears.

"By jove!" swore Lord Wesley under his breath. "Isn't she smashing, in the face of it all?"

Vivian tore her eyes from this mesmerizing vision. "She is suffering somehow?"

"Lost her husband three years ago. The Honorable Gervase Langhorne, third son of the sixth Earl of Langhorne. Killed in the Boer War."

Vivian recalled now that Lady Langhorne had been wearing a black voile jumper suit that afternoon, and wondered if it might be the English custom to observe so long a mourning. Not wishing to display ignorance, she pursued a different topic. "She has children?"

"Egad, no! Can't think how she'd hack it if there was that! There's enough in the kettle with trying to manage the Manor. Third sons don't fare so well, y' know."

"I see," murmured Vivian.

"Not that the present Earl hasn't helped out a bit. Viscount Langhorne, that is. Her brother-in-law. But the devil of it is, he's got Sutcliffe Hall to think about, and he lost even more than the rest of us a few years back when the crops failed. We've none of us pulled out of that."

"How difficult!" commiserated Vivian, her brain whirling with earls and viscounts, and not sure precisely what afflictions she was commenting on.

"Ah, well!" cried Lord Wesley suddenly, and despite his troubles turned upon her so cheerful a countenance that she was altogether disarmed. "Let's not be gloomy." A twinkle lit his eye. "Your husband is the very devil at cards, y' know."

Thinking of the financial embarrassment to which the young man had only just alluded, Vivian caught her breath. "I do hope you didn't lose too much!"

"Lose?" echoed Lord Wesley. "But, my dear Mrs. Mallory, I won."

"Won!"

At her incredulity, the most infectious giggle broke from his lips. "How flattering to your husband! I must tell him! He inspires great confidence in you. But does he usually win?"

"Always."

"No, but really."

She nodded emphatically. "In Atlantic City there are places—clubs and the like—where they won't let him play."

The teasing manner vanished and was replaced by something puzzled, alert in the young man's eyes. "You don't say," he drawled, and then, "Well, now, that quite sets me up, for we played all afternoon and I've won a packet."

"You must be very good."

"No, not good."

"Lucky, then."

"Yes," he replied thoughtfully. "Lucky, p'raps." He smiled. "But I say now, tell me a bit about yourself. You're not from around these parts, surely."

"Why do you say that?"

"Oh, I don't know. I can't put my finger on it. But something tells me." Against her ear, he whispered, "A little bird, no doubt." But upon looking into her face, amazement overcame him. "I say, now, not tears! Well, I mean, egad! I surely never meant to offend you. My dear lady, believe me—"

"Oh, do stop!" implored Vivian, hastily dabbing at her eyes with a handkerchief. "It's nothing you've done. Nothing at all. It's me. I can't carry it off."

"Carry it off? Carry what off?"

"The whole thing. It's all too much."

"But what's too much?"

"Everything! Trying to . . . to say the proper thing and do . . . do the proper thing. Trying to pretend . . ."

"My dear lady!"

"Oh, do stop saying 'my dear lady'! A lady is just what I'm not! A short time ago I was a lady's *maid*. Until I married Mallory I didn't have a penny to my name. I haven't done the proper things nor gone to the proper schools. Neither has Mallory." Having thus burned all her bridges behind her, she lifted her chin and added defiantly, "Money is all we've got."

* * *

Later that night, as they were preparing for bed, Mallory told her, "You made a big hit with Lord Wesley. He says we must visit him if we get to England."

"Oh, Mallory!" exclaimed Vivian with a light laugh, "that's what people always say."

"He means it."

"But we aren't going to England!"

In the mirror his eyes met hers. "I wouldn't say that."

20

To Vivian's surprise, the following day, Saturday, gave promise of going infinitely better.

Even before she had finished breakfast, served to her in bed on a prettily appointed tray, a firm rap came at her door, and who should enter but the Lady Langhorne.

"Such a glorious day, my dear!" cried the lady, sweeping into the room dressed for tennis and gracefully swinging her racket this way and that.

Vivian was so astonished she nearly choked on a bit of delicately sliced prosciutto served with the melon on her plate. "Indeed it is," she managed.

"And are you for tennis?"

"I don't know how to play tennis, I'm sorry to say."

"Well, why should you be? Altogether too much is made of the silly game. What would you say to a bit of a punt, then?"

"A punt?"

"On the pond."

"Oh!"

"Nothing to punting at all. Unless—" She stopped abruptly and fixed Vivian with a look. "I hope you're not afraid of water!"

"I? Oh, no."

"Well then, let's punt, I say!"

The woman smiled dazzlingly, and Vivian blinked her eyes in wonder and surprise. "It's very good of you."

"Not at all," declared Lady Langhorne. "My brother said you were feeling a bit blue last evening. He suggested I might have a go at cheering you up."

"How kind of him!"

"My dear, my brother is the most decent sort in the world. I don't know what I should have done without him when I lost Gervase."

"In the Boer War, I understand."

Lady Langhorne nodded with the spirited vigor she apparently brought to everything. "Three years ago, yet it seems like yesterday. Still, grief shouldn't make us impervious to the needs and feelings of others. Quite frankly, Mrs. Mallory, I feel I have slighted you."

"Oh, no!" cried Vivian, flushing pink.

"Oh, yes! Inexcusable, really. Never thought a thing about it 'til Robbie brought it up. He gave me a bit of a dressing down, I can tell you."

"No!"

Lady Langhorne lifted a hand. "All in a joshing way. Robbie could never be cruel. He's just not that sort. But I did take myself to task afterwards. 'Tanis,' I scolded myself, 'first thing in the morning, you must jolly well make it up to that girl.' So! Well, here I am!"

Vivian nodded. She could think of nothing to say.

"Robbie was so taken with your attractive husband, Mrs. Mallory," the Lady Langhorne continued heartily. "My brother gets these feelings. Intuitions, you might say. Quite uncanny, really. Makes me shiver at times when I think back to how right he has been. For instance, he predicted that awful drought we've had. Somehow, he just knew. Although of course he couldn't say how awful things would be; I mean, how much we'd all lose. But he was very definite that it would come. The drought, that is. And come it did."

"Your brother told me that you especially have suffered from it terribly," said Vivian.

"My dear, I have! But nothing compared to Robbie. I do, after all, have my brother-in-law, the viscount, to look to. If driven, I can at least bed down at Sutcliffe Hall. But if Robbie loses our lovely old Chittendon, he'll have nothing!"

Vivian made a mental note that she must implore Mallory to play no more cards with a young man in such straitened circumstances.

"Not to say that there aren't the tapestries and paintings and objets d'art," continued Lady Langhorne. "And of course the gems, *n'est-ce pas?* But to be forced to *eat* one's heritage, as it were . . . !"

"Indeed!" responded Vivian feelingly.

"Indeed!" echoed the Lady Langhorne. "But where was I? Oh, yes! I was speaking of dear Robbie's intuition. And I must confess that last night when he visited my room for our little ritual *tête-à-tête* before he trotted off to bed, he seemed quite beside himself with excitement. He told me that when he met Mr. Mallory he all but felt the clap of the hand of fate upon his shoulder. He knew he was standing in the presence of a great and powerful man."

"Not great, I think," answered Vivian, taking care to be honest. "But powerful for sure. Oh, yes! All the Amity Clubs in the City of Philadelphia are his to rule, and their treasuries as well. And if a man feels the want of the least thing, all he need do is go down to the Tip and have a word with my husband and it's like the wave of a magic wand."

Sitting up in bed, eyes shining and voice warm with such pride as put a throb to it, she pressed onward. "Senator Cavendish himself is beholden to him, for my husband is the man that sent him to the state senate in Harrisburg, and he's the one that keeps him there."

"Ah ha!" exclaimed the Lady Langhorne with sudden understanding. "So that is the basis of your friendship?"

"It is," said Vivian, glowing in glory.

"Then no wonder they entertain you!"

"No wonder at all."

"Things are different here than in England, which is why I ask."

"Ask away," cried Vivian, warm to her subject.

Lady Langhorne smiled. "I think you've answered my questions for now."

Ringing for a lady's maid to come help her dress for punting, Vivian wondered anxiously if she had displayed unseemly pride and perhaps boasted too much. After the snubs of yesterday it had been so hard to refrain from putting Mallory, and thereby herself, forward. But the Lady Langhorne—Tanis, as upon departing she had insisted Vivian call her—appeared to have been truly interested,

attending every word with such flattering absorption that
Vivian felt tingles run down her spine.

"Oh, it's so beautiful you look, ma'am," breathed the little maid as she hooked the high boned collar of Vivian's
white shirtwaist.

This was true. Few waists were nipped in so neatly, few
heads boasted such thick smooth coils unaided by puffs or
switches. Upon the white pique ascot now tied at her throat
was the emerald brooch Mallory had given her as her wedding gift. Presenting it, he had declared it no rival to the
emerald green of her eyes, and she had laughed at the extravagance of his compliment. But today the ornament
truly seemed less brilliant than the eyes that looked back
from her mirror.

"So beautiful you look!" repeated the little maid.

Something in the yearning voice recalled to Vivian her
own former position, and she felt a pang at the knowledge
of how heavy were the trays this child must carry, how
steep and wearisome the long flights of stairs, how narrow
the cot she slept upon, how few the pleasures. Impulsively
she swept the startled girl to her in a hug. Such behavior
defied all rules of etiquette, but she didn't care.

Although certain of the ladies continued to ignore her,
her budding friendship with the Lady Langhorne seemed to
encourage a few tentative if puzzled smiles. And any neglect on the distaff side was more than compensated for by
masculine attention.

After punting on the pond with Tanis, she found gentlemen vying for the pleasure of teaching her how a tennis
racket must be held. A picnic lunch of smoked trout sandwiches and sour cream strawberry cake, enhanced by a
fine chilled white Burgundy and served up from wicker
hampers in a cool glade, drew no one less than Senator
Cavendish to her side. Croquet saw Lord Robert Wesley
beg her as partner, tea brought a chat with Camilla Cavendish, dinner bequeathed upon her the honor of being escorted to table by Mr. Thomas Eakins; and the evening
found her content to sit quietly in the drawing room and
listen to musical renditions offered by an ensemble hired
up from Philadelphia, while the events of the day drifted
through her head.

"And how is dear Nancy?" Camilla Cavendish had
asked that afternoon over the teacups.

Vivian had replied that she was well, adding, "She is about to be married to my brother Neil."

"So I've heard," said Camilla. "And not one member of her family to be present at the wedding. Such tomfoolishness! All Alden's doing, of course. Obstinate as a mule, and his poor wife daren't lift a finger or say a word. But I told Irene, I said, 'Alden may stop you, but he can't stop me.' " She patted Vivian's knee and declared spiritedly, "I've had the where and the when of it out of Clinton, and you may tell Nancy I shall be at the church."

Recalling this conversation, Vivian felt gratitude swell in her heart. How kind and good Camilla Cavendish was!

Senator Cavendish, too.

"I consider Brian the luckiest of men to have won you, my dear," he had told her as they shared their picnic lunch together. "And not alone for your considerable beauty," he continued gallantly. "I believe you to be a sensible young woman who just may be able to keep that young man's feet on the ground.

"He adores you, you know. I've never known a man so open about his love for a woman. Very touching, to hear him speak of you. And, of course, he's a brilliant politician—a master of organization, which is pretty much what politics comes down to. But . . . well, do you know the story of Icarus?"

"No, sir," she replied.

"Then I shall tell you, little lady. The tale is out of Greek mythology. Icarus was a young man who couldn't find his way out of a labyrinth on the island of Crete. And so his papa, Daedalus, made him a pair of wings so he could fly out. But Icarus had big ideas and flew too high. In fact, Icarus flew so high he got too close to the sun. The sun melted the wax on his wings, and kerplunk, down fell Icarus into the Aegean Sea." The merry light faded from the senator's eyes, and he sighed. "Sometimes Brian puts me in mind of Icarus."

Vivian was struck by the tale. Although he expressed it so differently, Senator Cavendish seemed to share Ma Mallory's concern regarding her son's ambitions. Why should this be so? wondered Vivian. There could be no doubt Mallory cherished high aspirations, but not illogically, she felt. He had already come far. The gentlemen in the present company appeared to regard him with genuine interest and showed a great respect for his opinions. Their

wives, for all they might snub Vivian, reacted to him with
quite the same predictable smiles and titters as many a
blushing factory girl.

Why, then, these intimations of disaster? Ma Mallory
quite understandably might wish her son to forever remain
nearby on Butler Street. But what gave rise to Senator
Cavendish's fears? Might not it be that the senator hadn't
taken Mallory's true measure? Didn't know him as well as
he thought?

In Vivian's view few men seemed likelier candidates for
success, or achieved it so handily. She knew, for instance,
that her husband had set out to charm the ladies this weekend, and when he put his mind to it no one could charm so
well. His gregarious nature, quick wit, extraordinary good
looks, and something mocking and devil-may-care in his
nature combined to draw response even from the most unwilling. Several of the ladies were not above openly flirting
with him, including, Vivian had noted with some pique, the
Lady Langhorne.

She was reminded of this when, late that evening, Mallory said, "Sir Robbie tells me his sister is quite taken with
you."

Having, along with the other ladies, come upstairs early
in order to be helped by one of the maids out of her gown
and into a *peignoir*, Vivian sat at the dressing table taking
pins from her hair. "Sure, I think it's the other way
round," she replied tartly, "and she's taken with you."

"Why, Puss! Is it jealous you are?" he said, but she could
see very well that her observation had pleased him. As why
should it not? she thought, fuming—the Lady Langhorne
being endowed not only with great beauty but with royal
blood, a circumstance that in itself would recommend her
to Mallory.

"I've a fine regard for the truth," she told him. "And
anyone could see she was smitten entirely, swinging herself
about and smiling up in your eyes."

"And were you not doing the same whilst you played
croquet with Sir Robbie?"

"Indeed not. We spent the whole time speaking of you."

"Of me, is it?" asked Mallory with quick interest. "And
what did His Lordship have to say?"

"What a wonder you are and how he's never seen the
like. An American phenomenon, or some such, he called
you. He says it couldn't be done in England or in all of

Europe, what you've done in a few short years. Making your way up in life, I think he means."

Mallory grew serious, taking off his finely cut dinner jacket and loosening his tie. "Poor chap," he said. "He's down on his luck, which is why he's here in America; hopes to improve his fortune somehow."

At this Vivian turned to him. "Yes, Mallory, things have gone badly for him," she said earnestly, forgetting her vexation. "His sister told me as much. You mustn't take his money at cards. You mustn't."

"You've got it wrong, Puss. He's taking money from me."

"He's that good?"

Mallory moved to the open window to stand looking intently out into the hot night. He thrust both his hands into his pockets, jingling change. "I let him win," he said flatly.

"Let him win!" cried Vivian, incredulous.

"He needs some cash."

"But sure he'd never want to come by it in this way, and him a lord!"

"He doesn't seem to object."

"You mean he *knows* you're letting him win?"

"I think so."

"But why are you doing this?"

"It's not many men that can name a lord as a personal friend." He swung sharply round to her, and his eyes gleamed. "Everything has to be paid for, Puss. I've told you that."

In the deep, unfamiliar quiet of the countryside, where beyond the window furtive rustlings and harsh, stricken cries might of a sudden pierce the stillness, Vivian slept fitfully.

Mallory had made clear he didn't wish to discuss card games any further. But he did mention that Sir Robbie and Lady Tanis might be visiting Philadelphia for a while. At this news, unease had touched Vivian. The card games were to continue, then? Tanis was to go on batting those incredibly thick eyelashes and smiling up into Mallory's eyes? In the dark Vivian tried to duplicate that rapid flutter and gave it up in defeat.

Am I jealous, then? she asked herself. But what would this mean? That she was in love with Mallory? She knew she wasn't. He belonged to her just as she belonged to him, and no one had the right to take him away from her. But it was Jamie she loved.

Yet when, in reverie, she sought this lover, he wasn't there; she could no longer recall quite how he looked or conjure up the sound of his voice. Behind closed eyelids she could only see Icarus tumbling into the sea.

21

"It's all over, Puss," said Mallory glumly the next day as they rolled down the long drive between the beech trees and left Kimberly behind. "The good Lord only knows when we'll be asked to so grand an affair again."

He sounded like nothing so much as a small boy at the end of a party, with only bleak gray days stretching ahead.

"You've the convention to look forward to," she said.

"But there's no class to that, don't y' know. Butler Street types, for the most part. A lot of shouting and coarse talk. Politics is not for gentlemen, Puss; no, and it's not. It's not a gentleman's life." He surveyed the pretty little dirt lane onto which they had turned, wending its way under a leafy arcade through which shafts of sunlight streamed. "I think I'll buy me a farm."

Vivian gasped. "A farm, Mallory! And whatever would we do with that?"

"Why, the same as the Cavendishes do, of course. Hire us a man and his wife to caretaker it, and rent out the land to a farmer."

The prospect of spending days in the countryside, however lovely, with nothing but horses and cows for company and, on the weekends, guests who were loath to come, and who would snub and look down upon her as they ate her food and slept under her roof, was staggering. "And what would become of the saloon and all?" she asked.

"The saloon is not so important."

"Not important! Mother of God, Mallory, it's where your office is!"

"Sure and I'd go back and forth two or three times a week, don't y' know? With the Overland there's nothing to that."

"But people expect you to be there."

"They'd have to get over expecting that."

Vivian fell silent. She didn't care to distract her husband with conversation now they had reached the Old York Road and were traveling rapidly past carriages and trolleys and all manner of vehicles. But she found his inclinations even more alarming than the speed he so enjoyed, and she wracked her brain with thinking how best to divert them.

Such considerations flew from her head as they reached Philadelphia and rounded City Hall, a massive stone edifice planted squarely in the center of Broad Street with a statue of William Penn perched high on its top. From the south, in the far distance, a small, dark cloud boiled up into the placid Sunday afternoon.

"A storm?" said Vivian uncertainly.

"Fire," replied Mallory, and the Overland leaped suddenly forward like a bucking horse.

Hunched over the steering wheel, Mallory whipped the car in and out among the vehicles beginning to stream down Broad Street toward the dark stain that, more ominously now, was beginning to spread over an angry pink glow in the southern sky.

Clinging to her seat, Vivian was surprised she couldn't smell smoke, and then realized there was no wind. The day was a fine, balmy Sunday with a sky so innocent and blue as to mock the dark billows on its horizon. But in the vehicles they passed, people sat forward, urging horse or motor car onward toward the disaster, faces grim.

A mile or two more and all traffic was halted in an enormous bottleneck with only one narrow lane kept clear. Headed for this tunnel hurtled a fire wagon drawn by two horses, bell ringing wildly. Swerving in behind it, Mallory followed it through, drawing abruptly to a stop before a policeman who regarded him with fury from under his high-crowned helmet.

Pulling off cap and goggles, Mallory said, "Where is it, Patrick?"

Eyes starting in recognition, Patrick touched his hat. "The Wearever Waist Company, sir."

At his words, Vivian's heart leapt to her throat. "Rita!" she cried, clutching Mallory's arm. "The Wade girls!"

"It's Sunday," Mallory reminded her tersely.

"But there are people in there, sir," said the policeman. "They were working today. To make up for the strike."

The Wearever Waist Company was behind in its orders. Upwards of four hundred girls had come to work on Sunday, as they had on Saturday, to address the backlog. For the most part they were Italian girls from the tenements on Bryce Street. Many were the sole support of parents still living in "the old country." Others were saving toward their wedding day. When the fire was over, fourteen engagement rings were found.

They worked on the eighth and ninth floors of the Acme Building. Above them soared the twelve-foot ceilings that fulfilled the letter of the law, giving each worker the allotted 250 cubic feet of air, albeit their chairs were jammed back to back, and their sewing machines side by side. Stacked beside each girl were the cut piece goods waiting to be sewed into blouses and trimmed with the laces and ribbons set out before them upon the table that ran between the rows of machines. On shelves against the walls were stored bolt upon bolt of muslin, of voile, of lingerie. On great cutting tables patterns of tissue paper interposed layers of cloth. The male cutters who worked at these tables constantly smoked cigarettes. They blew the smoke under their coats so the floor manager could look the other way in winking defiance of the fire code. Under the cutting tables were large baskets of scraps that the ragman came to pick up and cart away. But he hadn't been by in some time, and baskets overflowed. There was one narrow passageway for the girls to leave by so their purses could be inspected in order to prevent the stealing of the odd bit of ribbon or lace: all other doors leading to the outside were kept locked.

Started perhaps by someone stepping on a match, perhaps by an ash falling from a cigarette, the fire caught and raced along, feeding upon the flimsy cloth, the tissue-paper patterns, drawn by drafts created by windows that had been opened to the fine day. Within minutes it became a roaring inferno.

The fire swept through the eighth and ninth floors. The ladders of the engine companies reached only to the seventh.

In the heat and dense smoke, the two elevator operators

kept working trip after trip, carrying the girls down, until other girls, crazed by fear, jumped into the elevator shafts, their wedged bodies forcing the elevators to a halt. Clothing afire, some rushed screaming into the flames, while still more, clinging together, jumped from the windows to certain death as police and firemen struggled futilely to break their falls with nets.

When it was over, 146 women had lost their lives.

"We run first to the door," said Eileen Wade, who, together with her sister Rosalie and Rita Celano, had managed to escape. "We run to the door, but it was locked and there was no key there . . . I tried to break it open and I couldn't . . . There was a woman forty years old there who was burned. And there were others, and they was next to me and with me at the door, and I said to the woman, 'You try. You may be stronger.' She said, 'I can't.' So then I said 'Let us all go at it.' And we did." They hadn't gotten it open, however, and had finally scrambled to safety by reaching stairs that led up to the roof.

Taking notes hour after hour in Mallory's office in the back room of the Tipperary, Vivian scribbled down bits and pieces of the tragic tale as, one after the other, Mallory questioned those involved in the fire. "My sister collapsed through fear," said a young woman, weeping. "I tried to drag her to the stairway. Another girl—I don't know who she was—tried to help me. The flames swept about us and I was literally brushed to the open door. I thought my sister was too. I slid down the cable of the elevator nine floors. My hands were torn and burned."

"The bodies didn't break through the nets," Fire Captain Ed Malone told Mallory. "They just carried them to the sidewalk. The force was so great it took the men off their feet, they turned somersaults over onto the bodies."

"We were there three minutes after the alarm," said Mickey Aherne of the Hibernian Fire Company. "And it took us four minutes to make our connections and 'stretch in.' By that time people were jumping from windows so fast that before we could turn the water on our line was buried under bodies and we had to lift them off before we could get to work."

"The girls behind us were screaming and crying," Rita Celano testified. "Several of them, as the flames crept up closer, ran into the smoke, and we heard them scream as the flames caught their clothes. One little girl who worked at the machine opposite me cried out in Italian, 'Good-bye, good-bye!' I have not seen her since. My cousin Gloria staggered through the mob and made direct for the flames. The next I heard of her was when they brought her body home from the morgue. She had jumped."

Just as searing, Vivian found, were the visits she made with Mallory to the bereft families, most of them living in the tenements that lined Bryce Street.

"I don't want you to go with me," he had told her.

"I'm going," she said.

And in remaining by his side as he tramped up and down stairs stinking of cabbage, of fish, of worse and worse, she learned of a poverty that was squalor, of suffering and privation such as, for all her own sparse early existence, she had never known.

At each stop they made, there was that moment when they were invited to view the fresh and smiling young face in the photograph—not by word or gesture, but by a mute leap of the eyes, an all but imperceptible nod of the head to the little cleared space on the table upon which rested the picture with, often, paper flowers tied to the frame and, always, a crucifix.

Our Carmella, our Maria . . .

"It will not happen again! No, by God, and it will not!" shouted Mallory. "It will not happen that doors are kept locked. It will not happen that windows are barred, that doors open inward, that stairways are dark. No, as God is my witness, it will not!"

In the rain, thousands of factory workers had silently walked up Broad Street to City Hall as thousands more silently watched. They marched to the muffled beat of a drum behind an empty hearse drawn by six white horses caparisoned in black. And now they stood in the drenching rain, their faces turned up like pale flowers to Mallory on the speakers' platform.

"I serve notice here and now," he cried, his voice hoarse with emotion, "that a code will be forged, laws will be passed, penalties fixed.

"I serve notice to landlords, to bankers, to employers that their hour has come.

"I serve notice and call upon the unions, the churches, the social workers, the reformers to join me and the Amity

Clubs of this city in ensuring that such a grievous tragedy
as the Wearever Waist Company fire will never occur
again."

Standing in the rain clutching her black silk umbrella,
Vivian listened to her husband's words, not realizing, any
more than he did, that he had just formed that first coali-
tion of labor and a party machine that was to transform
politics and, incidentally, make the political boss one of the
most powerful figures in the land.

Like the wave of a wand, Mallory's speech to the marchers changed the mood of the crowd, and they turned back
to their homes on that rainy Sunday with resolute step and
a gleam in the eye.

Not the least affected was Neil Randall. He seemed beside himself with a euphoria that brought two bright spots
of color to his lean face and a feverish brilliance to his
eyes. "There's no turning back now!" he cried jubilantly.
"The die is cast. The Rubicon is crossed. For the landlords,
the bankers, the employers, their hour has come!"

In Mamie Randall's kitchen the tea kettle simmered together with frying scrapple, with frying onions and potatoes as, with everyone hungry and chilled from the march,
the women of the family collided one with the other in an
effort to get a cloth spread over the table, to get bread
sliced and a batter of apple dumplings readied to be eased
gently into the pan of deep fat on the stove.

Laying places for all of them, Vivian felt a rush of happiness. After days of gloom that, along with the acrid odor
of smoke, had hung like a pall over the stricken city, a
sudden noisy gaiety infected the house. Even the quiet
Nancy Webb and the usually dour Ma Mallory seemed to
respond.

As always at such moments, Vivian felt a pang that her
father was absent. One never, it seemed, managed to get
life entirely to one's satisfaction. Always there was one tiny
piece missing, one small catch at the heart. Nonetheless she
took delight in having the family gathered together, and
special pleasure in the surprising new rapport that had
sprung up between her husband and her brother.

She hadn't realized this could mean so much to her, but
covertly watching Neil talk his heart out to Mallory caused
her to blink quick, bright tears from her eyes. Mallory, of
course, had heard these tales before. Hadn't she spent hour

after hour at his side, taking down notes on just such conditions as Neil was fervidly itemizing? But standing by the open back door as the rain beat down, Mallory gave the earnest young man his undivided attention, and for this kindness the most tender gratitude blossomed within her, like a rare new flower opening in her heart.

Indeed, so rapt was the gaze she fixed upon her husband, so intent her regard, that of a sudden he turned and their eyes locked. Blushing, she averted her head. But that leap of desire that had accompanied the moment did not now diminish, for all she sat at table murmuring responses to the conversation, passing platters of scrapple, of potatoes. Instead it raced and pulsed in her blood, making her breath come quickly and her hands tremble, making her impatient with the long meal, the desultory talk.

At last it was ended, the dishes washed, the kitchen put to rights, and Ma Mallory was saying she'd just as soon stay and spend the rest of the afternoon with Mamie.

Vivian and Mallory left the house. His hand at her elbow, the rain drumming on the taut black silk of her umbrella, they walked in silence, like strangers, albeit suiting their steps to one another. Down Butler they walked, away from Mallory's house, along a street bereft of anyone abroad save themselves in the midafternoon of this dreary Sunday.

Over puddles he helped her, but he didn't seem to care, or even to notice, that her black calf pumps were soaked through and the hem of her long black faille coat was wet and muddy. Twice she looked up at him inquiringly, but he didn't say where they were going, nor did she ask.

The corner where stood the Tipperary Saloon was deserted, as was the intersection itself. The saloon, the Keystone Bank, the grain and feed store, and the barbershop all had their window shades drawn down so that a passerby would immediately conclude the day was Sunday had he, perchance, forgotten.

Vivian thought Mallory meant to unlock the door of the saloon, with the intention of stepping into his office for a moment. But he steered her past, stopping instead at his mother's small clapboard house at the back and fitting a key in the lock.

Opening the door, he turned and gave her a look, and she entered. Her heart had begun to beat rapidly, for although the house had once been Mallory's, and might still be thought so, still she had the feeling of trespassing. She looked wonderingly at her husband as he shut the door.

They stood in a narrow hallway from which, almost immediately, rose steep stairs. To one side was a wide doorway fitted with sliding doors that, Vivian knew from previous visits, led to the interior parts of the first floor. These doors were closed now, leaving the hallway in almost total darkness except for pale daylight showing dimly from the top of the stairs.

Toward this staircase Mallory nodded and in puzzlement she followed him up. He led the way along a short upper hall to what she knew instinctively must have been his bedroom, although nothing she recognized as his gave evidence of this.

It was a rather large room with two windows at which needles of rain now pricked, overlooking an alley that ran behind the shops on Butler Street. It had a massive iron bedstead covered with a heavy, deeply fringed white coverlet, an oak washstand with two white towels folded upon the towel rack, a chiffonier, also oak, and by the fireplace, above which was a mantel fitted with an oblong mirror, an armchair upholstered in a dark figured velour.

As she stood looking uncertainly about her, Mallory quickly knelt, lit the gas jet in the fireplace, and then the two polished brass gas pendants on either side of the mantel. In the soft hissing glow that suffused the room, he tossed the packet of matches onto the mantel shelf and turned to her.

"You've been here often," he said.

"I?"

He nodded. "I've thought of you so. Coming here. Being here. I've seen you in every corner of this room. I've seen you here in all kinds of clothes you have never owned, nor are ever likely to. I've seen you in ball gowns, and in a purple satin cloak with a deep collar of gray fur. I've seen you all in white standing by the curtains with flowers in your hair. I've seen you sitting by the fire with your arms around your knees and your hair rippling down your back. I've seen you"—he turned to the bed—"naked there."

She gasped and, as though mesmerized, unwittingly followed his eyes to the heavy white coverlet.

"Since I've dreamed of you so often there, that way, I would like to have the sight of you."

"Here? Now?"

"You needn't whisper," he said matter-of-factly. "We are quite alone."

And but for the rain against the windows and the hiss of the gas jets, there truly was not a sound to be heard. Notwithstanding this encouragement, she stood transfixed, staring at this man. Once more he had become the stranger, in an unfamiliar room where he had imagined . . . why, she couldn't think, didn't want to think, what all! And this stranger had just suggested she take off all her clothes and lie on the bed!

"Only if you want to," he now added preposterously.

He moved impatiently, and the trace of a frown deepened between his eyes. Another second's hesitation and this disconcerting, distasteful moment would be over and they would be on their way down the stairs. And this would be fine with her—except for what she owed him. Yes, what she owed him for the way he had stood listening to her brother Neil, for the way he had helped all her family, for the gratitude that had swelled in her heart.

It was due him, this that he wanted, this that he asked.

Swiftly, so swiftly she wouldn't have time to think, her hastening fingers plucked jet hatpins from her black silk turban and cast it upon the armchair. Swiftly, her cheeks flaming, the long black faille topcoat was unbuttoned and removed. Following this, the little faille suit jacket with its smart trimming of soutache braid, the matching skirt, the white lingerie waist—oh, those little girls who might have sewn it! Those little girls whose deaths this man had sworn to avenge! Next, the flounced black taffeta petticoat, the black silk stockings.

"Leave your stockings on."

Startled, hands at one garter, Vivian stopped and looked up at him.

"I've pictured you with stockings. You may take off the rest."

Anger seized her. Was this her husband, the man she had married, speaking to her in this fashion? Giving her shocking commands as though—as though she must entertain him with some sort of bordello performance?

Kicking aside her wet pumps, she tore off the dainty white nainsook corset cover, the heavily starched muslin underskirt, leaving herself almost naked before his intent gaze in nothing but corset, sheer batiste underdrawers, and chemise.

He had never watched her undress, never watched her
take off her corset, parting it hook by hook down the front,
never watched her pull down her underdrawers. With a
sharp catch of her breath she now did this for him, kicked
them aside, pulled the fine crepe de chine chemise up and
over her mussed and tumbling hair, and stepped naked to
the bed.

Stretched tautly before him, consumed by fury, she felt
him, heard him, step toward her, and closed her eyes. A
rush of sound like waves breaking filled her ears, filling
the stillness. Then gently, ever so slightly, with his two
hands he parted her legs.

And from wishing it might never happen, she suddenly
wished it might never end.

22

In the days that followed, a blush crept up to flood Vivian's cheek whenever she recalled that rainy Sunday afternoon. Nonetheless, the visit to Mallory's bachelor room
gave her a new insight into this man who hazarded his
adult dreams on the skittish child she had been, who had
loved her so tenaciously and so long. How remote now that
vain and silly little creature! How changed she knew herself to be.

This was borne home by a chance meeting with Dolly
Muldoon in Hinkel's Ice Cream Parlor. The fire at the
Wearever Waist Company had erased all thought of the
Hibernians' carnival from Vivian's mind, but apparently it
remained paramount in Dolly's pert blond head.

"My Tom did very well with his jokes," she said.

Seated opposite Vivian at a small, round marble-topped
table, she sipped her strawberry soda and nodded her head,
causing the bunch of artificial cherries on her hat to
bounce beguilingly. "Very well indeed. There were those
who said he should go on the stage. Everything in the best
of taste, of course."

"Of course," agreed Vivian promptly.

"And I must say the platform did look spiffy. All that red, white, and blue bunting, and all. And Tom in his white suit with a red, white, and blue crepe paper rosette I made for his lapel."

"Very appropriate."

"Indeed. He wanted to wear just pants and a shirt, but I wouldn't hear of it. I told him what with the work Morrissey and Thurman and I had done to get his platform ready, he couldn't show up in just any old thing." She smiled, dimples springing to either side of the rosebud mouth. "I must say he did look handsome. I must say I was proud."

"Oh, Dolly," said Vivian impulsively. "I do hope you'll be very happy married to Tom!"

"I'm sure I shall be," replied Dolly, adding, "At least as happy as you, I expect. After all," she continued slyly, into the depths of her ice cream soda, "after all, we neither of us got what we wanted, did we?"

Vivian choked on her orange crush. "What do you mean?"

"You know very well what I mean. Are you going to see him out there?"

"See who?"

"See who-do-you-think, that's who. See who left you with your bags all packed in Morrissey's blacksmith shop."

So Morrissey had told! But Vivian had known he would. By this time everyone knew. She discovered, however, that she no longer cared. "Gracious!" she said, lightly, "how long ago that seems!"

Dolly's blue eyes went round. "You don't deny it?"

"That Jamie jilted me? Oh no, it's quite true. Thurman Foy took him to the railroad station in his milk wagon."

"That's just what Thurman said."

"That's just what happened."

Dolly leveled upon her a disapproving frown. "And you're willing to admit all this, Vivian Mallory?"

Vivian shrugged a shoulder. "It's the truth."

"Well, you are a cool one, I must say!"

She could hear the surprise in Dolly's voice, and in fact, she shared it. The truth was, she had changed. Being Mallory's wife had changed her, the trip through the tenements on Bryce Street had changed her; the fire had changed her.

But neither was she so cool as Dolly believed. In three

short days now, she and Mallory would board the train for St. Louis. Every time she thought of this her pulse raced and her mouth went dry.

Dear God, she prayed each night, *don't let us meet. Don't let me see him.* But even as she prayed she knew a wild rebellious hope that her prayers would go unanswered. Even as she knelt by Mallory's bed and folded her hands, her wayward fancy leapt to that one-in-a-million chance that she and Jamie might meet again.

Diverting her from such conjectures was a visit she received the day before their departure.

She was upstairs overseeing the packing, the bedroom strewn with Mallory's suits and her own gowns and hats and petticoats, when the doorbell rang and presently Halls appeared with the message that Mr. Clinton Webb waited in the front parlor.

At the announcement her thoughts flew instantly to the little packet of bills secured by a rubber band that must now be returned to him, and her breath caught as memory swept her back to Cavendish Square. Oh, the dread of that displeasure that could knit the smooth brow of master, of mistress! Oh, the consternation she had known at the drop of spilled tea, the forgotten task, the chipped cup!

No matter that the Webbs, one and all, had been unfailingly kind and considerate; no matter that she was far removed from the need to care what displeasure she caused, or to whom she caused it. Still, Clinton Webb couldn't fail but be annoyed upon receiving the return of the money his mother had so thoughtfully sent to his sister. This certainty unnerved Vivian as she unlocked the desk drawer and slipped the small roll of bills into her pocket.

That the result of such agitation made more dazzling the green eyes, cast a slight pallor over the delicately wrought features, and contrived to lend a certain diffident charm to the figure clad in an embroidered eggshell voile, was not lost upon Clinton Webb as he rose to greet her.

"I do hope I'm not being a nuisance," he said.

"Clinton, no!" she cried softly. "Not ever."

He held on to the hand she had given him, his dark eyes smiling down into hers. "I'm going to choose to believe you mean that."

"But I do! I'm always happy to see you."

The smile turned wry. "As, no doubt, you're always happy to see the greengrocer? The gardener? The scullery maid?"

He squeezed her hand rather too hard before releasing it, and the frown that had sprung between his eyes announced that somehow she had already succeeded in vexing him.

"Please," she said, gesturing to a chair and sinking down herself upon one of the gold-on-gold brocade divans.

In the cool, dim room he sat facing her, his shoulders ramrod straight beneath the navy blue serge blazer, as correct in his bearing as the knife-edged creases in the white ducks he wore.

"So you're happy?" he asked suddenly.

"Yes, I am," she said in surprise.

"You recommend the honorable estate, then?"

"Honorable estate?"

"Of matrimony."

He spoke in circles as, she had observed, many educated people did. One would have thought that much knowledge would help one express oneself clearly. But the opposite seemed to be the case. "I like it fine," she said simply.

"That's encouraging. I'm to be married myself shortly. To Miss Anthea Allenby."

"So I've heard."

"Have you?"

"Nancy told me. She had it in the letter from your mother."

"And how is my sister?"

"She is well." Taking a breath, she added, "She will not accept any funds."

What, she wondered, had she expected to happen? True, Clinton Webb was regarding her darkly, but the world hadn't come to an end. On the stairway the grandfather's clock ticked placidly and from outside came the snip of gardener's shears as Timothy Kerns trimmed back the new privet around the porch.

"Of course she knows this will cut my mother to the very quick," said Clinton.

"That is not her intention."

"What difference, if such is the result?"

"I believe Nancy means only to display an admirable independence."

"Admirable? My dear Vivvie, surely your experience of

life can't lead you to believe there is anything in any way admirable in a foolhardy refusal to accept assistance when it is needed."

Vivian could only agree, but one little ray of hope had appeared on the horizon. "Please tell your mother that things are going better for my brother. He is no longer working at O'Reilly's Market. He is otherwise employed."

"Oh? Doing what?"

"I'm not sure what it's called," she replied, frowning. "But he has a little office and he's working on getting laws passed. Laws about fire escapes and such. It comes of Mallory's interest in safety conditions after the Wearever Waist Company fire."

"Your brother doesn't scruple to accept nepotism, then?" he said sardonically. She had no idea what this might mean and tucked the word in the back of her head as Clinton continued. "I read the newspaper report of your husband's speech to the marchers. I hope you don't think all bankers, all landlords, all employers wear horns."

"I believe laws need to be made," she responded, perhaps more crisply than his mild observation merited.

He appeared not to take offense. "That's a popular belief these days. People seem to want laws about everything: laws about hours, laws about wages, even about children."

He looked at her in frank dismay. "Can you imagine a law telling a man he can't send off his child to work? Telling parents what they may and may not do with their own offspring? Why, I know for a fact that if the children in my woolen mills were forced by law to stop working, their families would perish!"

"But wait, Clinton!" she said, for she understood his feelings, having once shared them. "What must happen is that the men must be paid more. The women, too. Then the children won't have to work but may stay in school and learn something instead of doing as I did."

"Doing as you did! But look how far you've come. And your husband, also!"

"But others are held down."

"No, no."

"Oh, yes! Oh yes and they are! I could show you if you'd care to come with me. I could show you places not fit for a pig, and good rent charged for them."

"And what is to stop people from cleaning them up and making them better?"

"They haven't the heart."

"Now you sound like my sister."

"If I do, then I'm proud. For she sees what must be done, and Neil, too. They care what's what, and what happens."

"And I don't. Is that your implication? But my mills provide jobs for twelve hundred people. And my contributions support the art museums and the orchestra and the library; my donations support the hospitals, the orphanages, the poorhouses—"

"But maybe if things was to be more fair," she flung out, "poorhouses wouldn't be needed!"

She faced him defiantly, forgetting the gentleman he was, recalling the tenements, the Wearever fire—yes, and her own young life of drudgery. And to her surprise a look of such wry tenderness crossed his face as to quite disarm her.

"Ah, Vivvie," he said, "you remind me what worlds apart we are."

Like a curtain going down, the look, the tone, the moment vanished. He rose. "I predict we'll have lots of laws," he said flatly. "And men like your husband will make them."

That night, as she lay beside Mallory in the dark, she said, "What's 'nepotism'?"

"Nepotism?" repeated Mallory with a yawn. "It's when you give your relatives a job working for you."

"And can that be wrong?" she pursued, recalling Clinton Webb's thin smile.

"Some people think so."

"But why?"

"Playing favorites. Unfair advantage. Things like that. Puts noses out of joint."

She thought this over for a few moments, then, "Are noses out of joint because you hired our Neil?"

Mallory didn't answer. Perhaps, thought Vivian, he was asleep.

23

The rich, Vivian decided, had varied and interesting problems. For the poor, all problems were at heart the same, and money could nicely solve just about every one of them.

This was why, she reflected, looking out the window as the train sped toward St. Louis under a blazing sun, she favored Theodore Roosevelt and his "square deal for every American," although her preference scarcely mattered, since a woman couldn't vote.

Mallory, she felt, privately favored Roosevelt also, and certainly expected him to win the election.

"It doesn't matter who we nominate in St. Louis," he had told her. "We're not going to win in November. T.R. is going to be the next president. I just wish he was a Democrat!"

But if it didn't matter, Mallory nonetheless appeared to be working furiously to secure the nomination of one Judge Alton B. Parker. From the moment he had set foot on the bunting-draped special train that had come clanging into Philadelphia, already alive and swarming with the New York delegation, he had become enthusiastically embroiled in battle.

The "Tammany Boys," as he dubbed them, favored William Jennings Bryan, causing the Philadelphia delegation, under Mallory's direction, to rove red-faced and sweating back and forth through the swaying cars trying to drum up support for Judge Parker.

"Can you believe Tammany wants to run Bryan again!" demanded Mallory of Vivian. Straw hat on the back of his damply curling pitch-black hair, shirtsleeves rolled up, and sporting red, white, and blue galluses, he stared at her in baffled outrage. "Bryan!" he repeated. "He lost in '96 and again four years ago! The mood of the country isn't with him!" Recalling himself, he said, "Puss, you want me to bring you back a ham sandwich? A soda pop?"

He seemed not to have a moment's peace what with fussing over her, although she had several times assured him she was perfectly fine, ensconced as she was in the luxury of a private drawing room.

The fact that she had at last commenced upon what she felt in her bones to be a fateful journey, that every turn of the wheels was bringing her into closer and ever closer proximity to Jamie Fitzhugh, so unnerved her that she desired nothing so much as to be left alone to try to compose and calm herself.

But her restless mind swept from past to present, from present to past, like the constantly rotating beam of a lighthouse, pricking out Morrissey's blacksmith shop and Jamie's tall, lean body, stripped to the waist, shining with sweat, lit like a young Vulcan in the flare of the open hearth. Or again, Jamie, his eyes keen and dark above the determined mouth, explaining his experiments to her, using words she could not follow, a language she would never understand. But kindling belief in her all the same, belief as strong as her love.

Well, she had retained her belief in him. She had no doubt his theories would one day meet with success. As for her love . . .

Lying back against the seat, she gave a little moan. Oh, to have accepted Mallory's belated suggestion that she remain in Philadelphia! To be spared putting to the test that tormenting memory that could rise to tug at her heart so unexpectedly and invest even her happiest moments with anguished regret.

But even worse than the possibility that she might meet Jamie was the possibility—indeed, the probability, among so many thousands—that she might not. To be so near, and not see him? Not? Oh, it was unthinkable, like a thirst forever unquenched! She *must* see him. She must somehow make inquiry, find a way . . .

"Puss?"

Her eyes flew open, and she stared guiltily under her husband's intent gaze.

"I didn't mean to wake you, but you looked so . . . like you were in pain."

"It's so hot!" she cried distractedly.

"Why, then, come along to the lounge car and let me buy you a nice cold lemonade." He grinned. "I promised a few of the boys I'd introduce them to my beautiful wife."

She felt more wretched than beautiful in her rumpled and sticky clothes. "A Very Nobby Jumper Suit of Navy Blue Polka Dot Chally," the advertisement in the *Philadelphia Inquirer* had read, and she had rushed off to the John Wanamaker Store to purchase it, thinking it the very thing to travel in. But as she followed Mallory along the narrow, swinging aisles, she doubted that any garment could withstand such an onslaught of dust, dirt, and perspiration.

Mallory, though, appeared not to mind these conditions in the least, and their progress toward the lounge car took on aspects of a gala reception line as he stopped to introduce her on every side.

It never ceased to impress Vivian, this flattering attention her husband could command. At his voice, heads turned, smiles wreathed faces, eagerness leapt into eyes. He was good looking, of course, with a jaunty Irish handsomeness that had about it that which was cocky in the very moment it played itself down with a twinkle of the eye. And he was politically powerful, of this there could be no doubt, with a power the extent of which she was only beginning to grasp. But these things didn't fully explain why people fell over themselves to trade a quip with him, to extend a hand, nor, she observed gratefully and not for the first time, to turn upon her with warmth and love in their eyes.

Had she been snubbed by certain ladies at Kimberly, she was here treated like royalty. In the lounge car a bevy of delegates' wives quickly surrounded her. Far from bothering their heads with the relative merits of possible Democratic candidates, these women delighted in the gossip of the day.

Above all, the talk was of Alice Roosevelt, the president's lively and pretty young daughter—the parties she attended, the dinners, the balls, the clothes she wore, the beaus who had danced attendance on her, the way she fixed her hair. Europe and America alike were fascinated by her escapades. She scandalized and enchanted at the same time, smoking cigarettes, jumping fully clothed into swimming pools, dancing the immodest hula, playing poker with gentlemen and winning the game. She was, it appeared, every woman's ideal. Babies were named for her, as was an entrancing shade of blue, gowns of which color graced many a wardrobe. Alice Roosevelt flouted all the rules and did just as she pleased. Moreover, she got away with it, thereby putting ideas in other feminine heads.

So absorbing was this discussion that Vivian never noticed a new face joining the little circle until someone said, "By the bye, where's Gussie Doyle? Anybody seen her?"

A shocked silence descended upon the group as the newcomer looked about her. "What's the matter?" she persisted in some alarm. "Don't tell me something has happened to good old Gussie!"

"She didn't come this year," someone hastily explained. "Why not?"

A nearby woman whispered earnestly while a slow pink flush crept up the questioner's face. She darted a swift, hard look at Vivian and then murmured, "Gee, I'm sorry. I'm from New York. I didn't know."

Everyone quickly spoke of other things, but the little gaffe had left its mark. The mood was broken, replaced, on Vivian's part, by bewildered agitation.

The moment she could gracefully do so, she made her way back to the drawing room. It was here, somewhat later, that Mallory found her.

"I thought you were still in the lounge," he said in surprise. "Weren't you having a good time?"

"Something happened."

Instantly he was alert. "Yes?"

"Mallory," she said, "why aren't Gussie and Paddy Doyle on this train?"

Mallory hesitated not a moment. "Paddy isn't a delegate to the convention."

"Why not?"

"Because I said so, that's why not. No more conventions for Paddy, no more ice business, no more nothing."

She stared at him, incredulous. "All because of that silly party?"

"That's right."

"But Paddy was your best friend!"

"You're my wife."

Was she, Vivian asked herself, staring into the dark as the train rocked and swayed through the night, forever to regret that ill-starred evening at the Doyles?

But she knew it wasn't her own behavior, vain and foolish though it had been, that was to blame. Nor the drunken attentions of Paddy Doyle, however obnoxious. It was Mallory who was wrong, setting himself up like God to reward or punish, taking himself too hard.

As she recalled the bitter look on the face of the woman from New York, a chill presentiment trembled in Vivian's heart.

The city of St. Louis lay sweltering in the sun, but this didn't dampen the spirits of the multitudes who arrived for the Democratic convention, or for the Louisiana Purchase Exposition, more generally known as the World's Fair.

Everything in town was open: pool halls, saloons, hotels, theaters, ball parks, and, of course, the Coliseum, a great brick structure that housed the convention itself. In the new Jefferson Hotel, Tammany set up its headquarters to campaign for William Jennings Bryan, while at the Southern, Mallory and his Amity Club directed the fight for Judge Parker. And everywhere, in suffocating hotel lobbies, crowded restaurants, and hot, smoke-filled rooms, the delegates met and the deals were made.

Meanwhile, the delegates' wives spent their days out at the Fair Grounds in Forest Park. There, in awestruck wonder, they could observe the marvels of the new machine age: the Palace of Manufactures, the Palaces of Machinery, of Mines, of Education . . . That these ivory-white palaces, twelve in all, were pasted together out of a material called *staff,* a substance compounded of plaster of Paris and hemp fibers meant to last only for the few short months of the Fair, didn't detract one bit from the stunning effect of soaring fluted columns, of triumphal archways, of pediments and domes that turned the exhibit into fairyland. Tired of sightseeing, one might choose a stroll among the acres of gardens, a ride on the lagoons, or, more daringly, on Mr. Ferris's great Observation Wheel. Anything from a snack to a full-course dinner could be had at restaurant pavilions, including a comical new food called a hot dog, or tea served over ice for the first time when an enterprising young Englishman, finding few sales for hot in such weather, decided to try to increase business by serving it cold.

"You must just look to yourself, I'm afraid, Puss," said Mallory apologetically. "The Tammany boys are starting to promote a boom for Governor Pattison, and I'll have my hands full heading them off."

"And sure, Mallory, why would you not support a man who was a governor of our own state?"

"It's only a trick, don't y' see, girl? Only a ruse to force us to desert Judge Parker. But they'll not succeed in that!"

Vivian didn't attempt to follow these strategies. The excitement of the crowded city together with the prospect of the Fair had at last overpowered her anxieties, and she looked forward to each day with eager anticipation. In the company of two or three congenial women, she would set off every morning in a trolley for Forest Park, there to spend not only the entire day but frequently the evening also, for it was nightfall that introduced the most spectacular displays. Then it was that over 120,000 incandescent lamps twinkled on, outlining every palace, reflected in the water of the Grand Basin and the lagoons, changing colors under the Cascades that tumbled down from the brilliantly electrified Festival Hall.

"Oh, Mallory!" she would say upon returning. "If only you could see it! The largest organ in the world!"

Or, "A great sculpture made out of butter, and kept always cold! Think of it! However in the world . . . ?"

Or, "A tribe of Philippine natives who wear almost no clothes, and eat only dogs! Yes, dogs, Mallory! Twenty dogs a day, they say!"

Oh, if only he could leave off politics for just a few hours and see all the flags (ten thousand of them, it was said), and hear all the bands, and watch all the parades— cavalry, infantry, artillery, and John Philip Sousa himself!

If only he could stroll down the fabulous Pike and see the Illusions: "A representation of Hell, Mallory. Yes, Hell. One woman fainted and had to be carried off flat out." And other Illusions, also: the Galveston Flood, the Tyrolean Alps, Hagenback's Wild Animal Show.

And the flowers! The beautiful Sunken Gardens. And the giant clock. "All planted in flowers, Mallory! And hands that move around it and tell the time."

And the people! Eskimos, Russians, Indians, Chinese.

Was it any wonder that her thoughts strayed from Jamie Fitzhugh? Was it so surprising, then, that she looked up with no more than polite inquiry when, upon returning to the Southern Hotel late one afternoon, a young man approached her?

For a moment she stared at him in frowning puzzlement. Then recognition came flooding in upon a wave of vertigo, and she would surely have fallen had not Jamie tightened his grip upon her arm.

24

It had never occurred to Vivian that Jamie Fitzhugh might seek *her* out. In the elaborate pipe dreams she had fashioned, never once had she imagined he might make plans to find *her*. Nor was she aware that he had done so even now, believing their meeting to be the greatest coincidence as, hand tight at her elbow, he hurried her through the hot, crowded lobby and back out to the sweltering street.

Dusk was falling. Streetlights bloomed palely in the gathering dark, and lighted lamps bobbed on carriages. From restaurants laughter and golden pools of illumination spilled out to beckon the milling crowds moving at such indolent variance with the astonishing young man and woman who, like two demented creatures impelled by some dire emergency, plunged headlong through the crowd.

Trying to keep pace, Vivian clutched at her white dimity skirts, her folded eyelet parasol dancing against her side. For all their haste, her legs felt heavy, leaden. She moved as one in a dream, with no idea of destination, scarce able to credit what was happening, to believe it was Jamie at her side.

How alien he seemed—taller and thinner than she remembered, in the cheap gray crash sack suit and derby hat that he wore. Alien, yet as familiar as that leap of the heart she had known back at the hotel at the sound of his voice; as intimate as that moment when their eyes met.

He turned her into a side street, hurrying her along the uneven pavement. The neighborhood had a down-at-heel air although the houses were rather large, and sat above and well back from the sidewalk. Children played noisily in the early dark, and from the front of several houses hung a sign bearing the word Rooms.

Into one of these residences Jamie now swung her, all but lifting her up the steep porch steps, so urgent was his grasp upon her arm, flinging open the screen door festooned with chipped and peeling scrollwork.

The house was alive with the shrieks of children and the sound of roller skates on the uncarpeted hallway of the floor above, and a woman came from the back to stand in the light of the single gas fixture. She appeared to be in her mid-thirties, and was pretty in a careless way despite frizzy brown hair and a bit too much weight. With the keenest interest she inspected Vivian who, so finely dressed in embroidered dimity, stood clutching her dainty parasol, her breath coming quickly, tendrils of red-gold hair escaping from under a hat fashioned of white velvet violets.

"Connie, this is Vivian," snapped Jamie.

Bemused though she was, Vivian could see the woman seemed to apprehend and make allowance for that tension that had always marked Jamie and that sometimes caused others to think him arrogant and rude.

"Hi!" said Connie, and then to Jamie, with a jerk of her head toward the parlor, "You're in luck. Shaeffer is out for the night and old man Abramson is already upstairs. Go on in. I'll quieten those kids of mine."

She gave Vivian another look before moving to the scuffed wooden staircase, and Vivian sensed that the woman already knew something about her, perhaps even a great deal.

The parlor into which Jamie led her was as shabby as the foyer but possessed, withal, a certain liveliness—old magazines flung every which way on a table under a lighted gas lamp, a battered and abandoned doll on the sagging sofa, a child's shoes on the worn rug.

But her attention was not on these details as Jamie drew the double doors closed and, turning, rested his back against them. He looked almost ill, taut and tight-lipped as he closed his eyes and sighed deeply. Then he looked at her, shaking his head in disbelief. "I can't believe it," he said. "I can't believe you're here at last."

The implication in his words was so startling, so unwarranted as to instantly restore her to her senses. Why was she standing in this strange parlor in St. Louis? Why was Jamie smiling at her as though his treachery had never touched her? As though he had shared her aching yearning and now had the right to lay claim to her—to her, a married woman.

"I must leave at once," she said.

"Leave!" he cried.

"Yes, yes, at once."

With swift steps he was upon her, gripping her shoulders, his dark eyes burning down into hers. "For God's sake, Vivvie!"

She battled his grasp. "Jamie, please!"

"No! I'll not let you go. You must at least hear me out."

"I don't want to hear."

"You must! I love you."

A sob escaped her. "Ah, no."

"Yes. I love you. I've always loved you."

Stunned, she stared up at him, and he said, "Please, Vivvie. Hear me out, then go if you want. I won't try to stop you. But at least hear me out." His lips tucked back in the small, rare smile she had always treasured. "Please?"

Taking her silence for assent, he put a hand to her elbow and she let him lead her to the sofa. "Here," he said. "Sit here. You look so perturbed. Would you like some sherry?"

She shook her head and he lowered himself beside her, sitting forward, almost kneeling before her. "It was wrong to have left you as I did," he began.

Her hands fluttered up in protest but he said, "No, wait! How else can I say it? I was wrong, Vivvie, and I've hated myself for it ever since. Even when I was doing it, I hated myself; even when I was driving off in Thurman Foy's wagon and thinking of you hurrying back to Morrissey's with your bags all packed. Jesus!"

He sprang to his feet and paced away from her. When he turned back, a tight control marked voice and bearing. "But everything happened so fast: Mallory giving me the money, telling me a train was leaving almost right away, giving me two tickets. Yes, Vivvie, two tickets—one for you, he said, if I wanted to take you with me. But I didn't want to take you with me!

"Can you," he asked huskily, "possibly understand that? I weakened when you came running down to the shop, but after you left, I knew I didn't want you with me. Not then! Not when suddenly for the first time in my life I was free. Free!"

He plunged his hands into his pockets, his fiery dark

eyes staring down into the rug as though they would burn holes straight through it. "I came here and I got a room with Connie," he continued, "and for the first time in my life I did just as I pleased. I got up when I wanted, I slept when I wanted, I ate when I wanted. I walked over this whole city taking photographs, and I was *glad* I was alone! I was *glad* I didn't have anybody to answer to: not my old man, not Morrissey, not anybody."

He was silent a moment, standing gaunt and tall; abstracted. Then his head shot up and his eyes riveted themselves on hers. "But I thought about you all the time!" he cried. "All the time! It got to be like a sickness. I saw you everywhere. I followed girls in the street because they looked like you, walked like—"

"Jamie, please!" murmured Vivian out of the dazzle of his words. "You mustn't—"

"I must!" he shouted, and then, more quietly, "But still I wanted my freedom, don't y' see? Twice I started letters but each time I said, Not yet, not yet. And then one day . . ." He stopped and drew a deep breath. "One day Thurman Foy sent me a newspaper clipping. It was the account of your marriage to Mallory.

"I couldn't believe it! Oh, Vivvie, I was like a crazy man. I couldn't eat. I couldn't sleep. And then I got mad. I figured you had always wanted money and you finally got it. I decided I was lucky. Good riddance! I said. Good riddance!"

He shook his head. "But I couldn't get you out of my mind. When the Democrats came to town I checked all the hotels because I had to know if you were in one of them. I had to know.

"But I didn't plan to go near you. I was still that stiff-necked, don't y' see. And then today I couldn't stand it any longer. I knew time was running out and I had to have at least one look at you. So I hung around the lobby all day." He smiled wryly. "And when I saw you walk in, I couldn't stop myself from speaking to you, Vivvie. It just wasn't in me to stop myself."

Bright tears stood in Vivian's eyes. "I'm glad you didn't stop yourself, Jamie."

At her words he dropped down on the sofa, catching up her hands in both his own. "So am I, my dearest, my darling. And we'll never let it happen again. We'll never let anyone come between us, separate us."

She drew back sharply. "What do you mean? What in heaven's name are you saying?"

He returned her stricken look with one of baffled surprise. "Why, that we love one another and must always be together. " Again there appeared that rare smile that could so transform him. "Vivvie dearest, listen to me. We love one another. I knew it as soon as we met today. We still love one another. No matter what's happened, that's all that matters. You'll get a divorce and we'll be married as soon as possible. I know I've been wrong, but I swear I'll make it up to you." He stopped abruptly, and then, "Vivvie, don't look that way! What's the matter?"

"Mallory," she whispered. "What's to become of Mallory?"

"Who cares! He deserves no consideration. No, Vivvie, not one thought. He tricked us. Yes, tricked us both. He only wanted to get me out of the way. I see it all now. He bribed me so the coast would be clear for him with you."

"You took the bribe," she responded dully. But she didn't regret saying it; it had to be said.

Jamie's face twisted. "I explained all that! It happened so fast. And then I got mad at you. But now—"

"Now it's over."

"It's not over. You love me."

"If I love you, then it's a sinful love!" she suddenly cried.

"Don't talk that way!"

"Yes, Jamie, a sin! You know it, too. It's not only Mallory, it's the Church. No priest would marry us, and me divorced."

"Then we'll marry outside the Church."

"And be excommunicated?"

Jamie's jaw shot forward. "If need be."

A tremor rippled through her. "Oh, Jamie, don't say such a thing! Have you not been out to see the Illusions? Have you not seen Hell, and the devils dancing, and the snakes writhing over the lost souls in the fiery pit?"

"No, and I've not!" he exclaimed in fury. "Neither hellfire nor snakes nor devils have I seen. But I swear by God and all that's holy I'd rather live eternity in damnation than the rest of my days without you. And I'll not have any broadcloth bum tell me different."

Such shocking blasphemy brought Vivian to her feet. "Keep a civil tongue in your head, Jamie Fitzhugh! Yes," she continued wrathfully, "and turn your eyes and your heart to some other who can return the favor. I'm Mallory's now. I'm his wife and he loves me.'"

"And you love him?"

"That I do." .

"The way you love me?"

With a spring he was off the sofa. Pulling her to him, he bent her back over one arm and, forcing her face to his, brought his lips down on hers. Raising his head a moment, he looked deep into her eyes. "Well, well," he said tenderly, and once more covered her lips with his.

Shaken by the telltale ardor of her response, she ran from the house. Wrenching herself free of Jamie's grasp, she fled, refusing to let him accompany her, refusing to hear another word.

She was still almost running, as from perdition, through the slow-moving crowds in the hot St. Louis night. Oh, how wrong she had been to listen! How unwise to have heard him out! To have permitted the splinter of ice lodged deep within her to melt with understanding!

Yet, despite herself, happiness sang in her heart, and the heady vindication of her love swept in through the chinks and crannies of her soul, no matter that she fought against it. Oh, foolish to fight against it! Utterly useless! As well try not to breathe. But Mallory must not know. In this, at least, she must succeed. Please God, she prayed, don't let Mallory know. Don't let Mallory know, and I promise I'll never see Jamie again.

By the time she reached the Coliseum that evening, having first returned to the hotel to hastily change, with trembling hands, into a fresh white muslin skirt and blouse, twelve to fifteen thousand people jammed the vast arena, the delegates occupying what looked like a circus ring, and spectators filling the bleachers above.

Finding a seat, Vivian forced her attention upon the center of activity. Although she had arrived later than usual due to her tumultuous meeting with Jamie, she had no feeling of having missed anything, for the noise was so great it was next to impossible to follow the proceedings. Nor did she hope to catch more than a glimpse of Mallory in the multitude of sweltering, sweating masculinity milling about on the convention floor.

"They've just adopted the platform," a woman seated beside Vivian kindly volunteered. She smiled patiently, adding, "I guess that means another rendition of 'Hot Time in the Old Town.'"

And indeed it did, the band striking up and the delegates cakewalking through the aisles waving their banners, for with the adoption of the platform they would now, Vivian knew, put in nomination the names of the candidates for president.

"The Mallory men from the Keystone State declare it is all over but the shouting," said the headlines of the newspaper she carried. "Parker's nomination is expected tonight on the first or second ballot."

"We can't lose," Mallory had assured her in the early hours of the morning.

Red-eyed from lack of sleep, hoarse from hours of talking, he had stolen into their hotel bedroom with the dawn, cursing himself for stumbling against a chair.

"Six o'clock, Mallory!" she had cried, sitting up and glancing at her little gold-sheathed travel clock.

"Hush now, Puss. Don't let me be waking you."

"Have you been out all night?"

He sat heavily down on the bed beside her, brushing back the tendrils of hair clinging damply to her forehead. "It's that warm you are, Puss. Why not let me sponge you off with a bit of water?"

"And you needing your sleep?"

"I'll catch forty winks in a minute. The thing of it is, we've got the platform whipped into shape and a fight it was, what with trying to get in the Gold Plank. But that's neither here nor there, for we're finished at last."

Fully awake now, she said indignantly, "And you looking near ready to drop. It's you that's to have the sponge bath."

Over his protests, she insisted he undress and lie flat on his stomach on the bed. Pouring water from a pitcher into a basin that stood on the washstand, she dipped a washcloth into it, wrung it out, and, with towel in one hand, laved it over his great, sweating shoulders, gently patting dry as she went.

"You're that good to me, Puss," he murmured.

Smiling, she bent to kiss him, and discovered he had already fallen asleep.

How long ago morning seemed! she thought now, sitting high in the bleachers. And how unaware she had been, as she sponged Mallory's back, of all the day would hold in store for her.

Jamie . . .

Tears started to her eyes and she blinked them back, fiercely swallowing the lump in her throat. Judge Alton B. Parker, it appeared, had won on the first ballot. She fixed her attention firmly upon this, although the din was so great little could be heard. Mr. Davis was nominated to run with him, and with a final rousing chorus of "Dixie," the Democratic Convention of 1904 came to an end.

25

Upon her return from St. Louis, Vivian found a little pile of letters and messages awaiting her, neatly set out by Halls on the pretty japanned writing table in her bedroom. But contrary to her usual lively interest in the mail, she merely riffled through them, although she had spied a note from, oddly enough, Anthea Allenby, as well as an enticingly thick envelope from Gert Barkin in Newport.

"What's the matter, Puss?" asked Mallory, seeing her sway slightly as she thrust the lot aside. And in that moment a light-headedness seized her, the room spun round, and when she awakened she found herself lying in bed.

"You can expect the arrival along about February," said Dr. Cassidy, smiling down at her.

"A baby!" exclaimed Vivian. "I'm going to have a baby?"

"Yes, indeed," he assured her. "And now I'll be asking that husband of yours to step in so you can tell him. I don't believe I've ever seen a man so beside himself. Like to break down my door, he was, when he came after me. But he'll be pleased by the news no doubt."

In this last, Dr. Cassidy was mistaken.

"Aren't you happy about it?" asked Vivian in hurt bewilderment, gazing into her husband's stony face as he sat beside her on the bed.

"How can any man be happy about such an event, knowing the risks and the dangers?" he demanded. As always when upset and agitated, he rose to stride back and forth, his tread making the crystal vials and bottles tremble on her dressing table, setting, it seemed, everything in the room aquiver. "Only a poor dolt with neither sense nor imagination could be happy at receiving such news. Damn it, it's blaming myself I am for having got you in such a fix. And if I knew of a way—a good safe way, mind—to get you out of it, why, in a minute I'd do it."

"Mallory!" she cried, scandalized.

"I mean it, Puss."

"But don't you want children?"

"You're what I want. You."

Of this she had no doubt. At times the fierce intensity of his devotion leapt up like flames from a roaring furnace to illuminate the passionate depths of his soul, and at such times she was sobered by the awesome responsibility of such a love.

Engraved on her memory was the moment in the private drawing room of the train bearing them home from the convention in St. Louis. As it left the city and gathered speed, she had glanced up from her seat by the window to find Mallory in the narrow doorway, filling it with his massive presence, hands on either side of the doorjamb to brace himself. For seconds he stood there, swaying, silent, his eyes fixed upon her with a concentration so profound as to discomfit her.

"What is it?" she exclaimed. "What's the matter?"

"You're here," he said.

as to discomfit her.

"With him."

At the unvarnished truth of this, her heart bounded up in anguish and she turned from him.

"Ah, Puss," he cried, instantly beside her, "don't be cross! It's that harried I've been, each night coming back to the hotel thinking to find you gone and a note on my pillow; each morning asking myself, Is this the day? Not but what I wouldn't deserve it. It was wrong what I did to win you, and I wouldn't blame God for punishing me any way He might choose. Only not by taking you from me, for I couldn't stand that. Don't ever leave me, Vivvie. It would ruin me entirely. I can't do without you, Puss. I'd take a gun to my head, I swear it. It's as simple as that."

But when she had tried to assure him of her devotion, she knew he didn't believe her.

"Just don't ever leave me," he had said brusquely, and closed himself off to her in the way that he had.

Despite, however, the qualms Mallory felt about her pregnancy, his dark apprehensions that God might be sitting in judgment, pure joy filled Vivian at the prospect of a child.

Not for a moment did she doubt that all would go well, nor that her husband would adore the baby once it arrived. No shadow marred this happiness; no least twinge of regret, no touch of heartbreak flawed that sunny meadow to which her thoughts and fancies now persistently strayed.

Pleasure unalloyed, she would whisper to herself, smiling and hugging her stomach. She had no idea where she had heard this phrase, nor precisely what it meant, but it seemed to describe her feelings to perfection. Pleasure unalloyed.

This enchanted secret life growing within her gave her marriage to Mallory a new meaning and dimension. A bridge had been crossed, and there was no turning back to the person she once had been, even should she desire to do so.

It was this knowledge, perhaps, that sustained her when, a few days after Dr. Cassidy's visit, she happened to answer a tap at the front screen door to find Thurman Foy standing there.

"Mallory's at the Tipperary," she said, surprised that he wouldn't know this.

"I've come to see you."

Had she paled? she wondered, for a knowing smile curled under the small waxed mustache, lit the narrowly watchful eyes as, swift and sure, a foreboding seized her.

"Come in, then," she said, and reluctantly opened the door, hung his straw hat on the hall rack, and led the way into the front parlor.

The room was dark, and thunder rumbled in the distance with the sullen promise of a storm. On the massive center table, graced with a gold satin scarf heavily embroidered in Japanese design, a tall cut-glass vase of roses dispensed perfume that cloyed in the heavy air. No breeze stirred.

For another visitor Vivian would surely have lit one or two lamps, so easy to do these days with just the simple flick of a switch. But she had no desire to prolong this visit by implying a cordiality she didn't feel. Thurman Foy sat on a green velvet fauteuil, and seated opposite him, she found herself noticing how small his feet were in their sporty tan leather shoes. Small hands, too, with, she saw now, her heart leaping to her throat, an envelope in one of them.

Thurman had followed her gaze, almost, she thought, had felt the leap of her heart. Settling himself more comfortably, he raised one natty plaid leg and rested it, at the ankle, upon the knee of the other. Something in the utter insolence of this posture provoked Vivian into saying icily, "How can I help you?"

The thin smile returned. "It's more like how I can help you."

The white envelope dangling from his fingers urged caution. "And how might that be?" she inquired.

"I've heard from our mutual friend in St. Louis. He tells me he ran into you out there."

Oh how, fretted Vivian, could Jamie have done this? How chosen to confide in such a despicable little man? Briefly she considered denying the meeting. But she was not a devious person and possessed no talent for deception. "You mean Jamie Fitzhugh," she said.

"The same." He winked. "I guess you had a lot to talk about."

Vivian felt the blood rush to her face in a hot, guilty tide. He was playing with her, tormenting her like a cat with a mouse. Thurman Foy! A contemptible little weasel of a man who felt she thought too much of herself, had it in for her. "I'm sure you haven't come here just to tell me things I already know," she said scathingly.

"Ooh, now, don't get hoity-toity. I've brung you a message from your friend. It come in the mail just this morning and he asked me to make sure I delivered it to you *personal*. That's what he said: *personal*." He rose. "And that's what I'm doing."

Praying she wouldn't tremble, she took the envelope in both her hands. How thick, how heavy it was! How much he had written! How much he had to tell her!

She raised her eyes to Thurman. "How good of you," she breathed, and saw the tobacco-stained teeth that marked his smile. "Would you," she continued, "be kind enough to send my message in return?"

Triumph lit his eyes. "We aim to please."

"I won't be a moment," she said, rising.

"I ain't going nowhere."

"A moment, then," she told him and, moving serenely across the room, took a match from the painted tin box on the mantel. Dropping down swift as a bird before the dark fireplace, she struck the match. Instantly the blue-gold flame leaped upward, licking the letter she held above the grate, lapping it hungrily with voracious, racing little tongues, consuming it utterly.

She turned then, crouching like an animal, eyes blazing. "That's my message," she said. "Tell him what I've done. Tell him never to write to me again."

The letter, so quickly destroyed, proved not so easily forgotten. It teased her with the sentiments it might have conveyed, tormented her with the anguish of never knowing, of never hearing from him again.

Only you, Vivvie, he had said in that hot St. Louis night before she fled from him. *No one else. Not if I wait forever.*

More than once, consumed by longing, she had rushed to her writing table. But she was no longer the impulsive creature she once had been, and she replaced pen and paper, certain that cold silence was the best, the only course.

Mallory's happiness in their marriage and her own joy in the child she so eagerly awaited confirmed her in this decision. Nor were these her only considerations. Both Mamie Randall and Ma Mallory received the news of their first grandchild with Te Deums and a flurry of advice and novenas, while the Randall girls immediately purchased a sterling silver mug only waiting to be inscribed.

A boy would be named Matthew, after Mallory's father. But a girl—and in her heart Vivian was convinced that it was a girl she carried—a girl would be named after that woman whose exquisite manners and elegant ways had so charmed a little scullery maid on Cavendish Square. A girl would be christened Irene.

Vivian wrote to her father to tell him she was expecting. She wrote to him every week, long, chatty, loving letters filled with the things she felt he would like to hear, so far away from all of them in the mud and muck of the Klondike.

She wrote to describe Nancy and Neil's small wedding,

and to tell him Mallory had given Neil a job working to get laws passed about factory safety conditions. She wrote to tell him Mary Claire had moved into the front room of Mallory's house and begun the fall term at the Villa Maria Academy. She told him Bucky had a paper route after school, and that her mother liked sharing her house with her new daughter-in-law. Nancy proved eager to learn to sew and cook and do all the things Vivian was happy never to have to turn hand to again. Such enthusiasm flattered Mamie and, together with the girl's shy charm, completely won her. With a touch of envy, Vivian admitted Nancy got along better with her mother than she herself ever had.

There were things she didn't tell her father, of course. She didn't, for instance, tell him that her husband had been furious because Anthea Allenby had written a little note to ask if Vivian would wash and set her hair on the day of her marriage to Clinton Webb.

"What!" Mallory had thundered. "And is Miss Allenby thinking it's still a lady's maid you are?"

"No, now, Mallory, and it's not that at all," Vivian had answered placatingly. "It's only that she's got it into her head there is no one else who can do it so well. It's a grand compliment, really, and I'd very much like to oblige."

"Never!" cried Mallory. "Sure, it's an insult of the worst kind, and you may write and tell her I said so. Or maybe I should drive up to Cavendish Square and tell her myself."

It was all Vivian could do to persuade him otherwise. But the matter didn't rest there, for she believed this "insult" had confirmed him in the notion of making his presence felt in society.

"I want to give a grand reception for Sir Robbie and the Lady Langhorne," he announced at dinner one day.

Vivian's fork paused above her broiled lamb chop. "A reception, Mallory?"

He nodded. "Introduce him around. Sir Robbie needs to meet a few people who can be helpful to him with his investments. Besides," he added forthrightly, "is there many a man who can count a baron his very best friend? Not to mention your friendship with the Lady Langhorne."

"My friendship with the Lady Langhorne isn't as close as you seem to believe," said Vivian coolly.

"And that's your fault, Puss. Sure, she goes out of her way to be nice."

"So her brother will keep winning from you at cards."

"I'm thinking she knows nothing of that."

"Oh, Mallory, she must know!" cried Vivian in vexed exasperation at her husband's singular obtuseness where the Lady Langhorne was concerned. "Where does she think the money comes from that keeps them at Le Pierre?"

Le Pierre was one of the most fashionable hotels in the city, certainly not the address of impecunious guests. Yet the Baron of Chittendon and his sister had been living there for a month with, it appeared, no plans to move onward, or to return to England.

And why should they return? thought Vivian, her green eyes cynical. Two, sometimes three times a week, Sir Robbie dropped into the Tipperary to visit with Mallory in his private office in the back room. There he sipped framboise, the sweet raspberry liquor that Mallory unfailingly kept on hand for him, and told tales of English court life, of the sporting King Edward, of the Jockey Club in Paris, of races at Longchamp and Ascot and Epsom Downs— tales Mallory glowingly recounted to Vivian, and of which he seemed never to tire. There, too, as Vivian was well aware, Sir Robbie won at cards and, even more pertinently, gathered advice on those business enterprises upon which such winnings might best be spent.

While Sir Robbie visited the Tipperary, the Lady Langhorne as often as not took the opportunity to stop by Mallory's house in the smart little cabriolet they had hired and "look in" on Vivian. Lady Langhorne—"Tanis," as she insisted Vivian call her—confessed to loneliness and few acquaintances in "the States," and never failed to express the comfort she took in Vivian's friendship. But Vivian was finding it increasingly difficult to be cordial, suspecting, as she did, an interest based largely upon money.

However, when she mentioned this to Mallory, he only laughed. "Why, Puss, here I was thinking she had an eye for me, and that's the truth."

"Oh, you won't be serious," she declared, more irked than she cared to let on since she felt some credence might be placed in this view.

"You mean," he persisted, "you've never noticed how she flutters her lashes like so many butterflies, and gives me that bit of a look?" But not one to tease, he continued more soberly, "Let's say your surmise is correct. Let's say the Lady Langhorne is as penniless as her brother, and just as ready to put her friendship up for sale. My answer is that it's happy I am to buy, for I consider a lord and a lady good value and I mean to get my money's worth."

"Mallory!" gasped Vivian. "I'm shocked you'd admit such a thing."

He looked at her keenly. "It's more shocked you should be if I wouldn't. I'm no fool, Puss, to think such a one as Sir Robbie would value me just for myself. We both have our uses, me for him and him for me. I can well afford what I slip him at cards, plus the few tips on how best to use it. In return I get what I want."

"Which is what?"

"Why, I told you. To live in a certain way. That's what I'm after. To live in a certain way. It's been the goal of my life since I was ten years old and was made to go round to the back."

"The back door?"

"Yes, I was made to go round. That's the first time I knew there were those that thought me beneath 'em. And that's when I made up my mind. No back doors for me, Puss. Not anymore. I'm buying my way and happy to do it. It's only money, after all."

She drew in her breath as at blasphemy. Only money. Never would she get used to her husband's cavalier way with it, for all he must surely have so much. But she could understand very well about back doors, having gone in many a one herself, and so she said no more.

Nonetheless, she felt some qualms when, a few days later, he went off to order five hundred invitations to be engraved.

"Mother of God, Mallory!" she exclaimed. "Are you inviting all the Amity Clubs in the city?"

"Why, no, not a one," he replied. "It's not that type of affair."

"Then who do you think will come?"

"Why, everyone that's asked. Those that were at that weekend at Kimberly, for one thing."

Vivian recalled the frozen faces of the Kimberly ladies, and her heart sank. "They'll not come because they want to, only because they must."

"No, Puss, I'm thinking you're wrong there. When people receive an invitation requesting their presence in the Grand Ballroom of the Bellevue Stratford to honor the Lady Langhorne and the Baron of Chittendon, I'm thinking they'll be wanting to come."

Mallory was to be proved correct. In the flood of wealth that poured like a golden tide over the country, people of means wished to put their humble origins as far behind them as possible. This resulted in an emphasis on fine clothes, luxurious furnishings, and the fussy, time-consuming formalities that marked the lady and gentleman and set them safely apart from the lower classes from which they so recently had come.

The desire for social prominence grew into a mania, and in the frantic climb up the social ladder any least acquaintance with royalty was avidly sought. Mallory's reception, therefore, promptly found its way into the society pages, where, thanks to the glamour of the royal guests of honor, it was heralded as a major event of the new social season. Far from being loath to attend, as Vivian had feared, everyone in Philadelphia apparently wanted to come.

"So how come Harry and me haven't got an invitation yet?" demanded Gert Barkin.

They sat, just the two of them, in the little sewing room on the second floor, one of Vivian's favorite spots these days, busy as she was with making things for the baby. In her hands was a small cream-colored silk sack she was hemming with tiny, careful stitches. "I'll have to speak to Miss Vernon," she murmured, knowing full well the Barkins weren't on Mallory's list.

"Who the hell is Miss Vernon?"

Over the summer Vivian had forgotten how vulgar Gert could be. "She's my social secretary."

"Social secretary! You can tell her for me she must be some social secretary if she forgets to invite your very best friend."

As always, Vivian was put off by this assumption. And as always, she decided to ignore it. From the three bay windows that formed an alcove in the room, sunlight streamed in upon her slender shoulders. It felt warm and good.

"Do you like doing that?" asked Gert suddenly.

Something wistful in the question made Vivian look up from her sewing. "Why, yes. I love to make things for her."

"Hah! Already she knows it's a girl!"

"With skin as white as snow," said Vivian, her smile deepening, "lips as red as blood, hair as black as ebony."

"Snow White." Gert nodded, the nest of frizzy curls on top of her head bobbing approvingly. "No kiddin', I bet

that's just who she'll look like. For instance, look how black
Mallory's hair is. Jet black. And I'll bet you're right. She'll
be a girl. What will you call her?"

"Irene."

"Irene Mallory. I like it. I really do. I bet she grows up
to be quite a dame."

"She's going to be a lady, Gert," said Vivian, surprising
herself by the intensity that quivered in her throat. "She's
going to have everything I never had. Good schools, pretty
clothes. Everything."

"I believe it. She's gonna be a lucky kid. You're gonna
be a good mother, I can tell." She laughed. "Now me! Any
poor kid that got me would pull a real clinker. Which is
why it's good I can't get pregnant."

Vivian stopped sewing. "Gert, you can't?"

"Nope. Me and Harry have tried everything."

"Gert!" cried Vivian softly.

"Oh, what the hell!" cut in Gert sharply. "But hey," she
exclaimed, brightening, "how about making us the godparents of Snow White?"

26

Vivian would have been hard pressed to say which riled
Mallory the more: her insistence that Gert and Harry receive an invitation to the reception for Sir Robbie and his
sister, or the impulsive promise she had made to Gert that
the Barkins would be godparents to his child.

The Barkins, he raged, weren't the type he had in mind
for godparents. No, not the type at all. Not an ounce of
refinement between them. Why, if the good Lord should
call him before the child was raised, he'd never have a
moment's peace lying beneath the sod.

He was mollified only when struck by the recollection
that the Barkins were not Roman Catholic. "And so," he
cried, jubilant, "they'll not do after all."

Belatedly Vivian realized he was quite right, the laws

of the Church being such that only those within the Faith could stand in the parents' stead. But this turn of affairs served only to make her adamant that Gert and Harry be invited to the reception. "Or I'll not go," she told him, eyes flashing. "Mark my words, Mallory. I'll not go."

A handsome engraved invitation went off to the Barkins that very day. But there were those who wouldn't receive one.

"Such a fuss!" grumbled Ma Mallory. "Why, you'd think it was a reception for the King of England the way everyone's going on. Making himself more enemies than friends out of it, that's what he's doing. Making himself more enemies than friends. But you tell him for me I'll thank him to send an invitation to Dolly Muldoon for her and her intended."

Though she saw her son at the Tipperary every day of her life, Ma Mallory had developed the habit of passing on her less welcome requests and observations through her daughter-in-law.

"Oh, Ma," sighed Vivian, "you always think I can get him to do things I can't."

"And if you can't, who can? You're the only one that's ever been able to sway him. I give thanks to God for the day you were married."

Remembering a certain bribe of ten thousand dollars, Vivian said crisply, "You weren't all that thankful in the beginning."

"Well, there now, that's all in the past, and we'll let bygones be bygones. It's a fine wife you've made him, and I'm the first to say so."

They sat in the small, elegant back parlor, where a coal fire offered comfort against the rainy Sunday afternoon while gusts of wind rattled the windows and shook leaves from the trees. Mallory had long since departed to make a speech urging Judge Alton B. Parker for president. With the November election just one month away, he seemed always to be off making a speech somewhere.

"Is His Lordship with him again today?" inquired Ma sardonically.

"I believe Mallory went to pick him up at Le Pierre. He's interested in our elections. He says they're different from his own country."

"Hmph!" sniffed Ma. "And when is he going to pick up and go back to his own country, him and his sister both?"

"Not for some time, I'm afraid."

"Just like my father, Mallory is," said Ma, nodding darkly above the baby blanket she was crocheting. "Just like my father, wanting always to run with the gentry and neglecting his own kind. Then one fine day didn't a new man come along and in no time at all wasn't my father's practice góne entirely? And it can happen again in this family. Indeed it can, it can happen again."

"Oh, Ma," murmured Vivian, for how many times had she not heard this tale?

But Ma continued more vigorously. "Yes, indeed. And something else, something I've never told you, something I've not told a soul."

She stopped abruptly and cocked her head heavenward as though seeking divine guidance. Having apparently received direction, she gave a tight little nod and fastened her eyes upon Vivian. "There was a gentleman I once knew, now dead," she said. "Brady, his name was, may his soul rest in peace. This was after my Matt died that we were friendly. And it was him that took my boy in hand, for no woman could manage him.

"Not that he was mean, now," she hastily amended. "My son hasn't a mean bone in his body, even if I'm his mother saying it. But stubborn then as he is to this day, and needing a man set over him; feeling the lack of a father and needing a man to take an interest, which Brady did as a kindness to me."

She dropped her eyes, and a painful flush suffused the strong features. "Brady was a married man with his own family to look after, but he brought Mallory up and taught him and watched over him and made him his right-hand man.

"He got him elected our district leader, which he holds to this day as you well know. Only three thousand Democratic votes it took to elect him, the same as now. And you may say district leader isn't much of a job, and for sure you'd be right. But what it did, don't y' see, was put Mallory on the county committee of the Amity Club, and that was his start.

"It was as a favor to me Brady did it. Not that he didn't see talent in my boy. But it was a favor to me that gave him his start in the district. And if I did wrong, why then, it was in a good cause. It was in a good cause that I did it. And now you know why it pains me to see my son neglect what he's been given. Now you can see, I betrayed my dead husband for the good of my son. You can see the cost of it."

Vivian studied the downcast, penitent head. How much to believe? How much to believe of this outrageous, wily old woman who still wore black, but whether out of mourning or an inherited sense of drama, who could say? And had Ma shown nothing but gratitude to the popular Brady? Left a widow in her thirties, still passionate, still young, had she expressed only gratitude? Or, to so devout a Catholic, was her son's welfare the devious but necessary excuse?

Whatever the reason, there could be no doubt that the young Mallory had benefited from the alliance. But things were different now, thought Vivian, and for all Ma seemed not to realize it, her son's influence extended far beyond the South Philadelphia wards over which Big Bill Brady had once held sway.

Vivian was well aware that there had been a change in her husband's fortunes. From the day of his speech about fire laws after the Wearever Waist Company fire, he had been taken up by two new and disparate groups of people. On the one hand were the Quakers. Discreetly wealthy, quietly powerful, from the time of Willian Penn they had constituted the social conscience of the city, and they now invited Mallory to address their committees, to speak at forums, engage in debate. On the other hand, and of even greater significance, the struggling labor unions had heeded his call for cooperation, and hailed him as a champion of their cause. As a result, Brian Mallory had become a powerful figure, not only in Philadelphia, but in the highest councils of the Democratic party.

None of this had Vivian learned from her husband. Like all men of the day, he didn't discuss such matters with his wife. As closemouthed about political affairs as he was about his myriad financial dealings, he spoke little of such concerns, and Vivian wouldn't have thought of asking questions that were deemed none of a wife's business.

However, her green eyes were as alert as ever they were when she was a little lady's maid, her ears as sharp, and it was surprising how much information she was able to pick up and fit together. She would agree with Ma, for instance, that Mallory had put some noses out of joint. But she would wager that this had more to do with a split in the party over a young congressman named Anthony Frazzio than with invitations to a reception.

"Was Tony Frazzio on the platform with you?" she asked Mallory that evening.

"He said he was going to show and he didn't," replied Mallory, and added, "So to hell with him."

"People like Tony Frazzio, Mallory."

"He's just a cocky kid."

"People like him all the same. They understand his position."

"He's not loyal."

Nothing, Vivian knew, could be more damning in Mallory's eyes than this. Anything could be forgiven, overlooked, winked at except disloyalty.

Staunchly faithful himself, a man of his word regardless of the cost, in order to keep a promise Mallory would go to lengths Vivian had sometimes marveled at. She didn't realize that it was just this absolute fidelity that characterized the political boss. With nowhere else to turn, people were forced to rely upon this most paternal of urban figures. Venal he might be, tolerant of vice and corruption, but he could be counted on to take care of his own in whatever way was needed. He never forgot either a promise or a favor, and he asked only one thing in return: unquestioning, undeviating loyalty.

Now, having returned from his own loyal speechmaking soaked by the chill October rain, Mallory sat at the kitchen table over the late supper she had fixed for him, tie loosened, shirt collar open, curly black hair glistening and damp.

"It's good, Puss," he said of the steaming bowl of pepper pot soup and freshly baked milk biscuits. "Real good."

Following, as she meticulously did, the practices learned during her days in the Webb household, she regularly let the servants go off after the long midday meal on Sunday. Ma Mallory, having spent the afternoon, went back to her own house toward dusk, and Mary Claire seemed always to have plans of some sort. This left Vivian alone with Mallory on Sunday evenings, and she discovered she liked having the house just to themselves.

Especially did she enjoy being in the kitchen, although she knew Mallory preferred the formal elegance of the dining room. She loved this big, warm room filled, tonight, with the delicious aroma of baked biscuits and freshly made coffee. Everything winked and gleamed: the blue and white diamond-patterned linoleum, the silver nickeled handles on the big, shiny range, the polished wood of the kitchen cabinet with its built-in flour sifter and bins for storing coffee and sugar, its compartments and shelves and drawers. And every one of them—oh, the wonder of it!— every one of them filled with the choicest items O'Reilly's Market could provide.

Thinking of O'Reilly's, she said, stirring the coffee in her cup, "Ma says she'd thank you to send an invitation to Tom O'Reilly and Dolly Muldoon."

"And I'll not do that."

"Mallory!" she gasped in surprise, for though he might grumble at his mother's many requests and directions, Vivian had never known him to refuse a one.

"Well, I'll not," he repeated, fixing her with a look before which she had seen others quail.

Displeasure glinted in his eyes, and the day's growth of beard lay like a blue-black shadow along the outthrust jaw. Surely he must have found the afternoon in the cold and wet a penance, but he gave no sign of this. An animal strength emanated from him, implicit in the strong, thick neck, the massive shoulders, the hands with their immaculate square cut fingernails that were so unequivocally masculine despite a weekly manicure.

"Young O'Reilly is part of Frazzio's crowd," he continued. "He tried to tell me his friend Tony is afraid he won't win reelection if he sticks with the party too close."

"And likely he won't."

"Then let him go it alone," snapped Mallory. "Let him go it alone."

Vivian considered the bits of gossip she had heard. "He just might win on his own, Mallory. Yes, he just might win if he can separate himself away from Judge Parker. Why," she added, "you told me yourself Judge Parker is bound to lose."

"Told you in private, Puss," said Mallory warningly. "In confidence, don't forget."

"But all the same . . ."

"All the same, you're right. Parker can't win against Roosevelt. I'm not sure anyone could win against such a man. But that's neither here nor there," he observed, impatiently brushing aside this consideration as though it were an annoying gnat.

"The point is," he continued flatly, "the point is that the Democratic party nominated Judge Alton B. Parker for president, and it behooves the Honorable Anthony Frazzio to stand up and support him."

"Even if it means he might lose his seat in the Congress?"

"Those are the rules, Puss. Every party man knows you got to support the party no matter what. Even if it means you lose, you got to support the party because your turn will come again, and the party will remember your loyalty and be right there to help you. You got to bear in mind that without the party organizing things, where would you be? Without the party, where would Tony Frazzio be?" He stopped eating and stared off, cold contempt in the stunningly blue eyes.

"I made Tony Frazzio," he said. "He was nothing, a nobody. I picked him out of nowhere because he was young and bright and I liked him. I worked my tail off to get people to remember his name." An angry flush suffused the darkly handsome features. "I sat him in the damn Congress of the United States! *I* did, nobody else. And now he can't make one lousy speech for Judge Parker, after me promising he'll be there? Now he leaves me sitting up on that platform in the rain beside an empty chair? Now he embarrasses me before all those people? Before the Baron of Chittendon? Letting everybody think Brian Mallory can't deliver on his word? Christ!" He slammed his fist down on the table, making the dishes rattle.

"But one thing sure," he continued quietly, "one thing sure: this is one election the Honorable Anthony Frazzio is going to lose."

He smiled suddenly, and it was as though some other person had inhabited his body, some dark, dangerous, inconsolable creature, and now he was returned to it again.

"I don't want any more supper," he said.

He rose and moved around the table to stand behind her chair, and she felt him slide his hands down under the deep V of her collar to capture her breasts.

She leaned back against him and looked up to meet his eyes.

"I could use a little loving, Puss," he said. "Let's go to bed."

27

Perhaps, Vivian was to think later, she should have paid more heed to Mallory's grim prediction that Anthony Frazzio would lose the election. She might at least have wondered how he could be so sure. But her attention that night was abruptly diverted to her sister Mary Claire.

Just before going to sleep, Mallory said, "By the way, where is your sister?" And when Vivian replied that Mary Claire was spending the weekend with a new friend from the Villa Maria Academy, he added, "Well, you ought to keep a better eye on her. I hear she spends a lot of time at Lawson's Music Store when she should be in school."

At this news Vivian's eyes flew wide open even as Mallory turned on his side and went soundly to sleep. Hands resting lightly on the gentle swell of her stomach, she stared into the darkness. How did it happen that Mary Claire spent time at Lawson's when she was supposed to be in school? Vivian didn't for a moment doubt the accuracy of Mallory's information, but how, she asked herself, was this possible?

From all accounts, the days of the young women who attended the Villa Maria Academy were full and busy from the time they arose at six-thirty in the morning to attend mass in the school's chapel, until lights out at nine o'clock each night. Vivian had listened unmoved to Mary Claire's tearful complaints about this regimen, and to the girl's exasperation with the close surveillance the students received: the notes required from home for permission to visit the dentist, to go shopping; to, in short, leave the well-cared-for, stately grounds of the Villa Maria for any purpose whatever. It was only on weekends, from Friday afternoon until Sunday evening, that, released into the custody of their parents, the girls had any freedom at all. And it was these weekends that Mary Claire had taken to spending with her friend Drucie Stella.

Filled with unease, Vivian realized that she had never met Drucie and knew nothing about Mary Claire's visits to Lawson's Music Store. Mallory was right. She should have been keeping a better eye on the girl. She would correct this oversight the very next day.

The Villa Maria Academy resembled a small castle. Once the home of a wealthy and devout elderly spinster, it had been bequeathed to the elite order of nuns who ran it as a private school for young ladies.

To reach it one rode out along the Schuylkill River, leaving this pleasant, winding drive at a place called East Falls to climb steeply upward past a brewery in whose beer garden boisterous catfish and waffle parties were held each summer, past a carpet mill with its rows of windows deeply set into a drab gray stone facade, and thence past working-class houses that stretched ever upward cheek by jowl. At the summit, the land seemed to heave a sigh of relief and spread itself out in broad lawns guarded by high wrought-iron fences, dotted with tall trees and graced with abodes worthy of those captains of industry who owned the mills and breweries below.

Driven by Bunty O'Hare up to the school's imposing front door, Vivian alighted from the carriage and with some diffidence mounted the stone steps.

She had taken special care with her costume, at pains to conceal a "condition" that soon would be so apparent as to keep her at home. Indeed, it was just this consideration that lent a special urgency to her mission, for in a few weeks it would be improper for her to go about in public. But under the most severe scrutiny before her pier glass that morning, she had concluded she didn't really "show" as yet. Too, the clever style of her navy blue voile suit, the top of which was trimmed with folds of fine white lawn, diverted the eye, as did, she felt, the navy blue leghorn hat trimmed with white daisies that perched upon her upswept hair.

Together with attending to her ensemble, she had given the utmost consideration as to how she would comport herself—or rather, how Irene Webb might comport herself upon such an occasion. Therefore, when she stepped into the foyer and a fresh-faced little nun glided from an anteroom to greet her, she said in cultivated tones, "I'm Mrs.

Brian Mallory. I wonder if I might possibly have a word with my sister, Mary Claire Randall."

Most certainly Mrs. Mallory could, the little nun informed her. Would she just step into the reception room and have a chair?

Vivian sank down upon a divan upholstered in rose colored petit point as, with a gentle clicking of the rosary beads that depended from the waist of her habit, the nun excused herself and disappeared.

How serene everything was, thought Vivian, looking about her. And polished to a fare-thee-well. October sunlight sifted through spotless, deeply hemmed white curtains that hung before tall gleaming windows. A coal fire burned behind a fender of burnished brass, and a perfume combined of beeswax laced with the suggestion of incense, most likely from the chapel, filled the air.

Classes must be in progress, Vivian decided, her heart racing with the excitement of being in so scholarly a place. Classes must be in progress, for voices floated to her, young voices speaking in unison, chanting things she would never know. Might it be Latin? French? Or the recitation of poetry. Shakespeare, perhaps. Shakespeare was one of the few great writers she knew of, although she couldn't have named anything he wrote.

Mary Claire, of course, would know. Or if she didn't know right now, she soon would, thanks to Mallory for generously paying the academy's shockingly high fee. A smile caught Vivian's lips, and she touched her stomach. And Irene would know. Irene would read all the books, learn all the languages, do all the things Vivian had never done. Oh yes, Irene would know.

"Mrs. Mallory?" said a voice at once so quiet yet so filled with command that, snatched from her reverie, Vivian sprang to her feet.

"Ma'am?" she replied instantly, and for all the world like a guilty parlormaid caught malingering.

"My dear, I didn't mean to startle you," said the nun, and in that moment Vivian had the feeling that all her thoughts were known to this woman, all her vanities, her wearying pretenses.

"Do please sit down. I'm Mother Marie de Chantel. I'm the Superior of our school."

Vivian sank back down on the divan. The Reverend

Mother's voice was like a musical instrument, deep and sweet as a viola, a cello. Sheer goodness informed the face framed by the starched white guimpe that seemed to cut like a knife into the flesh.

"You've come to speak to Mary Claire," she said. "But of course she's never here at this hour on Mondays and Thursdays. She goes to the conservatory for her lessons in piano and music theory."

"The conservatory," repeated Vivian.

Reverend Mother nodded. "We feel so fortunate in having one of our girls accepted there. Particularly Mary Claire because . . ." She hesitated and added, "I'm sorry to tell you we feel your sister isn't happy here."

"She isn't?" said Vivian, wondering how anyone could fail to be happy in such surroundings.

"She seems not to get on with the other girls. We believe she doesn't enjoy being with them, doesn't enjoy being here. Certainly it's too early to draw any conclusions. The school year has only just begun, and it takes a while for a new girl to feel comfortable. But she has made only one friend, Druscilla Stella, a new girl, too, and not very academically inclined, I'm sorry to say."

"I see," replied Vivian, her brain whirling with questions she would never put to this good and trusting woman.

Reverend Mother smiled. "Of course, there is her wonderful aptitude for the piano. As I wrote in answer to your letter, we are happy to cooperate in fostering such God-given talent. One of our girls is fortunate to be studying mural painting twice weekly with Miss Violet Oakley at her studio, and two others take regular classes at the Pennsylvania Academy of Fine Arts. It has been quite simple to arrange Mary Claire's Mondays and Thursdays at the conservatory. With our Mr. Clafferty and his ability to drive our splendid new motor bus, it's been possible to arrange such things."

Anger, cold, hard, and unforgiving, shook Vivian. She could see it all now: the scheme, the forged letter requesting permission to study at the conservatory, even the letter written by the Reverend Mother in return, intercepted for Mary Claire by, in all likelihood, the slow-witted downstairs maid, Peggy Garvey, willing to keep an eye on the daily mail in return for a bit of change.

"Mrs. Mallory, are you all right?" asked the nun in sudden alarm.

"Thank you, Reverend Mother, I'm fine," replied Vivian.

But inside she was seething. She could scarcely wait to lay hands on Mary Claire.

"But I told you I didn't want to go to that school!" cried Mary Claire, tears streaming. "I told you that from the beginning!"

"And why would you not?" demanded Vivian, white-faced with fury as she confronted her sister in the girlish bedroom on the second floor front of Mallory's house.

Upon leaving the Villa Maria she had told Bunty O'Hare to drive to Lawson's Music Store. Arriving there, she directed him to go inside and summarily fetch the truant out. Surprise, guilt, and outraged dignity had followed in tumultuous succession across Mary Claire's pretty face, reducing her at last to this tearful laying of blame.

"Why would you not want to go to such a fine place, I'm asking?" persisted Vivian in enraged bafflement, forgetting the delicate inflections that had so recently graced her speech. "Why would you not? Would you be telling me that?"

"Because I like playing the piano at Lawson's, where there's fun and larking about."

"And is there no fun and larking at the Academy?"

"I don't like those tony girls."

"You don't know them."

"Yes, I do! Except for Drucie, they're all stuck up!" In tearful mimicry she pressed onward. " 'Oh, do play "The Muthic Box Waltz." It's too dee-vine! Oh, do let me hear a bit of "After the Ball." It's thimply devastating!' "

"They don't all talk like that," responded Vivian, giggling despite herself.

"They do!" insisted Mary Claire, much encouraged. "And when their beaus come to tea it's even worse!" Fluttering her eyelids she trilled, " 'Oh, Jack, I must hear "Heart's Desire." Oh, dear me, I think I may thwoon!' "

"You won't feel this way when you turn sixteen and have a beau of your own."

"Pooh, I could have plenty of beaus right now if I'd a mind to. And not like their Jacks. My friends are more larky."

Vivian could easily believe how larky they might be. Lawson's catered to low show-business types who hung around the music store trying out new material on the piano, trading gossip of shows, auditions. How happy she had been to rescue her young sister from such unwholesome associations.

"In time you'll make friends with the young ladies at the Villa Maria," she said firmly. "Don't turn your face against them."

Mary Claire's small round chin shot forward and her lower lip trembled. From childhood, this pitiable tremble could pierce Vivian to the heart. It still moved her. But she couldn't let Mary Claire turn from all that the bright future offered. She couldn't, and she wouldn't.

"It's easy enough to find things not to one's liking if one sets out to do so," she continued severely. "But I'll not see you back playing the piano at Lawson's and frittering away your best chances. You have a fine opportunity. I mean you to make the most of it."

"I don't want to make the most of it!" protested Mary Claire, bursting into fresh hysterics. "I don't care about fine opportunities!"

"You'll feel differently in time."

"I won't. I never will!"

"Just wait and see."

"I won't wait and see! I hate that school! I won't go back to it!"

"You will!" countered Vivian, swift anger seizing her at such blind obstinacy. "You'll go back, or you'll leave this house!"

"I'll leave this house!" cried the girl, and dashed headlong from the room.

As though slapped, Vivian stood transfixed. Then she recovered her senses. "No, wait!" she implored, rushing after her sister. Tears filled her eyes, all but blinding her. "Come back!" she begged, starting down the stairs. "Come back, Mary Claire!"

She felt her foot catch in the hem of her skirt, felt herself step out into air, and then plummet downward.

The baby wouldn't be harmed by the fall, Dr. Cassidy assured her. Nature took better care than that, he said. The baby would be born right as rain, but she must stay off her feet as much as possible and avoid going up and down stairs.

Lying on the chaise longue in her bedroom, Vivian had

no trouble accepting this opinion. Somehow she felt sure
the child would be healthy and all would be well. But Mallory was beside himself.

"I'd begun to want it!" he said, as though charging himself with some incomprehensible lapse of judgment. "I'd begun to believe everything would be all right."

"Everything will, Mallory," she told him.

He was not convinced. "The risk to you now," he said
distractedly, shaking his head, pacing back and forth before her. "The risk! As for your sister . . . ! Never is she
to set foot in this house again!"

Alone, Vivian recalled these harsh words, and tears
flowed out from under closed eyelids to roll unheeded
down her cheeks. If only she hadn't lost her temper . . .
If only she had calmly reasoned with Mary Claire . . . If
only, if only.

"Now, girl, don't be torturing yourself." It was Mamie
Randall come to visit. "Your sister is back in her own
home where she belongs. It was wrong, I'm thinking now,
to try to make her into a lady. How could she get along
with those girls and them raised so grand and used to
everything, and her with nothing at all?"

Maybe mama is right, thought Vivian, remembering her
own snubs from the Kimberly ladies. It's too late for me,
for all Mallory believes to the contrary. And it's too late for
Mary Claire. But my Irene will start out on the right foot.
Irene will start right from the beginning. It won't be too
late for her.

"Does Mary Claire hate me, mama?" she asked.

Mamie sighed. "It's herself that she hates, blaming herself for what's happened."

The tears that seemed always just beneath the surface
welled up in Vivian's eyes. "I don't want her to. It was my
fault. Will you tell her it was my fault and that I'm sorry?
So sorry, mama."

"I will." The firm, cool hand pressed upon Vivian's forehead, bringing a world of comfort. "Everything will come
right once the child is born. You'll see. This time will be
forgotten and we'll all be happy together again."

Moving cautiously down the upper hall to stand in the
doorway of Mary Claire's deserted bedroom, Vivian found
it hard to believe this. Why had it gone so wrong when she
had wanted everything to go right so badly? How pretty
and inviting the room looked, sunlight falling upon the

brass bed dressed in its dainty white plissé counterpane. An embroidered pink organdy scarf covered the top of the birdseye maple chest, and in one corner stood a large armoire. But dresses no longer peeked from out it, and no stockings or ribbons spilled from half-open bureau drawers.

Hattie Flanagan had packed up all of Mary Claire's things, and Bucky arrived with his express wagon to cart them back to Mamie's small house. No careless girlish habits marred the room's perfection. Looking at the fruitwood rocker upholstered in pink silk, at the garlanded Aubusson carpet, the mantel above the fireplace with the dainty figurines of shepherd and shepherdess, Vivian felt tears rush to her eyes.

Due to her confinement, her presence at the coming reception for Lady Langhorne and the Baron of Chittendon was of course proscribed. Mallory had wanted to cancel the affair entirely, and it was only upon her insistence that it was to go forward as planned.

"But my heart won't be in it, Puss," he told her. "How can I take any pleasure and you not there?"

She knew that more than ever he was feeling the shadow of the avenging angel, ready to punish him for the way he had gotten her from Jamie Fitzhugh. It did no good to tell him she felt life stirring within her and that if they were just careful and patient all would be well. He spent every available moment with her in their bedroom, into which a cot for him had been placed.

"Suppose I should roll over against you in the night," he said when she protested this arrangement. "Why, I'd not sleep a wink for fear of hurting you."

He slept poorly anyhow, and often she would be awakened in the early hours by his restless turning and thrashing about. Not only, she knew, was this occasioned by the superstitious unease he suffered in regard to her condition, but by the increasingly frenetic pace of the approaching election. Cursing the rallies, the meetings that took him from her side, he nonetheless shouted himself hoarse in behalf of Judge Alton B. Parker.

"But it's going pell-mell in Roosevelt's favor," he would tell her upon returning from these sorties. "Nothing can stop that man."

It wasn't *that* man, however, that Mallory cared about stopping. It wasn't, Vivian knew, Theodore Roosevelt who kindled that implacable blue gleam in the depths of his eyes. It was Anthony Frazzio.

For her part, she rather enjoyed being indulged and fussed over by Mallory and everyone else. Only the rift with Mary Claire cast a shadow upon days that never failed to bring a pleasant little surprise—a bouquet of flowers from an unexpected source, a little note, a visit. Wearing a becoming negligee and seated among the pillows of her chaise longue as Hattie Flanagan brushed and dressed her hair, she would wonder what new delight the day might hold in store. Her bedroom at times resembled a garden, so many were the plants and flowers that arrived, frequently sent by friends of Mallory's, people she had never met.

With a sharp eye and a nod of the head he took careful note of these kindly expressions as well as the avalanche of letters and cards that poured in. Each morning as soon as the postman stopped by, Halls would carry the mail up to Vivian on the silver mail tray and Mallory would sit by her side, reading each and every message before leaving for the Tipperary.

It was thus that Vivian's fingers, eagerly sorting through the pile one sunny morning, jerked to a halt and her breath caught as she came upon a letter from Jamie Fitzhugh. It was addressed not to her but to her husband—a long white envelope with, in the upper left-hand corner, his name and return address c/o Mathews in St. Louis, Missouri.

As she stared down at it her throat constricted, and all pleasure drained from the crisp October day. In the fireplace a coal fire continued to blaze brightly. Sunlight streamed through the lace curtains, and a sleek gray Miss Prim, come to call less for sociability than to seek the broad band of golden warmth that fell across the flowered carpet, lay stretched out in trustful oblivion.

Around her the house hummed just as usual. Hattie Flanagan had carried off her breakfast tray with its blue and white Meissen-ware chocolate pot. She could hear Mrs. Doughty scolding Peg Garvey down in the front parlor and Maureen running the sweeper in the upper hall. From the kitchen came a muffled pounding that meant the butcher boy had arrived from O'Reilly's with the veal for dinner and Clarissa was readying it for breaded cutlets. From outside, the bustling presence of the city insinuated itself reassuringly. Everything, in fact, was usual, peaceful, pleasant, except her wildly fluttering heart.

What, oh what, might the letter contain? More than once she had considered telling Mallory about seeing Jamie in St. Louis. Each time she had decided against it, as much to keep the memory of that precious final meeting hers alone as to spare Mallory any pain he might feel. Surely, she told herself now, Jamie wouldn't attempt to effect through Mallory what he had been unable to achieve through her—namely, a recognition of their love that would lead to a dissolution of her marriage. More likely the letter had something to do with business, with the investment in Jamie's invention that Mallory had made. But though her quick wits fixed upon this as the logical reason, it was all she could do to keep her voice from shaking as she said, "You have a letter from St. Louis from Jamie Fitzhugh."

"From Fitzhugh, is it?" said Mallory, and, taking it from her, slit the envelope with his thumb. "Well, he's sold his formula," he told her, scanning it. "Yes, sold his formula, he has, and looks on his way to being a wealthy man. Twenty-five thousand down, and royalties. He encloses the agreement I'm to sign to get my share."

Vivian felt such a rush of vertigo that she was grateful she was lying on the chaise longue. The invention sold! The bright promise realized! Everything they had hoped for, talked about on countless winter evenings, summer afternoons—all their dreams come true!

The rip of paper, sharp, crisp, final, startled her. She looked up to see that Mallory had torn the contents of the envelope in two.

"In the name of God, what have you done?" she gasped.

"Fitzhugh doesn't owe me anything," said Mallory, eyeing her keenly. "I've already got my share."

28

In the days that followed, Vivian began leading a double life.

There was her daily outward existence wherein she pursued her usual activities—sewing clothes for the baby, entertaining visitors in the pretty bedroom that, having acquired additional chairs and hassocks, doubled as a sitting room, arranging menus, consulting with Halls or Mrs. Doughty on household affairs.

But during the many hours she perforce must spend alone, she lived more fancifully in vivid daydreams. And lived so happily that she must hide her annoyance when someone dispelled this imaginary world by entering the room.

The dream she dreamed never varied. It commenced on that late spring evening when, seeking Jamie, she had flown down the alleyway to Morrissey's blacksmith shop. But from this point reality was forsaken in favor of a more satisfactory construction. Much less begging Jamie to take her to St. Louis with him, in her dream she spurred him on alone, content to await his return. In her dream, they exchanged letters, his always as thick as that letter he had sent by way of Thurman Foy, that letter she had burned without opening, whose contents she now achingly longed to know.

They were filled with love and yearning, these letters, and of plans for their future together, as were the ones she wrote to him. As though a dam had burst, outpourings of tenderness gushed from her heart in flights of fancy that momentarily assuaged her anguish but left her, when reality swept back in, completely hopeless, with unshed tears thick in her throat and a head that throbbed.

As a result of this double life, this blissful imaginary existence and the frustration of her true position, she became frequently short-tempered, abrupt, unlike herself. With the

servants she was often sharp and demanding, hating herself
for the kind of mistress she had become, trying to make up
for curt ways by being overly lenient, granting little favors
that should not be granted, overlooking things that should
have been done. With Ma Mallory and Mamie she was
tearful and querulous in the face of their baffled concern.
She listened to Mallory with only half an ear when he
came home from his speechmaking, glad his only touch
was a light kiss on the forehead, glad he slept on a cot
instead of beside her in bed.

The dream had become infinitely more absorbing than
the workaday world. She would pull it like a blanket over
her head, snuggling down into it with a smile on her lips.
Everything in the dream arranged itself to her satisfaction.
Any guilt she might have felt regarding Mallory was
evaded by imagining him conveniently married to Dolly
Muldoon.

She didn't bother her head about who might then be
paired with Thomas O'Reilly. Mallory was happy with
Dolly, leaving her free to marry Jamie Fitzhugh. This she
did, walking down the aisle to him in St. Bonaventure's
just as they had planned. The dream enthralled her so completely, she slipped off into it so frequently, that reality
paled, and at times it seemed even the child she carried
must be Jamie's.

"You look queer," Gert Barkin told her, stopping by one
day. "Your eyes look funny. What ails you?"

"Nothing ails me!" countered Vivian.

"Well, don't take my head off."

"I'm sorry, Gert," she apologized, truly contrite. "I guess
maybe I'm tired of this room."

"I don't blame you," said Gert promptly, quick to forgive.

She had driven down from her house on Broad Street to
ask Vivian's opinion as to what gown she should wear to
the reception for Lady Langhorne and the Baron of Chittendon that, at long last, would be held that very evening in
the Grand Ballroom of the Bellevue Stratford Hotel. Holding up two possibilities, one a striking white velvet with
gold sequins, the other a pale blue silk, she looked at
Vivian inquiringly.

"I think you may feel more comfortable in the blue,"
Vivian told her.

"Cripes! I *knew* you was gonna say that."

Seeing her friend's disappointment, Vivian said quickly, "Oh, wear what you like, Gert."

"Nope," replied Gert. "I'll wear the blue and act like I'm a lady. I don't want to embarrass Mallory. He's got enough trouble on his hands."

Jolted, a frown sprang between Vivian's eyes. "What trouble?"

"What trouble?" echoed Gert. "Why, the election next week."

"But Mallory doesn't expect Judge Parker to win."

"Who said anything about Judge Parker? It's Mallory or Tony Frazzio in this one, and it looks like Mallory is going to lose."

"Lose!"

Gert stared at her, dumbfounded. "Don't tell me you didn't know!"

"Know *what*, in the name of God?"

"Cripes!" Gert groaned. "I should be strung up by my toes."

"Gert, tell me," commanded Vivian. "You must tell me. What's been going on? What don't I know?"

"Oh, cripes!" moaned Gert again.

"Gert, tell me!" cried Vivian. "Tell me, or I swear I'll get dressed and go down to the Tipperary and ask Mallory himself."

At this Gert's face jerked up out of her hands. "You're not to let on I told you, Vivian Mallory! You're not to let on. Like as not he wanted to spare you because of your condition. Oh, cripes!"

Broken as it was by Gert's remorseful asides, the story was not easily come by, but at length Vivian had it from her. Anthony Frazzio wanted to run on his own record and keep the distance between himself and Judge Parker, the ill-starred presidential nominee. This much Vivian knew. "But Frazzio wouldn't of stood a chance," said Gert, "if it wasn't for the big support he's been getting. Without big support he wouldn't of stood no chance at all bucking Mallory, my Harry says."

"And who is supporting him?" asked Vivian.

Gert's eyes slid away. "Oh, lotsa people. Lotsa people around."

"People like Paddy Doyle?" pressed Vivian with sudden comprehension. "People with money, like Paddy's father-in-law, Mr. Ritter? Like Paddy's brother-in-law, Heinz?"

Gert nodded tightly. "A lot of people in the district like Paddy. He has a lot of friends."

"Who else?" continued Vivian, rapidly turning over names and faces in her mind like so many playing cards. "Thomas O'Reilly," she cried, pouncing. "Mallory told me Thomas is for Anthony Frazzio. And because of Tom, why then Dolly's father, Mr. Muldoon, like as not. And Thurman Foy! Yes, I'm sure of it. Thurman Foy, and Morrissey, too, I just bet."

"Give the little lady a great, big hand," said Gert wryly.

"But they can't win!" protested Vivian. "They can never win against Mallory and the machine!"

"Harry says they don't aim to win against the machine. They aren't dumb enough to buck that. All they want to do is spit in Mallory's eye and get Frazzio elected. If Mallory can't call the turn on that, he's on his way out."

For a long time after Gert Barkin left, Vivian sat unmoving on the chaise longue, staring into the coal fire that burned in the dusk of the waning afternoon. No least trace of Jamie remained in her mind. Her thoughts were all of Mallory, of the nights when he had come wearily home and she had asked few questions, had scarcely listened to his answers. Anxious about her, of course no one had told her how badly things were going—not Ma, not Mamie; never Mallory.

Within her the child stirred, and with a catch at her heart she put her arms about her stomach, recalling that only that morning she had wished it were Jamie's. So absorbed was she in these reflections that she was unaware of Mallory until, home early to bathe and dress for the reception that evening, he stepped quietly, fearful as always of perhaps waking her, into the room.

When, she thought now, was the last time she had really looked at him? In the firelight she could see that he had lost weight. There were deep shadows like bruises under the steely blue eyes that softened the moment she lifted her arms to him.

In swift strides he was across the room and, sinking down beside her, swept her to him. Remorseful tears filled her eyes and spilled over, wetting his cheek as well as her own. He didn't ask what might be the cause of such sorrow. He simply held her. For a long moment they remained so, clinging together. Then he said brokenly,

"You've been that unhappy for so long, Puss. I've had it in mind you might be wanting to leave me."

"I'll never leave you, Mallory," she answered fiercely. "No, never will I leave you. No matter what."

Election day dawned unseasonably warm for November, with sunny blue skies to encourage a large turnout.

The polls would not open until seven o'clock, but by six in the morning the fire trucks had been removed from the Hibernian Firehouse, polling place for Mallory's Third Ward, and stood ranged along Butler Street, bright red and winking in the sunshine at the carters and wagoners and trolley motormen who all day would curse them for being there.

Inside the firehouse a long trestle table had been set up on sawhorses. Three voting booths stood waiting, draped with curtains to insure privacy. Nearby was a large ballot box painted with a fresh coat of white gloss and locked with a padlock prominently displayed for all to see. Solly had already carried the ward books from Mallory's office in the Tipperary and delivered them into the hands of Bunty O'Hare. Bunty was judge of elections, and fully prepared to adjudicate any dispute as to who might and might not be permitted to vote.

Even at this early hour a number of policemen were about, nattily turned out in dark blue serge, the polished badges on their high-crowned helmets catching the first shafts of the sun. Swinging billy clubs, they sauntered casually back and forth in front of the Hibernian Fire Company's doors. Under Mallory's direction, it was a scene repeated at every polling place in the entire city.

Noting this marked presence of the constabulary, early risers on their way to work or to mass observed that for sure "Mallory's men," as they were called, were out in force. "To keep things proper," said some, adding with a wink of the eye, "There's many a man gone to his Maker whose name will be borrowed today. Aye, with things so dicey, they be voting the graveyards today. And among the living many a man will find himself richer for voting more than once."

Never were truer words spoken, for the election about to take place on this day was to go down as the meanest, the dirtiest, and, finally, the most scandalous in the history of

Philadelphia. And contrary to the fears of Gert Barkin, Mallory was to win.

Not knowing this, Vivian saw him off in the morning with anxious eyes. "It won't really matter so much if you lose, Mallory," she said, trying to soften in advance the blow she felt sure was coming.

"Not matter!" exclaimed Mallory. "Why, Puss, don't say such a foolish thing. Winning or losing makes all the difference in the world. What would I do if I lost? Tend bar the rest of my life at the Tipperary? Is that what you're thinking? No, no, Puss, I don't mean to do that."

The gleam, hard, cold, implacable, that so puzzled her, struck his eyes, changing his expression, making of him once more the stranger. "Ah, no," he said, but it was no longer at her that he looked. "Paddy Doyle's out to get me, that's the nub of it. Paddy's out to get back his ice docks. He's out to get back the power he once had that was the only reason Heinz Ritter and his old man had any use for him." Such an iron-hard determination stole into his eyes, into the thrust of his jaw, that he seemed carved from stone. "But Paddy," he said softly, "is going to lose."

This prophecy was fulfilled basely, mercilessly, and with blatant disregard of the laws governing elections. Victory could be achieved only by a fine knowledge of how individual voters were likely to vote. This knowledge Mallory and his ward leaders possessed, honed to perfection. Quite simply, those who might have voted for Anthony Frazzio were warned to stay away from the polls. Bands of young toughs such as the Bryce Street Alley Rats lay in wait for the more venturesome. Bloody battles broke out while the police stood idly by, watching Frazzio's supporters get sorely licked in the fray. Meanwhile, throughout the city, carefully chosen men like Bunty O'Hare, charged with arbitrating any vote that was challenged, came down firmly against Anthony Frazzio every time. Complaints that ballot boxes were being stuffed, that votes were being bought, that the names of voters long since dead or moved away were being used—all this fell upon deaf ears. There was no authority to whom Frazzio's people could appeal because, even in the very corridors of City Hall, Mallory was the authority.

"He's a fiend!" cried Neil, bursting into Vivian's bedroom late that afternoon. "A fiend out of hell!"

"Neil!" gasped Vivian from her chaise longue. "What are you talking about? What do you mean?"

"I mean your husband!" White-faced and almost demented he stood before her, fury in his eyes. "To think I worked for him! To think I ever trusted the man!"

"Are you speaking of Mallory?"

"Who else!"

"But what has he done?"

"What has he not done!" exclaimed Neil, running a hand through his hair. "He has subverted the entire democratic process. He has taken liberty by the neck and choked it in both hands! He has made a travesty of the right to vote!"

"Neil, do please be calm and tell me what has happened. I feel sure Mallory will be able to explain whatever little problem—"

"Little problem!" shouted Neil. "He's stealing the election."

"You mean . . ." faltered Vivian. "You mean Mallory is winning!"

"Yes!"

"Neil, are you sure?"

"Of course I'm sure! I've been back and forth across the city. Frazzio's losing everywhere."

Relief overwhelmed Vivian, and she fell back among her pillows. "Thank God!" she breathed.

"You can thank God?" asked Neil incredulously.

"Neil, you don't understand! They were out to get him. Paddy Doyle and Heinz Ritter and—"

"I don't understand!" cried Neil. "I don't understand!" A grim smile twisted his mouth. "Oh, my dear sister, it's you who don't understand! You are married to a ruthless bully who will do anything—yes, anything, to keep power in his hands."

With a harsh laugh and a shake of his head, Neil spun round and left her. She heard his angry footsteps pounding down the stairs and then the front door slam shut.

Sighing, she bit her lip. She hadn't been able to follow all the incoherent things her brother had said, but she was sure Mallory would be able to explain any misunderstanding. In the meantime, he was winning! Winning! All those weary nights of speechmaking, the mortification at Frazzio's hands—more, all those weddings and funerals and bar mitzvahs attended, all the hours spent listening to tales of woe—it was all paying off at last!

"He's winning, Ma! I hear he's winning!" she exclaimed joyfully as Ma Mallory entered the room early that evening. People had been back and forth to her bedroom all afternoon, bringing her news. Harry Barkin, Solly, Judge Wickersham, even Sir Robbie had dropped by. "Isn't it grand, Ma!"

It was then she noticed the look in Ma's eyes, saw the gray tinge to the woman's face as she lowered her girth down into the chair beside the chaise longue. It was then, too, with an ominous pounding of her heart, that she saw others easing into the room, silent as shadows: Harry Barkin again, and Solly; Mamie, her mother, and, most surprising of all, a policeman.

"What is it?" she asked wonderingly, staring from face to face. "What is it? What's happened?"

"My son," said Ma, "is dead."

A frown touched between Vivian's eyes as she struggled with this information. "You mean . . . You are saying . . . You are telling me Mallory is dead?"

Ma nodded. "Shot dead."

"Shot dead?"

Again Ma nodded. "Paddy Doyle."

Part III

29

The baby was a girl. Irene Mallory, born on February sixteenth, a little over three months after Mallory's funeral.

"With skin as white as snow, lips as red as blood, hair as black as ebony, just like you said," observed Gert Barkin standing above the big bed and studying the bundle Vivian held in her arms.

Remembering that happy, long ago moment in the sewing room, Vivian had all she could do to keep her voice steady as she replied, "That's right, Snow White."

Beyond the windows, snow was falling, sifting silently downward to pile up in drifts on the window ledge outside Mallory's old room. Vivian had accepted Ma's invitation to move in with her as soon as she understood the precarious financial position in which she found herself.

In a terrifying session with Mr. Bert Davison of the Keystone Bank she had learned that interest on the many notes Mallory so dextrously juggled would be coming due, not to mention ongoing expenses like heat, food, and wages for the large household. There was no insurance. Vivian didn't think this strange, for at the turn of the century only the most enlightened carried life insurance. And Mallory had thought he'd live forever, as Ma said. Or if not forever, at least long decades that would see his fortune secured. Under present circumstances, Vivian was grateful for Ma's generosity, and didn't mind in the least being here in his old bachelor quarters. In fact, she rather liked it. It made her feel close to him.

"If only he had seen her once!" exclaimed Gert on a sob, adding quickly, "I'm sorry, Vivvie. Cripes, I didn't mean to come here and blubber!"

"It's all right, Gert. I've cried gallons." She looked down at the tiny round face. Such a little, little baby! But exquisitely formed, nonetheless. "I believe Mallory somehow sees her, somehow knows." She shook her head. "It just seems so strange to me, though, to remember that he was always afraid something was going to go wrong, that his happiness would be taken from him and he would be punished somehow."

"Punished for what?"

"For . . . Well, for something he'd done," replied Vivian evasively.

"But he was a good man, the best!"

"Yes," she agreed softly, thinking: And bad, too. How bad she had only gradually come to discover, putting together the accounts of the election; hearing some things, remembering others. *Have you ever killed a man?* she had once asked. *No,* he had said, *but I've hurt 'em real bad.* And another time: *One day you'll find out I'm not the man you think I am, and I say to myself, what then?* Knowing what she knew now, would she have loved him less? How could she tell, having only now realized that she loved him at all.

"I miss him, Gert," she said, tears welling to her eyes. "I miss him so."

"Sure you do. Like I said to Harry the other night, Mallory was the kind that only comes one to the package, know what I mean?"

Despite her tears, Vivian smiled. One to the package. Throughout the funeral service, the eulogies, the hundreds of cards and notes that poured in, there had been more florid assessments, but perhaps none more apt.

Senator and Mrs. Cavendish came to visit, also, sitting upright and elegant in straight-back chairs pulled up to the big iron bedstead that dwarfed the room. There had been a recount of the vote. The senator had joined with Anthony Frazzio in demanding it.

"I couldn't have let it stand as it was," he now told her. "A blot on the electoral process." He shook his head. "The thing of it is, Mallory won anyhow. He needn't have got carried away."

A wry smile touched Vivian's lips. "Icarus?" she said.

"You remember the tale?"

"Always! I've thought about it so often." Cocking her head to one side, she fastened deeply green, speculative eyes on the senator. "But tell me, is it written anywhere that Icarus was happy when he was flying so close to the sun?"

Senator Cavendish smiled. "I wouldn't know about Icarus, but of one thing I'd like to assure you, Mrs. Mallory, and that is: I've never known your husband happier than in his marriage to you. He preferred you—yes, preferred you to the sun, the moon, and the stars. I cannot imagine more solace to any woman than this."

It was solace, for Vivian knew this was true. She had made Mallory happy. She clung to the knowledge. Together with his child, it helped fill the aching void within her.

"Life will go on for you again, Vivvie dear," said Camilla Cavendish. "Just make up your mind not to settle for less than you've had, not to slip backwards. You're no little lady's maid anymore."

"But I can't think what else I can do," replied Vivian honestly. "Ma has been so good to take us in. But we can't become a burden on her. She's getting along in years and, well . . . business isn't good. People don't seem to fancy the Tip as much now that Mallory's gone."

Camilla Cavendish fastened snapping black eyes on her. "Vivvie, you are a remarkably beautiful young woman with lovely ways. It's far too soon to say it, but I feel I must just put a word in your ear. You must marry again."

"No!" responded Vivian sharply, unable to tolerate even the thought of such disloyalty to Mallory's memory.

"Yes, my dear, you must. If not for yourself, then for the sake of your daughter. A beautiful young woman often gets the chance to marry up, and when she does it's as if someone thrust in a hand to pull her out of the bog she's stuck in. With a man, it's different; he can work himself out of the mire and amount to something all on his own. But a woman must be careful and clever and make a good marriage. For a woman, there's no other way."

Nancy Webb, now Nancy Randall, had other ideas. "Do as I do, and go to typing school," she urged. "These days a woman shouldn't be a parasite living off a man. Nor a lady's maid. The whole world of business has opened up."

Vivian was truly astonished to see how Nancy had blossomed since her marriage to Neil. Always forthright and of firm convictions, she had proved herself in a dozen ways.

"I feel so *capable*!" the girl continued, laughing lightly. "I can cook, sew, bake, *and* earn my own way. Sometimes I believe Neil feels he got more than he bargained for."

Vivian thought this just might be true, especially since Nancy didn't stop with her own accomplishments but urged

Neil onward also, succeeding in getting him to apply for a clerkship in a law office. Neil was successful in this application largely through the contacts and expertise acquired while working on factory fire laws for Mallory, and one day he rather shamefacedly confessed as much.

"My trouble," he finished ruefully, "was wanting Mallory to be more than he was, more than he wanted to be. He could have done so much, Vivvie! Changed things, made them better."

"Don't talk against him to me, Neil," she said swiftly.

Neil reddened. "I'm not talking against him. I'm complimenting him in a way, saying he could have done more."

"He did a lot!" declared Vivian. "He did a lot, and I know it better than you do, better than anybody. He helped people. He got them jobs, food, a place to live. He got them started here."

She wouldn't tolerate anything said against him, not from anyone—not from Ma talking about all the money he had let run through his fingers, not from Mamie, wondering what was to be done; not from Clinton Webb, come to call.

"He should have left you provided for!" Clinton spat out, seeing where she was forced to live.

It was a blustery March day and the wind shook and buffeted the small frame house huddled up against the side of the Tipperary. Ma was, as usual, at her station in the saloon, and Trudie, the maid-of-all-work, had opened the door to Clinton.

He and his bride, Anthea Allenby, had just returned from a prolonged honeymoon trip through Europe. Wearing English tweeds, he sat in the dark little front parlor whose graceless ambience was increased rather than diminished by the two lamps Vivian lit.

"How," he demanded, looking about him with distaste, "can you possibly abide here?"

"It's quite cozy," replied Vivian.

"Cozy! Why, it hasn't an ounce of comfort or cheer. Must you stay here?"

"I can't go to mama's, and her with Nancy and Neil and Bucky and Mary Claire."

"It's infuriating!" exclaimed Clinton. "Yes, Vivvie, it infuriates me to see you here. It's like—well, damn it, like some rare jewel threaded onto a grimy piece of string!"

Clapping a hand to her mouth, Vivian laughed aloud, but Clinton continued, glowering. "Well, it's true! It offends me, my sense of the fitness of things; puts me in a vile humor."

"But you didn't have to come see me," she responded teasingly.

"Of course I did! Only decent. Although now I'm almost sorry. Your situation will bother me, stay in my mind."

"Let me show you the baby, then you'll feel differently."

"Feel differently! But the child is simply an added burden to you."

"Clinton, no!" cried Vivian, her eyes suddenly soft under the piled-up coppery red hair, a happy flush riding into the creamy white of her complexion. "She's what I live for. And you surely must admire her!"

When Trudie was summoned to bring the child in, warm and rosy from her nap, Clinton grudgingly admitted she was a pretty baby. As, thought Vivian, how could he not? The tiny fingers curling like unopened flowers, the flushed, tissue-paper-thin skin, the eyes, blue as Mallory's ever were under a cap of black hair, combined to achieve, in Vivian's view, utter perfection. Just looking at her brought pleasure; yes, thought Vivian, despite all the heartbreak and sorrow, pleasure unalloyed.

"What's her name?" asked Clinton crisply.

"Irene."

Jolted, he turned to her. "Irene! You mean, after . . . ?"

"After your mother, yes."

"That's what I always thought to name a child of mine."

A stillness grew and hung in the air between them as Trudie left with the baby. It was as though a gaffe had been committed, and for a moment neither could think of a word to say. Then Vivian said softly, "I admire your mother more than any woman I know. I can only hope my Irene will grow up to be like her."

To her amazement, tears sprang glistening to Clinton's dark eyes. "Oh, don't hope that, Vivvie! My mother . . . my mother is losing her mind."

"Clinton!" cried Vivian.

Anguish twisting his face he turned from her, fetching a handkerchief from his pocket.

Swiftly she went to him, placing a hand on his arm, turning him toward her, reaching up to pull his cheek down against hers. "Clinton! Oh, my dear!"

A strangled cry broke from him and his arms went about her, straining her to him, hoarse, dry sobs shaking him. She stood in the circle of his arms, gently crooning, patting the expensive tweed that tautly covered his shoulders, tears in her own eyes.

At length, releasing her and straightening, he said, "I apologize, Vivvie, for losing control of myself. Unforgivable!"

"Unforgivable!" she cried. "Clinton, no! Don't say that, dear. Why shouldn't you relieve your feelings with an old friend? What are friends for? With your mother ill, you have been under a great strain."

"It's more than mother," said Clinton tightly. "Not that that wouldn't be enough. It's Anthea and I." He smiled wryly. "I seem not to possess the talent for making a wife happy. I can't believe Anthea would mourn me as you mourn Mallory."

The sad little admission in so new a marriage haunted Vivian long after Clinton said good-bye and left her. It joined a host of other melancholy companions that seemed to have taken up permanent residence in her breast. Out of the blue, remorse would seize her, vain regrets surged against her heart. She blamed herself for all that had happened, including Mallory's death. How could she not? After all, but for her flirtation with Paddy Doyle on that fateful night of the party, the two men would most likely still be the best of friends. Paddy and his in-laws would still have the ice docks, they would never have supported Anthony Frazzio, Mallory would never have felt it necessary to rig the election, Paddy would never have got raging drunk, taken a gun, and shot Mallory dead as he came smiling and victorious down the steps of the Butler Street Amity Club.

I mustn't think such thoughts, she would cry out to herself in silent anguish, pressing fingers to her throbbing head. But never a day, sometimes, it seemed, never an hour went by that she didn't think of Paddy Doyle serving, thanks to a sympathetic judge and jury, a minimal eight-year sentence in Moyamensing prison; of Gussie, his wife; of all the sorrows, enmities and disasters that had resulted from the foolish, ill-considered behavior of a silly girl.

As she had so frequently done since childhood, Vivian brought her low spirits not to the already overburdened Mamie, but to her aunts, the Randall girls. She never failed to benefit from her visits to these two maiden ladies, returning from contact with their orderly, generous, reassuring lives feeling heartened and refreshed.

Together with her quest for comfort and conversation, Vivian had a more practical reason for calling on the aunts these days. Without a word being said, they had resumed paying her for washing and dressing their fine silvery hair, and these small amounts were gratefully received. So it was on this rather chilly early April day that the Randall girls' kitchen had once again been turned into a beauty salon, and Vivian stood above the dry sink gently massaging Opal's head.

"No one has your touch, Vivvie," she said, sighing luxuriously. "I can feel all the little tensions running away."

Vivian smiled. It was Dr. Webb who had taught her those areas at the base of the skull, at the nape of the neck, and just below the temples that responded to massage. She had instructed her own lady's maid, Hattie Flanagan, in this method, and therefore knew from personal experience its deeply relaxing, salutary effect.

Thinking of Hattie, of Halls and Clarissa, of Mrs. Doughty and the rest of the staff who, with glowing notices from her, were now working for others, a sigh escaped her.

"What's the matter, Vivvie?" demanded the sharp-eared Sarah.

"Nothing, really," she replied. "I was just thinking of all the people who worked at Mallory's house, and wondering how they are."

"You always called it Mallory's house," said Opal. "I hope you won't think it rude of me to say, but Sarah and I always considered that strange."

"Speak for yourself, Opal," said Sarah.

Opal regarded her sister mildly. "Well, Sarah, you know we did. We mentioned it many times."

"I suppose it was strange," agreed Vivian. "I never thought of that 'til now. But somehow, it always *was* Mallory's house, not mine."

"That's because he built it before you were married," observed Sarah. "If you had built it together—or bought it together—you'd have felt differently."

"I expect so. Maybe that's the way it will be with Dolly and Tom O'Reilly. I'm showing them through later today."

"You don't say!" exclaimed Opal.

"I thought they were living at the funeral parlor with the Muldoons," said Sarah.

"That's all changed," said Vivian. "At least, I hope so. Dolly has decided she wants a house of her own and really, they are the only ones who could afford such an expensive property in a location like Butler Street.

"Then too," she continued, brushing Opal's hair, "Tom likely will win Mallory's old position as district leader. Everybody seems to like him and want him, but it means they'll have to stay in the Third Ward. Mallory's house makes sense for them."

If only, she silently prayed, Dolly and Tom realize this! If only they would like the house when she showed them through, would buy it, would take it off her hands! Delinquent interest on the enormous mortgage was piling up month after month and she had no way of paying it, much less the principal amount.

"Oh, it's an awful thing," sighed Opal. "An awful thing that you should lose it all!"

"Now don't talk that way, Opal," scolded Sarah. "No use crying over spilt milk. Vivvie has simply got to turn her mind to the future and do something, that's all."

"What can she do?" asked Opal.

"Get to work, just as I did."

"But you had pa's store, Sarah."

"That's true. I had the store, and that made me an independent business woman. That's what Vivvie must do."

"Run a store, Sarah?"

Sarah nodded emphatically. "Run a hairdressing salon."

The aunts frequently talked as though others were not present, but never had anything they said struck Vivian's imagination with the force of a bolt of lightning, galvanizing her attention as she continued dressing Opal's hair.

"A hairdressing salon?" asked Opal in wonderment.

Sarah nodded. "Is there anyone better at it? And not only that. Think of all the wealthy ladies Vivvie knows. Why, they'd all come to her shop if it's placed in the proper location. Location is very important in a business enterprise. I've been thinking it might be located just off Cavendish Square."

"Sarah!" cried Opal. "How brilliant you are!"

Vivian felt so weak she let brush and comb fall, groped for a chair, and sat down.

"You'll need money, of course, to get started," continued Sarah, giving Vivian a shrewd look.

"Yes, money!" cried Opal. She looked eagerly at Vivian. "Have you any money, dear?"

"Indeed she has," answered Sarah. "She has an interest in Mr. Fitzhugh's successful invention."

Opal clapped her hands. "Mr. Fitzhugh's invention! Of course!"

"She must just get in touch with him."

"Yes!" exclaimed Opal. "Just get in touch!"

30

Vivian left in something of a daze.

Carrying her small jug of special liquid soap, she proceeded back to Butler Street, a slim, lithe figure under the newly leafed out trees that arched, fragile and lemon green, above her.

On little gusts of wind all manner of pods and dandelion puffs whirled and eddied about her, bearing seeds of future growth, of renewal, busy about *next* spring already. Irene would be over one year old by next spring, walking, beginning to talk. And, in not too many years, ready to start school.

The haunting memory of the visit to the Villa Maria Academy rose before Vivian. But no lady's maid could afford to send a daughter to the Villa Maria, with its broad green lawns and wrought-iron fences and soft voices speaking foreign tongues. No, no lady's maid could give her daughter that, nor any of the other advantages she had promised herself Irene would have one day. Whenever she thought of the child growing up in Ma's dark little house at the side of a saloon, with nothing but back alleys to play in and no prospects at all, panic seized her, making her hands tremble and a cold sweat break upon her brow. The ugly specter of poverty had slipped from behind the door, this time to bend above Irene's cradle, filling the air with its rancid breath. Until today, however, Vivian had averted her eyes.

But Aunt Sarah was right. She was penniless, absolutely penniless, with a child to support. She must leave off mooning about the past and turn to the future. She must *do* something. And nothing, oh, nothing beckoned and beguiled her so much as the thought of a beauty salon. The times, she felt, were right for it. Women no longer remained at home or spent their days working in sweatshops. As Nancy had said, the typewriter was their liberation, and while their nimble fingers earned them twice what they had been paid heretofore, their days were enhanced by a heady independence and a certain flirtatious boldness encouraged by a new and suddenly accessible world of men.

Nor did a young matron necessarily rest content after having exchanged her parents' residence for that of her husband. Women's clubs abounded, and far from displaying a devotion to cooking and sewing, a lady might plunge wholeheartedly into the quest for culture; learning, often to her husband's discomfiture, to converse in French or Spanish, developing opinions on the world through travel talks, or dedicating herself to ameliorating the lot of the less fortunate whilst beginning to consider improving her own.

Aiding and abetting this somewhat alarming new woman was a whole array of exciting new products devoted to her appearance and to her jingling purse: La Dore's Bust Food for the lady who might regret that, as the advertisement politely stated, her form was not what she would like it to be; the Dupre Massage Cup, "a beautiful nickel-plated suction cup for bringing color to the cheeks"; Mrs. Gervaise Graham's Face Bleach for the removal of sallowness; and a host of others.

Also appearing were all manner of new hairdressing equipment: curlers, crimping irons, hair straighteners. Vivian had bought and experimented with all of them. Her interest and pleasure in coiffure had never diminished. Among any group of women she would sooner or later catch herself observing the arrangement of their hair, deciding which styles were the most becoming, studying how even the best might be dressed to greater advantage.

Long ago she had become convinced that a woman's hair had by far the greatest effect on her appearance. Even a poor figure could be somewhat compensated by a healthy, shining, attractively created hairstyle. Conversely, the finest clothes, the most artful cosmetics could never dispel the effect of an ill-cared-for, poorly arranged head of hair. At times her fingers itched to sit a woman down, pull out combs and pins, and start over from the beginning.

Now, she told herself with a thrill of conviction, was the time! She had no least doubt of her success in this venture. Was she not willing to work hard? Had ladies not clamored for her services in the past? And she quite agreed that Sarah was right: location was everything, and what more convenient, more desirable, more perfect location than Cavendish Square? Only one aspect of the enterprise gave her pause: the necessity of having anything to do with Jamie Fitzhugh.

The guilt she bore over Mallory's death cut even more deeply when she remembered that only hours beforehand she had delighted in imagining herself shed of him entirely. These flights of fancy returned again and again to condemn her for the traitorous heart that had been hers, with the result that she now could scarce tolerate the thought of Jamie at all.

If only Mallory's house could be sold for a bit more than the principal and interest due on it! Observing Dolly and Tom O'Reilly waiting for her on the front porch, she moved up the walk, palms damp with nervous greediness and fire in her eye.

"Good afternoon, Vivvie," said Tom O'Reilly, stepping smartly forward to extend his hand.

How trim he looked! thought Vivian, in his dark blue striped suit and derby hat. Trim and well off. Dolly, too, in a powder blue linen that bore a frothy white lace jabot and was topped by a large blue linen picture hat. Surely, surely Dolly O'Reilly might become a prime customer at the salon. Alert to this possibility, Vivian turned to the newly married Mrs. O'Reilly and said fervently, "Dolly, how utterly smashing you are!"

The phrase—from the Lady Langhorne–Baron Chittendon past—had just slipped out, causing Dolly's rosebud mouth to drop open in surprise. "Why, thank you, I'm sure!"

"You're looking mighty good yourself, if I may say so," offered Thomas. "Always said you and Mallory made the best-looking pair in the parish, didn't I, Dolly?"

"Yes, Tom, you always did," responded Dolly sourly.

"And, Vivvie," he continued earnestly, "I want you to

know it gives me no pleasure to think of living in your house, walking through your rooms."

"Thomas O'Reilly," snapped Dolly, "if it will give no pleasure then why are we looking at it?"

"Why, Tom," said Vivian, jumping into the breach, "I can't think of anyone I'd rather have living in it than you and Dolly. And I'm sure I speak for Mallory, too. Why, I think it would be just too bad if some stranger came along and moved in. I've been so *afraid* that might happen! I'm not sure I'd even sell to a stranger, no matter what the price."

"Gol' darn, now, Vivvie, that is mighty nice of you. Dolly and I sure do appreciate that, don't we?"

Was it possible, thought Vivian in a surge of hope, that the O'Reillys had already decided to buy the property? She felt in her bones that they had! Yes, she felt they had, for all Dolly said sharply, "Thomas, we haven't inspected it yet," and swept imperiously to the front door.

But it was the price that was all-important. To command the price Vivian wanted, needed, *must have,* the house had to appear irresistible. Standing beside Dolly in the front hall, she slipped an arm about the young woman's waist, murmuring, "Oh, Dolly, I just know you can appreciate the dimensions of this vestibule. My dear friend the Lady Langhorne says nothing sets the style of a fine residence so well as a noble entrance. And do look," she breathed, "at how well the Remington bronze complements the console. The Webbs of Cavendish Square have the identical piece in their front hall."

"And is it for sale, that bronze?" asked Dolly.

"All the furnishings . . . everything is for sale." She raised her hands. "Where would I put such treasures? What would I do with them? But Dolly, it's not only that. You can see for yourself how everything suits this house. Not," she added hastily, "that these are *my* ideas. Oh, no! Why, I can't tell you how much I've learned about the proper way to furnish a house. This is because I sought advice from experts. I didn't trust myself. I wanted to rest assured that everything would be in the best of taste."

"Oh, it's grand, Vivvie!" exclaimed Thomas appreciatively. "Just grand!"

"Why, thank you, Tom," replied Vivian absently, and turned back to Dolly. "Now, Dolly, the dining room . . . I just bet your eye picks up right away how the blue in this rug matches those fireplace tiles over there. It's such a subtle little thing, isn't it, and yet it makes all the difference, don't you agree?"

Through the house they went, Vivian and Dolly together, Thomas trailing behind, down to the cellar, still stocked with jams and jellies, with piccalilli and the jars of beets, beans, corn that Clarissa had put up only that fall, still holding bottles of wine, including the framboise Sir Robbie had so often enjoyed, and bins of potatoes, turnips.

Up into the kitchen. "A wonder!" declared Tom. And through the upstairs: sewing room, master bedroom, Mary Claire's room. . . .

On the landing the grandfather clock cooperated by chiming the hour. Holding up a hand, Vivian stopped to listen ecstatically. "Such a beautiful tone, hasn't it? The Westminster chimes: the very same sound as the chimes in Westminster, London, England. So comforting to awaken at night and hear that lovely reassuring sound. The Baron of Chittendon once stood right here and observed that a ticking grandfather clock was the heartbeat of a house."

She must, she thought, have read that somewhere, as was true of just about everything else she had said. The remark proved telling. She looked at Tom to catch him swallowing hard, and Dolly's blue eyes were frankly covetous. "How much?" she asked Vivian.

It was the question Vivian had been praying for. "You mean," she asked with bated breath, "for the house alone? Or for everything?"

"Everything."

Vivian knew to the penny precisely how much she must have. Twenty-five thousand was owed on the mortgage, plus interest at one and one-half percent; to this must be added fifteen thousand on notes for the furnishings, for a total of forty thousand, three hundred, and seventy-five dollars. But this amount would only pay off Mallory's debts. To start her beauty salon she must have more. "Forty-five thousand," she said.

Dolly nodded. "We'll let you know."

Standing at the open door, she watched them move down the front walk. As they went, Tom turned smilingly to Dolly, taking her arm. Observing the small, solicitous gesture, Vivian felt such a yearning for Mallory beseige her, such a wave of loss and loneliness overwhelm her that she felt she must cry aloud with the pain of it.

Tears blinded her, bulged in her throat. Shutting the door, she turned and leaned back against it. Now that it was over, now that she had made the sale—for she felt certain the O'Reillys would buy it—the beauty of the place, its sweet appeal pierced her to the quick, clung to her, it seemed, pleading not to be let go. How could she bear to do so?

Tears coursed unheeded down her cheeks as she looked about her. Mallory was everywhere. His footsteps echoed on the porch, on the stairs; the sound of his voice was in every room. Upon a hundred surfaces his hand had rested, his fingerprints remained. His desk stood in the library; in the dining room, his chair. It had been his house—his, not hers. No matter who bought it, he was here still.

This last thought brought with it a measure of calm. Slowly, as though her bones ached, she went up the stairs and into the bathroom of which Mallory had been so proud. Letting water run over her wrists, she bathed her face and patted it dry with an embroidered linen towel. Then, methodically, she went from room to room, taking her time, letting her eyes travel over each object, chosen, not long ago, with such painstaking care.

After she finished with the upstairs she went down to the cellar, marveling afresh at so much food, so many beautiful jars of food. In the kitchen she stood at the giant range, running a finger over its cool nickel trim, hearing the voices that had filled the house—the soft Negro slur of Clarissa, of Halls; the Irish lilt of Mrs. Doughty and the Garvey girls.

On the lustrous surface of the dining room table a speck of wax from some long-ago candlelit evening had hardened. With her fingernail Vivian carefully lifted it off, and then paused beside Mallory's chair, thinking of him. How he had filled her life in those few brief months! She knew such intimate details about him—the things he liked to eat, his favorite colors, the way he made love. But there was so much she didn't know, so much she kept finding out, things that weren't nice, that gave her pause. He had shown her the best side of himself. But there was still the stranger, whom she now would never know.

Didn't want to know? With a shiver she shook off the notion and moved into the library with its neat rows of books that neither of them had ever read, or had ever meant to read. Dolly and Tom had been impressed, but she was ashamed of them, although they once had made her proud. She wouldn't do that again, have books just "for show." She didn't care that much about "show" anymore.

Swiftly she took a turn through the two parlors, front and back, admiring the furnishings but feeling more detached now. Then she went into the hallway and out the front door. She turned the key in the lock.

Mallory wasn't here. There was nobody in this house anymore.

Tom O'Reilly looked embarrassed. Derby in hand, he stood before Vivian that evening in Ma's little parlor staring down at the linoleum rug on the floor, shifting his large feet, unwilling to meet her eyes. In her arms Irene fussed, and Vivian patted her back and jounced her gently up and down, but her mind wasn't on the child.

"Thirty-six thousand, Tom!" she cried, aghast. Far from giving her a bit extra, the offer wouldn't pay off Mallory's debts.

"Thirty-six thousand," replied Tom awkwardly. "That's what Dolly said to say."

"But I can't sell for that!"

Instantly his head bobbed up. "How about forty then?"

"Forty?" she repeated, nonplussed.

"Dolly said to start out with the thirty-six and then, if you were determined to hold fast, to offer the forty. Shoot, Vivvie, I'd like to make it forty-five. But it's Muldoon money, and that's as high as they will go."

She looked at him through narrowed eyes. "Really, Thomas?"

"Gol' darn, Vivvie, do you think I'd lie?"

Looking into that open face, she knew he wouldn't. She listened attentively as he went on to explain that the Muldoons had somehow discovered the exact amount of the mortgage on the property and the interest due. Further, that Dolly had toted up the probable cost of the furnishings and come up with forty thousand as about the correct amount. It was the poor location that had led to the low first offer. In fact, the elder Muldoons felt the property might be purchased for thirty-six thousand if only they waited awhile.

"I'm not sure whether they're right or they're wrong," said Tom. He looked at her with concern. "Don't you know someone with your interest at heart who could advise you on this?"

Clinton Webb jumped instantly to mind. Beyond the shadow of a doubt she knew she could trust him, that he would, as Tom said, have her interest at heart. And he was a highly successful businessman. Surely he would be able to tell her whether to take this offer, or not.

"There is someone . . ." she said.

"Then best you should talk to him," Tom solemnly advised. "With the little one to think of, it might be best you should not jump at the first offer but try for another sale."

She saw him off with a smile more gallant than secure, all the time wondering if she shouldn't have given a firm yes to the forty thousand. Only her reluctance to go to Jamie Fitzhugh for money had led her to delay in the hope of a better offer. But had she been right in this decision?

Clearly Ma thought she had not.

Although no longer speaking to her erstwhile bosom friend, Regina Muldoon, due to Mr. Muldoon's support of Anthony Frazzio in the election, Ma nonetheless retained a healthy regard for Muldoon solvency. "And would you be telling me why in the honor of God you'd turn down a good offer like that?" she demanded later that night.

During the week the Tipperary Saloon was less busy than it was on the weekends, and Ma usually returned to her house about ten o'clock. It was then she would cook up her supper of fried potatoes and bacon or scrapple, helped down by a pot of tea laced with warm milk.

"I need more money," said Vivian, seated at the round dining room table watching Ma eat. "I want to go into business."

Ma set down her fork with a thump. "Business, is it? And what business are you fit to go into, may I ask?"

"I want to open my own hairdressing establishment, a beauty salon."

Ma's gray eyes riveted themselves upon Vivian's determined green ones. "A beauty salon!" she said at last. "Well now, I'm thinking that's a grand idea at that! Sure, it's the coming thing, and you're clever about it. And the best part is, you can open your business right here and without any risk."

"Here?"

Ma nodded. "You can have the saloon. To tell you the truth, I've no heart for the drink since my boy lost his life to it. But a fine corner property it will make for your hair-dressing establishment."

Vivian's heart sank. All the frustrations of the day—her need for money, her dashed hopes for the sale of the house, her reluctance to approach Jamie combined with this suggestion of Ma's to make the difficulties of opening an elegant shop off Cavendish Square seem insurmountable.

Contributing to this sense of defeat was the very reason-ableness of the proposal. Ma owned the saloon lock, stock, and barrel. Too, it was singularly suited to renovation, equipped as it was with a big sink, a huge mirror behind the bar, cupboards, shelves, tables, even towels. The invest-ment would be minimal, but she could never charge the high prices she felt sure she would command in a more stylish location, and as much to her own wavering courage as to her mother-in-law, she cried out, "No! No, Ma! No!"

"How's that?" said Ma, mystified and affronted.

"My shop will not be down here on Butler and Bryce. My shop is to be just off Cavendish Square."

"Cavendish Square," said Ma slowly, as though this in-formation must sink down, down into some deep well within her. Then a red flush of fury suffused her face. "Cavendish Square!" she cried scathingly. "And has there not been enough of that kind of folderol in this family? Has there not been enough of that, with my son lying dead?"

"That's not why he died," countered Vivian sharply.

"Is it not? Is it not why he lost his constituency, running around with the royals and giving himself airs?"

Under the table Vivian squeezed her hands into tight balls, digging her fingernails into the palms. Would it never end, this harking back, this laying of blame? Some-times she thought Ma's bitter words were wearing her down, breaking her spirit the way drops of water, drip by drip, at last succeed in eroding a stone. Sometimes, for all Ma's goodheartedness in taking her and Irene in, it seemed that the price was too high.

But where could she have gone? Not back to Mamie's already overcrowded small house. No, her only hope was to fight her way up somehow, fight up and out of Butler Street. Above all, fight up and out of that contented de-pendence that sucked you down and forever bound the poverty-stricken together, ineffectually aiding one another instead of concentrating on helping themselves.

She needed Ma now. She needed help with Irene, she

needed food, a roof over her head, everything. But the day would come—yes, the day would come when she wouldn't need anything from anybody.

Money, she had learned, couldn't buy happiness. But it could buy independence. This was her goal.

31

Her high resolve faltered somewhat the next morning when Bunty O'Hare, having secured from somewhere the loan of a horse and carriage, drove her over the Belgian block courtyard of the Webb Woolen Mills.

She had had no idea of the vast size of the place. Solidly built of a dark gray stone, four stories high, its front pockmarked with tall dingy windows, it seemed to stretch for miles, obliterating trees, hills, river, every least bit of greenery. But what struck Vivian most forcibly was the constant clatter of the looms that filled the air with a racket that was all but deafening—that indeed *did* deafen, "weaver's deafness" after long years in the mills being a common complaint.

The courtyard itself was crowded with draft horses and wagons, and draymen shouted and cursed as they sought a place from which to unload bales of wool yarn or cart away finished yard goods. Mill workers passed by shod in the wooden clogs worn at the dye vats where spilled dye covered the floor. At the windows above, a woman's head now and again appeared, for women tended the looms almost to the exclusion of men now that the men had unionized and demanded higher pay—women, and children.

Along the side of the building a broad iron stairway rose two flights to a platform upon which opened a door.

"Bunty," said Vivian, spying this, and shouting to make herself heard, "do you just go up those stairs and ask where Mr. Clinton Webb can be found."

Her voice shook a bit under her words as, dressed in black widow's weeds, she sat ramrod straight in the carriage. Dealing with business, with more than just the household money, was a frightening experience. The truth was that just walking into a bank could cause her pulse to race. So like jails they were, bars everywhere and clerks frowning as though you had no right whatever to be under that coffered ceiling, to tread upon that polished marble floor.

But Clinton Webb was used to such things. How self-confident he looked, thought Vivian, as the door at the top of the stairs swung open and he came running down them followed by a less sure-footed Bunty O'Hare. The dark gray frock coat he wore sat perfectly upon his shoulders, his sleek dark head was immaculately groomed, and an air of assurance invested every move. Seeing him, her own spirits rallied. She *knew* he would help her.

"Vivvie, what a delightful surprise!" he cried, coming to the carriage and extending his hand. "But we can't talk here, it's bedlam. I've asked your man to drive us down to the river to a restaurant I know. The shad is running, we'll lunch on 'em. Will that be all right?"

It occurred to Vivian as they were seated at a table on the attractive dining porch overlooking the Schuylkill that she hadn't thought twice about this invitation to be Clinton Webb's luncheon guest. How all-but-forgotten, that wide-eyed little lady's maid who would have trembled at such a notion!

She was again penniless, but she was well aware that she was far removed from the simple girl she had been. In the six brief months of her marriage Mallory had provided her with a lifetime of experiences, acquaintances, perceptions. But his greatest gift was the sense he had given her of her own worth. She had charmed him utterly, this man of discrimination, this connoisseur of women. She knew the power she had held over him, and she was never to lose the self-confidence this inspired.

Looking across the table at Clinton, she smiled. "I've come to ask a bit of financial advice."

Over a bottle of chilled Chablis and a luncheon of shad roe straight from the Schuylkill River, garnished with new potatoes and fresh asparagus with hollandaise sauce, Vivian explained her present position, her plans to open a beauty salon off Cavendish Square, and her quandary as to whether to accept Dolly's offer on the house.

Clinton listened intently, his dark brown eyes informed

by the fine intellect behind them. When she had finished, he said, "I believe you should hold out for your price on the house. I believe you'll get forty-five thousand."

"You do?" replied Vivian dubiously. "In that location?"

"Oh, you've got your buyers. From what you tell me, I'll wager Mrs. O'Reilly won't rest until the house is hers. Just be patient and sit tight. You'll get your price."

"Clinton, how wonderful!"

He raised a hand. "Well, the cat's not in the bag yet, so we'll not celebrate. But, Vivvie, you should have more capital before you open your shop."

"More than five thousand dollars!"

Years later she would remember those words and be grateful he didn't smile. "Five thousand dollars," he said, "is very little for a woman who wants to go into business, and who, while she is getting started, must support herself and a small child."

"Oh, but Irene and I will continue living with Ma."

"Are you sure? Are you sure the woman will keep you if you refuse to accept her offer of the saloon? If you refuse to do things her way? Is your mother-in-law likely to be any less resolute than my father when he turned my sister out of the house?"

Vivian set down knife and fork. How likely that Clinton was right. Nothing riled Ma more than what she considered extravagance, putting on airs. She had, in fact, already expressed herself on the subject of Cavendish Square.

"Come now, Vivvie," said Clinton, "don't be gloomy. You need a bit more money, and I'll be more than happy to make you a little loan."

As she opened her mouth to protest, he said quickly, "Now hear me out. I have great faith in your ability as a hairdresser. The Lord knows I ought to, after having to listen to Anthea constantly bewail the fact that no one but you can do the right things with her hair. And of course you must establish yourself not on Butler Street but on Cavendish Square. You'll make more money there. But not only that—it's where you belong. Vivvie, you *belong* in an elegant shop on Cavendish Square."

He said it with such earnest conviction that a thrill of confidence, heady and sweet, coursed through her. This was what she needed, this beautiful reassurance, this encouragement in undertaking such an enticing but awesome enterprise. Without thinking, she reached across the table and covered his hand with hers. "Thank you, Clinton," she said gratefully.

She felt his hand tremble under hers, part of a tremor that passed like a spasm through his whole body, causing her to jerk her hand away in dismay.

He grinned at her wryly. "Now you can see your effect on me. I may add I'm only surprised I was able to keep it a secret so long."

"Clinton!" she gasped.

"Oh, don't worry, I'll not press my suit. After all, I'm a married man. But I'm in love with you, Vivvie. I've been in love with you for Lord knows how long. I only wish my upbringing and my devotion to duty hadn't prevented me from asking you to marry me long ago." He raised a finely shaped dark eyebrow. "Would you have had me? Don't answer that. I prefer to live with my illusions. And divorcing Anthea is something, of course, I'd never do."

Vivian stared at him, filled with tumbling emotions that seemed to have lodged in her stomach. But one thing was clear. "Clinton," she said, "I truly appreciate your offer, but I don't want the loan."

"Oh, Vivvie, for God's sake!"

"No," she said firmly, striving to keep her voice low, her face serene for the benefit of hovering waiters, the other diners. "The point is, I don't need it. I have . . . I have another source of funds."

"What? Someone else wants to marry you?"

The words, meant to tease, clutched at her heart. Since Mallory's death she hadn't let herself think of this possibility, but it was there, tucked in the back of her mind. She was free, in the eyes of the world and the Church, released from her vows. Jamie and she could be married.

More calmly than she would have believed possible, she said matter-of-factly, "Mallory invested a small amount of money in a new chemical formula useful in developing photographs. Just before his death he learned that the inventor had been successful in selling it." She went on, explaining the details but not mentioning that Mallory had torn up Jamie's letter and the contract.

"Do you know where the inventor can be reached?" asked Clinton.

"I'm sure I can find out."

"Then you must do so! You owe it to yourself and to

your child. You should receive not only a lump sum payment but a share in the royalties for as long as royalties are paid—which may be for years! You'll need a lawyer. I'll send you the name of a competent one. Vivvie, this is the best stroke of luck!"

Leaving the restaurant on his arm she scarcely listened further. Luck . . . fate . . . the heavens above had conspired to force her to see Jamie again. The thought of him consumed her.

She didn't know Jamie's address in St. Louis, but she had an idea who did, and so, upon returning to Butler Street after her luncheon with Clinton Webb, she asked Bunty to drop her off at Morrissey's blacksmith shop.

Arriving there, she saw she was in luck, for although the wide old wooden door in the grimy plastered stone building stood open to the April sunshine, no fire glowed in the hearth, and the usual idlers who collected to watch Morrissey hammer a red-hot horseshoe or turn glowing pig iron into wrought-iron twists and curves were absent.

"You want I should wait for you?" asked Bunty, helping her alight from the carriage.

"No, thank you, Bunty," she answered. "I'll walk home."

How she was to regret this decision! But she waved a careless hand as Bunty heaved his short round person back up onto the carriage and, with a click of his tongue, moved off.

Lifting her skirts, Vivian moved cautiously into the half-light of the dingy room with its smoke-blackened walls and, hanging along them, the hammers, tongs, chains that looked like nothing so much as instruments of torture. Even more true was this when the furnace was raging and Morrissey stood above it, stripped to the waist, his belly bulging under a soiled leather apron. Vivian had never quite lost her childhood fear of the place despite all the time she had come to spend here with Jamie.

Eyes growing accustomed to the dimness, she looked about her. No one appeared to be around. The place had the feeling of emptiness. To the rear of the building was a wheelwright shop; upon inspection she discovered it, too, to be deserted. Impelled by a wave of nostalgia, she moved to the door of the lean-to that had been Jamie's darkroom, pushed it open, and stepped inside.

The glass of the single window of this small room had

been painted black in the interest of photography, and the window draped in a black flannel curtain she herself had sewn up. This was now pushed to one side, as was the curtain on the door leading to the alleyway.

How many times, she wondered, had she opened that door to perch upon the high stool beside the dry sink and sit silently attentive as Jamie, with eyebrow tweezers and bated breath, lifted a photograph out of one of the baths he had concocted? All her hopes, her whole future had seemed to swim in those solutions he mixed, pouring in a little of this, a little of that from the row of apothecary bottles on a shelf above his head.

Having prayed so hard, hoped so long, believed so completely, why was she surprised that Jamie had, in fact, brought it off, that his ideas had worked, that he was a success? Perhaps because things so seldom turned out as expected. Deep inside sat the Skeptic, ever waiting to skip out and cry, See, see, I told you so! But Jamie had vindicated the dream. Jamie was one of the rare lucky ones whose dreams had come true. For him . . . and for her.

She felt, rather than heard, someone behind her, knowing this as surely as, a while ago, she had known the shop was empty. For some reason the knowledge made her breath catch in her throat, and she spun round.

Morrissey lounged in the open doorway of the lean-to. Beyond him she could see the blacksmith shop and then bright daylight, which, for the most part, his obesity blotted out. Her eyes darted to the other door, the one to the alleyway.

"It's padlocked," said Morrissey. "No point leaving it open for you after Jamie went away." He smiled, creases of fat pushing up to all but close his small eyes. "Saw you drive up and get out. I was across the street."

So he had deliberately stolen in, intending to startle her.

"What can I do for you?" he asked lazily.

Controlling her agitation, she said, "I was wondering if you could give me the address of Jamie Fitzhugh."

"Ha!" He spat onto the hard dirt floor. "Can't you wait to take off your widow's weeds first?"

The insolent implication turned whatever unease Vivian had felt into anger. But she knew she mustn't let this show. She must get Jamie's address, and she was sure he had it.

"I must reach him about a business matter," she said.

"I bet!" He grinned. "Maybe you shouldn't of been so

quick, throwing that letter Thurman Foy brung you into the fire. Maybe you should of first looked at the return address."

She felt her cheeks sting at the thought of the seamy gossip that had surely transpired between these two, but she made no answer.

Her silence apparently changed Morrissey's mood. "What do you think?" he demanded, suddenly surly. "Do you think you maybe shouldn't of burned up that letter?"

"I have no doubt of it," replied Vivian, temper flaring, "seeing how difficult it is to get the address from you."

Her loss of composure seemed to delight him. "Oh, I'll give you his address. Be happy to. But first let's decide what you're going to give me in return."

Useless to continue the conversation, Vivian silently admitted. He was baiting her, making sport of her, like a cat with a mouse. Once, as a small child, she had stood horrified and watched a cat play with a mouse, picking it up, shaking it in its teeth, almost but never quite letting it get away. She wouldn't let herself be put in this position. She would have to swallow her pride and go to Thurman Foy, hoping he would prove more cooperative.

And then it came to her. She could ask at the post office for Jamie's forwarding address! The solution was so simple, so obvious, that she almost laughed. Walking directly to Morrissey as he stood blocking the doorway, she raised steely eyes to his. "Let me pass," she said.

Morrissey didn't move. "Aren't you going to say please?"

Fury seized Vivian. "I said, let me pass!"

"I'll let you pass all right!" retorted Morrissey. Wrapping one huge arm about her, he bent her backwards and with his free hand grasped her chin, jerking her face up to his. "But first I get a kiss."

"No!" she cried, turning her head this way and that in her efforts to avoid the leering face and foul-smelling breath above her.

"Shut up!" he snapped. "Shut up or I'll not stop at a kiss."

At his words cold reason gripped her and she stopped struggling, having not a doubt in the world he would do just as he said.

"Now," he continued, more agreeably, "it's not going to be so bad, is it? Just a kiss, that's all I'm after. Open your mouth."

Vivian felt her jaw being pinched between his thumb and his strong, stained, dirty fingers.

"Open your mouth, I said!" he commanded hoarsely.

Closing her eyes, Vivian did as she was bidden and felt his thick tongue thrust like a snake into her mouth, seeking her own tongue, finding it. At the contact, revulsion streaked through her and with all her strength she thrust against him, taking advantage of his insecure stance to twist from his grasp and race wildly toward the daylight.

"Wait!" he thundered.

Shocked into immobility, she froze in the open doorway and turned to face him.

"Now I keep my part of the bargain," he told her. "Jamie came back from St. Louis. He's got himself a picture studio. Number 804 Chestnut Street, right here in Philly."

32

Teeth chattering despite the mild spring afternoon, Vivian left the blacksmith shop and moved along the crowded street where all manner of vehicles passed, where busy pedestrians hurried by and children played. Yanking her handkerchief from her purse, she jammed it into her mouth, roughly wiping her tongue and then flinging the scrap of cloth into the gutter.

She had no intention of returning to Ma's house. What she wanted was Mamie, and home.

"What in the world has happened to you?" exclaimed Mary Claire, turning from the piano as Vivian flung open the screen door and burst in upon her.

"Where's mama?" demanded Vivian.

"Mama's not here."

"Not here!"

It seemed the ultimate desertion. Frustrated tears filled her eyes.

"Vivvie!" cried Mary Claire, springing up. "What's happened?"

For answer, Vivian said harshly, "Is the water hot for tea?"

"Yes," replied the mystified Mary Claire. "In the kettle."

"I want some," announced Vivian. "The hotter the better."

She couldn't get it hot enough, rejoicing that it scalded her tongue as she stood outside the back door taking sips from the cup in her hand, swilling it around in her mouth and then spitting it into the backyard.

"Have you gone crazy?" cried Mary Claire.

"Morrissey kissed me," said Vivian between sips.

"He what?"

"He kissed me."

"Kissed you?"

"Yes! Kissed me! Kissed me!"

Looking round, she caught sight of Mary Claire's baffled expression, and something so comic, so utterly ridiculous in this backyard performance struck her with such force as to dissolve her into wave after wave of laughter, which only pealed out afresh each time she beheld Mary Claire's vexed face.

It was some time before she could calm down sufficiently to explain her behavior to her offended sister, who observed, "Well, I don't see any call to take on this way over a silly kiss. You half scared me to death, bursting in that way."

Vivian had no desire to inflict upon Mary Claire just how distasteful the episode with Morrissey really had been. It was so pleasant sitting together on the back steps in the sunshine, just like old times. Next door the Curtins' ancient apple tree was in flower, clumps of daffodils bloomed against the picket fence, and down at the end of their yard, the forsythia that had so recently been a golden glory now modestly screened the privy with a haze of green.

Things, perhaps, weren't as bad as they might have been, Vivian decided. Upon consideration, she doubted now that anything worse than a kiss might have transpired at Morrissey's. He was a bully, but he had a business and a reputation to maintain. She would never put herself at his mercy again, but there was no call to take on, as Mary Claire said. And Jamie was back in Philadelphia! Somehow, despite her distress, the number and name of the street had lodged securely in her memory.

She thought of sharing this information with Mary Claire, but changed her mind, saying instead, "I'm thinking of opening a hairdressing salon."

Mary Claire listened with polite interest to Vivian's plans. A new and vastly different relationship had developed between the two of them. There was a wariness now, a carefulness of things said. Childhood roles of older and younger, of leader and follower had vanished forever, replaced by attitudes more remote, if more mature.

Vivian regretted the lost closeness. It was as though some part of Mary Claire shrank away from her, ever on guard. She believed their argument and her tumble down the stairs had hurt her sister far worse than it had hurt her. Mary Claire blamed herself for it, and Mallory's punitive attitude hadn't helped matters.

It was because Vivian longed to bridge this chasm between them that she listened with a show of sympathy she didn't feel as Mary Claire said, "I'm embarking upon a new career, also. This morning I had an audition with Mademoiselle Fleurette. I'm to be one of the Florodora Girls."

Vivian's heart sank to her toes. Everything in her urged protest, but she said, "The Florodora Girls? They're dancers, aren't they?"

"You've seen them?"

"No, I haven't," she replied, adding stiffly, "I believe Mallory knew Fleurette."

"I wouldn't be surprised," responded Mary Claire. "Everybody knows Fleurette. She's so larky and gay. I'm really lucky. You see, just by chance I found out at Lawson's that one of the Doras is leaving the show because she's in a family way. And it just happens she's the same size as me, so I'll fit into all her costumes, which is what decided Fleurette."

"But you can't dance," objected Vivian faintly.

Mary Claire giggled. "Oh, there's no terpsichore, as Fleurette calls it. We just parade around to the music and form a background for Fleurette when she sings."

Quite an extraordinary background, thought Vivian, observing her sister's remarkably fresh beauty—the startlingly white, flawless skin, eyes sparkling like brilliants, cloud of curling blue-black hair, and figure achingly youthful and lovely.

"Mary Claire," she burst out, flying in the face of past

experience, "what would you say to learning hairdressing and coming into my shop with me?"

Mary Claire jumped up from her perch on the steps. "You haven't been listening to one word I've been saying! Not one word! You never do!"

"But I have! And it's just because I know something of the life of a showgirl that I can't bear to see you on the stage."

"And how would you know about showgirls?"

"I've met some through Mallory, and I've heard of others. Their lives aren't nice."

"Nice! Ha! I should think not. I'd die of boredom if I had to live a nice life. I don't like things nice. I like things gay and larky."

Vivian sighed. Useless to try to dissuade her, and the very last thing she wished was another argument. "What does mama say?" she asked.

"Mama can't stop me," replied Mary Claire, snapping her lips shut tight over the words in the very incarnation of Mamie Randall herself. "Besides," she continued. "She's got enough to tend to. Nancy's going to have a baby, and papa is coming home."

Dumbfounded by such an abundance of news, Vivian's thoughts instantly leapt to her father. "Papa is coming home? From the Klondike?"

"Of course from the Klondike, where else? And," she added bitterly, "it's just the same as all the other times: not one penny to his name, done out of his share by the others, treated unfairly, and not his fault."

The scathing words twisted within Vivian. Mary Claire had always carried a resentment against their father. Whereas Vivian blew hot and cold, alternately adoring this man who swept in and out of their lives and rejecting him for the inept poseur she feared him to be, Mary Claire knew no such agonizing ambivalence. Mary Claire despised him, pure and simple.

Knowing this, Vivian hid the surge of happiness she felt at the prospect of his return. "Poor mama," she said, thinking of Mary Claire's decision to go on the stage, of the burden, precious though it might be, of a baby in the small house, and, finally, of the return of a moneyless, unwelcome husband.

"And to make matters worse," said Mary Claire, as if matters could be worsened, "Bucky is running with bad companions. Jerry Doheny and that set. The Bryce Street Alley Rats."

"Papa will put a stop to that," declared Vivian firmly. And just possibly, she silently prayed, to a daughter of his embarking on a life upon the stage.

As though reading her thoughts, Mary Claire said, "Well, I'll be gone by the time he gets here. You can tell him for me I'm going to get rich and famous and take care of mom."

Vivian left her mother's house sunk deep in thought. Mary Claire, she knew, hadn't been jesting when she said she meant to get rich and take care of Mamie. It was a dream the whole family shared, including, perhaps it was even engendered by, their father. The family had always wanted to make things easier for Mamie. And things had never been worse!

Oh, if only her hairdressing salon were already an established success! If only she could afford to keep Mallory's big house and move the family in there, all of them! If only she had money! Money!

There it was. Money, again.

Beyond the bedroom windows the sky lightened inch by imperceptible inch. A single bird twittered, fell silent, twittered again, the sound precisely duplicating those last sleepy settlings-down of dusk, only now the call acknowledged a new day.

From the crib beside the big iron bed came also a single tentative cry and then a more affirmative gurgle, good-humored, as Vivian had been spoiled into expecting from this amiable child. Rising, she picked up Irene, marveling yet again at her rosy perfection, burrowing her face into the tiny neck.

Mallory's figured velour armchair stood waiting. Vivian had turned it to face the window so that, as she gave her breast to Irene for this first feeding of the day, she could look out at the sun climbing up the sky, glinting on the golden spire of St. Bonaventure's in the distance, glistening on slate rooftops still wet with morning dew. She liked sitting here. It was as though Mallory were holding both of them in his arms. She had once mentioned this to Gert Barkin, and Gert said, "You better cut out that kind of stuff, Vivvie. You can go loony thinking things like that."

But Vivian continued to take comfort in the notion. She liked to believe Mallory was watching over her and Irene, although how anguished he would be had he observed what had happened in Morrissey's blacksmith shop yesterday. And how, she asked herself, might he feel about seeing her travel up Chestnut Street to see Jamie Fitzhugh today?

At the very thought of the mission that lay before her, her heart took a leap and she sucked in her breath, causing Irene to stir in her arms. How would Jamie receive her? Did he know she was now a widow? How long had he been in Philadelphia?

Fortunately she could reach his establishment by walking up to Chestnut Street and thence west to Eighth. She would have hated to ask Bunty O'Hare, devoted to her though he had been since Mallory's death, to borrow someone's horse and carriage again today. But she would have to ask Ma to mind Irene once more, and this she disliked. Not that Ma ever objected to caring for the child. She adored her granddaughter and was good to her. But she was less than happy with her daughter-in-law, especially after the little altercation over a site for the hairdressing salon.

Slipping into a light, figured lawn kimono, Vivian quickly tied back her hair with a ribbon and carried the baby down to the dining room. Ma, at this hour also in a capacious kimono, raised her arms to receive a squirming and delighted Irene, bequeathing on the child a smile that did not include Vivian. Trudie, the maid-of-all-work, brought in a bowl of hot oatmeal together with a pot of fresh coffee, and Vivian spooned brown sugar over the steaming cereal, floated cream on top, and tucked into her breakfast.

Barely had she swallowed a mouthful, however, when Ma said, "I've thought over the advice your Mr. Webb gave you yesterday about my son's house. I think he's wrong."

The phrase "my son's house" wasn't lost upon Vivian, nor the gratuitous "*your* Mr. Webb." But it was Ma's tone that was most offensive: peremptory, arrogant, domineering. It was the voice of the old days just after Vivian had married Mallory and "taken" Ma's son away from her. Now death had taken him away, but nonetheless Vivian was to be made to bear the brunt.

Still, conscious of the many favors received at Ma's

hands, Vivian said mildly, "It can't hurt to hold out for a while, can it, Ma? I feel sure Dolly wants it rather badly."

" '*Rawther* badly,' " mimicked Ma. " '*Rawther* badly.' That's from those royals who never bother to see or come near you anymore. Is that the way you're going to teach my granddaughter to talk?"

Vivian felt Irene could only be counted fortunate if she grew up to speak in so cultivated a manner, but she made no comment, spooning up the cereal, which now seemed to have lost all its savor.

"The Muldoons aren't ones to be trifled with," continued Ma, deftly dealing with Irene's kicks and squeals while returning to the fray. "They know you've got a white elephant on your hands. That's what it is, and that's what I told my son it would be from the day they thrust the first shovel into the sod. Who do you think is going to buy it if the Muldoons don't take it off your hands?"

"I think the Muldoons will buy, Ma. If it looks like they won't, I'll lower my price."

"It may be too late by then."

"No, it won't."

"Miss Know-it-all, eh?"

"Oh, Ma!" cried Vivian, losing patience at last. "I just know how badly Dolly wants the house. And how badly I need the money."

Less belligerently, Ma said, "And what are you needing all this money for? I'm perfectly happy to have you here, you and Irene both, for all your days. And the place comes to you when I'm dead, who else? Who else have I got to leave it to? Who else have I got left in the world? And you needn't worry with the hairdressing. I've been thinking we'll keep the Tip just as it is. Income is off a mite, but we'll have enough. It's a business that's always got custom. You can live like a lady and sew a fine seam. Now, what do you say to that?"

How Vivian wished she could accept this generous and undoubtedly sincere proposal! How she wished she could be just as frank in turn and tell Ma that, far from thinking to go into business, it was marriage to Jamie Fitzhugh that now filled her head.

"I appreciate your offer, Ma, but it wouldn't work out," she said in a low voice. She added swiftly, to forestall argument, "I have a favor to ask of you. I need you to mind

Irene for me this morning while I go to visit Jamie Fitzhugh."

Had she thought for a day and a night, no subject could have more surely claimed Ma's full attention. "Jamie Fitzhugh," she whispered, her voice so stunned that little Irene grew quiet in her arms. "You are going to visit Jamie Fitzhugh?"

Vivian nodded. "He owes Mallory money. Mallory invested in a formula that Jamie sold to a photographic company. Mr. Webb says I should receive a lump sum payment and royalties as my share. He says the royalties might last a long time."

"Jamie Fitzhugh is in St. Louis."

"He's come back. He's opened a photographic studio at Eighth and Chestnut."

The flat gray gaze hardened. "You've found out a lot, running around behind my back."

I've done nothing wrong, thought Vivian, standing before Ma like a prisoner in the dock. Why do I feel guilty?

But as Ma cried roughly, "Go then! Go to him!" guilt she did surely feel.

33

Unseasonably warm for April, the sun beat down, piercing the black silk of Vivian's parasol to lie along her slim shoulders as she moved up Chestnut Street.

It was really much too hot for the faille suit she wore, but there was no help for it. She must wear black for one more week, until—she had long since noted the date—May Day, the first of May, and how happy she would be to shed these garments that for long months she had worn everywhere!

The only possessions she had left from her marriage were her clothes and what jewelry Mallory had given her. Everything else was pledged, but for these he had paid cash, she discovered, sifting through his papers in a determined effort to understand his tangled financial affairs. And how like him, she thought, smiling, to want everything about her to be totally his. There were no strings attached to her personal belongings, and she would give thanks when she could slip back into her lovely clothes and once more wear bracelets, brooches, rings.

Perhaps, she thought apprehensively, catching a glimpse of her somber figure in the reflection from a store window, she should have delayed this visit until she could dress more becomingly. The women she passed all seemed especially smart in their spring suits and straw boaters. Frequently, however, their hairdos lacked. Yes, there were things she would definitely have liked to try with some of the coiffeurs. Her fingers started to itch, but the likelihood of her ever having anything to do with hairdressing now appeared to be remote.

A pity, she reflected, that married women couldn't go out to work—married women, that is, of the class to which she would belong if married to an inventor and man of means like Jamie. The shame this brought upon a husband, proclaiming as it did that he was unable to support a wife! No, it wasn't done, *couldn't* be done. But that she truly regretted this state of affairs indicated how far she had wandered from earlier predilections, although she was far too excited at the prospect of seeing Jamie to observe this interesting change in herself.

Number 804 Chestnut Street, when she reached it, proved to be a serviceable-looking red brick building, tall and narrow, and wedged between the Regal Shoe Store (Shoes: $3.50) and a watch repair shop that advertised its presence by a huge gilt-painted pocket watch hoisted above the sidewalk.

The front of Jamie's establishment was divided into two sections. On the one hand was a large plate-glass window curtained by a green baize cloth depending from a rod and brass rings. In front of this was a sign: James Fitzhugh, Photographer. On the other, set into an alcove, was an entrance door, its upper half glass. Through this Vivian could see stairs leading steeply upward to the second floor. To the side of the stairs was yet another door, also half glass, its face lettered with the same information as on the sign in the window. A light glowed within; someone was there.

Standing outside, Vivian's heart hammered so alarmingly she felt she could scarce catch her breath. A roaring filled her ears, perspiration broke upon her lip and forehead, and her hands shook. Everything within her seemed to be quivering with such a mixture of anticipation and apprehension, such a desire to rush in and a like inclination to rush away, that she stood rooted to the spot and might have remained there for heaven knew how long if Jamie hadn't casually brushed aside the green baize curtain and looked out at her.

For a moment both were transfixed, staring at one another in surprise. Then Jamie let drop the curtain, and in seconds was ushering her into his studio.

Grateful for his hand at her elbow, she let him lead her to a bench cushioned in brown velvet. This bench was used to pose Jamie's clients and had been placed in front of a canvas backdrop artistically painted to suggest a summer garden in full bloom. The drop could be raised like a window shade and exchanged for a drop depicting Grecian ruins, or one providing simply an expanse of blue sky. Before the bench was a camera on a tripod, and beyond this a desk heaped with letters, newspapers, magazines. But along with such prosaic furnishings were accents of a curiously unprofessional character: a child's roller skate peeking from under the tripod, a skipping rope loosely lassoed to the desk chair, while from overhead came the muffled sound of children's voices.

Vivian took scant notice of all this.

"You've been here some time, Jamie?" she asked softly.

"A month," replied Jamie.

"You've heard about Mallory, then?"

He nodded, his eyes on her as though he could never look his fill. "Thurman Foy told me."

"And you did not wish to come by and call on me?"

"And you still in your widow's weeds?"

She met his eyes squarely. "Until May Day I'll wear them. Until the first day of May."

"I'll be dropping by then."

"I'm living with Ma now."

"This I know."

"And also . . . also, I have a child."

"This I know, too. And I'm telling you right now I'm marrying you. I'll be by on the evening of the first day of May."

Out on the sidewalk once more she walked along in a

daze, scarce able to believe she had heard what he had said to her, scarce able to trust the happiness that sang in her heart. Yet she could recall every word he had spoken, every nuance, inflection, every expression that had crossed his face. Over and over in her mind, like a scene in a play, she reviewed all that had transpired. They had spent only moments together, but her whole life had changed. Why, he had proposed to her!

Without realizing how far she had walked in such blissful rapture, she saw now that she had arrived at Cavendish Square. It spread out in the sunshine, the fountain dancing in the center as children hung over its sides with small boats, nursemaids chatting together on benches while keeping an eye on their prams, ladies with parasols and gentlemen in derbies moving along the broad pavements under the feathery young green leaves.

Drugged with happiness, Vivian sought out a vacant bench and sat down. She wasn't at all sure what she had expected when she called upon Jamie, but certainly an immediate proposal of marriage had been far from her mind. And she suddenly remembered, she hadn't said one word about his invention, or Mallory's share in it. A smile touched her lips. Small matter, since now it would merely be taking money out of one pocket and putting it into the other.

Engrossed though she was by such pleasant considerations, her eyes widened as they chanced to rest upon two figures approaching her from the distance. The one, dressed all in white, was clearly a nurse. But the other . . . oh, how could she forget that graceful carriage, that movement that was more floating than walking? Irene Webb, of course. But as the woman drew closer, Vivian noted marked changes. The thick beautiful hair, formerly always arranged in sculptured perfection, was haphazardly done up, as though no time or interest had been taken, and the once serene visage was creased in frowning anxiety.

As the two women came near, Vivian rose and stepped forward. "Mrs. Webb," she said gently, not wishing to startle her.

The nurse looked askance but Irene Webb's face brightened. "Why, Vivvie dear!"

"Oh, Mrs. Webb, I'm so happy to see you. It's been such a long time. May we sit down and talk a moment?"

Irene Webb turned inquiringly to her nurse, who replied, "For a moment, if you like," although she didn't sound pleased.

With all three seated on the bench, Vivian said, "I've so much to tell you! I have a little girl . . ." She chattered on, describing Irene. "I named her for you," she offered shyly.

"For me!" echoed Irene Webb. "Why, how nice of you!"

"Not at all, ma'am," responded Vivian, slipping back into a role long since shed. "I always thought you the grandest lady in the world. I'd love you to see my baby. Could you come to tea sometime?"

"Oh no, dear, never. I seldom leave my home even for a walk in the Square. I'm afraid to be outside, you see."

It was then Vivian noticed Irene Webb's jeweled fingers clutching her nurse's hand, and in dismay she understood the effort this little conversation was costing her former employer.

"But perhaps you will bring your baby to visit me," Mrs. Webb continued. "I love babies. I'm hoping my son and his wife will present me with one."

Dare Vivian mention that Nancy was now three months pregnant? Fearing to upset what might be a delicate balance, she held her tongue. Only if Irene Webb asked about her daughter would she feel free to speak.

But when, moments later, Mrs. Webb rose from the bench, saying she felt breathless and dizzy and must return home, she hadn't uttered Nancy's name.

The little meeting took the edge off Vivian's euphoria. She moved along past the Episcopal Church of the Holy Trinity, in whose Romanesque interior Webbs, Cavendishes, and Allenbys worshipped and married, past the massive stone residences in which they and their neighbors lived, and, leaving the Square, past the stylish little shops along Walnut Street that serviced them.

These shops were as far removed from the stores and business enterprises of South Philadelphia as were the mansions on the Square from the row houses of Butler Street. Their windows, whether offering flowers or jewelry or bonbons, were alike in an air of nonchalance that veered on hauteur, and it would not be too much to say that only those who lived on the Square, or in proximate locations, possessed the savoire faire to enter them.

It was beside a tobacconist's that Vivian came upon an empty shop with a sign in the window: To Let. See Mr. Boyd next door. Spying it, she stopped dead in her tracks, oblivious to pedestrians who eddied about her as though she were a small, inconvenient island. Never would she be able to sleep without knowing the price of the rent. With some diffidence she regarded the wooden Indian guarding the tobacconist's door, then she screwed up her courage and entered.

Inside, in gleaming cases all manner and styles of pipes were set out, displayed on black velvet cushions like rare jewels. Myriad kinds of tobacco were stored in large glass jars stoppered with ground-glass tops. Hung from chains about the necks of these jars were sterling silver tags bearing romantic names of tobaccos: Perique, Burley, Latakia. The whole was infused with an enticing aroma that made the head spin.

Part of this aroma was supplied by a dapper little man who, smoking a pipe, came forward from the back of the store.

"Are you Mr. Boyd?" asked Vivian politely.

"I am," he replied.

"I'm inquiring about the shop next door."

"Who is to be the propietor?"

Nonplussed, Vivian said, "Why, I am."

Mr. Boyd shook his head. "Won't rent to a female," he snapped.

"Why on earth not?"

"Females have no head for business." He squinted up at her. "What kind of business have you got?"

"I haven't got it yet. I haven't started."

"See what I mean? No head for business. Here you come in and want to rent a shop in one of the most exclusive locations in the city for a business you haven't got."

"An exclusive location is just what I need."

"Why? What kind of business do you want to start?"

It had never crossed her mind that she might have to justify herself to a landlord, but summoning all her dignity, she replied, "I am a hairdresser, Mr. Boyd. I wish to open a hairdressing salon."

"A hairdressing *what*?"

"Salon. Ladies will come to my shop and I'll wash and dress their hair."

"You mean a female barbershop?"

"Well, more or less."

"I never heard tell of such nonsense."

"It's the coming thing," she assured him.

But he was not to be won. "Not next door to me, it's not."

Vivian stared at him. There was no doubt he meant what he said, but her stubborn nature wasn't about to let her depart without even having learned the rent.

"How much are you asking?" she said.

Her persistence clearly annoyed him. "I just now raised the price from thirty-five dollars to fifty-five."

"May I inspect the property?"

"No!" he hollered. "Didn't I just get through telling you I don't rent to females? Now clear out of here. Go on, clear out!"

Cheeks burning with humiliation, Vivian did as she was told. She had come to the end of her courage. What's more, she wasn't going to open a hairdressing salon. She was going to marry Jamie Fitzhugh!

Slowly, slowly the last few days of April slipped by. Minute by minute, time slid into eternity and at last it was May Day, the first of May.

During this period Ma had scarcely spoken to Vivian, and what words she uttered were barely civil. Vivian knew this was due in part to her visit to Jamie's photography studio, and in part to the fact that she had written a note to Dolly and Thomas O'Reilly, informing them she couldn't accept their offer on Mallory's house.

Neither of these developments was designed to put Ma in good humor, and only the thought of Jamie sustained Vivian—the prospect of an end to this unpleasant sojourn and the start of a happy new life. Even the weather appeared to augur well. Doubtless due to the unseasonable warmth, Butler Street had burst into luxurious bloom. White and purple lilacs filled the air with their fragrance, pansies and tulips graced backyards, and here and there a dogwood tree blossomed, its petals clouds of pink or creamy white.

Not even Ma's dour expression could dampen Vivian's spirits.

"Jamie Fitzhugh is coming to call on me this evening," she told her mother-in-law on that first morning in May.

"Hmph!" said Ma. "I see you're wasting no time."

"It's been six months, Ma."

"I can count. Every day I tick off the time my boy has been in the grave. Every day."

Vivian had learned that her only defense was to firmly ignore such invitations to sentimentality. "May I invite Jamie into the parlor? Or would you prefer I meet him outside?"

"I'm sure I don't care in the least."

"I'll invite him inside, then," replied Vivian, no longer caring that her answer was sharp.

In the parlor she threw up the windows to the May breezes. A five-piece matched parlor set graced this room, ranged round a massive center pillar oak table. Upholstered in fancy brocaded plush of red and black, with deep diamond-tufted backs and corded seats, the chairs and divan alike offered curved dragons' heads on the arms, and claw feet.

Asking Trudie to give the room a special dust-up, she went into the backyard, cut purple lilacs, vigorously shook the ants from them, arranged them in a cut-glass vase, and set them in the center of the table. Then she washed her hair with her own special soap and slowly brushed its coppery length while sitting on the back stoop. It was midafternoon when, having put Irene down for her nap, she stood at her wardrobe considering what she might wear. Not black, saints be praised! Her inclination ran to either a fine percale with blue figures on a white background or a pink silk mull with a valenciennes lace yolk trimmed with black velvet ribbon.

She had just decided on the latter when a light tap came to the bedroom door. Trudie stood in the hallway. "There's a woman come to see you, ma'am."

"Who is she?" asked Vivian.

"I don't know, ma'am. She wouldn't give her name so I didn't let her in."

Thrusting the two dresses back into the wardrobe, Vivian whipped off her work apron and hurried down the stairs, a puzzled frown between her eyes. When she opened the front door her mystification deepened, for though she recognized the woman who stood before her, she couldn't place her.

"Hi," said her visitor. "I'm Connie, from St. Louis. Remember me?"

Instantly everything fell into place: the rooming house to

which Jamie had taken her, the good-looking, rather blowsy young woman who had appeared in the hallway, the sound of children's voices, of roller skating, in the hall upstairs.

Like a companion piece, certain details from her recent visit to Jamie's photography studio now returned with an ominous relevance, although she had scarcely noticed them at the time: a skate under Jamie's tripod, a jump rope tied to a chair, children's voices from the floor above.

"I do remember you," she said wonderingly.

"I'd like to talk to you. Can I come in?"

"Certainly."

She stood back to let the woman enter and then, in something of a daze, led her into the parlor. A conviction of doom, heavy as a hand on her shoulder, enveloped her as she motioned the woman to the divan and sat down herself upon a chair.

The feeling deepened when the woman said, "I don't like what I'm doing. But I know Jamie's coming here to see you tonight so I may as well get to the point." She paused for the space of a breath, then added, "I'm pregnant with his child."

Vivian made no reply. She could see that the woman, cheaply but not unfashionably dressed in a black and white checked jumper suit, was clearly pregnant. She could see, also, that some comment was expected from her, but it was as though her brain had been frozen by this news. She was unable to think, let alone speak.

Failing to elicit a response, Connie pressed onward. "Like I say, I hate to do this. I know all about your husband being shot. Jamie told me. I felt real bad about that, especially you being true to him. Jamie told me about that, too. Believe me, I admire your type of woman."

"Mrs. Fitzhugh," began Vivian faintly.

"Hey now, wait a minute! Don't get me wrong. I'm not Mrs. Fitzhugh. Don't I wish! Mathews is my name. Connie Mathews. That's my married name. And I got three kids, not counting this one here in the oven. Three years ago my husband ran off and—"

Vivian raised a hand. She felt ill. "Mrs. Mathews, I don't want to hear—"

"You gotta hear!" the woman cut in sharply. More quietly, she said, "Like I just told you, I don't like what I'm doing, but I got nowhere else to turn. I know Jamie's coming here tonight and I know he's wanting to marry you. He's crazy about you, I know that; I've always known that right from the beginning. But I did it because . . . well, Jamie's been good to me and my kids. And when Thurman Foy wrote and said you burnt up that letter of his in the fireplace—"

"Mrs. Mathews—"

"Damn it, shut up!" cried the woman. "I've got more to lose in this than you do! I'm carrying his kid!" More calmly, she said, "I was good to Jamie after he got that letter. He liked me. I always knew that. I suit him better than you do. He'd never be the gentleman you want him to be. Jamie's a free spirit. What he really wants is to roam around the world with his camera and still have someone waiting for him when he gets back home. Right now, he's planning to go across the country taking pictures of poor people."

She laughed shortly and shook her head. "Can you beat it? Taking pictures of poor people! Documentary photography, he calls it. Pictures that show how bad things are for folks. He sells them to magazines. He's been in six different magazines so far. Sometimes he doesn't come back for two, three weeks at a time. I never ask where he's been. Jamie's touchy about questions." She laughed. "As long as he comes back, what do I care?"

She fastened frank, undeluded eyes upon Vivian. "But now something new has been added," she said bluntly. "You. He wants to marry you."

Like match to tinder, the words kindled sparks within Vivian. "And I want to marry him!"

Connie Mathews sighed. "I know."

The irrelevance the woman seemed to attach to this declaration served to incense Vivian even further. "How do I know you're telling the truth?" she cried.

"Ask him tonight," responded the woman flatly. "You gotta. It's the only way you'll ever rest easy. If he denies it, just ask him about that strawberry he's got. He'll know where."

A tremor gripped and shook Vivian. "Please go," she said.

"Look, don't be mad—"

"I would simply very much appreciate it if you would leave."

"Now, wait. I got my conscience to live with, too. The

only reason I come here is like I said, because of the kid. Jamie had me and now I gotta get him to marry me because—"

"Get out!" screamed Vivian at the top of her lungs. "Get out! Get out! Get out!" Turning to Trudie, who had appeared wide-eyed and curious in the doorway, she said in a voice shaking with fury, "Trudie, show this woman the door."

34

With the shutting of the front door and the sharp little clicks of Connie Mathews's heels receding in the distance along the sidewalk, Vivian stood rigidly upright in the center of the parlor and pressed the tips of her fingers against closed eyelids.

It was thus that, upon entering the room, Ma found her.

"Sit down, daughter," said Ma gently, using the appellation for the first time. "Sit down."

Vivian opened her eyes to find Ma regarding her with the utmost seriousness.

"I heard every word," said Ma. "Sit down."

Of their own volition Vivian's knees seemed to obey this injunction, and she sank down upon a chair.

"Now listen to me, daughter," continued Ma solemnly. "I know what a blow this visit has been to you. I know you were thinking to marry the man. But you can't do it now."

"And why can't I?" cried Vivian, life flooding back into her. "Why can't I when it's him I've always wanted and now I'm free?"

Ma shook her head. "You know why as well as I do. He's got this woman in trouble. There's an innocent child coming into the world that must be considered."

"And how do I know it's his?" raged Vivian, goaded beyond endurance. "How do I know she's telling the truth?"

"Daughter, daughter," said Ma sorrowfully. "Does a man bring a woman and her children all the way from St.

Louis out of the goodness of his heart? Isn't it more likely that it's just as she said? He lives with her. I hold no brief for her, but her tale smacks of the truth. And you could tell by the looks of her whether she was pregnant or not."

"And if she's that kind of woman, it could be by any man."

"True," sighed Ma. "Only likely it's not. You must ask him tonight, just as she said. He must have his chance to deny it, if deny it he can."

Vivian stared at the woman standing so placidly just inside the doorway, hands folded over her stomach, calmly making pronouncements, uttering these implacable words that lacerated the soul.

"And why should I care if he can't?" she demanded, grief and fury overwhelming her. "Why should I care? It's no doing of mine. Why should I give up my happiness?"

"Because," said Ma somberly, "you can't build happiness on another's sorrow. No, and you can't. If Jamie Fitzhugh got this woman with child, if he took his pleasure with her and has made her pregnant, then he must stand up like a man and accept his responsibility. He must seek to marry her and give the child a name and a father. Now there's nothing in heaven or earth that can twist it or turn it from that.

"Ah, daughter," she pressed onward, "don't be thinking I'm not wanting to see you happy. Life stretches so lonely and hard without a man at your side. But you'll not be happy with him—no, not with the likes of Jamie Fitzhugh. Sure, he'll bring you only grieving and heartache, just as he did before."

"He didn't!" cried Vivian sharply, a flush rising to her face.

"There now, everyone knows all about it, him running off to St. Louis and leaving you. And mark my words, a man that does it once will do it again, just as he's about to prove with this woman today, by the look of it."

"You've not heard his side!"

"That I have not, and neither have you. All I'm saying is, you're a good woman, Vivian Mallory. You must answer to your conscience and your God."

From upstairs came the baby's sudden demanding cry.

"I'll see to her," offered Ma. "You take a little rest."

Vivian sighed. "No, Ma, I'll go. I'm all right, really I am."

But as she went up the stairs, a deep bone weariness assailed her, and it was all she could do to lift one foot after the other. The baby seemed unbearably heavy in her arms.

Out of her crib Irene switched from tears to companionable cooing, but Vivian paid scant heed to the wiles that usually so charmed her. She carried the child down the stairs and went to sit on the back stoop to feed her, staring off down the alleyway with turbulent green eyes.

The sound of Jamie's voice rang in her ears, and every detail of their recent meeting sprang vividly to life before her.

"*You've been here some time, Jamie?*"

"*A month.*"

"*You've heard about Mallory, then?*"

"*Thurman Foy told me.*"

"*And you did not wish to come by and call on me?*"

"*And you still in your widow's weeds?*"

"*Until May Day I'll wear them. Until the first day of May.*"

"*I'll be dropping by then.*"

"*I'm living with Ma now.*"

"*This I know.*"

"*And also . . . also, I have a child.*"

"*This I know, too. And I'm telling you right now I'm marrying you. I'll be by on the evening of the first day of May.*"

Oh, how she had counted the hours, the minutes to this day, and now it had arrived to no purpose. Worse, to the end of everything she had hoped for, dreamed of; indeed, had come to expect. One small glimmer of hope like a wavering candle began to glow within her heart. Jamie might assure her that he wasn't the father of Connie Mathews's child. If he did, she would believe him. Yes, believe him against the world!

And why, after all, should this not prove to be the case? Connie Mathews had everything to lose by Jamie's taking a wife. Such a woman, pregnant and with several other children, could be expected to try the most desperate means to secure her livelihood. Such a woman might well say anything, stop at nothing.

The more she thought about this, the more reasonable it seemed. Her brow cleared. She looked down and smiled at her baby and, as soon as the child finished feeding, sat her in her high chair in the kitchen. Then she took the ironing board from the closet and pressed her pink silk mull.

By six-thirty she was dressed and ready. Supper was over; Ma had gone next door, as usual, to her post at the Tipperary. Trudie was upstairs crooning to Irene before tucking her in for the night. Every red-gold hair in place, eyes bright with excited anticipation, Vivian sat in the waning day at one of the open windows in the parlor.

It might, she fretted, be construed as overly eager should Jamie find her at the parlor window, straining her eyes down the street for the first sight of him, but she was powerless to stop herself. Each time she left the window, she found herself hastening back again. Far better to sit down and compose herself.

But sitting quietly, gazing out into the street in the gathering dusk, she felt how slowly the minutes passed. On the mantel the clock ticked, seeming to fill the room with sound, and the perfume from the vase of lilacs she had fixed earlier that day lay on the air, heavy and sweet.

Hennie Greene, the lamplighter, came by, stopping at the street lamp on the corner of Butler and Bryce just outside the Tipperary saloon. Knocking back the cap on the lamp with the prong of his pole, he lit the wick. A medallion of yellow light bloomed above the sidewalk, illuminating the foliage of an overhanging branch, turning each quivering leaf to gold.

More people were about and the street was livelier now that the dinner hour was passed. Vivian, peeping out, recognized more than one neighbor on his way to the Tip to lift one before going back home to bed. Had she better, she thought, just light a lamp or two in the parlor? The house mustn't look dark and unwelcoming. Jamie should be along any minute. It was now eight o'clock. Moving about the room, she lit first the green domed student lamp above the bent glass bookcase, and then the large parlor lamp on the table with the wild geese painted upon its beaded porcelain shade.

"Ma'am, I'll just be saying good night, then," said Trudie from the doorway. "The little one's sleeping as fast as can be."

At the girl's words, alarm washed over Vivian. Was it really so late? Time for Trudie to go?

"Thank you, Trudie," she said.

The girl smiled, transforming the plain young face. "I hope you enjoy your evening. You look ever so grand."

"Thank you."

"I'll be off, then."

Vivian listened to the stolid footsteps thumping through the house and heard the back screen door swing shut. From the Tipperary came sounds of activity. Someone was playing the piano, and voices were raised in that favorite Irish pastime, a little sing-song.

Vivian sat on a straight-back chair before the mantel, unable to take her eyes off the clock. Quarter to nine. Later than she had expected him to be. But instead of walking he might have elected to take a trolley and then missed it, having to wait for another. All sorts of things could conspire to delay one.

Taking a handkerchief from out of the tight cuff of her sleeve, she dabbed her forehead. She wished she hadn't worn the pink silk mull, for all she loved the net yolk under which her shoulders gleamed. It was warmer than her percale would have been. And the night itself seemed to have turned warm, much warmer than recent evenings. Her face was very likely as shiny as the brass coal bucket on the hearth, and her hair, with which she had taken such pains, was surely curling into damp ringlets.

Rising from her chair, she hastened to peer into the oval mirror above the mantel, and it was at this precise moment that a firm rap came to the front door. At the sound her heart gave such a leap that she felt it would choke her. She coughed and, whirling, rushed to the door, flinging it open.

Solly, the bartender, stood there. Only the grace of God had prevented her from flinging herself into his arms, so sure had she been that it was Jamie.

"Ma sent me over," said Solly, "to see how you're coming along."

So keen was her disappointment she could scarce get out the words to assure him she was perfectly fine.

Slowly, like a sleepwalker, she shut the door, moved back into the parlor, and sat down. It was nine-thirty. As the clock struck the half hour, she acknowledged the fear that for some time had lain at the back of her mind like a thief waiting to snatch the last of her happiness.

It was getting late, quite late. He should surely have been here by now had he meant to come.

She was still sitting upright on the straight-backed chair when Ma came in from the Tipperary just a bit past eleven o'clock. Vivian heard the door open and close; heard the heavy sigh that frequently accompanied Ma's ungainly movements, heard her move into the parlor. But she didn't turn, or look up from the hands tightly clenched in her lap.

"You must start your hairdressing business," said Ma. "Yes, that's what you must be about. You must start your hairdressing business on Cavendish Square."

It was, thought Vivian the next morning at breakfast, the most vexatious injustice that, instead of being permitted to lick her wounds in silence, tend her broken heart, she must perforce listen to Ma take on about a hairdressing salon on Cavendish Square.

"Why *won't* Mr. Boyd rent to a female?" Ma demanded.

"Ma, I told you. He thinks females don't have business sense." She sighed and added, "Maybe he's right. I certainly know nothing about running a business."

"Well, I do, and I shall instruct you. Now," said Ma with renewed vigor, "you liked this shop, did you? You felt it was just the thing?"

"Ma, he even raised the rent while I was standing there, from thirty-five dollars to fifty-five!"

"But is the shop what you're wanting?"

Unable to endure the interrogation longer, she rose from the table, saying feelingly, "Ma, there's not one thing left in this world that I want."

As always when distressed, she flung herself into an orgy of physical labor. She didn't want to think. She wanted, for the moment, to blot Jamie, Connie Mathews, and the events of the past few days from her mind. Jamie, for whatever reason, had chosen to stand her up, just as, not so very long ago, he had chosen to go off to St. Louis without her. But she wouldn't permit this knowledge to intrude on her consciousness. His failure to arrive or at least send word had left a wound too fresh, too hurtful to allow for probing. Someday she would think about it, sort it all out. Someday, but not now. Instead, she took Irene into the backyard, put her in her carriage, and began hoeing the small kitchen garden.

"Bunty always does the garden," said Ma at lunchtime.

"I'm going to do it this year," replied Vivian.

"Wearing yourself out," grumbled Ma, but she turned her attention to the new mattress she wanted to purchase for her bed. "There's one right here in the Sears' catalogue," she said, moving her tea cup and opening the thick book before her. " 'Genuine elastic felt mattress,' it says. 'Ten dollars and ninety-five cents.' And with a six months' free trial offer."

She glanced at Vivian to make sure she had full attention before proceeding. "Here it says right here: 'Send us your order for this Genuine Whitmore Luxury Elastic Felt Mattress, enclose the price, $10.95, and when you have received it, compared, examined, and tested it, by sleeping on it for six months, we give you the privilege of returning it to us and we will immediately refund your money together with the freight charges.' Now, I'm after asking you," concluded Ma, "what could be more honorable than that?"

But impressed though Ma was by the fair dealing of the Sears, Roebuck Company, she nonetheless informed Vivian that she would just take herself off to John Wanamaker's grand new department store and inspect the mattresses they had there.

Vivian was happy to see her go. More than anything she wanted to be alone and, most especially, spared Ma's heavy sighs, sorrowful glances, and attempts to draw her into conversation about mattresses and salons.

Left to her own pursuits, Vivian continued to work in the garden, and it was here that Trudie brought her the letter.

"The postman's just come, ma'am," she said, a knowing sympathy in her eyes. "There's a letter for you."

Thanking her, Vivian took it and, less from choice than from a sudden weakening of the knees, sank down upon the ground. She had instantly recognized Jamie's hand. For a moment she held the envelope before her, fearful of opening it. Then she slit it with a grimy thumb.

> *Dearest Vivvie,*
> *When you receive this I shall have commenced upon the first leg of a journey across the United States, taking photographs for* The Social Survey Magazine. *I consider this work my mission in life—namely, forcing the American people to look into the face of misery created by a money-grubbing society.*

The fee is decent enough and I believe it will lead to other assignments.

But there is a special reason I'm taking the trip right now. Someday I hope I will be able to explain the necessity for it. Presently, suffice it to say that Connie Mathews was quite correct in informing you that she is bearing my child. But I don't love Connie, and I have never once told her I did. I'm only sorry she didn't give me the opportunity to tell you of her pregnancy myself, as I had meant to do until she wrecked my plans by taking these matters upon herself.

You are the only woman I have ever loved or wanted to marry. I love you still, but I no longer know what you may be feeling for me. Can you, my darling, possibly want me for a husband? Will you write and tell me so? My editor at The Social Survey *will have my itinerary and forward my mail. At every stop I shall be looking for word from you.*

Always,

Jamie

For a long time after she read the letter she remained in deepest thought. Faithless, yes, he had proved faithless once again. Faithless to the unwanted, illegitimate child, and to her—sneaking off without a word of explanation, sending her a letter. The humiliation of that long night of waiting, sitting upright in the parlor wearing her pink silk mull and staring at the clock, now joined that other night when she had flown down the alleyway to Morrissey's only to find him gone. Her heart grew hard as stone.

Carefully she replaced the letter in its envelope and put it in the pocket of her apron. She wouldn't destroy it as she had his other letters. She would keep it always. Whenever, in the future, she would be tempted to think yearningly of Jamie Fitzhugh, she would open it and read again those callous, self-centered words.

35

The shop on Walnut Street was right. It was the right size, it had the right appearance; above all, it was in the right place.

Returning to it the day after Jamie's letter arrived, Vivian stood across the street and gazed longingly over at it. She had arisen that morning determined to put the past behind her and open her hairdressing salon. So firmly resolved was she that she was scarcely aware of the steady spring rain drumming down on her black silk umbrella, or the carriages that passed by casting up a great spray of water that rapidly dampened her skirt.

For most of the night she had lain awake planning what she must do to get started. She would, she decided, ask the lawyer whom Clinton Webb had recommended to get in touch with Jamie about Mallory's share in the formula. And she must wrack her brain for a way to inveigle Dolly and Tom O'Reilly to buy Mallory's house at her price. She must, after all, have money to make the shop the elegant, luxurious establishment she intended it to be.

She knew very well the atmosphere she meant to create. She wanted her patrons to look forward to their appointments as a unique part of their week, one they would anticipate with pleasure, cancel with reluctance. She wanted them to emerge from her ministrations looking as beautiful as it was possible to look. But more, *feeling* beautiful: relaxed, pampered, rejuvenated.

She had no doubt she could achieve these results, for hadn't she proved this over and over again? Hadn't even Anthea Allenby—now Anthea Webb, and one of the hardest women in the world to satisfy—hadn't she begged Vivian to dress her hair on her wedding day?

Thinking of Anthea, Vivian was struck by an idea so novel, so audacious as to take her breath away. For a few moments it rolled around in her head as she continued to look hopelessly but covetously at the shop across the street. Then, with a determined lift of her chin, she turned and proceeded toward the home of Clinton Webb situated, like the Webb, Sr., residence, on Cavendish Square.

Anthea Allenby Webb's cool blond beauty shone in marked contrast to Vivian's rain-bedraggled appearance as, following her request to see Mrs. Webb, she was ushered into Anthea's boudoir.

Fleetingly, Vivian recalled a time when, at nine o'clock in the morning, she too was having toast and tea. But it was not a thought that made her in the least regretful or cast down. On the contrary, she felt nothing but an eagerness to get on with her plans.

"Vivvie!" exclaimed Anthea with a vexed frown. "Why in heaven's name do you come calling so early? I've got The Fiend and feel just terrible. The worst cramps and an absolutely splitting head."

Informed opinion would one day ascribe the monthly difficulties suffered by so many women of the times to the tightly laced corsets that achieved the popular hourglass figure, to lack of exercise, and, most particularly, to the general expectation of misery once each month as part of woman's lot. To this Anthea added a self-pity that now moved her to tears as she astonished Vivian by saying, "Don't you just despise being a woman?"

"Why, no," replied Vivian promptly.

"Oh, come, come, now," pressed Anthea, sniffling into a dainty hankie. "You can't tell me you enjoy this messy business every month. Not to mention the coarse, common things men expect of us."

Vivian grew hot with an embarrassment she had never once felt while meeting the "coarse, common" expectations to which Anthea so strongly objected. She dropped her eyes, electing to make no response.

Silence seemed only to incense Anthea. "Come, come, now," she said again. "Don't tell me you didn't grit your teeth when Mr. Mallory climbed into bed. Don't pretend."

The charge brought Vivian's head up. "I'm not pretending."

"You mean," demanded Anthea incredulously, "you *liked* it?"

This was certainly not the topic Vivian had intended to

address, but out of a deep honesty she looked levelly at Anthea and said, "Yes. I liked it."

A smile curved the thin lips. "How interesting! But then, our backgrounds are vastly different, aren't they? If you had been raised as I have, you would no doubt share the opinion of me and my friends that no real lady can possibly like it."

"Are you sure your friends are telling the truth?"

Anthea's eyebrows climbed up her forehead. "But of course! Why, it's simply not a ladylike thing to do. I mean, one knows there have to be children. I'm willing to be co-operative on that score. But only up to a point. I've tried to explain this to Clinton. I've tried to tell him a gentleman understands that it's no pleasure to a lady. Quite the reverse! I've tried to point out that he should never have married a lady if he wants to be always . . ." She fell back among the pillows, tears welling into her eyes. "Oh, dear, what's the good of talking? I'll never make him understand."

Pity for the young woman filled Vivian, chasing her own concerns from her mind. Never to know the release that was part of passion, the ecstasy that could make you let the everyday world slide away, make you permit the body to take over and follow its own sweet dictates! Remembering how wonderful Mallory had been, she wondered, was Clinton gentle enough with Anthea? Did he take time enough? Time was important to a woman. Did all men understand this Questions, she concluded ruefully, that could never be asked of the prone figure on the bed.

"I'm wondering," said Vivian, "I'm wondering if you wouldn't like me to shampoo and set your hair?"

Instantly Anthea's lips parted with childlike eagerness. "Oh, Vivvie, would you! There's nothing that makes me feel so good!"

Forbearing to comment, Vivian set about her task.

Leaving the Webb residence a good hour later, Vivian had the promise of Anthea's help in renting her shop. This was not accomplished without some difficulty, however.

"But, Vivvie," Anthea had protested, "you don't need a shop. You can simply arrange to go from house to house to your patrons. It will be much more convenient."

For whom? thought Vivian, brushing the long blond tresses. But she said, "Heavens, no! I can give superior service only in a shop where I'll have all the emollients and equipment right at hand. For instance," she said, lifting several strands, "I can see your hair is very dry. It looks just like straw, if I may say so. What it wants is a good hot-oil treatment to restore its healthy luster and beautiful sheen. But this can best be done in a salon."

Anthea's pale hands flew to her hair. "It's that bad?" she cried, horror-struck. "Vivvie, when do you plan to start?"

"Well, as I say, just as soon as I get my shop. Now if you could take a moment to drop by Mr. Boyd, the tobacconist, and put in a good word for me. Assure him of my character, my responsibility . . ."

"Boyd?" said Anthea. "Is that the man's name? I know the place. Clinton buys his tobacco there. I shall speak to him."

Camilla Cavendish, when Vivian called at Cavendish House just across the Square, proved a less reluctant advocate.

"What!" she cried. "Won't rent to females! Preposterous! Believe me, dear Vivvie, I shall make it my business to let Mr. Boyd know just what I think of such antediluvian nonsense. Won't rent to females, indeed!"

A smile on her lips, Vivian left Cavendish House and proceeded to Broad Street and Le Pierre Hotel. She hadn't seen hide nor hair of Tanis, the Lady Langhorne, nor Sir Robbie, Baron of Chittendon, since Mallory's death. They had proved fair weather friends, indeed. This didn't especially surprise Vivian, nor did she very much care, never having felt at ease with either of them. But now she needed them, and meant to use them just as, in the past, they had used Mallory and her.

"I'm here, your ladyship," she told Tanis, "because I've a favor to ask."

In the comfortable parlor of the suite on Le Pierre's sixth floor, far above the noise of the city, the Lady Langhorne sat on a divan and rolled her eyes toward her brother. "A favor?" she inquired guardedly.

"Ah," said Sir Robbie, nodding. "A favor."

Vivian had no doubt both brother and sister believed she had come to beg money, and the desire for a little mischief danced through her head. "As perhaps you know," she said with a sigh, "my husband had quite overextended himself. Had he lived, he would have fulfilled all obligations, but as it happens . . . Well, I am left heavily in debt."

"Tst, tst," commiserated the Lady Langhorne.

"Tst, tst, tst," echoed Sir Robbie.

"Yes. The house must be sold and all the furnishings. I've nothing but my clothes and a few pieces of jewelry." She threw them an appealing look. "Out of sentiment I feel one must keep such personal things."

"Oh, one must!" cried Tanis.

"Indeed!" said Sir Robbie.

"But one can't eat one's jewels, after all, as I'm sure you well understand."

"Precisely," replied Tanis and, from Sir Robbie, "Hear, hear!"

"And so I considered all the people to whom I might turn with some expectation of assistance . . ."

Brother and sister blanched.

Vivian smiled. "Naturally I considered my first court of appeal must be to you." She fixed Robbie with a gentle look. "You know how deeply fond of you Mallory was. He counted you his dearest friend. I think I'm not wrong in believing you returned the sentiment. You spent so much time in his company. All that framboise . . ."

"Quite," responded Sir Robbie.

"I believe he was helpful to you in many ways: introductions, timely advice, not to mention the pleasures of the gaming table. And so now I would like to ask you . . ."

"Yes . . ." breathed brother and sister with one voice.

"Would you be kind enough to put in a good word for me with the tobacconist, Mr. Boyd, on Walnut Street? You see, I desire to open a hairdressing salon . . ."

She quickly explained her predicament. Tanis and Sir Robbie listened, and relief lacing their assurances, they promised they would indeed put in a good word.

Leaving them, Vivian traveled back to Butler Street, intent on her next project.

She had given the most serious consideration as to how she could get Dolly and Thomas O'Reilly to decide to buy Mallory's house at her price. Now, turning up the front walk, she hitched up her skirts and gingerly made her way to the For Sale sign that Bunty O'Hare had painted and put up on the front lawn. The rain had stopped but the ground was still soggy. When she reached the sign and gave it a tug, it came readily out with a soft sucking sound. Carrying it up to the house, she deposited it under the front steps, well out of sight. She then made her way to O'Reilly's Market and took her place in the line at the meat counter.

Tom's father, Mr. O'Reilly, Sr., held sway over this department, and it was with him that she wished to speak. Patiently she waited her turn as, clad in a large white apron, he quartered chickens, trimmed chops, sliced bologna, and weighed bacon, the while carrying on a sprightly conversation enhanced by whatever news had reached his ears that day.

Gossip made going to the store a treat, and everyone came home the wiser from a trip to O'Reilly's Market. Therefore, when it came Vivian's turn and Mr. O'Reilly said, "Well now, Vivvie, and what can I do for you today?" she replied, "Oh, dear! I've been so busy I can't even think! A pound of top of the round, I guess."

Mr. O'Reilly lifted down a piece of beef from a hook on the wall behind him and smartly cut off a chunk.

"Busy, is it?" he said, slicing the beef into cubes and placing them in the top of the meat grinder. "Putting in Ma's garden for her, I hear."

"Oh, it's not that!" exclaimed Vivian. "It's my hairdressing salon that I'm opening up just off Cavendish Square."

Mr. O'Reilly tore off a sheet of brown paper, placed it under the meat grinder, and commenced to grind away, but his eyes had grown round. "A hairdressing salon, is it? You don't say!"

"Yes, indeed. I hope to open it soon with all the money I'm getting from a fortunate investment that Mallory made. I already have patrons like Mrs. Cavendish, the senator's wife, and the Lady Langhorne. I hope to be such a success that I won't have to sell Mallory's house. I really want to live there myself. It seems only right I should raise my daughter in her father's house."

Mr. O'Reilly had stopped grinding meat. "You know," he said confidingly, "my Thomas says he don't mind being in the undertaking business but he sure don't fancy living in the same house with his work. He and Dolly like that place of Mallory's just fine."

"Well, anyone would, Mr. O'Reilly. I just love it myself. That's why I went up there and took that old sign off it today."

"You mean, it's not for sale?"

Oh, God forgive me! she prayed, and took a deep breath. "Not anymore."

One hour later the front doorbell rang, and Vivian opened the door to Dolly and Thomas O'Reilly.

"We've come to buy your house," said Dolly, fire in her blue eyes. "Now don't tell us it's not for sale, Vivian Mallory, because you said right to our faces that you wanted us to have it, you wanted to sell it to us."

Clinging to the door jamb, Vivian replied faintly, "I know I promised you . . ."

"Well?" demanded Dolly. "Are you going to go back on your solemn word?"

"Oh, I never would! Never! But, Dolly, the price . . ."

"We'll pay your price."

The following day, Sunday, Vivian had another visitor. Mr. Boyd, tobacconist, sat on the divan in Ma's parlor. Everything about him shone: rimless spectacles, pink cheeks, bald head. Outside the front door his carriage waited, and it too sparkled in the Sunday morning calm.

However, there was nothing in the least calm about Mr. Boyd's demeanor. "I can only say," he told Vivian, "that if you had mentioned your connections, young lady, it would have put another complexion on the thing, another complexion entirely."

"Mrs. Cavendish came to see you?" asked Vivian wonderingly. "Mrs. Cavendish, the senator's wife?"

"The very one!" cried Mr. Boyd, his reedy voice rising several decibels in agitation. "The senator is one of my very best customers, as you might expect. Together with Mr. Clinton Webb."

"Mrs. Webb visited you also?"

Ticking off on his fingers, he said, "Mrs. Cavendish, Mrs. Webb, the Lady Tanis Langhorne along with the Baron of Chittendon. And Mrs. Harry Barkin."

"Mrs. Barkin, too!"

Just for good measure Vivian had nipped next door to the Tipperary the day before and talked to her friend Gert Barkin over the telephone.

Mr. Boyd's voice quivered. "As brazen a piece, as brazen a *hussy* as I ever hope to meet. She threatened to sweep all my tobacco jars off my shelves with her parasol."

"I'm sorry for any distress you've been caused," murmured Vivian. "They're such dear ladies, and so eager to have a salon convenient to the neighborhood. They simply can't understand why you won't rent to a female—"

"Please!" implored Mr. Boyd, holding up both hands. "Please, Mrs. Mallory, my one desire is for the goodwill of my customers, especially, the wives of my customers. As I said, if only you had mentioned your admirable connections . . . But no matter. I've come here today to tell you I'll be more than happy to have you as my tenant, more than happy."

Remembering how he had shouted at her and ordered her out of his store, a thrill of triumph surged through Vivian. There is a way to get what one wants! she told herself. There is always a way!

Regarding him coolly, she said, "I appreciate your change of heart. But what with raising the rent to fifty-five dollars—"

"A mistake!" put in Mr. Boyd quickly. "A mistake pure and simple. My dear Mrs. Mallory, to you the rent is thirty-five."

36

The key to the front door bit into the palm of Vivian's hand, and the pain was pure pleasure. The key was hers, the shop was hers, the lease for one year was in her purse.

The shop consisted of a long narrow room devoid of everything except a water closet at the far end, but to Vivian, seeing it as it would be once she had gotten through with it, it was beautiful.

Together with the lease in her purse was a bankbook, the first she had ever possessed. In it was noted down $4930.00, which, together with the first and last month's rent just paid out to Mr. Boyd, represented the amount borrowed from the Keystone Bank.

Thanks to the kind suggestion of Clinton Webb, she had a lawyer, the courtly and elderly Mr. Hiram Custis, who had explained to her that the agreement of sale Dolly and

Thomas O'Reilly had signed on Mallory's house could be used as collateral for a small loan, thus enabling her to immediately rent and equip her salon.

Mr. Custis would also deal with Jamie Fitzhugh in securing an equitable interest in the proceeds of his successful formula.

"Will I have to meet with Mr. Fitzhugh?" she had asked anxiously.

"No, indeed," replied the lawyer. "There'll be no need of that at all."

With his words a weight seemed to fall from her shoulders. She had no desire to see Jamie ever again. On the new road she had taken she would permit herself no looking back. Nor, in truth, had she any wish to do so. Much more enticing was the future she meant to build for herself and her little daughter, a future unbeholden to anyone in the world, completely within her control.

She had already written up a list of possible patrons to whom announcements would be sent. Drawing as it did upon Mallory's wide acquaintance, this list was both lengthy and impressive. Although Vivian had quickly realized she would never become friends with such as the Kimberly ladies, she was hopeful they might patronize her salon. After all, with Mrs. Cavendish, Mrs. Clinton Webb, and the Lady Langhorne as customers, it could well become the thing to do.

And once the ladies were enticed inside, satisfaction was assured. To this Vivian had made up her mind with such resolve that at times, rapt and transfixed, she would stand rooted to the spot, consumed by the will to succeed. This determination that burned like a white-hot flame within her was fed by every desire to better herself that she had ever known, every aspiration, every dream. It was kept alive by every memory of pain, effort, and weariness, every recollection of worry and want. It leapt up raging with the thought of what Jamie had done to her, of Thurman Foy's smirk, Morrissey's kiss, Mr. Boyd's contempt.

Now she had this one chance, and she wouldn't fail, couldn't fail; failure mustn't enter her mind. Problems existed only to be solved, and she meant to solve every one of them. Thinking of the lease in her purse, the money in her bankbook, and the advantageous agreement of sale on Mallory's house, she smiled. She had already solved quite a few.

"You're working too hard," Neil told her.

Each night after work he came by the shop. Vivian felt he should go home and study, for she knew that a clerk in a law firm had a lot of homework to do before even thinking of taking bar exams. But he insisted upon helping her to get started, and at present was painting walls the palest pink while she gilded a latticework trellis that would screen the work area from a little reception room.

"If I'm working hard it agrees with me," she answered. "I've never felt better in my life."

This was true. She didn't care how long or how hard she worked. She loved every minute of it, for all there was so much to do.

Pink and gold were her colors. Across the plate-glass window was inscribed in large gilt letters the name of the shop: Vivian's. Each day before entering, she stood across the street and gazed upon it. Under the name was a great gilt swirl, the tail of which ended by describing a gilt rose. Shirred window draperies in pink crepe de chine were even now being run up on Mamie Randall's sewing machine, and Ma Mallory was embroidering dozens of white towels with a large pink V.

Vivian had determined that everything possible must be done to insure a pleasant atmosphere and maximum comfort. To this end she had purchased swivel chairs that could be conveniently raised or lowered before each of two marble sinks. These chairs she paid to have padded and then covered in red plush, together with similarly upholstered hassocks. A lady might lie back in total comfort for her soothing shampoo and massage.

Seeing this arrangement, Mamie Randall shook her head. "Spending too much," she pronounced. "Just like your father, you are."

This gentleman had returned from the Klondike at last and now slept peacefully each night at his wife's side. If the arrangement discomfited Mamie, she made no mention of it, just as she seldom mentioned Mary Claire's departure with the Florodora Girls, or Bucky's friendship with the Bryce Street Alley Rats. Tight-lipped and increasingly stoical, Mamie said less and less as more and more of life's options swirled out of her grasp, seeming to take her greatest pleasure in Nancy's company. This daughter-in-law, so different from her own children, apparently offered a comfort and closeness that Vivian had never achieved.

With Edward Randall, it was different. Vivian *was* like her father. Along with his astonishing good looks, she had inherited his zest for living and his stubborn optimism if not, fortunately, certain quixotic ways.

"You're right to strike out for yourself, Vivvie!" he declared ringingly. "Looking back upon my life, I consider it a great mistake always feeling it best to go in with someone or have a friend or two at my side. The truth of the matter is, it's my friends that have done me in and kept me poverty-stricken. But you, now, you're doing it right, and I glory in your spunk!"

Mamie disagreed. "Spending the little bit of money that is all she has in the world," she muttered.

"It takes money to make money, Mamie my love," observed her husband.

"So I've heard," sniffed Mamie. "So I've heard, but I've seen no results as yet."

"Are you directing veiled criticism at me?"

"If the shoe fits . . ."

It distressed Vivian to hear her parents bicker in this fashion. She couldn't help comparing their marriage to her own. How happy she and Mallory had been. Had she known it then? She surely knew it now, often regarding little Irene through tears. With every passing day the child seemed to become more like him, a dainty feminine version of the father who would have adored her.

"That's the worst," Gert Barkin remarked ruefully. "Not even to have seen your kid. Especially with a winner like Snow White."

Gert had astonished Vivian, perhaps even surprised herself, by converting to Roman Catholicism in order to become Irene's godmother—further, by talking her husband Harry into converting, also.

"What's the diff?" she replied when Vivian questioned this. "Harry and me never had any church. Now we got one."

Vivian consulted with Father Shields. "Father, I must tell you that the only reason the Barkins are becoming Catholics is in order to be the godparents of my child."

"And who is to say that's not a good reason, as long as they mean to sincerely practice the Faith?" asked the priest.

Thus counselled, Vivian offered no further comment,

and soon discovered Gert to be a far more devout Catholic that she herself.

"I like having a religion," explained Gert. "I've been lonely ever since Harry struck it rich. I don't cotton to a lot of these *nouveaus*. Now I've got some place to go, somebody to talk to." She winked. "And the Man upstairs don't answer back."

Whatever solace Gert received from her church, she returned tenfold. It was thanks to the Barkins that St. Bonaventure's received a splendid new baptismal font in time for Irene's christening, electrical wiring, and, luxury of luxuries, padded kneeling benches, "because," said Gert, "I'm wearing calluses on my knees." Every Thursday the Barkin carriage arrived at the rectory to pick up Father Shields and transport him to dinner at the Barkin residence off Broad Street. "A priest is a lonely person," said Gert. "I been lonely, too, so I know."

Her devotion to Snow White, as, to Vivian's annoyance, she persisted in calling Irene, knew no bounds. The time she spent with the child, feeding her, changing her, rocking her, singing to her, was never enough.

"Just you go along to that salon and get it fixed up," she would tell Vivian. "Irene and me will make out fine." And off she would take her in the ridiculously ornate perambulator with its ruffled pink parasol attached to the top, one of dozens of christening gifts presented "With love, from godmother and godfather."

Ma could get quite snappish about Gert's frequent appearances, and Vivian wasn't above a flick or two of jealousy herself. Too, she worried about the strong objections Mallory had once voiced about the Barkins as godparents. Certainly Gert's blunt ways, especially her ungrammatical use of the English language, provided a poor example for a child. But errors, Vivian reasoned, could be corrected as Irene grew up, and she could only benefit from exposure to Gert's loving and giving heart.

Actually, Vivian was happy to have Gert take the child off her hands, for each day laid some new demand on her time and energy. Large gilt-framed mirrors were delivered and must be installed over the vanity tables. A hot-water heater arrived. Purchases of combs, brushes, switches, rolls, and crimpers of every kind must be made.

Nancy volunteered to compose the engraved cards that would herald the opening, and see to the addressing and mailing of one hundred and fifty of them. Bucky used his express wagon to fetch things from hither and yon. Bunty O'Hare was always able to borrow horse and carriage from someone whenever Vivian needed transportation. Everyone pitched in and helped, but there was always more to be done.

One of the most pressing problems was the manufacture of the special soap she would use. Heretofore she had made it herself, brewing a jug at a time. But now she would need far more, and the process of making it was a lengthy one, requiring, as it did, that the mixture be boiled down, cooled, and skimmed three different times.

"Can't you use just ordinary soap?" asked her father, dropping by the shop as he did every day to inspect the progress she had made.

She looked down at him from the ladder on which she happened to be standing. He was, she had to admit, what would be called a fine figure of a man. He possessed few clothes and those that he had were ancient, but such care did he take of them, such brushing and spot cleaning, such a polish did he put to his shoes, such a shine to the brass knob of his cane, and, finally, such a jaunty angle did he give to his high-crowned hat, that the picture he presented was that of a person of consequence. Both Mamie and Mary Claire scorned such styles as hypocrisy. There were neighbors on Butler Street who shared this opinion and laughed behind his back, knowing he hadn't a penny to his name. But Vivian admired his panache. There was something dashing and brave in his swagger, and the very first thing she meant to do when she made a little money was redeem the gold watch chain notably absent from his vest.

"I must use this special soap, papa," she said now. "It's a formula Dr. Webb gave me."

"A secret formula, eh?"

She smiled, recognizing that love of drama that had led him instantly to dub the formula a secret. "It works miracles," she said. "The hair is left with a beautiful sheen."

"You don't say," said her father, and took a few steps back and forth, twirling his cane. "Well now, Vivvie, I'm thinking you might have a nice little sideline confronting you. What you must do is have a bit extra done up and ready to sell. Then, when your ladies are ready to pay up and leave, you say, 'Oh, madame, may I recommend that you purchase some of my Miracle Shampoo to take with you and keep handy in your home?' " He nodded sagely. "Many's the lady that will buy, I've no doubt."

On top of the ladder, Vivian set down her paint brush, thoughtfulness deepening the green in her eyes. Though she had not as yet been asked what she would consider the reasons for her success, indeed had yet to achieve the success that would give rise to the question, nevertheless, the requisite qualities were firmly ingrained in her nature. Her stubbornness, her self-confidence, her radiant health all played a part, together with a truly sympathetic nature and deft hands. But prime among these characteristics was an open mind, a willingness to truly listen instead of merely using the time to formulate a reply, a curiosity about other points of view, an ability to jettison certain opinions, however cherished, if other considerations proved worthy.

"Why, now you mention it," she said, "I don't doubt but I could sell a bottle to every lady who comes into my salon. But the formula isn't mine. It belongs to Dr. Webb."

"Then we'll just step around to Cavendish Square and have a word with that gentleman. I doubt he'll be averse to making a mite on each sale, would you think?"

Thus was agreement reached, Edward Randall assuring a surprised but not uninterested Dr. Webb he would mix and bottle the formula himself and defend its secret with his life if need be.

"Vivvie, my girl, we'll make our fortune!" he cried, upon the success of this visit. Luckily, he continued, she had a lot of money in the bank. They would purchase a building, equip it with a stove, tables, shelves, whatever was needed. They would sell the soap everywhere! To think he had traveled all the way to the Klondike, only to come home to strike gold!

Vivian heard him out. Then she said, "We don't have to purchase a building, papa."

"We don't?"

"We have the room Mallory used for his office at the back of the Tip."

"Ah!" replied her father, but with rather a drop to his voice.

"And we don't need shelves and tables. A few planks and two sawhorses will do. As for a range, we'll find one secondhand. But you'll make the formula and we'll sell it, papa. However," she added, "only to the ladies who come to Vivian's."

* * *

Vivian's opened on the first day of June 1905.

The gilt lettering on the plate-glass window shone in the sunlight and the shirred pink crepe de chine draperies gave a pearly pink glow. The gilded latticework divided the work area from the front of the shop, which was furnished with a little appointment desk on which sat a telephone and, in a cut-glass vase, a single rose. The painted pink cupboards were stocked with white towels embroidered with a pink V, shelves held bottle after bottle of Miracle Shampoo, and marching up Walnut Street in the early morning came the first two customers, the Randall girls.

37

On Saturday night, as Vivian was about to lock up at the end of her first week in business, Clinton Webb opened the door of the salon.

"I just thought I'd look in to wish you luck. Not," he added, smiling, "that you need it, for I'm hearing your praises sung on all sides."

At these warm words, weariness dropped from her. "Clinton, do let me show you around. I'm so proud of it."

"I don't wonder." Tall and slim in a light beige summer suit, he looked about approvingly, and she was interested to note that he commented on the more subtle things: the way the setting sun cast a flattering glow upon the room, the single rose in the cut-glass vase on the reception desk, the embroidered V on the towels. He also was quick to note the exhaustion that, despite her smile, stamped itself on her face, and with a concern that couldn't help but strike a chord within her, he said, "Vivvie, you look very, very tired."

"I am," she admitted, adding, with a deprecatory smile, "I'm afraid the salon is a little too successful. I've never worked so hard in my life. And next week is already almost filled with appointments."

"Are you trying to do all this by yourself?"

"Papa is helping me. He mixes the liquid soap I use. And," she added, "he has become my receptionist. He dropped by on opening day and found me so busy that he stayed to answer the telephone and usher the ladies in and out. He's been here every day since. He adores it. The ladies make such a fuss over him, and he returns the compliment. I do believe he has at last found his life's work."

Clinton smiled. "I've heard about your father. I believe he escorted old Mrs. Eugene Westbridge home under an umbrella when it began to rain the other day."

"Oh, he does all sorts of things! Fetches cabs, passes bonbons, hands out magazines. But his greatest appeal is that he's an incorrigible flatterer. The ladies like it."

"They like you, too, Vivvie. I can't begin to tell you the good things I've heard. You're off and flying, no doubt of that. But can you keep up the pace? You look ready to drop."

She had no doubt of this last. Every bone in her body ached. The fiery hot pain that always lay like a molten rod across her shoulders when she was fatigued had been a constant companion for the past few days. The small of her back ached from bending over wash basins, while her arms were so sore that it was an effort to raise a hand. Her feet were swollen and cramped and even her fingers hurt, but she said offhandedly, "Oh, I'll be all right. I just have to get used to hard work again."

"You shouldn't have to!" snapped Clinton. "Your husband should have left you better off."

"Clinton, please."

He reddened. "Oh, I don't mean to broach that touchy subject again. But, Vivvie, you're going to be a success. You're a success already. You must hire help. Surely you know likely prospects after your years in service."

Vivian cocked her head thoughtfully. "Hire lady's maids? Why, Clinton, that never occurred to me, but . . . Hattie Flanagan! I've taught her my method. Why, she's the very one!"

"You mean, ma'am," said Hattie a few days later, looking around the salon in awe, "you mean you want me to leave my present position and come to work here?"

"Yes, Hattie," said Vivian. "I want you to work here."

"But ma'am, I'm no hairdresser. I'm just a lady's maid."

"So was I. Have you forgotten that? You know my beginnings."

"But I'm not like you."

"Hattie, you are good, kind, diligent, and competent. And you know how to dress hair every bit as well as I do."

"Oh, ma'am!" protested Hattie.

"Hattie, you know very well that you do, for I've taught you precisely what must be done. You know how to massage, how to shampoo. You know my entire method. All you need do is follow my instructions. And, Hattie, I'll be right here, working beside you."

Hattie shook her head. "It all seems so queer."

"You mean our working together?"

"No, ma'am. I mean not being a lady's maid anymore. Not—well, being looked out for, if you take my meaning. Where would I live? How would I eat? Who would I know?"

Vivian sighed. It was the end of the day. She was tired and longed to have done with this conversation and go home to little Irene and a bite of supper. But she needed Hattie Flanagan. What's more, looking at the dowdy clothes, the woebegone face, Hattie Flanagan, she decided, needed her. At the reception desk, she sat up straight. "How old are you, Hattie?"

"Twenty-four, ma'am."

"Do you have a steady beau?"

"Ma'am, you know I never had a steady beau."

"Then," persisted Vivian relentlessly, "are you prepared to spend all your days as a lady's maid, living in somebody's attic, eating somebody's leftover food, wearing somebody's hand-me-down clothes, without anything in the least interesting or exciting happening to you at all?"

"I never thought about things like that, ma'am."

"Well, think about them now," suggested Vivian spiritedly. "This is a chance to better yourself, but you don't deserve it if you only put obstacles in the way. As to where you'll sleep and eat . . . Why, heavens! I'll rent you a room in a boardinghouse. As to friends, you'll keep the old and doubtless make lots more. And," she added, on the wings of inspiration, "if you decide you don't like it, you can always go back to being a lady's maid."

Hattie brightened. "Yes, there's that. I could always go back. One thing I know, I'm a fine lady's maid."

"And you're a fine hairdresser. I have faith in you, Hattie. You're more than you think you are, better than you know. All you want is a little confidence. But that will come. You're frightened now because things are new to you. But once you start doing them, you'll find that you'll lose your fear. You'll find you've entered a whole bright new world."

Vivian leaned forward. Her eyes burned like green fire and she was no longer tired. "Hattie," she said, striving to reach the girl, "it's good to be in control of your life. It's good to feel you can look out for yourself. And there's no secret to it. All you need are two things: persistence and a willingness to work. You needn't be beautiful or specially blessed. You need only work hard and persevere. That's all it takes, Hattie. And if you do that, you needn't strive for success. Success will come to you."

She sank back in her chair, feeling she had just run a race, a race, it appeared, that she had won.

"Why, then, I'll give it a try, ma'am," said Hattie. "Yes, ma'am, you've got me so fired up I'll give it a try."

Miss Harriet, as Vivian elected to call her, plunged into her work with the fierce dedication of the neophyte.

"If all it takes is perseverance and hard work, I'm on my way," she told Vivian.

Unquestionably, she was. Her desire to please, combined with her skill, quickly earned the loyalty of patrons, who soon began to specify they wanted no one but Miss Harriet to do their hair. Vivian was delighted with this development and couldn't help but notice the effect it had on the young woman.

Slowly but surely, confidence crept into her manner, and as the weeks went by, she began to speak up more firmly and offer suggestions her patrons might wish to try. There was a marked change in her appearance, also. No longer did she try to make do with cast-off clothes. Though plain, with a broad, flat face and a rather bulbous nose, she had a dignified style, and there was no doubt but that the personality flowering at last in the warm sunshine of success was both forceful and sweet.

"You'd best have a care," Edward Randall would tell his daughter, not altogether in jest. "Miss Harriet may waltz off one day and start a salon of her own. Of course," he added, perhaps to calm his own fears, "she'll not have our famous formula."

He guarded this secret concoction as though the crown jewels. No one was permitted in the back room at the Tipperary while he was engaged at his work. He was, Vivian sometimes declared with amusement, even sorry *she* knew how to mix it. He badgered her to let him sell it outside the salon, but she was adamant: it must be sold only to her patrons. And more of these arrived every day.

By October the burgeoning business had required her to employ two more assistants. Miss Mavis Donovan and Miss Rosalie Curran were former lady's maids recruited by Harriet Flanagan, whose accounts of salary, independence, and prestige put lights in their eyes. Vivian interviewed them, exercising that same shrewd observation she had once turned upon the ways of Cavendish Square. Having satisfied herself that their seriousness of purpose, warm personalities, and ready smiles augured well, she rented rooms for them at her own expense in a boardinghouse nearby and commenced to train them in her method.

It was a procedure she was to follow in years to come. The boardinghouse, she had made it her business to learn, was clean and the food wholesome. But most important, the proprietress, Mrs. Benson, was a plump, motherly little person who could be relied upon to keep an eye on the inexperienced and naive young women whom Vivian so blithely placed under her roof. This was the sheerest good luck for, young herself, it wasn't until years later that Vivian would look back with a shudder at the audacity of taking simple, ignorant servant girls out of the sheltered society of "below stairs" and introducing them to life on their own in the city.

At the moment no such consideration entered her head, consumed as she was with high hopes, not only for herself but for "my girls" as she came to think of them. And indeed she had enough to occupy her since, together with increasing her staff, she was looking for a house to rent in a convenient location.

She could well afford this move, for not only was the business making a good profit and showing every indication of growing better, but she had received a lump sum payment of five thousand dollars on Jamie's invention, plus the first of regular quarterly checks on the royalty.

These amounts were sent to her by Mr. Custis, her lawyer. The checks were signed by Jamie's bank. She thus had no contact with Jamie at all, no idea as to his whereabouts or anything else about him other than the name of the magazine for which he worked.

She never chanced to see Connie about anywhere, and had made it an inviolate rule not to walk past the photography studio. It was therefore something of a shock when, one day in November, she overheard a patron give the name of a millinery shop at 804 Chestnut Street. Vivian's hands went still as she heard a second woman say, "Oh, but I think you must be mistaken. There's a photographer's studio there."

"Not anymore," replied the first. "He's moved away."

Unable to contain her curiosity, Vivian took the time to go by the address that very night. Her customer proved quite correct. The green baize curtains were gone and the window was full of hats. Standing on the sidewalk, Vivian looked upward and, in the light from a street lamp, saw that a For Rent sign had been placed in a window on the second floor.

Had Connie and her family left with him, then? Had her child been born? Oh, why do I care? she asked herself, out of patience with an interest that should have long since died. But as she continued on her way, a strikingly attractive young woman in a modish blue wool suit, its blue velvet collar and cuffs echoed in the velvet picture hat upon her upswept hair, she knew there was some deep part of her that still did care, would always care.

Her house was found at last.

Built in the Federal period, when Philadelphia was the capital of a new young nation, it rose straight up from the sidewalk, a charming pink brick residence with a fanlight over the door and a lamp post at the bottom of its broad marble steps.

"I want you to come live with me," she told Ma.

It was a November evening, and she had come down to the parlor after putting Irene to bed. Since the start of the cold weather this year, Ma had discontinued her practice of going next door each evening to her post at the Tipperary, where a blast of chill air swept in upon her with everyone who opened the door. She sat by the coal fire in the fireplace knitting a little sack for Nancy's baby boy, Clinton, who would be christened the following week.

"And what," demanded Ma, "would I be doing in that fancy big house you've rented?"

"The same things you do here," replied Vivian.

"But not liking it half so well."

"You will, Ma. You'll get to like it if you give it a chance. And just think how much more comfortable you'll be. This house is like a sieve. You're always cold unless you're huddled up beside the fire. And there's no electricity, no bathroom—"

"Now just you be tending to yourself. I've got everything here the way I want it."

Vivian decided to change tactics. "You'll be missing Irene."

"I've got used to missing people in my lifetime. I'm used to people up and leaving me. I'll get along. I've done it before, I can do it again."

Vivian overlooked the grumbling self-pity. "Well, I'm not sure I'll get along so well without you," she observed, and quite truthfully, aware of the peace of mind that was hers going off to work each day and leaving Irene in the loving care of her grandmother.

"You'll find good help, no doubt," said Ma with a sniff, and leveled a look at her daughter-in-law. "Are you after being able to get that Mr. Halls and his wife to come back to you?"

"Yes, I am."

"Well, they'll take an interest and see that the baby comes to no harm. And you're going to have Bunty O'Hare around."

"But I'll miss you, Ma."

She didn't add, as well she might have, you'll miss me, too. But the thought of Ma eating a solitary meal each evening and then sitting by the fire all alone was the one factor that had made Vivian hesitate to sign the lease on the house, much as she desired to do so. This worrisome concern led her to take a step that, were Ma to learn of it, would surely bring wrath upon her head. Yet Vivian felt she must chance it and so, on Sunday morning, returning from the ten o'clock mass, she paid a visit to Ma's erstwhile bosom friend, Regina Muldoon.

"I know how much Ma has missed seeing you, Mrs. Muldoon," she said, looking earnestly into the woman's kind, homely face.

"And haven't I missed her?" countered Regina. "Friends all these years, and now her walking by me without so much as a word!"

"It was because of Mallory and the election."

"God love you, don't I know the cause? And then her losing her boy . . . Believe me, I've shed many a tear about that."

Vivian felt a sudden lump in her throat. The mention of Mallory's untimely death was still sometimes more painful than she could bear. "If you could just find it in your heart to go to her, Mrs. Muldoon," she said. "Try to make it up. I know she misses your company and wants to be friends again more than anything in the world. But Ma has a stubborn streak—"

"And you needn't be telling me that! Morna Mallory is stubborn as a mule. But since you say that underneath she wants to be friendly, I'll give it a go. Is she likely to be home today?"

"She is."

"Then I'll knock on her door this afternoon."

In view of the delicacy of Mrs. Muldoon's mission, Vivian felt it would be best if she took herself off for the day. It was therefore close on dusk when, having spent the afternoon with her parents, she returned, pushing Irene in her carriage.

"Well, you'll never guess who stopped by while you were away," said Ma the moment Vivian opened the front door.

"Who was that, Ma?"

"Regina Muldoon. Came crying to me, saying how she wants us to be friends again."

"I hope you were cordial."

"And what else could I be, with her taking on in such a way? I promised I'd go to the novena with her on Tuesday night. Seeing it means so much to her, it's the least I can do."

Vivian forbore a smile, but the next day she felt no compunction in signing her lease and commencing upon her new life.

38

Although Ma persisted in calling it a fancy big house, the property Vivian had rented on Spruce Street, a short walk from her salon, was really quite modest.

The moment she saw it she had fallen in love with it, despite the rather topsy-turvy living arrangements it dictated. Meals would be taken on the first floor, where a room just off the kitchen served as dining room. But one must walk upstairs to the parlor, which utilized the entire second floor, with a wrought-iron balcony just off the front windows overlooking the street and a garden under the windows at the back. On the floor above was the master bedroom and dressing room, the nursery, and a room for the nanny who would care for Irene. Halls and Clarissa would have their quarters on the ground floor. All in all, it promised to work out very well.

"We're mighty glad to be back with you again, ma'am," said Halls on the day they moved in.

"I'm mighty glad to have you," replied Vivian. "I hope we'll be together now for years and years."

"Amen to that," said Clarissa, smiling warmly. "Amen to that."

It was Gert Barkin who procured a governess for Irene.

"English," Gert informed Vivian. "Just what we want so Snow White will learn to speak proper."

Mrs. Swan, a widow of middle age, proved right in every way, her serenity and her dignified bearing reminding Vivian of nothing so much as those gliding, self-composed creatures whose name she shared.

With the house as small as it was, little was required in the way of furnishings. Vivian installed Mallory's great iron bed in her room. They had once, on a rainy Sunday afternoon, made love in this bed, but they had never slept in it together. It had, however, been Mallory's bed for most of his adult life, and retained a trace of him—an indenta-

322

tion in the mattress, a faint fragrance. Vivian liked sleeping there. She would almost have said she *needed* to sleep there.

For the rest, Gert Barkin was invaluable.

"Look," Gert would say, "I got nothing to do but go to church. Just tell me what has to be done."

"Gert, I can't impose on you this way," protested Vivian. "You've done too much already, taking care of Irene, finding a governess . . ."

"So what? Aren't we best friends?"

How irritated, mused Vivian, she once had been by Gert's use of this possessive phrase. Now there was no one of her acquaintance, including her own family, whom she counted more dear.

The things Vivian asked Gert to hunt up were far different in style and feeling from the type of furnishings Gert would have chosen.

"Why don't you forget that Chippendale sideboard and spend your money on a really classy dining room suite?" Gert would ask, eyeing the cheap mission-style table and chairs that were to join it.

"Because," said Vivian firmly, "I love that sideboard. And someday I mean to have a dining room that will live up to it."

Gert might shake her head, but off she would march on the next project, a bounce to her step and a glint in her eye.

By the week before Christmas the house was, to all intents and purposes, complete. A small Christmas tree trimmed with popcorn and baubles stood on a table in the parlor, and there was a wreath on the door.

"I want you and Harry to be my first dinner guests, Gert," said Vivian. "Irene and I are going to mama's for Christmas, so why don't you plan to come to me on Christmas Eve?"

"Let's wait 'till after the holidays, kiddo," Gert suggested. "You're too busy at the salon right now."

This was true. Even with the two new assistants, Vivian had all she could do to keep up with appointments. By the day before Christmas she looked forward to nothing so much as returning to her home, playing with Irene for an hour, taking a long, hot bath, and toppling into bed. Already she had given Halls and Clarissa the day off in order to let them have an early start to their holiday. At the salon she would have liked to dismiss Harriet, Mavis, and Rosalie a bit early also, especially as, toward dusk, snow began to fall. But it was after six before the last customer left.

"I have a little gift for each of you," she told the girls when every last brush and comb had been put away and the salon returned, as Vivian always insisted, to perfect readiness for the next business day. "I hope you'll like it. I came upon it just by chance, but the idea appealed to me."

Tired though they were, the three young women were intrigued, and as much by the giver as whatever the gift might be. She had changed their lives, this slender, vibrant woman who was so beautiful, who expressed herself with such ease and possessed such a warm interest in others. They had forgotten that she was not yet twenty. She possessed a quiet command that led them to think of her as several years beyond that age, and without doubt she looked elegant and sophisticated in the bottle green wool suit she wore, its skirt and jacket trimmed with black silk braid.

Holding three small packages enticingly wrapped in gold paper and tied with red satin ribbon, she said, "I have a little speech to make first," and a smile danced in her eyes. "I want you to know how proud of you I am. But more, I want you to know how proud you should be of yourselves. By your hard work and dedication you have made yourselves into full-fledged, competent beauticians. You are professionals, with a career you can practice anywhere in the world." Her smile deepened. "I hope you will always stay with me and work here in my salon. But you have provided yourselves with a knowledge, an ability no one can ever take from you. Never treat your career lightly, never let down your standards, always strive to improve. And always, always enjoy your work, for if you do you will surely make your patrons enjoy coming to you. And now . . ."

She presented the gifts, having first warmly shaken hands with each one. Then, with eagerness in her voice, she said shyly, "You may open them now, if you like."

Instantly ribbons and gilt wrappings came off, and to exclamations of delight, boxes were opened to reveal, resting on black velvet, brooches fashioned as a single gold rose.

The three girls left shortly, each wearing her gift pinned to her coat and hurrying off into the night with cries of

"Merry Christmas." From the employee cloakroom Vivian fetched her hat and went to a mirror to put it on. Under its green satin brim, her eyes looked back at her with infinite satisfaction. Only six months since she had opened her salon, but what a triumph they had been. She could scarce believe her good fortune, not realizing it was shared by entrepreneurs everywhere.

Times were good and people were happy, with money in their pockets, hope in their hearts, and stores filled with things to buy. If Vivian believed problems existed only to be solved, so did everyone else. There seemed nothing this young nation couldn't do. In the space of a hundred years it had changed from a few largely rural states along the East Coast to the greatest industrial colossus in the world, its railroads crisscrossing a continent, its ingenuity changing the course of rivers, building harbors where none existed, digging a canal in Panama that rivaled the feats of the Romans. "The will to grow," wrote Henry James of the period, "was everywhere written large, and to grow at no matter what or whose expense."

Admittedly, there were sweatshops, poor working conditions, child labor. But so swift were the rewards of enterprise that an individual could vastly better his position in life in the space of a few years. Newspaper boys did in fact grow up to become captains of industry. The moral of the Horatio Alger stories, with their exhortations to hard work and their promise of riches, did indeed often prove true.

With never so popular a president as Theodore Roosevelt, with hundreds of thousands of immigrants arriving to provide brute force, with steam, steel, and electricity taking over where brute force must fail, money was everywhere. It was the Age of Optimism, the Age of Confidence, above all, the Age of Innocence, for times would never be so carefree and happy again.

Standing before the mirror, Vivian tied an ermine ascot around her throat, pulled on her gloves, picked up a small ermine muff, and, after a last look around, turned off the lights and left the shop. She had just locked the door when she felt a hand on her arm.

"Vivvie . . ." he said, and turning, she looked up into the face of Jamie Fitzhugh.

39

How long had they stood there? She had no idea. Jamie's sudden appearance, his voice, his touch took her breath away. For an awful moment she believed she had gone mad, conjuring this vision out of the swirling snow.

"I must talk to you," he said.

"No, no!"

"I must! If I don't, I swear I'll kill myself."

Her eyes widened. He looked ill. Under the battered, wide-brim felt hat, rather like a cowboy hat, his coal-black eyes burned in a face that could only be described as ravaged. He wore an overcoat and had tied a long knit scarf about his neck; nonetheless, he appeared to be shivering.

"You're cold!" she exclaimed.

"Am I? Perhaps I am. I've been standing out here for an hour, waiting for you."

At such a foolhardy procedure, impatience seized her. "You might have opened the door and come in. Well, come along then," she continued, not suspecting how the new tone of command in her voice surprised him. "We'll go to my house."

With Jamie at her side she moved, brisk and unspeaking, past shop windows that were now dark. But the streets were lively with hansom cabs and carriages, and when they reached Cavendish Square the windows of the big houses that gave upon it were bright with beckoning light. Lights glowed, too, behind the windows of her own small house. Since no Halls or Clarissa would be about, she fitted her key into the lock and opened the door.

Jamie followed her inside.

"May I take your things?" she asked.

They were the first words she had spoken since their meeting, and again without her realizing it, they rang with quiet command. Like an obedient child Jamie handed over the soggy hat, coat, and scarf.

"I'd best put them in the kitchen to dry," she said, and bore them off, hanging them on the coat rack beside the back door. Quickly divesting herself of her own outer garments, she gave them a good shake to rid them of snow and hung them, too, up to dry. Then she stood perfectly still, talking silently but furiously to herself, steeling herself against the pity his appearance had evoked in her, reminding herself that this was the old Jamie, the very same.

Returning to the front hall, she said, "The parlor is upstairs," and led the way, hearing his footsteps heavy behind her, feeling those dark eyes burning into her back.

Mrs. Swan came down from the nursery, eyebrows lifting in polite surprise as she saw the stranger.

"Will you put Irene to bed, please, Mrs. Swan? I'll come upstairs a bit later." Turning to Jamie, she said, "Do you care for a brandy? You must be chilled to the bone."

"Nothing, thanks."

"Do sit down, then."

She herself sat down with a composure she considered nothing short of remarkable. Her entire performance, for such her pounding heart assured her it was, astonished her with its self-confident serenity. She felt as if she had stepped outside herself and were regarding the proceedings as though attending a play.

She saw herself, clad in long green wool skirt and white shirtwaist with high shirred collar and tall, tight cuffs, her hair burnished by the light from the lamp on the table beside her. She saw Jamie, tense as ever, mouth grim in the angular face, jaw thrust forward. He seemed out of place in the ordered room, at variance with polished tables, the tinseled charm of a Christmas tree.

He sat before her, feet planted firmly, both hands on his knees, his eyes gripping hers. "Connie Mathews has borne my child," he said. "A son. Daniel."

Vivian sucked in her breath at the blunt announcement, clinging to her resolve to be removed, disinterested. But when had she ever displayed disinterest in Jamie Fitzhugh? Although she had assiduously avoided that part of the city in which he and Connie lived, she had never once gone abroad in the past months that her eyes hadn't sought him—often without her knowledge, certainly without her permission, unconsciously scanning the crowd even when she knew he must be far away. Hard though she worked, tired though she was each night, his face all too often swam before her when she closed her eyes to sleep, his voice to frequently invaded her dreams. Unlike Mallory, he brought no happy memories, no solace. But forget him? No, she had not.

It was because of this inability to rid herself of him finally and forever, because the proof of her defeat now quivered in every nerve, throbbed in her throat, spun in her brain, raced in her blood, that fury seized her and she cried out scathingly, "Why are you telling me this? Why do you think I care?"

Ignoring her questions, he said, "I finally caught up with Connie's husband in 'Frisco. I told him that I had been living with Connie and that she was carrying my child. I said I had made twenty-five thousand dollars on a chemical formula, plus royalties. I said I had a partner whose widow would receive a cash payment of five thousand dollars and twenty percent of all royalties. For the rest, I explained that I had set up a trust fund to be administered by my lawyer and my bank. Under the terms of it, Connie will receive the interest from the fund until Daniel is twenty-one, when the trust will be dissolved and the capital will be his to start off in life."

Stunned, Vivian said, "You've given it away? You've given it all away?"

Jamie smiled, the faintest trace of amusement. "That's exactly what Ed Mathews said to me. He also allowed as how he'd better patch things up with his wife because someone would have to help her manage all that money and give my kid a name."

It was all so like Jamie, forever extricating himself, explaining things away. "And," said Vivian scornfully, "having provided your son with a name and a future, you feel you have fulfilled your parental responsibilities?"

"I haven't come to ask your approval of the arrangement," he replied coldly, and Vivian felt her face burn as from the sting of a slap. "He'll have more than many do," he continued matter-of-factly. "Connie will love him, she adores kids. As for Ed Mathews, Daniel represents far and away the most valuable asset the man will ever have, so I doubt the lad will be mistreated.

"Other than this, I confess I have little interest in the boy, since I felt no love for his mother. I told her as much when I came home nights to find her waiting in my bed.

Yes, that's where Connie liked to wait for me. And I own to having come home a mite drunk more than once."

A shudder ran through Vivian at the thought of the blowsy Connie waiting among the bed covers for a man to come to her, drunk and uncaring, satisfying upon her body only carnal desires.

"I don't wish to hear any more," she said.

"Then you'll miss the best part."

She looked at him sharply.

"I refer," he went on, "to my bout with malaria in the stench and steaming tropics of the Canal Zone where, in my delirium, they tell me I constantly cried out your name."

"Don't!" she protested shrilly.

The word was wrung from her, for at his careless admission a leap of joy so sharp and keen it was almost like pain had shot through her.

"Don't what, Vivvie?"

"Don't say such things! I won't listen! I won't have it to do all over again!"

"Have what to do?"

"I won't let you lead me on only to abandon me once more! No, and I'll not! I won't let you play this cat and mouse game and then go off whenever it pleases you. I've forgotten you. Yes, forgotten you. You are a thing of the past, do you hear? I no longer need you or want you. I no longer care about you. I have what I need: my work and my dear little girl. And I'm happy. Or I was until I saw you again. And now . . . and now . . ."

She stopped, willing back the tears that swelled hard and tight in her throat and threatened to overwhelm her. Rushing to the doorway she flung out a hand. "Get out!" she cried. "Get out of here!"

Breast heaving, tears on her cheeks, she watched him slowly arise. He moved to the doorway and stood looking down at her. His presence enveloped her, making her head swim.

"And so," he said, "it's really good-bye?"

She closed her eyes, nodding. But her lips were raised to his and suddenly she was in his arms and he was straining her to him, bringing his mouth down on hers in a bruising kiss whose pain brought the keenest pleasure, and all her days of aching yearning and loneliness were eclipsed in an ecstasy of delight.

Part IV

40

They were married as soon as the Church would allow.
Quite a different wedding it was from her marriage to
Mallory. Jamie hadn't wanted all the fuss of an elaborate
affair, and she readily agreed. Except for Gert and Harry
Barkin, only family were included. A handful of people sat
huddled together in the front pews of St. Bonaventure's
while a January rain drummed on the roof.

At the altar Jamie awaited his bride. Beside him stood
his best man, Thurman Foy. This gentleman was the last
person in the world whom Vivian would have chosen to see
at her wedding. But Thurman was, Jamie said, his good
friend, and his only guest, so she hadn't wanted to object.

Her father gave her away. This made her happy, but
somehow things lacked the air of celebration that had attended the last time. The luncheon that followed the ceremony, and that, at some expense, she had arranged in a
small private dining room at Le Pierre, taking pains with
the menu of smoked salmon, beef Wellington, and me-
ringues, possessed little true spirit. Except for her father,
exuberant in the role he played, gaiety seemed forced.
This, Vivian knew, was only to be expected, given the
strained relations between her mother and the Randall
girls, her own less than cordial feelings toward Thurman
Foy, and Ma Mallory's barely veiled contempt for the
groom.

Wearing a lace gown of French blue, with ostrich feathers dyed to match in her hair, Vivian was conscious of
smiling a lot, trying to make people see how happy she
was, an exhausting performance until, as frequently happened, she looked to Jamie and their eyes met. Then her
smile came easy and true. She adored him. What else mattered? She couldn't wait for the luncheon to end.

Immediately they took the train to New York City,
where they would spend their honeymoon. Jamie had

333

wanted to see Paris and deluged her with brightly colored travel folders in efforts to entice her. Vivian studied the information, longing to go for his sake, but she didn't see how she could possibly leave her fledgling business for the several weeks that even the most cursory trip to Europe would entail. Hating to disappoint him, she returned again and again to the literature he had so enthusiastically presented, delaying a decision until forced, at last, to admit her dilemma.

"Well then, of course we mustn't go," he responded amiably, waving aside her profuse explanations and apologies. "A trip is no pleasure if you've got one eye on the calendar. Perhaps in another year you'll feel free. Certainly you'll have more cash."

It was understood she would be the one to pay for their honeymoon trip, wherever they would go, just as she would continue to meet all the expenses of running the house.

"I haven't a dime, Vivvie," Jamie had told her candidly. "You're getting your bit from the sale of my formula, and Connie and the boy get the rest. I earn peanuts from magazines like *Social Survey*. They're big on prestige but they don't pay. I'm happy to share what I have, but it won't ever be enough for you. Fortunately, you've got the salon."

"You don't mind if I keep it?" she exclaimed.

"I very much hope you do. I'll never be able to support us in such style. Besides, I know how much it means to you."

Vivian could only be grateful for an attitude so sharply at variance with the prevailing thought of the day. Vivian's meant more to her than she could express in words. She was so proud of it, so absorbed in every aspect of it, so exhilarated by the success she had made. Her assumption that, with marriage, she would just naturally be expected to abandon it, had been the only cloud on her happiness. Jamie whisked it away. "I'll be your star boarder," he said, lips turning up in the wry self-deprecating smile that he had.

Vivian wasn't sure she liked this description, but she counted her blessings. Mallory, she knew, would have insisted she give up her business. He had indulged her, adored her, but he would never have understood her feelings in the matter; nor, she felt, would most other men. But then, Jamie had never been like anyone else. Most men didn't invent formulas that sold for thousands of dollars; most men didn't then turn around and give away all they possessed; most men didn't go to places like the Panama Canal, risking their health in order to snap a few pictures.

"Why in the world did you want to go *there?*" she had asked with the mystification and curiosity he always inspired in her.

"To capture time," he said.

Time. It was something Vivian sought only to put to good advantage, never having enough of it, something it wouldn't have occurred to her to try to capture or detain, eager as she was for what might happen next. But when he spoke of such things, her interests seemed shallow, her goals petty.

"Photography can change the world," he would tell her, his lean face averted, eyes far away, seeming to speak to himself. "It will change the world because it can capture the moment, the way things are—the truth. And when people see the truth, they'll do things differently. When they see the truth about hunger, about disease, about the exploitation of man by man, they'll change things."

"But what about," she ventured, "happy things? Things people should value, should keep. Don't they need to be captured by photography, too?"

She saw she had vexed him, broken his mood by her trivial question. But he said, "Only when they're as lovely and luscious as you," and pulled her to him for a bruising kiss.

Her lips often hurt from the way he kissed her, pressing his mouth against hers so that his teeth sometimes drew blood, and more than once, undressing after he had left, she had discovered purple discolorations on her breasts under the layers of cloth that had foiled him. She was happy they were at last married and that such urgent passion, having its natural outlet, might grow more gentle, evoking in her the delight she had known with Mallory.

Sitting on the green plush seat of the train as it sped onward, Vivian studied her new husband. His battered, wide-brimmed hat pulled forward over his eyes, he slumped back against the seat, lost in oblivion. She knew he was exhausted. Not completely recovered from his bout with malaria, he had enjoyed several glasses of champagne at the wedding luncheon and now, as he was lulled by the rocking motion and hypnotic clatter of the wheels, sleep claimed him. But still there was an air about him, a subtle distinction that smacked of the adventuresome, the picaresque, and caused those who boarded the train at its several stops to look at him as they passed by, and then, intrigued, look again.

Vivian turned away and stared out the window. Unable to pierce the cold, steady downpour for a glimpse of countryside, she absently followed little rivulets of water down the pane. Together she and Jamie presented an oddly matched pair: she, glamorously stylish in a black suit of chiffon panama with velvet collar and silk buttons, a tam-o'-shanter hat of rosettes and black silk perched upon her shining upswept hair; Jamie, having removed the morning suit he had rented for the wedding, wearing ill-fitting and rumpled store-bought brown corduroy.

Used to Mallory's impeccable appearance, Vivian had suggested Jamie visit a tailor, or at least invest in ready-to-wear clothes of better quality. He had resisted.

"Is it because," she asked gingerly, "of the expense?"

"Oh, I'm sure you'd be happy to pay my tailor," he replied easily. "But clothes don't mean much to me. I haven't the time for such things."

Ashamed that "such things" meant a great deal to her, Vivian struggled to overcome her distaste for Jamie's carelessness, his disregard of worldly possessions making her admire him only the more. He had always been mysterious to her, exciting, unlike anyone she had ever known. Of a forthright, practical nature herself, and with little formal education, she was deeply impressed by scholarship in others. From childhood she had accorded awed respect to her brother Neil and his bookish ways, but nothing had prepared her for Jamie's brilliance. His seemingly limitless knowledge was a sorcery that held her enthralled. The more incomprehensible his vocabulary, the more inexplicable his theories, the more he dazzled. She felt privileged that he had singled her out, chosen her from all others to be the one to whom he confided his exotic conjectures. For the life of her she couldn't fathom what had prompted his selection, fearing always to bore him, say the wrong thing.

Although aware of her own beauty, she wouldn't have dreamed of equating such physical happenstance with real intellectual achievement, and she felt that Jamie too must find her somewhat lacking, despite hair that in the sunlight looked like spun red-gold, despite eyes that put one in mind of dark forest pools at one moment and sparkling emeralds the next. But for all her misgivings, she sensed that Jamie somehow needed her. Without his ever once having told her so, she knew this absolutely, the way she knew right from wrong. The conviction had slowly grown within her and was no longer subject to question or debate. It existed, immutable as a natural law. He needed her. It was why he kept returning, why he had married her.

The rain stopped as the train moved over the dismal marshlands of New Jersey. Beside her, Jamie stirred, caught her hand, his thumb finding the broad gold wedding band he had so recently put on her finger. "Jersey City, is it?" he said. "Almost there."

Vivian caught her breath. Almost there. Almost in New York City, almost in the hotel Jamie had chosen for them in what he called the Village, almost alone together in that unfamiliar bedroom that awaited them somewhere.

She settled her stylish hat on her head and pulled on kid gloves.

They elected to stand out upon the deck of the ferry. There were few passengers who joined them, for it was cold and a wet wind blew off the Hudson, bearing with it the scent of the sea. Jamie held her before him within the tight circle of his arms, but Vivian's teeth chattered, whether from a sudden attack of nerves or from the chill she couldn't have said. In the late winter afternoon the setting sun struck the myriad windows of Manhattan with a fiery metallic glow.

"Skyscrapers," Jamie murmured against her ear, and Vivian nodded. How apt the conceit that they scraped the sky! They were taller by far than any building in Philadelphia, taller than anything she had ever seen in her life, rising like so many shiny needles from out of a giant pincushion. Round about, all manner of ships and boats rode the dully gleaming water, horns blowing mournfully, stacks belching smoke. With a throb to his voice, Jamie said, "Look, Vivvie. The Statue of Liberty."

She turned her head to the right, and there, a ways off but clearly visible, was the huge monument she had seen only in pictures.

Quietly, Jamie recited:

> "Give me your tired, your poor,
>   Your huddled masses yearning to breathe free,
>   The wretched refuse of your teeming shore
>   Send these, the homeless, the tempest-tossed to me;
>   I lift my lamp beside the golden door."

Vivian had heard the scrap of poem many times, knew the words had been inscribed at the base of the statue. But it would never have occurred to her to memorize them. How like Jamie to do so! Gratitude filled her for this tall, rawboned young man who quoted poetry and held her so tightly in his arms. Happiness, brimful and flowing over, engulfed her, and the statue blurred before her eyes.

The dock, when they reached it, was crowded with horses, carriages, carts, and all kinds of conveyances, with wagoners shouting, people shoving, humanity gone berserk. Pedestrians in New York, observed Vivian, moved faster than in Philadelphia. There was a self-absorbed, enclosed aspect to their countenances as they hurried along; excitement, at once seductive and intimidating, crackled in the air. She was glad Jamie knew his way about this redoubtable city. With camera equipment slung over his shoulder and luggage in both hands, he plunged into the throng.

"Where are we going?" cried Vivian, clutching two hatboxes and struggling to keep up with him.

"I hope to catch an omnibus."

"But what about the carriage from the hotel?" she persisted, recalling the comfortable conveyance that had been at the train, ready and waiting to transport her with such dispatch on her previous honeymoon.

Glancing back over his shoulder, Jamie flung out, "Oh, they've nothing like that. It's not a fancy place."

Never, thought Vivian somewhat later, standing in a bedroom in the Hotel d'Étoile, was truer word spoken. The name of the hotel, Jamie informed her, derived from the Place d'Étoile, a square in Paris, from whence came the bowing and scraping, and, yes, smirking little man who had greeted them and escorted them upstairs. Apparently he knew Jamie and called him *Le Sérieux*, which, Jamie further informed her, if somewhat unnecessarily, meant The Serious One.

"Lots of us have sort of tags here in the Village," explained Jamie. "They'll no doubt give one to you. *La Magnifique.*"

Without further preamble, she found herself summarily pulled into his arms. He was bending her backwards, kissing her, and then, to her consternation, she felt a hand thrust between her legs, grasping for her through the many layers of her clothes.

"Jamie!" she gasped protestingly.

He gave a brief strangled cry. "Don't you know how long I've waited? How many times I've wanted this?"

Straightening, he wrapped both arms about her, lifted her off her feet, and, taking two complete turns in the small room, arrived at the bed and fell upon it with her. Unadorned lust distorted his features as he grimaced down at her pinioned beneath him, and she felt skirt and petticoats being flung up to her waist like so many coverlets swept from a bed.

She thought to scream for help but was stopped in confusion by her circumstances. This is my husband. I *must* let him, she told herself as, exposed in the fine lawn umbrella drawers she was wearing, she felt his hand slip under the wide pant leg.

"No!" she cried out, but even as she did so she knew a swift, sweet surge of desire and moved her hips a little, wishing now he had waited until they were shed of hampering garments, wishing, suddenly, to be naked against him. With a small moan she fell back on the bed, only to frown in displeasure when he abruptly left her and arose. But his departure was merely, she saw, to rid himself of his clothing. A smile touched her lips and she closed her eyes, every nerve quivering with anticipation of those caresses that would slowly, inexorably transport her out of the everyday world into inexpressible ecstasy.

She felt him sink down beside her, his hand seeking once more. Then her eyes flew open and she sucked in her breath as, like a knife, he entered her, plunging again and yet again into her unready body. Withdrawing at last, he let himself sink downward upon her. "*Magnifique!*" he sighed.

He had been overly eager, overcome by emotion, she told herself as she lay in the tub of scented water she had crept shakingly into in the bath down the hall. Its being the *first* time, she assured herself, was what had caused his total disregard of her; it was having waited so long, just as he said. Still, his attack—for how else could she think of it?—had left her appalled.

Odious though comparisons might be, she couldn't help but remember Mallory's quite different behavior. In reverie she went back to their arrival in Atlantic City, bellboys snapping to attention, the airy bridal suite filled with fresh flowers, violinists instructed to play her favorite tunes during dinner in the dining room. But more clearly than this evidence of thought and attention she recalled his exquisite consideration on their wedding night, the infinite tenderness and complete unselfishness with which he had introduced her into the mysteries and pleasures of which she had been so innocent.

Annoyed to find herself thinking longingly of one husband while newly married to another, she turned such reminiscences aside. Naturally the two men weren't alike. Mallory had captured her heart because it had been impossible not to respond to so devoted a husband. She had come to love him dearly, but he had never excited her as Jamie did, never presented her with a single new thought or forced her to look at things in new ways. He had never quoted poetry or told her of far places. And most certainly he would never have tolerated her salon. In Mallory's view success in business had been something to which only men might properly aspire.

How fortunate, she thought, brightening, that Jamie didn't share this opinion, or by this time the door to Vivian's would be firmly closed. Yes, she concluded, laving water over satin-smooth shoulders, she must be thankful for Jamie's free thinking. If he had a few things to learn in his ways with a woman, she must just instruct him. Mallory, after all, had doubtless benefited from wide experience with highly sophisticated and knowledgeable ladies. Whereas Jamie, on the other hand, had had only poor Connie, blowsy and undemanding, waiting for him in bed. It wasn't fair to compare the two men; no, it was not.

Slipping into a soft white wool dressing gown, she roundly berated herself and, in the process, very nearly forgot Jamie's gross violation of her.

41

The restaurant to which Jamie escorted her that evening was, like the Hotel d'Étoile, also French.

Although they hadn't boarded an ocean liner, it struck Vivian that they seemed to have arrived in Paris after all. Certainly this Greenwich Village that Jamie so adored appeared altogether foreign. Its many cafes featured checked tablecloths and candles guttering in empty wine bottles, bookstalls piled high with used books leaned against the sides of buildings, and funny little shops offering strange exotic merchandise beckoned everywhere. A gigantic limestone arch dedicated to the honor of George Washington rose above a thoroughfare, looking for all the world like the grand triumphal arches she occasionally had seen in pictures of Paris and Rome. But it was, finally, the residents who most surely gave the Village its alien cachet.

"Of course they speak perfect English!" exclaimed Jamie with his wry grin when she expressed surprise at this. "They're as American as you are."

Vivian's eyes widened, for if these young men and women—frequently scandalously *unescorted* women—who stopped by Jamie's table were Americans, they surely didn't dress or comport themselves as such.

"They're artists of one sort or another, most of 'em," said Jamie. "Writers, actors, painters, sculptors. It's their artistic temperament that makes them seem, well, what some people call them: Bohemians."

"Bohemians?"

"Gypsies. But when people use the term about my friends here, they mean people who aren't all bound up in stuffy conventional ideas. People who aren't afraid to be themselves and do as they choose, who aren't stereotypical."

Vivian nodded. She would never manage to twist her tongue about that unwieldy word, but she could see very

341

well what it meant, for at a table not far away hadn't an elderly and dignified looking gentleman just kissed a loosely bloused young woman full on the mouth while putting a proprietary hand on her breast as, at another table nearby, a woman dressed in what looked to be man's clothing was lighting a cigar!

She brought her eyes firmly back to her plate. Jamie had assured her that the food in this restaurant was cheap but good. It was called Le Crapaud. "Meaning 'The Toad,'" Jamie told her, adding to the shocks she had already gamely withstood this evening by saying offhandedly, "Naturally everyone calls it Le Crap."

Toying with a piece of fish served in a watery white sauce, Vivian decided Le Crapaud was merely cheap. Jamie appeared to relish his meal, however, along with the raw, inexpensive wine that burned the throat. When they returned to Philadelphia she would have Clarissa fix him filet of sole with nutmeg sauce and serve it with a fine wine. It was one of Mallory's favorites, she mused, and found herself thinking about him again. How he would have objected to this undistinguished dish, to the spotted tablecloth, the slapdash service by waiters with soiled aprons and untended hair.

Slashing across her reverie came Jamie's voice, peremptory and harsh. "Tell me what you're thinking."

She looked up in sharp surprise. It would never have occurred to her to ask such a question of anyone, to so impinge on privacy. But he was waiting for her response, regarding her narrowly, displeasure in his dark eyes. Hastily casting about, she said, "I was thinking that when we return to Philadelphia I must ask Clarissa to fix you sole in nutmeg sauce. It's more delicate than this."

"And therefore better?"

"That depends," she hedged.

"On?"

"One's taste, Jamie."

"So this doesn't meet the approval of your cultivated taste buds?"

She stretched out a conciliatory hand to cover his. "Jamie . . ."

He shook it aside. "Don't play games with me, Vivvie. Do you think I'm deaf, dumb, and blind? Do you think I don't know you've been in a snit with everything about this honeymoon? Do you think you didn't make it plain that I

should have had a private cab, at least, waiting for you at
the ferry? Do you think I didn't see you looking down your
nose at the hotel? At this restaurant? Making it clear you
can't abide the food on your plate? Do you think you didn't
let me know you took offense when I exercised my rights
this afternoon? My rights as a husband? Don't you know
that kind of a look on a woman's face is the worst thing she
can do to a man?"

His words were none the less vitriolic for being delivered
in so low a voice—more, with so inscrutable an expression
on his face as surely to fool all but the most attentive.
Vivian provided herself with no such camouflage. Stricken,
she stared incredulously back at this young man whom she
had felt she knew so well, yearned after so keenly, married
so recently.

"I don't mean to offend . . . to look down . . . I
don't . . ."

"Oh, for God's sake, grab hold of yourself! I shall have
to explain that you can't hold your drinks and suffer
crying jags."

The threat, hissed out with such venom, brought to an
abrupt end the last tears he was ever to see in her eyes. "I
believe I have a better suggestion," she said coolly. "Simply
explain that your wife got bored with your company and
returned to her hotel."

Jamie didn't follow after as she left the restaurant and
retraced her steps to the Hotel d'Étoile. The desk clerk
regarded her with more than a little interest as, in that
voice whose clear articulation carried such quiet command,
she asked for her key.

Although she gave it no consideration, everything about
her was at odds with the bedroom she entered. It wasn't
that the room lacked anything: a sturdy bed, a dry sink
with basin and pitcher, two horsehair-covered armchairs
standing before a fireplace whose gas log she quickly lit.
But she presented a striking contrast to the prosaic décor.
Over a fine pearl gray wool skirt, its hem trimmed with
black soutache braid in a Roman key design, she wore a
short, sheared beaver jacket nipped in at the waist, from
which flared a peplum. On her head was a knitted black
fascinator that permitted the sheen of her red-gold hair to
gleam through. A black morocco vanity purse hung from
her wrist.

As soon as the room was warm enough she took off these things, hanging them in the wardrobe. Then she opened her overnight case and took out the fine batiste gown through whose sheer folds she had planned first to reveal her body to Jamie's eyes. Dressing herself in it, she thought how different had been her expectations of this night. Certainly she never dreamed she would be spending it miserable and alone. Picking up the matching batiste negligee, she regarded its deep ruffles admiringly and then folded it and set it aside, slipping into a warmer if less glamorous white wool robe, since clearly there was no reason to play the bride.

Standing at the dresser she took the pins out of her hair, and it fell in heavy silken loops about her shoulders. As she brushed it, her eyes in the mirror were dark with the most grave concern. Jamie had been absolutely correct in his assessment of her opinion of the hotel, of the restaurant, yes, even of that quite ridiculous dash for an omnibus when they might have so easily engaged one of the many hansoms waiting by the dock.

She hadn't realized she had shown her disappointment in these matters, except, of course, for her quite uncontrollable dismay at the unbridled passion Jamie had unleashed upon her. But even this she believed she had taken in good grace. Not so, however, according to Jamie. A shudder ran through her, shaking her from head to toe. With such a disastrous beginning, what would this marriage be like?

She had been sitting curled up in one of the armchairs by the fireplace, staring somberly into the dancing little gas flames, when, an hour or so later, Jamie returned and she opened the bedroom door to his light tap. For a moment he looked searchingly into her face and then, to her complete astonishment, abruptly fell to his knees, grasping both her hands, pressing his lips first to one of them and then the other before flinging back his head to say, "Forgive me!"

Overcome with embarrassment for him, Vivian said, "Jamie! Get up!"

Wrapping his arms about her legs, he pressed his face against her. "Not 'til you say you'll forgive me."

"There's nothing to forgive."

"There is, there is," Jamie insisted. "I've done it all wrong. All of it. I knew you wouldn't like this hotel, the restaurant. I knew we should have stayed uptown. As for what I did to you . . . the way I . . ."

What he had done had filled her with no more revulsion than this abject plea through which her pity now struggled to rise.

"I do forgive you," she said, to end the maudlin scene. To her infinite relief, he stood up, and she returned to the sanctuary of her chair. "We must talk."

"Yes," Jamie agreed. "But first I want a drink. Do you want one?"

"I'm not thirsty."

He laughed shortly. "Oh, not water. Wine."

"No, thank you," she answered, once more surprised. She had had only one glass of wine at the restaurant and Jamie had finished off the bottle. Now she watched him go to his suitcase, extract a fresh bottle, open it, and pour the ruby-red liquid into a tumbler, filling it to the top. He took a sip and then returned to her, sitting in the armchair on the other side of the fireplace.

"Tomorrow," he said, "we move out of here. Where would you like to go? The Waldorf-Astoria?"

"No, Jamie, really! I'm quite happy here."

"Don't kid me, you hate it."

"Jamie," she said earnestly, "how can we ever learn anything about one another if we don't speak the truth? I admit I was a bit surprised at the hotel because I was expecting something altogether different. But it's clean and we're settled here. Besides, you like the Village and I feel sure I shall, too, when I come to know it better. It's just that it seems strange at first. I feel as though I'm in a foreign land."

"That's it!" cried Jamie approvingly. "That's just why I prize it. It's precisely what I believe Europe must be like."

Delighted with his cheerier mood, Vivian fell in with conversation about Italy, France, disregarding the nagging little reminder at the back of her brain that this wasn't the topic she had had in mind when she suggested they talk.

But there could be no arguing it was a livelier, more suitable subject for bride and groom, and one Jamie pursued enthusiastically, refilling his glass with wine and at last persuading her to have some, chatting into the small hours when, wearied by the long and eventful day, they went light-headedly to bed and fell instantly asleep.

The upper reaches of Manhattan, especially broad and elegant Fifth Avenue, were devoted to mansions like the

Vanderbilts', the Astors', the Goulds', and the Rockefellers', together with sumptuous restaurants like Sherry's, Delmonico's, Rector's, and fancy stores like Tiffany's for jewelry and McCutcheon's for fine linens. But the lower end, at Washington Square, had its share of money and dazzle also, if displayed in a different, and many would say regrettable, form. Here certain sons and daughters of the rich had dug in and established themselves in opposition to the thoughts, habits, and mores of their parents.

At "evenings" in Washington Square, lectures on the new Freudian psychology could be heard, and discussions on Free Love. Amid supplies of food and wine paid for by those very examples of bourgeois mentality being denounced and damned, anarchists preached anarchy, suffragettes preached women's right to vote, and passionate quarrels broke out about the concept of the soul, and the purpose, if any, in living at all.

To Vivian, so recently enjoying the security and comforts a bit of money could provide, these people sounded like raving maniacs. Jamie, however, was entranced. Each evening after dinner at Le Crap, as he persisted in calling it, they would go hurrying through the cold night to someone's warm and welcoming salon, most frequently to one established by the popular Lulu Miller.

Miss Miller's father, as everyone knew or quickly learned, owned some of West Virginia's biggest coal mines. Lulu kept saying how she hated to be reminded of this, hated to be forced to accept money from such an enterprise, and could only salve her conscience by dedicating all her strength and energy to bringing the capitalistic system down. She never said what might then become of her, perhaps because, as she stated sadly, this feat would never be achieved within her lifetime.

When, after returning to their hotel one evening, Vivian pointed a finger at a certain hypocrisy in this young woman's attitude, Jamie said, "Look, Vivvie, this is what she means," and from his valise took out a copy of the *Social Survey*. There, spread before her eyes in black and white, were photographs he himself had taken of children, boys from perhaps eight to twelve years of age, at work in a coal mine. With the riveting clarity for which he would one day become famous, he had caught the very coal dust suspended in the air as the youngsters bent over their work, an older boy standing by with long pole in hand to prod those who dallied or fell behind.

"Breaker boys, they're called," Jamie told her. "All day long they sit on those benches. The coal comes rattling down on them through the chutes. Their task is to pick out the pieces of slate and stone that won't burn. Sometimes the coal dust is so thick they can barely see. It gets in the eyes, the throat, the lungs. The stones cut their hands, and their backs get so tired they like to break."

Plunging his hands in his pockets, he paced up and down the room consumed by a kind of fury. "This is what I'm going to make the Millers of this world look at! This is what I'm going to shove under their snotty noses after they've eaten their big dinners in their big, comfortable homes. By God, they're going to know the true price of it!"

He had a vein that ran down along one temple. It grew swollen and pulsated when he got excited. At one time his plans for his chemical experiments could induce this phenomenon. Now it was the things his camera had seen. Always it alarmed Vivian, made her fearful for him.

"Hush, Jamie," she said. "It's not to get wrought up."

"Not to get wrought up!" he cried, running a hand through his dark hair and staring at her like some stranger he had never laid eyes upon before. "Not to get wrought up when cruelty such as this exists? And I can show you more, much more. Things that break the heart. Yes! Things that . . ."

Voice catching raggedly on a sob, he stopped abruptly and, raising a hand, pinched the bridge of his nose.

Vivian rushed to him, putting her arms about him, pulling his head down against hers. "Hush, hush," she crooned. "You'll give yourself such a headache again. Come, we'll lie down."

Urging him to the bed, they lay down together.

"I'm all right," he said flatly.

"Hush, hush. I know you are." After a moment she felt his hand at her skirt. She should really, she thought, tell him how she would like it, the time she wished he would take. But somehow this wasn't the appropriate moment for such instruction. Nor, she knew sadly, would there ever be such a moment for, in the year 1906, how could a respectable woman bring herself to say such things to any man?

* * *

To her surprise, and to Jamie's satisfaction, she began to enjoy their sojourn in the Village.

A quite acceptable omelet could be got at Le Crapaud, and she developed a fondness for Vichy water, leaving to Jamie the full bottle of wine he ordered with each meal. She no longer was shocked at gratuitous displays of affection in public, and Jamie had educated her to the preference on the part of certain women for men's trousers and cigars.

The suffragettes she applauded, the anarchists she deplored. As to Free Love, this she didn't understand at all. The very words seemed a contradiction in terms, for surely to love meant to be tied by bonds of greatest affection. She would look at Jamie, so lean and gaunt yet with a kind of dark intensity about him as he engaged in some fiery debate or other, and her heart would all but burst with pride and love of him. There was nothing in the least "free" about her feelings. How could there be?

Nonetheless she came to be captivated by this insular little world and its exuberant high spirits, by the refreshing honesty that at times blew through it like a cleansing wind, by its pervasive sense of fun. She adored the evenings devoted to charades that mocked the affairs of the day, or to amateur theatricals that presented plays with such titles as *The Poisoned Pancake* or *The Streetcar Conductor Takes His Revenge*. But what she loved best about the Village was the world of painting that, like an exotic garden, had opened before her eyes.

Knowing nothing of art, she didn't understand that these paintings she admired were the avant garde of a realism that, although dubbed the Ashcan School, would soon challenge the venerable National Academy of Design and bring it to its knees. At first she had been put off by these glowing works because their subject matter seemed not worth the painting: two slatternly women walking along a shabby street, a horse-drawn lunch wagon in the bleak solitude of a rainy night, weary passengers riding an elevated train. They certainly weren't like the pretty landscapes or the portraits of carefully dressed ladies and gentlemen that adorned the houses of Cavendish Square. But she was drawn to these ordinary people, these everyday scenes.

"They're like your photographs, Jamie," she told him. "They speak the truth. No wonder everyone admires you."

"Do they admire me, Vivvie?"

"Yes, indeed!" she said, pleased that her words pleased him. "Only the other day I heard you compared to Mr. Stieglitz."

"Stieglitz, eh? That's high praise." And then, "Lulu wants to mount a show for me."

"A show of your photographs!"

He nodded. "Here in the Village. But I'm not ready yet."

"Not ready? Why, you've hundreds of pictures to choose from."

"Not that I really like. I'll have to take a trip again."

Her heart sank. "So soon?"

"It's a great chance for me. Surely you understand that."

"I was just thinking of leaving Irene, and the salon."

"Oh, you won't come with me."

"No?"

"What would you do on such a jaunt?"

"How long will you be gone?"

"I'm not sure yet."

"Where will you go?"

"For God's sake, don't ask so many questions! How should I know?" Catching sight of her face, he softened and took her into his arms. "Look now," he said, and kissed the tip of her nose, "once you get back home you'll have Irene and your house and your business, plenty to keep you busy." More somberly he added, "Don't make me feel hemmed in, Vivvie. It's something I'll not abide."

Hurt and angry, she pulled away from him, seeking the capacious depths of the horsehair-covered armchair that seemed to have become something of a sanctuary for her in the small hotel room. There she sat for the remainder of the lowering January afternoon, staring into the tiny blue and gold flames that danced like so many small devils on the gas log in the fireplace.

Jamie had long since left her, clapping on his wide-brimmed felt hat with an exasperated sigh. She didn't blame him, since all his efforts at conversation had been met with stony silence. She knew she should have responded, helped make it up, but the stubborn core of her wouldn't permit it. This was such new behavior on her part, so petulant and childish, that she was dismayed at herself. Had she been utterly spoiled by Mallory, then? Her wishes always first and foremost? Her slightest suggestion his command? Could she not adjust to a less indulgent husband?

When, toward dusk, Jamie returned, she ran to him, conscience-stricken and contrite. "I'm sorry," she whispered, her head burrowed against his chest.

He kissed her brow and looked solemnly down at her. "I forgive you," he said.

Their quarrel was over, but it struck Vivian as strange that, like their lovemaking, his absolution gave her little joy.

42

Difficult though it was to believe, the glamorous crea-ture seated across the table from Vivian was unquestionably her sister Mary Claire.

"You and Jamie mustn't come backstage after the show tonight," this vision was saying. "Mr. Ziegfeld won't permit us to be seen with all that heavy stage makeup on our faces."

They sat, just the two of them, at lunch in the hushed grandeur of Henry Maillard's Retail Confectionery and Ladies Lunch establishment on Broadway. Above their heads, handpainted nymphs in pastel garments floated across a pale blue ceiling, while moving silently over a thickly carpeted floor, waitresses dressed in black sateen and frilly white aprons served tea and sandwiches and *pâtisserie*.

"My chums and I come here a lot," confided Mary Claire. "It's near the theater, of course, but the real reason is that they've got the best chocolate éclairs."

That Ziegfeld Follies showgirls might harbor such girlish desires was no more surprising to Vivian than that they should be Mary Claire's "chums."

Ravishing in a suit of rose pink taffeta with wine velvet facing at wrists and lapels, a wine velvet Gibson girl hat filled with pink silk roses on her dark hair, Mary Claire smiled sunnily and nibbled a sandwich, happily aware that around her she was creating a little stir.

Two months ago the great Florenz Ziegfeld had spotted her dutifully parading about a stage along with a bevy of Fleurette's Florodora Girls. With an unerring eye for feminine appeal, he had plucked her out of this troupe, promised her the enormous salary of seventy-five dollars a week, and made her a star in his newest revue.

Ziegfeld showgirls need only be able to walk down stairs without tripping, but in this age of opulence they were the extravagant centerpiece in Broadway's most opulent show. On them Florenz Ziegfeld lavished infinite care, striving to bring out each young woman's special quality. Thousands were spent on the stage settings that would display her like a new and precious jewel, thousands more on the costumes that turned her into an exotic bird, a flower, a Miss December dressed as a Christmas tree, a Miss June dressed as a bride, or, in the current new show, a ship in a gala patriotic representation of Teddy Roosevelt's Great White Fleet.

"I'm a United States battleship," announced Mary Claire proudly.

"How can you be that?" demanded Vivian, wide-eyed.

"On my head, you see," said Mary Claire, "I wear this fabulous headdress fashioned like a battleship. All the girls wear different ships on their heads. And after we walk down the stairs and parade around, why, click! all the lights on the stage go off and we switch on the lights in our headdresses. It looks like the whole Great White Fleet on the ocean at night. The audience goes wild!"

Vivian could very well believe it.

"After the show," continued Mary Claire, offhandedly, "we'll go to supper at Rector's. Max is taking us."

"Max?"

Mary Claire wrinkled her nose. "Max Delacey. A very rich man. But not larky. I've just started seeing him."

"Why see him if you don't like him?"

"Oh, Vivvie, don't *be* that way! All my chums have rich boyfriends."

Recalling the outcome of an earlier disagreement, Vivian held her tongue. But she found herself looking forward to seeing Max Delacey with even keener interest than she felt in Mr. Ziegfeld's rendering of the Great White Fleet.

* * *

The string of shops that comprised the Delacey Arcade on upper Fifth Avenue was only the most visible of the Delacey family assets, which included part ownership of a railroad, stock in a steel mill, and partnership, albeit silent, in a prestigious publishing house known for its scholarly imprimatur.

Inheritance had bequeathed the administration of these holdings to Max Delacey at the age of twenty-four, thereby making his name a legend among those people—bankers, entrepreneurs, mothers of marriageable daughters—who are apt to know of such things. The sudden death of an uncle had thrown this responsibility upon the young man. Thus it was that the considerable energy and acumen Max Delacey had intended to apply to archaeology was instead turned to the care of that family fortune on which he himself depended, together with his gently abstracted father, a renowned medievalist; his charming but impractical mother, and his three pretty, unmarried sisters.

He shouldered this burden by applying himself with unrelenting diligence to mastering the intricacies of the vicious rate wars that plagued the railroads; the vagaries of the stock market, and those mercantile practices that, under his uncle's management, and now under his own, had made a success of the elite establishments renting space in the Delacey Arcade. This dedication, absolutely essential if the family was to continue living in its accustomed splendor, had in the past few years left him with little leisure to devote to personal concerns. He wished to sell off the family interest in the railroad that was keeping him embroiled in constant fights; with the profits he wanted to purchase controlling stock in the steel mill; he wanted to help his father fulfill a life's dream of building a replica of a medieval monastery on the upper Hudson River; and most especially, he wished to see his sisters happily married to gentlemen who would cherish them as tenderly as he meant to cherish his own wife.

He intended to marry, and had highly developed notions as to the kind of husband he wished to be. But as yet he had too much to do to *be* that kind of husband. He harbored, nonetheless, a fine regard for feminine companionship, which he sought outside that class in which he expected eventually to marry, his sisters unwittingly having taught him the cruel false hopes an eligible bachelor can arouse. Having no wish to encourage unwarranted expecta-

tions, he felt most comfortable with attractive young
women who quite unceremoniously used him, his gifts (expensive), and his attentions (considerate) in return for accommodating his demands (reasonable).

A brief introduction to Mary Claire Randall had revealed her to be a likely candidate for such friendship, and
so Max Delacey had gone to considerable trouble arranging
this evening, engaging a box at the theater, reserving a table at Rector's for supper after the show, sending a basket
of two dozen white roses backstage. Now, faultlessly
dressed in formal clothes, broad shoulders enhanced by
careful tailoring, strongly etched features set off by the
stark masculine attire, he waited with amiable curiosity to
welcome his guests, Mary Claire's sister and her new husband from Philadelphia, Mr. and Mrs. Jamie Fitzhugh.

With far greater concern, Vivian approached this meeting.

"Mary Claire has a beau," she had told Jamie upon returning to the Hotel d'Étoile after luncheon with her sister.

"Oh?" said Jamie. "Is it serious?"

"They've just met. She says he's very rich."

"It's not serious, then."

"Jamie, how can you say that? How can you know?"

Jamie tossed aside his magazine and pulled her down
into his lap. "Listen, my little innocent. How many very
rich men marry Ziegfeld showgirls?"

"Some do."

"But most don't. Most do you-know-what."

Blushing furiously, Vivian nevertheless had little doubt
that, on the whole, Jamie was right, and so she leveled cold
green eyes upon Max Delacey that evening as she entered
his box and he rose to bow graciously over her hand.

At sight of him every story she ever had read of the rich
and handsome despoiler of feminine virtue, every tale ever
told of innocence defiled seemed to stand incarnate before
her, looking down at her with a quizzical smile. How, oh
how, could Mary Claire resist someone so attractive, so
debonair, so obviously engaging? Why, the devil himself
must have sent him to test her.

"Mrs. Fitzhugh?" said this emissary from Satan.

Vivian recalled herself. "Yes?" she whispered.

"I was suggesting we sit down."

She collapsed onto the gilt chair he offered, placed between Jamie's and his own. He helped her off with her

sheared beaver jacket and didn't look askance at the gray
wool suit she wore, inappropriate to the occasion but selected in order not to put Jamie's rumpled brown corduroy
to shame. He opened her program for her, asked if she
were comfortable, if she would like the use of his mother-
of-pearl-encased opera glasses, and begged her to rise
briefly so that he might position her chair to better advantage.

In each small attention, each charmingly expressed solicitude, he reminded Vivian of no one so much as Mallory.
Unlike him though Max Delacey was—in appearance, in
the quiet self-assurance that yet bespoke command, in the
modulated voice—still there was that about the man that
sent through Vivian so searingly vivid a recollection of her
first husband that she felt suddenly light-headed and faint.

She was grateful that the houselights went down, plunging the audience into velvety darkness, although Jamie
muttered in her ear that he hadn't finished reading his program. In the expectant hush that followed, when the theater itself seemed to be holding its breath, a longing for Mallory seized her, a memory of him so sharp and true, a
yearning so excruciating that sudden tears slid down her
cheeks and she was shaken by a stifled sob.

As she fumbled for a hankie, her morocco purse escaped
her and slipped to the floor. With a mild oath Jamie dove
for it. While he rooted about in the darkness, Vivian felt
Max Delacey grasp her hand and press into it a smooth
folded handkerchief. Then the curtain rose.

"Why were you crying?" he asked.

They were at the famous Rector's, and Vivian sat beside
Max Delacey. In the brightly lit room with its hurrying
waiters and finely dressed patrons, their large table was the
cynosure of all eyes, just as Mary Claire had expected it to
be. The party, Mary Claire had airily informed Max Delacey, had grown to include, together with boyfriends, a half
dozen of her chums who earlier had been seen wearing battleships on their heads, and little else.

Unlike Jamie, at the opposite end of the table, Max Delacey appeared unfazed by these exotic companions. Or
perhaps he was merely disinterested in the banter that occupied his guests and frequently convulsed them in gales of
raucous laughter. It was as though, having seen to their

wine, their crab ravigote, their lobster thermidor, he had sat back and said, Well now, children, enjoy yourselves.

There was a reserve about him that one might almost have called hauteur until catching the good humor informing the candid gray eyes. His forehead was broad under hair that was a glossy honey brown, smooth-textured, thick; straight heavy brows were separated by a deep declivity like a permanent frown above a strong, fine nose. Tall, well coordinated, his movements marked by grace and ease, he was direct in manner. Who, thought Vivian, could dissemble to such a man? She liked him as well as anyone she had ever met. Foolish though the thought might be, she wanted him to marry Mary Claire.

"Certain ways you have remind me of my first husband," she said simply, by way of explaining her surprising behavior in the theater.

"He is dead?"

"Yes."

"You must have loved him very much."

"I did. I do still. Death doesn't change such things."

"But now you are married again."

"Yes. Very happily so."

She regretted that hasty assurance. Why had she felt it necessary? Some guilty sense of disloyalty to Jamie, she supposed. But she had never loved Mallory as madly, as recklessly, as selflessly as she loved Jamie.

Her eyes flew down the table to him. How aware she was of him always! How difficult to keep her eyes off him. Mallory had used to do that with her. Often she would look up to find him watching her. She had felt flattered at such attention, but Jamie detested it. "Vivvie, why must you forever spy on me?" But how hard to tear her eyes away.

"Are your two husbands alike?" asked Max Delacey.

"No, no. Quite different."

In contrast to the noisy party, her voice was quiet. Everything about her, in fact, set her apart from the other young ladies in their colorful gowns. But for her striking beauty she might have appeared quite innocuous, dressed as she was in gray skirt and white leg-of-mutton shirtwaist.

"I would have thought," said Max Delacey, "that one would be drawn to the same type of mate, as one is inclined to the same kind of friends."

"I haven't found it so. For me, the difference is that in my first marriage, my husband loved the more. In my second, I love the more."

"Is that so?" His eyes flicked to Jamie, then back again. "May I say I find your second husband hard to understand?"

Later she was to wonder what had led her to such candor. At the moment, Mary Claire archly insisted Max rise so that she could sit beside Vivian. "That's Dolores," she announced, singling out a statuesque beauty. "Mr. Ziegfeld discovered her modeling clothes in a fashion salon. You know how tony she looks on the stage? That's the way Mr. Ziegfeld wants her to behave, but she's really larky, look at her now."

Mary Claire chattered on, commenting on this one and that; assuring Vivian that Mr. Ziegfeld was the soul of propriety. "For instance," she said solemnly, "we must never go about without wearing gloves. And we must always have our hair perfectly dressed. And we must own at least one tailored suit for when we travel. Wherever we go, we must remember we are the representatives of Mr. Florenz Ziegfeld and conduct ourselves as such."

Vivian was hard put to believe she wasn't hearing the code of deportment set down by an exclusive girls' school.

"It sounds," she observed, "like the Villa Maria."

Mary Claire giggled. "Well, it's not! How do you like my beau?"

"Oh, so much! I do think he has such a lot to him. He's so intelligent, so considerate."

"So dull."

"I think he may surprise you when you're alone with him."

"Oh ho!"

"Now you know I'm not meaning *that*. What I'm saying is, I think he's the nicest gentleman in the world, and I shall start a novena to St. Jude that you marry him."

"St. Jude!" cried Mary Claire. "But he is the patron of impossible causes."

"Yes," agreed Vivian with a nod. "And for sure I think it's well nigh impossible that Mr. Delacey will want you. But if he does, I'll count you the luckiest girl in the world."

43

They returned, she and Jamie, to a Philadelphia in the
throes of a January thaw. The sun shone with traitorous
splendor, melting icicles, turning gutters into streams, beguiling some to go about minus coat or scarf. It was sheer
deception but pleasant while it lasted, adding to Vivian's
joy in being home and, most especially, with Irene once
more.

At not quite a year old, the little girl was a beauty, her
quite extraordinary natural endowments enhanced by the
sunniest of temperaments. Even Jamie, who admitted to little interest in children, was captivated out of self-defense.
Used to smiles and approval from everyone about her,
Irene seemed to accept Jamie's initial indifference as a
gauntlet thrown down. With the persistence of one who has
never known rebuff she pursued him, catching at his
hands, gurgling archly, and one day fluttering thick, spiky
black eyelashes at him.

"Little flirt!" said Jamie, laughing, but he was caught at
last, if caught he could be, for no one held him long. His
work was his first love, his true mistress.

"I'm not in the least possessive," Jamie told Vivian, and
this proved true. Not for a moment did he object to the
long hours she spent at the salon or at her desk in the
parlor in the evening, poring over figures, making plans.
That he lived in her house, among furnishings that were
hers, waited upon by her servants, disturbed him not at all.

Entering her bedroom on their return from New York,
she had discovered Mallory's big iron bed removed, and in
its place an equally large brass bed. "We can't have the star
boarder climbing into the master's bed," Jamie told her.

It was the only change he made in the house, the only
bill he paid, the only domestic decision for which he took
responsibility. At first she had made a point of consulting
him on household affairs until one day she realized this

annoyed him. He didn't *care* what color rug she had in the hallway, it didn't *matter* to him whether he ate roast beef or baked ham.

Clarissa, and even Halls, Vivian could tell, were disappointed in him, used as they were to Mallory's warm praise of a dinner, Mallory's eye for the well-polished brass doorknob, the telling detail.

Once, after a particularly fine meal, Vivian said, "Jamie, did you enjoy dinner?"

"Yes, I did," he replied.

"Then you might say a word about it to Clarissa. It would please her."

"Vivvie, for God's sake, don't start telling me what to say!"

But the next morning she overheard him in the kitchen stiffly complimenting Clarissa on the roast duck. Clarissa's response was equally self-conscious. The exchange appeared only to have caused embarrassment all around, and Vivian resolved to make no more gratuitous suggestions.

However, if he took little interest in domestic matters, he was fascinated by her hairdressing business.

"What's in this liquid soap you peddle to all your ladies?" he asked.

When she told him the ingredients, he said, "It's the sulfur that's your secret. I'm wondering if you might not just substitute sulfated lauryl alcohol for the castor oil that's your base. It would be a good foamer and very likely do better in hard water."

Thus was born Vivian's Hard-Water Shampoo, to be followed by Vivian's Hair Groomer, a solution of gum in water that, after application and drying, left a residue that kept hair beautifully in place. These products not only sold well but, since they could be obtained only by patrons of the salon, brought more and more customers.

At first her father had objected to admitting Jamie to his private sanctum in the back room of the Tipperary.

"What!" he cried, when Vivian told him she had revealed the secret soap recipe. "You've told him what's in it!"

"Jamie knows a lot about chemistry, papa," she said. "He wants to come down to the Tip and watch you mix it one day."

"Never!"

"Now, papa."

"Never!" repeated Edward Randall.

But Jamie managed to get round him, largely, Vivian suspected, because her father was flattered at finding himself part of experiments in chemistry. Ensconced behind the appointments desk, he now spoke knowledgeably of sulfates and emulsions, to the edification of the ladies to whom he sold his wares. Vivian was delighted that the two men, so different in their ways, got along together.

This wasn't true of her mother and Jamie, alas.

"What sort of man lets a woman keep him and pay all the bills, will you answer me that?" demanded Mamie. "What man lies around doing nothing all day?"

Jamie had asked Vivian if he could fix up the second floor of the empty carriage house at the end of her property as a darkroom and study. She readily agreed, and he now spent most of his day there, reading, looking over photographs, lying on the floor on a mattress he had covered with a paisley quilt.

"He's going to be off on his trip very soon, mama." explained Vivian. "He's going to be traveling through New England taking photographs for his one-man show."

"And who is paying him for this?"

"He hopes to sell the negatives to magazines."

"Meantime he makes no objection to seeing his wife go off to work every day."

"You've never liked him, mama."

"That's neither here nor there. It's just a wonder to me how you put up with him."

Vivian might have answered that she adored Jamie. Not given to introspection, she couldn't have said why this should be so, had never so much as asked herself the question. Dr. Freud's new technique of psychoanalysis might label her predilection an obsession of sorts. She herself would be more inclined to say with Pascal, had she known of him, "The heart has its reasons which reason does not know." Jamie made her happy. So far as she was concerned, this was the long and the short of it. At sight of him a smile danced to her lips. He made her happy; this was enough.

True, there were things she would have preferred to be different. She had wished, for instance, to continue her custom of inviting Ma Mallory for Sundays. But while Jamie made no objection to this, he refused to be present. He said he couldn't abide "that egotistical old woman," as he called her, so Vivian arranged to visit Ma instead of having her to the house.

She scarcely saw Rita Celano and the Wade girls anymore. Jamie declared he could find nothing in common with the "insular Butler Street mentalities" of the men these girls had married, and with a pang Vivian watched these friendships grow cool.

But she suffered real anguish at strained relations with Gert and Harry Barkin.

"Never mind!" advised Gert when, full of apologies, Vivian turned down an invitation to dinner for the third time. "Look, kiddo, I know his highness don't like Harry and me. We don't like him, either, to tell you the truth. But the important thing is, he suits you. For the rest, you and me can still get together now and then, can't we?"

Jamie would, Vivian knew, make no objection to this any more than to anything else she did or didn't do, so long as his participation wasn't required. A unique arrangement had evolved wherein they shared the intimacies of marriage but led quite separate lives.

Friends came to visit Jamie in the carriage house at the bottom of the garden all the time. Often in the evenings he entertained there. With the black draperies necessary to a darkroom pulled across the windows, with candles lit, bottles of wine out, the room took on an exotic air. He unfailingly invited her to join him on these occasions, and unless Morrissey or Thurman Foy were to be present, she frequently did so, taking pleasure in sitting quietly by his side as heated arguments on the new thought of the day raged on past midnight. But she felt he would have enjoyed himself just as much if she weren't there, knew he often forgot she *was* there.

One cold Sunday afternoon toward the end of March, after putting Irene down for her nap, Vivian felt lonely and at loose ends in the quiet house. A restlessness touched her, making her loath to settle down to the desk work forever awaiting her. Moving to a window, she looked out over the frozen yard to the carriage house. Suddenly, unexpected and unbidden, desire shook her. So overpowering was its assault that she trembled and closed her eyes, as though withstanding a wave of acute pain while her heart pounded and her head swam.

Their lovemaking in the three months of their marriage,

often abruptly concluded by Jamie just as she was becoming fully aroused, had seldom satisfied her. Now such an insistence drove her that she flung a shawl about her head, went out the back door, and ran down the slate walk to burst into the carriage house.

"Jamie?" she called imperiously, and at his answer ran up the wooden stairs.

She found him seated at a long table he had fashioned out of a few boards set upon trestles. Coals glowed red hot in a potbellied stove, and he had some photographs in his hand. He turned to greet her as she came to a halt at the top of the stairs, her breath coming quick and shallow, cheeks flushed, the shawl slipping from her hair. Stock-still she stood, looking at him with parted lips, eyes glazed.

"What is it?" he asked, puzzled, uncertain.

"I came . . . to see you." Her voice was strange, unlike itself—guttural, throbbing.

He continued staring at her, and as he did so his eyes changed, the light in them leapt and brightened as though kindled with the twin flames in her own.

"I'll put more coal on the fire," he said.

"The fire's all right."

"Then take off your clothes."

With impatient, hastening fingers she did as she was bidden, flinging skirt, shirtwaist, petticoat from her. Naked, she moved to the mattress on the floor, flung back the paisley cover, and lay down.

I shall perish if he makes me wait, she told herself.

But he didn't make her wait. As always, he was upon her instantly, and she was ready. With an eagerness born of past denial, her passion rose to his, her desire as insistent as his had ever been, her own needs clamoring to be met. She would not brook frustration this time, not be thwarted. She moaned aloud with pleasure as he plunged within her, abandoning herself to utter ecstasy.

Instantly, she felt a change in him. Eyes flying open, she saw surprise touch his face. He stared down at her, incredulous. Then panic seemed to seize him, horror spread across his features, and in that moment she felt his presence shrink within her.

"No, no!" she lashed out, clinging to him in cheated fury. "No!" she implored, as with a single harsh sob he flung himself from her.

It was this cry that brought her to her senses. The high blue March sky came sailing back beyond the windows; within the potbellied stove a piece of coal shifted and fell. As though recovering from some malady, Vivian raised herself on a bare, slender arm and looked to where Jamie lay, face down. "Jamie . . ."

When he didn't answer, she drew the quilt up over him. "You'll take cold."

"Leave me alone."

"Jamie, please . . ."

He rounded on her. "Leave me alone! Don't you know what's happened? Don't you know what's happened to me?"

Her heart went out to him. "Jamie, you'll be all right. Why, sometimes with Mallory—"

"Don't speak to me of Mallory! Is this the way you were with him? This wanton, demanding way?"

She shrank from him, pulling up the quilt to cover her breasts.

"What kind of woman are you?" he raged. "What kind are you? No lady acts that way. No lady likes it. Is this how Mallory taught you to behave? Like one of his whores?"

She had no recollection of whether she attempted to answer these questions, to defend herself. She remembered running back over the yard, hastily clad only in skirt and shawl, her shirtwaist and underclothes clutched in her arms.

It was just before supper that Jamie returned to the house, to find her sitting in the half-light in their bedroom.

"Forgive me," he said, kneeling beside her chair. "Forgive me. You surprised me, Vivvie, that's all. I've always thought of you as so . . . well, superior." He chuckled and gently cuffed her chin. "You know, me way down here, and you up there. I never thought of any other woman that way. Only you. It's why I always said you were the only woman I'd ever marry. And it just never occurred to me that you would . . ."

"Jamie, please," she begged, face burning with embarrassment.

"No, wait, Vivvie. Christ, I owe you an apology. I'm enlightened. I'm informed. I know a lady can like it. I've thought it all through, and what I'm saying is, it'll be different after this. I mean, now that I know that you . . . Well, it'll be different now."

Vivian made no answer. She doubted she would abandon herself in such a manner ever again.

44

Stunned by Jamie's behavior, mortified by her own, Vivian thrust that devastating afternoon to the back of her mind, concentrating on those aspects of life that pleased her.

Much did. Her salon was becoming famous. The women who passed through its doors were among the cream of Philadelphia society. Far from being daunted by this elite clientele, she had learned from her long experience as lady's maid that all lives are burdened, rich as well as poor, that all seek a bit of kindness. Thus it was that, seeing Camilla Cavendish's face as that elegant lady swept into the salon one April morning, Vivian knew something was terribly amiss.

"Mrs. Cavendish!" she exclaimed softly. "What has happened?"

"Oh, Vivvie, dear!" replied Camilla Cavendish, her usual poise deserting her. "Irene Webb has been found dead!"

Found dead. It sounded different from *being* dead, from dying. Vivian went cold. Her thoughts leapt instantly to Clinton and Nancy.

As though reading her mind, Camilla said, "Clinton has gone down to Butler Street to inform his sister. Poor, dear Clinton! It was he who found her."

All day the salon buzzed with stories. Irene Webb, it was reported, had suffered a fatal heart attack. Irene Webb had been ill for some time with an unnamed malady and had slipped away. Irene Webb had suffered a stroke and never recovered; no, a burst appendix. No one said the one thing on so many minds, that, sinking deeper and ever deeper into melancholy, Irene Webb had taken her own life.

As soon as Vivian had locked the door of the salon that evening she hurried through the soft twilight to Cavendish Square. She blamed herself for not having taken the time to visit Irene Webb more often. Just once after their meeting in the Square she had brought little Irene to see her, but it had been stiff and awkward trying to make conversation with a nurse standing by. The air was filled with questions that couldn't be answered, things that shouldn't be said. She hadn't gone back.

She mounted the smooth marble front steps, lifted the polished brass knocker, and rapped at the front door. Somerby opened it. She could tell he didn't recognize her, modishly dressed as she was in a tailored suit of dove gray linen and a hat trimmed with gray mousseline de soie.

"Good evening, Mr. Somerby," she said. "I'm Vivvie. Vivvie Randall that was; I'm Mrs. Fitzhugh now. I've come to pay my respects to Dr. Webb."

Somerby appeared dazed. "Step inside, ma'am. The doctor is not receiving, but would you have a word with his son?"

"Oh, yes! Please!"

He led her into the center hall she knew so well, whose newel post, mounted with a bronze statue of a naiad holding aloft a globed electric light, she had dusted so often. This globe was lit now, as were lights in the rooms on either side. People waited about, and a sibilance filled the air, murmurous and subdued.

"Why, Vivvie!" cried Clinton in surprise, chancing to come from out the library, and Somerby turned to gape, recognizing her at last.

Vivian went to him. "I'm sorry. So very sorry."

"We can't talk here. Come along, into the morning room." So saying, he swept her off, flinging back over his shoulder, "Hold the fort, Somerby. I'll be but a moment."

Once inside the pleasant room, its wallpaper still the pretty flowered pattern Vivian remembered, all pretense of composure fled Clinton. Anguish stood in his pinched white face, made all the more pale by contrast with his black hair, small, neat black moustache, somber black frock coat.

"I found her, Vivvie," he said, grasping her hands in

both his own as though he were imperiled and she might save him. "I knew she had been feeling blue lately. More blue than usual, that is. In the past two years she's been blue enough, God knows. She had gotten it in her head that she must see Nan's boy. She somehow had the notion that there was something wrong with him, some defect, and that we weren't letting on. I begged father to permit it. He wouldn't; said seeing Nan and the baby would only stir things up again and upset her." Letting fall Vivian's hands, he flung himself from her. "Upset her! Does he prefer to see her calmly dead?"

"Clinton!"

He swung to face her. "I'm sorry, Vivvie. I believe he was doing what he felt best. I *must* believe this, or I'd go up to that room in which he has enclosed himself with his sorrow, and kill him with my bare hands!"

"You mustn't talk this way," said Vivian severely. "No, and you mustn't. There's too much to be done right now, too much to be seen to. You can't indulge yourself."

"Indulge myself!"

"Yes, that's what it is; that's what you're doing!" Going to him, she placed her hands on his shoulders. "Now listen to me. There'll be plenty of time later to fix blame. Right now, this time belongs to your mother, to see her decently to her grave. You've got a part to play and you must play it. There are people here in this house come to pay their respects to her memory. You've no call to think of yourself. It's your mother that claims your attention, to be laid to rest with dignity and honor. She was a great lady. She wouldn't have liked things this way. Now, Mr. Clinton, sir, you must just take hold of yourself."

A dry sob escaped him. " 'Mister Clinton, sir.' " He smiled. "Dear, good, wonderful Vivvie. If only we could go back to those days."

"Well, we can't. But we can remember them, the best of them. We can remember the musical evenings and the parties. We can remember the good times. That's what I plan to do."

Clinton nodded. "Yes, Vivvie. I, too."

The set of Nancy Webb Randall's face was hard, unforgiving.

"Sometimes," Vivian was gently saying, "it's better to receive than to give."

"I need nothing from him," said Nancy.

"But Clinton needs to give. He needs to give to you. It will help assuage his grief."

"Why should his grief be assuaged? Mine shan't ever be."

Vivian sighed. In the May evening, three weeks after Irene Webb's funeral, she sat beside her sister-in-law on the back steps of the Randall house. The fragrance of lilacs filled the air, for the backyards of Butler Street boasted many a lilac bush. The mild evening gave up a fresh, sweet scent of turned earth, of growth and promise. But the young woman who sat opposite Vivian on the worn wooden step appeared impervious to such blandishments. Wraith-like in her white muslin skirt and shirtwaist, she stared off into the distance, unmoved.

"Your brother has changed, Nancy," continued Vivian, refusing to relinquish the mission she had undertaken. "I believe what especially troubles him is the lack of an heir. He has a real interest in young Clinton. He would like to meet him."

Silence greeted this information, and Vivian pressed onward. "It will be a long while before our Neil is a successful lawyer. Why, he has yet to take his examinations for the bar. Meantime, young Clinton is growing up in this little house that is far too crowded, and with none of the advantages your brother is so eager to provide if only you'll let him."

"Oh, Vivvie!" cried Nancy impatiently. "You make me out some kind of ogre. I know very well how cramped the house is! It's not only difficult for Neil and the baby and me, but for your parents, especially your mother. It would be just lovely to accept a loan from Clinton to buy a place of our own. I'm not a complete ninny. I've learned at least a little about the importance of a bit of money. But loans always come with strings attached."

"In this case," said Vivian, "I think the only strings would be those of real affection for you and young Clinton. Your brother needs you."

"Is that what he told you to say?"

"No."

"The one he really needs," burst out Nancy unexpectedly, "is you." She nodded sharply. "It's true. Mother knew it. I remember her once saying what a pair you'd make, and what a pity it was that such things could never be. But

Clinton could have married you if he had really wanted, just as I married Neil."

Despite her rebellion against her family and their ways, clearly Nancy still felt the Webbs held the prerogatives. Amused by the unwitting little condescension, Vivian said slyly, "Why is it that you named your son Clinton if you dislike your brother so much?"

Nancy bristled. "I don't dislike my brother. It's just that all this that he suddenly wants to do . . . It's too late."

"Too late for what?" snapped Vivian, losing patience at last. "Too late for your poor mother, that's for sure. But not too late for Clinton and you."

To Vivian's delighted satisfaction, Nancy and Neil decided to accept Clinton's offer of a loan with which to purchase a house. "You'd think," announced Anthea Webb one day to anyone in Vivian's who cared to listen, "that my husband didn't have a home of his own. He's forever at his sister's."

And there came a time when Dr. Webb accompanied his son on a visit.

"I couldn't believe my eyes!" proclaimed Anthea. "Off they went together, the two of them. The doctor wanted a look at his grandson. Heavens, I'm glad he's willing to own up to the child at last. Now maybe he'll stop dropping hints in my direction. After all, it's not my fault I'm not *enceinte*, when his son never opens the door to my bedroom."

Anthea's listeners tittered as Anthea had invited them to do. Vivian made no response. It wasn't her practice to comment on the revelations to which a hairdressing establishment is singularly privy. But she couldn't help wonder if Anthea would be quite so ready to gossip about her husband were she aware of the unflattering speculations such disclosures raised about herself.

Jamie returned from New England late in June, laden with photographs that he immediately set about developing for his show in the fall. The results were stunning in the way he meant them to be: the skillful work of a gifted photographer condemning a society that tolerated such conditions as his camera revealed.

"Vivvie, look at this, just look," he would say, and she would stand transfixed before some picture of hopeless poverty, utter weariness, palpable despair. "Such conditions are obscene!" he would fling out in helpless fury. "Obscene!"

After poring over such pictures all day, he couldn't sleep at night and his head throbbed with the violent headaches to which he was prone. Roused by his discomfort, Vivian hurried to fetch cold compresses, to fan him in the hot, muggy nights when not a breath of air stirred. She worried about him. He was so thin, and he had never recovered a good color after the malaria. "You can't change the world, Jamie," she would say.

"I'll be happy if I can change conditions in just one small part of it."

The magazines in which his work appeared didn't pay much, but he was beginning to make a name for himself. The stark faces peering out from his photographs were like a pointed finger: "*J'accuse*." More and more assignments came his way. As a result, he was at home less and less.

Knowing how important his work was, Vivian tried to make no protest at his frequent absences, his lack of concern for household affairs. But she found it increasingly hard that he took for granted that the larder would always be full, the coal in the coal bin ready for winter, the leak in the roof mended, the chimneys swept clean. He just isn't aware of such things, she would reason, persuading herself that her husband's mind was on far more important concerns.

It was a conclusion supported by any number of books and periodicals. In order to stir up a public intent on its own pleasures, the most shocking stories were being published. Books such as John Spargo's *The Bitter Cry of the Children* and George Kibbe Turner's *Daughters of the Poor* addressed themselves to child labor, to prostitution and the white slave traffic. Upton Sinclair's *The Jungle* assaulted sensibilities with its study of Chicago food-packing methods and the conditions of the immigrants who worked in the stockyards. Fearful that some of these tales were irresponsible, Theodore Roosevelt likened such reporters to the man with the muckrake in Bunyan's *Pilgrim's Progress*. Offered a celestial crown, this man would not so much as look at it, continuing to fix his gaze upon the muck on the floor. Thus was born the term *muckrakers*.

"As though any one of us cares what we're called," observed Jamie with fine contempt.

He applauded the fact that Vivian's girls were former

lady's maids. "You've taken them out of a life of servitude, Vivvie," he told her. "You've trained them and given them dignity and a real chance. I wish there were hundreds like you."

Not only did he praise her, he praised them to their pleased, rosy faces.

Understanding how tiresome boardinghouse food could become, Vivian often invited her young assistants home for the excellent roasts and stews presented by Halls and Clarissa. At such times Jamie outdid himself, teasing the girls, making them giggle, but also driving home a few points as he held center stage.

"You must help others who are still held down. You must smarten yourselves up. Here, read this newspaper, this book."

The girls adored the attention of this lean, fiery Irishman whose adventures in far-off places were so exciting, whose photographs could be found in the pages of magazines. That he troubled himself to cajole and instruct them appeared to them remarkable.

"It's good of you to take an interest," Vivian told him. "I believe they're half in love with you."

"And are you?" he asked suddenly.

"Am I what?" she parried.

"In love with me?"

"You know I am."

"I hope so," he said, adding plaintively, "Sometimes you don't seem like the girl I used to know at all."

"Nonsense," she responded.

But she knew she wasn't that girl anymore. Mallory had changed her. The salon had changed her. Success had changed her. Assurance was in her step, confidence in the curving smile. She went next door to Mr. Boyd, the tobacconist, and arranged to expand her establishment by renting the floor above her salon. Dazzled by proven performance, he drew up a lease, no questions asked. Harriet Flanagan recruited three new apprentices who aspired to be more than lady's maids, and Vivian settled them in Mrs. Benson's boardinghouse.

Busy about so many enterprises, she had little time to moon over Jamie's now-you-see me, now-you-don't arrivals and departures. And she had made a discovery: she was more relaxed when he was away. The ecstasy he now expected her to reach in their lovemaking eluded her completely. Since that fateful Sunday afternoon in March she had been unable to abandon herself in his arms, and the performance she felt constrained to give left her out of sorts and secretly resentful.

Was she not, she wondered, to experience again the bliss she had once known with Mallory? The question was about to be answered, but in a way she would never have wished.

45

Mary Claire was to be married.

The news arrived at the end of August. Returning from the salon one broiling hot day, Vivian found her sister's letter among the pile awaiting her on her desk in the cool, dim parlor, at whose windows awnings had been lowered.

Hastily scanning it, she glanced at Jamie, who sat on the divan reading and sipping iced tea. "Mary Claire is to be married," she said.

"Oh?" responded Jamie. "Who to?"

Vivian sank down beside him. "Well now, let me see. It says, 'I expect everyone to approve, for he is the most adorable of men. Robert Harris is his name, but we all call him Bobbie. He's ever so cute and not the least snobby for being so rich. He's not an R.C., but he's a fine person all the same. We plan to be married in the rectory at St. Bonnie's on Saturday, the fifteenth of October. The wedding will be small—just the family and Max Delacey, because Max introduced us. But I plan the reception to be large. Lots of my chums will be coming from New York. Maybe even Mr. Ziegfeld. I'll write more later. But, Vivvie, I would be grateful if you'd reserve the ballroom at Le Pierre for the reception at twelve noon . . .' "

"October fifteenth," said Jamie, when she came to the end. "Damn!"

Disappointed that the successful suitor had not been Max Delacey, as she had expected to learn, Vivian looked up, bemused, and then remembered Jamie's photography show in New York.

"Wouldn't you know," he groaned, leaving the divan. "October fifteenth, out of all the days in the year! Do you think it can be changed?"

"Your show?" asked Vivian uncertainly.

"Lord, no! Lulu Miller laid that on months ago. October first to the fifteenth. That's sacred."

Vivian looked at the letter in her hand. "I wouldn't want to ask Mary Claire to change her wedding. Do you," she asked, "feel you must be at your show until the very last day?"

Jamie raised helpless hands and let them fall. "What can I say? I mean, of *course* I'll arrange to come back a day early if you *insist*. It's just a question of how important this is to you. I'm sure Mary Claire won't mind my absence in the least."

"But I will," said Vivian stubbornly.

"Isn't that what I'm trying to say? Not," he added, "that you'll have time to miss me, with all the fuss. But it's up to you. You decide. I can get a train back to Philadelphia first thing Saturday morning if that's what you want me to do."

"Saturday morning?" Vivian caught her lip between her teeth. "But there ought to be a little family celebration the day before. I'm thinking we might entertain at a small dinner here on Friday evening."

"You mean you'd want me for that, too?"

She had, she saw, pushed her luck too far. "No, no! Not for the dinner. You needn't return for that. Take the train on Saturday morning, that will be fine. And, Jamie, you'll take lots and lots of pictures, won't you?"

He brightened, she was glad to observe, since she had no wish to have her happiness at Mary Claire's engagement dampened by one of her husband's dark moods. Up until this moment she hadn't realized how anxious she had been about the temptations to which the life of a beautiful show-girl must expose one. Much as she admired Max Delacey, she had been well aware marriage might not be uppermost in his mind. That, far from compromising her sister, this charming and attractive gentleman had played match-maker brought Vivian to her knees in thanksgiving that evening. After all, even though St. Jude hadn't quite managed to arrange the impossible, he had surely come close.

✦ ✦ ✦

As in all major events of Vivian's life, Gert Barkin was there with assistance.

It was Gert who helped arrange for the reception at Le Pierre; who found the perfect wedding gift: a charming anniversary clock fashioned in brass and resplendent under a glass dome; who helped Vivian select the dress that, as Mary Claire's only attendant, she would wear: a gown of primrose silk taffeta trimmed with antique lace, bands of brown velvet ribbon defining the narrow waist. She would fasten three ostrich tips in her hair.

"Unless you want to borrow my tiara," offered Gert. "You know that gold tiara I got?"

"Thank you, Gert. The ostrich feathers will be fine."

"You should have some jewelry."

"I'm going to wear the pearls you and Harry gave me. And Mallory's emerald brooch."

"You'd have a lot more stuff if only Mallory had lived longer. More jewelry, you know what I mean?"

"Soon I'll be able to buy some for myself."

"Yeah, but what fun is that?"

Gert was right, thought Vivian absently. Buying jewelry for oneself wouldn't be much fun, but it was the only way she'd ever acquire any. Even were he able to afford it— which he certainly was not—Jamie would never think to buy her such things. He simply wasn't a romantic. Much less jewelry, she had long since stopped looking for those little surprises Mallory had regularly brought home: the bunch of flowers, box of candy, amusing trinket.

But as she reminded herself, Jamie was thoughtful in other ways. In the past summer he had frequently taken her brother Bucky off with him on photography jaunts. "Get him away from those Bryce Street Alley Rats" he said.

The suggestion was not without the little tinge of self-interest that Vivian was beginning to note in all Jamie's ways. With the amount of equipment a photographer must carry, Bucky's presence would come in handy. Still, Jamie had given the boy an old camera and taught him how to use it. In consequence, Bucky was more likely to be off taking pictures these days than getting into trouble. Did it matter, then, that Jamie didn't bring her gifts?

✦ ✦ ✦

Three days before the wedding, a chauffeur-driven
black limousine appeared at the front door of the Randall
house on Butler Street and Mary Claire stepped stylishly
from it, a white ermine toque on her blue-black hair, a
matching scarf topping a bright purple wool suit tailored to
that perfection of which Florenz Ziegfeld might well approve.

That evening found the two sisters perched once more
upon the lumpy bed in the room they had shared for so
many years.

"I don't mind for me if his snobby parents won't come to
the wedding," Mary Claire was saying. "I mind for Bobbie."

"Have you met his parents?" asked Vivian.

"They don't want to meet me. They don't want anything
to do with me."

"That may change with time," said Vivian, thinking of
the Webb household. "Wait until a child or two comes
along."

"Who cares?" responded Mary Claire in a tone that announced that clearly *she* did. "Like I say, it's for Bobbie
that I feel it. He's so darling, Vivvie. So larky. But he has
his serious side, too. Life isn't all just fun and games, y'
know."

Vivian could only hope she concealed her astonishment
at the source of this wisdom. Fetchingly clad in white batiste gown and wrapper, curls caught up in a cherry-red
ribbon, Mary Claire let her brow clear. "Of course," she
continued, "it's lucky Bobbie has lots of money in his own
name and doesn't have to look to his parents. A grandmother left him a furniture factory in Grand Rapids,
wasn't that nice? *Santé, grand-maman!* That's what Bobbie
always says." A relieved little sigh escaped her. "I pray for
the repose of that woman's soul every night of my life."

The telephone call came on Friday night just as the
small dinner party—the Randalls, the Barkins, Mary
Claire, Bobbie Harris, and Max Delacey—sat down at Vivian's candlelit table. Its imperious summons sounded
through the house, and moments later Halls appeared at
Vivian's side. "It's Mr. Fitzhugh, ma'am," he murmured.
"He'd like a word with you."

"Please tell him we've just sat down."

Halls departed, only to return immediately. "Mr. Fitzhugh is most anxious to speak with you, ma'am. He says it's an emergency."

Directing Halls to remove her own first course of smoked salmon and caper sauce, Vivian urged her guests to begin, and hurried to the telephone in the hallway.

"Vivvie dearest, forgive me," said Jamie. "I know it's the worst possible time to call. But Lulu has just told me Stieglitz is coming to see my show tomorrow afternoon."

At the famous photographer's name, Vivian's heart leapt. "Stieglitz! Jamie, how wonderful for you!"

"Isn't it? But the thing is, I should be here to greet him. I mean, it would be insulting if I weren't, don't you agree?"

"Oh, Jamie!" she wailed, grasping the point of his call.

"Look, Vivvie, I won't stay if you don't want me to; not if you want me back home. But . . . well, that's why I'm calling. If you want me to take the train back to Philadelphia tomorrow morning, just say the word."

"Oh, Jamie!" she said, and sighed.

"How is everything going?" he asked somewhat irrelevantly into the silence. "Did everyone get there tonight? Your parents? Delacey?"

"Yes, yes. Everyone."

"Well, what do you say? About tomorrow I mean."

"I don't *know* what to say."

"Look, sweetheart, you can't keep your guests waiting for you forever. I wouldn't have called except . . . Well, who would have thought Alfred Stieglitz would come to a show of mine? He's got that magazine, too. It could mean some interesting assignments. But . . . well, I guess you want I should come home, so . . ."

"No, no," she said quickly, her mind made up. "No, I'm sure you should stay. It's a very great honor. I'm sure you should be there. It wouldn't be right, not."

"That's what I've been thinking. But it's up to you. If you want me to come home . . ."

"No, Jamie. Of course you must stay. I want you to."

"Well, if you're really sure . . ."

"I am."

"All right, then," he said, reluctant, now. "You tell Mary Claire I'll be thinking of her."

"Yes."

"Love you, Baby."

"Yes."

"And?"

"And what?"

"Don't you love me, too?"

"Of course."

"Then tell me so."

"Jamie, my guests . . ."

He chuckled softly. "Say it."

Embarrassed, she whispered the words and hung up, returning to the table flustered and distracted. Inquiring eyes sought hers, but Max Delacey was talking about an archaeological dig he once had joined in Egypt and, to Vivian's relief, proceeded with the story.

Meanwhile, Halls bore in the second course, displaying to the table a fragrant crown roast, each chop dressed in a white paper frill, the center filled with Clarissa's excellent bread dressing and topped with glazed carrots. Having served this, Halls poured a chilled Anjou rosé into each glass, regarded the table with satisfaction, and retired to the kitchen.

Candlelight played on faces, glasses were raised in toasts; everyone was affable and smiling. Vivian was grateful for these high spirits, inasmuch as she seemed unable to focus her attention upon the happy scene. Trivial though it might be in light of the great honor being done Jamie, she was more annoyed by his telephone call than she had let on.

It did no good to tell herself she was being unfair, to remind herself that she had urged him to remain in New York, assured him this was the best plan. Resentment filled her, coupled with a sense of abondonment so all-consuming that she was no longer aware of the conversation at table, of the lovely rum cake that Clarissa had baked in a heart-shaped mold and garnished with a rich hard sauce dotted with candied violets. Only the euphoria that infects celebrants on the eve of a wedding permitted Vivian to ride the crest of the wave with so little participation.

But not, it appeared, without bringing herself to the attention of Max Delacey.

"Mrs. Fitzhugh," he said, under cover of the general high spirits, "would I intrude if I asked what has happened? You seem distressed, and you've touched scarcely a morsel of food."

Surprised out of her dark ruminations, Vivian said, "Oh,

Mr. Delacey! How observant you are. It's nothing, really. Just a bit of inconvenient news from my husband. He had meant to take the early train from New York tomorrow in order to arrive in time for the wedding. Now he finds he must absent himself altogether. Mr. Alfred Stieglitz will visit his photographic display in the Village, and my husband must be on hand to greet him."

"Stieglitz? That's a great honor."

She managed a smile. "So I keep reminding myself."

"Your sister has told me Mr. Fitzhugh is a fine photographer, but I've not had the pleasure of coming across any of his work."

"There's lots in the studio. Would you care to have a look?"

"Very much."

"After dinner, then."

And so it was that, leaving the gentlemen at table to their cigars and brandy, and seeing the ladies settled in the parlor where Halls would serve them coffee and liqueurs, Vivian led Max Delacey out the back door and down the walk to the carriage house and Jamie's studio.

She wore a gown of cream-colored rosepoint lace. The lace formed a pattern of leaves and flowers over the entire gown, which was of a fitted style with a high boned neck and long, tight sleeves. She picked up her skirts, the better to walk, and Max Delacey's firm hand came instantly to her elbow. The night was chill but clear, with a moon so bright as to cast shadows. Everything stood out sharp as an etching. Struck by such magnificence, Vivian stood stock still. "So beautiful!" she murmured.

"Yes."

Impelled by a quality in his voice, she glanced up sharply, to find him staring down at her with an intensity that took her breath away. She had no idea how long she stood there as he towered above her, his grip tight on her arm. It was, she knew, only with difficulty that she wrenched her gaze away. The very ground seemed to have shifted, and her step was no longer steady as she proceeded along the path, every fiber of her being acutely, quiveringly alive.

The heels of Max Delacey's shoes rang out on the slate walk; his shoulder grazing hers was a caress. Reaching the carriage house she lifted the latch on the side door and stepped within, readily finding the light switch by the stairs. She paused then, while in her blood thundered a message: Go back to the house, go back. She turned to him to suggest this, and met his eyes riveted upon hers, the crease between them deep as a gash in the harsh overhead light that illuminated the staircase.

In utter frankness she met this gaze, and knew she hadn't the least desire to return to the house, that the insistent force that gripped her demanded to be served; refused to be denied as it had been for so long. Turning, she purposefully mounted the stairs, the silence broken by each inexorable footfall. At the top she snapped off the light.

Moonlight streamed into the room in a bright, broad band, picking out potbellied stove, trestle table, mattress. Her heart fluttered wildly, and she ran a tongue over dry lips. She stood looking at him, unable to make him out as more than a shadow, silent, unmoving. Then, just as she gave up all hope of a response, he reached out and drew her to him, straining her against the length of him as at long last his lips came down upon hers.

46

"I've wanted you, Vivvie, from the first moment I set eyes on you," said Max Delacey.

"Don't!" she cried. "Please, don't! That's no excuse for . . ."

"It's not a question of excuses," he cut in gently. "We neither of us intended what happened last night. You must remember that. But it was wonderful and good. You must remember that, too."

She stifled a small moan and turned from this elegant stranger—this lover—on the divan beside her. Outside, in the late afternoon, his shiny black Daimler waited. It still bore the white crepe paper streamers appropriate to the conveyance of a bride and groom. In it, Max Delacey, with Vivian as matron of honor by his side, had driven Mary Claire and Bobbie from the rectory of St. Bonaventure's to

their wedding reception at Le Pierre, and thence to the
Delaware Avenue docks and the ocean liner that would
carry them off to Europe on their honeymoon.

Standing among the crowd of well-wishers, Vivian had
told Max Delacey that the Barkins would see her home.
She hadn't met those gray eyes she felt upon her. Could
she ever meet anyone's eyes again?

"I insist upon seeing you home," he had responded,
voice low but unmistakably determined. "I must speak to
you at least this once. Surely you owe me this."

She had agreed, not knowing whether to do so was right
or wrong, having lost all sense of right and wrong in the
abandon with which, the night before, she had heedlessly
indulged herself.

"I've thought about you ever since we met," Max was
saying now, and in some cool, detached part of her, she
thought what a fine gentleman he looked in the meticulously tailored frock coat, how at ease and confident as he
sat beside her attempting to explain the inexplicable, the
unthinkable, the unforgivable.

"I plied Mary Claire with questions about your whole
family," he continued. "Your parents, your brothers, the
Randall girls. By the way," he asked teasingly, "why weren't
the Randall girls at your dinner party last evening?
Isn't a wedding a good time to patch up family quarrels?"

"Mr. Delacey—"

"Vivvie, don't!" he said swiftly. "Don't spoil it. I could
do that, too, and with more reason: a guest in the house,
availing myself of the mistress while the master is away,
grossly abusing the hospitality shown me. But I'll not do it.
Last night was enchanted. I've never met a woman like
you. So beautiful, so good."

"Good!"

"Yes, Vivvie. You are good. Goodness shines out of your
eyes as though there's a lighted lamp inside you."

"Oh, please!"

"It's true. I can't tell you how much I admire what you
have done with your life; how you coped after your first
husband was assassinated; the success of your salon. I can't
imagine my sisters, the women friends I know, doing what
you have done."

Could he imagine them creeping up the stairs of the carriage house? Making love with a man they scarcely knew?
Thinking nothing of husband? Family? Marriage vows?

Not likely. For this, one looked outside one's class to a former lady's maid. Oh, the shame of it! Abruptly, she rose. "Please go now."

He rose, too. "Vivvie . . ."

"I don't blame you for what has happened," she said coldly. "Only myself."

He moved to grasp her hands. "Vivvie, you mustn't—"

"Please!" she interrupted curtly. "I'll see you to the door."

For a moment he stood looking at her, concern in his eyes. Then he said gently, "That won't be necessary. I'll see myself out."

The church was dark and full of whispers. Only the lighted vigil lamp glowed in its ruby red glass cup. On either side, in the shadows, were statues: St. Bonaventure, St. Joseph, the Virgin Mary. Banks of votive candles burned before the statues, their sweet, waxy odor heavy in the air.

Vivian knelt on the hard wooden kneeler in the inky blackness of the confessional. The palms of her hands were sweaty. She could hear Father Shields counseling the penitent in the stall on the other side, hear the murmur of their voices, the heavy sighs.

When the wood partition on her side slid open, she jumped in surprise and struck her nose against the screening. She made the sign of the cross. "Bless me, Father, for I have sinned."

Father Shields sat in the dark on the other side of the little window. He inclined his ear to the screen but he didn't turn to her. Priests in the confessional always looked straight ahead, although you knew they could usually tell who you were by your voice. Some people traveled miles from their parish to get to a priest who wouldn't recognize their voice.

"I've been with a man not my husband," she said, bracing herself for the condemnation that must surely follow.

But Father Shields said mildly, "Was this once, child? Or many times?"

Mortification overcame her. Could he believe such transgression was frequent! Did he think that she, Vivian Fitzhugh, baptized by him, taught by the nuns, twice married at the altar . . . Did he think that she often forgot the vows she had made? But if once, why not many times?

"Once, Father," she answered, cheeks flaming in the dark.

"And will you be seeing this man again?"

"Never, Father." Those gray eyes under the thick brows, the kind concern in them, the tenderness . . . "No, never."

"Does your husband know?"

Her husband! My God, was she supposed to confess to him, also? But she wouldn't. No, never. Not if she were refused absolution and must therefore burn eternally in hell fire.

"I'll not tell my husband, Father."

"That is kind and wise."

She hadn't expected approval. Gratitude welled up in her.

"For your penance say the Five Sorrowful Mysteries of the Rosary every day for one month. Meditate on the purity of Our Lady, and the example she has set for us all. Think of the Holy Family and the sacredness of the marriage bond. But do not permit yourself to dwell on the past nor belabor yourself for the sin you have committed. Resolve to put it behind you, for you have no right to be more unforgiving than He Who in His infinite mercy forgives you. Now make a good Act of Contrition."

" 'Oh, my God,' " she dutifully whispered, " 'I am heartily sorry for having offended Thee. I detest all my sins because I dread the loss of Heaven and the pains of hell. But most of all because they offend Thee, my God, Who art all good and deserving of all my love . . .' " As she continued the ancient prayer the priest's words of absolution washed over her, and peace of a sort stole into her soul.

But it was hard, she discovered, not to dwell on the past. Jamie returned from New York ebullient with the success of his show, with his meeting with Stieglitz, which had resulted in an assignment. He was filled with remorse at having missed the wedding and profuse with apologies, which fell uncomfortably on Vivian's guilty ears.

She lived in dread that she might have become pregnant. Jamie wanted no more children.

"You have Irene," he would say. "And I have Danny."

"But you never see him."

"Nonetheless, he fulfills any need I may harbor to replicate myself. Let's face it, Vivvie, I'd hardly have the freedom to roam about as I do if I got you with child."

Knowing his feelings in the matter, how had she dared risk becoming pregnant with the child of another? Soon, however, she could forget such worries. No danger, either, of having Max Delacey turn up again in her life. Late in November, when Mary Claire and Bobbie returned from Europe, they stopped off in Philadelphia before going on to Grand Rapids.

"Guess what," said Mary Claire offhandedly, "Max Delacey has got himself engaged."

Vivian caught a breath. "Oh? To whom?"

"Some New York society girl. Bobbie won't be able to take time off to come back for the wedding, more's the pity. It will be quite a bash."

"When is it?"

"February ninth."

On Sunday, February 10, 1907, Vivian, coming home from mass, made it a point to purchase a copy of the *New York Times*. There, in the society pages, was an account of Max Delacey's marriage to Nadine Townsend Folinsby, daughter of Mr. and Mrs. Hobarth Folinsby of Newport and New York City. A picture of the bride accompanied the story: a pretty young woman with dark hair, the hint of a smile on her lips.

Vivian read every word. The next day, tidying up the parlor, Halls found the newspaper tossed aside, and threw it away.

47

Countries were building battleships. The United States sent its Great White Fleet on a cruise around the world: sixteen battleships, 12,000 men. But the United States was not alone. The arms race was on. Britain, France, Germany, and Russia were increasing their armies with almost the same speed with which they signed alliances: the Triple Alliance, the Anglo-Japanese Alliance, the Dual Alliance, the Entente Cordiale.

Meantime, business continued good everywhere, and wonders never ceased. Thanks to Mr. Henry Ford and his new idea of an assembly line, the luxury of a Model T was now available to the average man. The *Lusitania* crossed the Atlantic in five days; the Wright brothers perfected their airplane; the Great Caruso could be heard on a phonograph record right in one's living room. There was no end to the things one could buy, and no end to the money with which to buy them.

In 1909, two years after expanding her business establishment by utilizing the floor above the salon, Vivian turned her attention to the house she had been renting, and decided to purchase and expand that, also. It was convenient to her work but too small for the family's needs, so she had a large addition put on the back.

Jamie took no part in this. Vivian had become used to his disinterest in domestic matters; at times she even relished the fact that he made few suggestions and let her do as she pleased. How burdensome if, like the ladies who came to her salon, she must needs consult a husband at every turn. But it could be equally onerous to have sole responsibility for everything. Jamie, however, complaining of the inconveniences of living through the renovations, took himself off to Paris, and she hurried over to join him there when he wired that she simply *must* come learn the new way of curling hair called the Marcel.

His instincts about her business proved excellent. Introduced into her salon, the Marcel wave was an immediate success, as was the glamorous aura the trip cast upon her own persona. Women liked to feel they wore the latest Paris coiffure. Things European, especially things Parisian, were regarded as infinitely superior to things *des Etats unis,* and during the next few years Vivian returned to France from time to time.

With shrewd insight she understood the necessity for these trips, the value of the cachet they gave her. But she was always glad to have them over. Unlike Jamie, who grew easily bored and restless at home, Vivian discovered she didn't really like to travel. Cathedrals and museums all day and, in the evenings, studio parties filled with cigarette smoke and incomprehensible arguments on subjects such as the nature of Man, of Time, of Heredity versus Environment, wearied her. She couldn't make sense of such things nor see any reason to bother one's head about them. She much preferred the challenge and stimulation of what she considered the *real* world, and spent her happiest hours in her salon, or with her daughter Irene.

As the child grew older, Vivian could see Mallory in her more and more. Sometimes the likeness was so sharp it took her breath away, for the resemblance was more than physical. The little girl displayed Mallory's warmth, his tenderheartedness.

"I miss him, Gert," she said. "Miss him still, after . . . What is it now? Almost eight years?"

"He'll never be dead while Snow White is alive."

Vivian smiled. "I treasure that likeness in her; treasure *him* in her. And yet I didn't love him when I married him."

"Mallory was one of your more lovable types. You take Jamie, now . . . Yeah," amended Gert sourly, "take him. You can have him."

Vivian laughed as she was meant to do, but it troubled her that the past few years had brought her husband and the Barkins no closer.

The truth was, the Fitzhughs as a couple possessed few friends in common, just as they shared few activities. One couldn't, after all, expect to have everything, and Vivian would be the first to admit to having a great deal. No other woman of her acquaintance ran a successful business, or had a husband who had achieved the national—more, the international—prominence that was beginning to be Jamie's. Distinguished visitors climbed the stairs to his studio in the carriage house these days; well-paying popular publications sought his work, admiring neophytes his advice. Still, she was finding it increasingly difficult to come to terms with a marriage more anomalous than most.

Jamie was away more and more often, consulting editors, giving illustrated lectures on social conditions, taking pictures hither and yon. Their friends weren't the same. His, Bohemian types for the most part, visited him in the studio; hers, usually local merchants and their wives, occupied the parlor. At times, saying he needed to be alone, Jamie would take it into his head to spend several nights in the carriage house, with the result that their paths didn't cross for days.

Proud of this arrangement, Jamie chuckled over the gossip it caused in more traditional circles, the eyebrows it raised. And he was fulsome in his praise of her success, congratulating her upon being unlike other women who, he said, would try to keep him "tied down"—the surest way, he declared, of losing him forever. But although she strove to retain his high opinion, Vivian sometimes found herself envying the closeness of those more prosaic marriages at which Jamie loved to poke fun.

Usually, however, she was far too busy to spend time fretting about such things. Her days started early. Up at six o'clock, she dressed and breakfasted with Irene, now a day scholar in the second grade at the Villa Maria Academy. Seeing the child off on the omnibus sent round to fetch her, Vivian briskly walked the short distance to the salon, reaching it punctually at seven-thirty, well in advance of the first appointments.

This little period at the start of each day afforded her time to speak to her girls, iron out any problems or difficulties, and see that all was in order. So it was that, arriving at the salon one morning in the fall of 1912, she found things at sixes and sevens, all her girls with long faces and Harriet Flanagan in tears.

"Oh, ma'am," Mavis told her, "Harriet must go off to help take care of her family in Washington, D.C."

"Harriet," said Vivian, "is this so?"

It was so, Harriet assured her, fresh tears starting to her eyes. Her brother-in-law had suffered a heart attack at "the works," as he called it, and had died, leaving her sister with five children, two elderly parents, and nowhere to turn.

"So I must go right away and lend a hand," she finished.

"Can't you move your family up here to Philadelphia?"

"Ah no, ma'am," replied Harriet. "I couldn't do that. My father and my mum have lived in St. Martin's all their lives, God love them. I doubt I could get them to leave their priest and their parish however hard I tired."

Recalling Ma Mallory's stubbornness in a similar situation, Vivian had no doubt Harriet was correct. "But what will you do in Washington?"

"I'm thinking I'll try first for employment in this profession I've learned. If there be no takers, I can always go back to lady's maid."

All day the possibility of Harriet's going back into service irked Vivian. The memory of her own experience as lady's maid returned in its dreary hopelessness. Much less no future, the position offered no present, living life, as one did, forever at second hand, looking forward only to continued servitude.

And was Harriet to sink back into this limbo? Indeed not! fumed Vivian, noting the young woman's expertise as a stylist, her warm confidence with patrons—all the result of six long years of patient effort on Vivian's part, never mind Harriet's contribution. Indeed not! Not if she had to march down to Washington, seek out hairdressing establishments, and speak up for the girl. Anyone who would employ Harriet would never be sorry. Why, the young woman could just as well run a first-class salon all by herself!

Like fireworks going off, the idea exploded in Vivian's brain. Why *not* a salon of Harriet's own in Washington? Why *not!* All it took was a bit of courage and the willingness to work hard. Harriet had long since proved these qualities. And she possessed a singular advantage. She would have Vivian to help her.

Shaken at the prospect, Harriet nonetheless agreed to the suggestion—more accurately, the command—that she open her own salon. It was Vivian's father, Edward Randall, who raised objection. Involved for the first time in his life in a successful enterprise, he was outraged at the proposal.

"Didn't I caution you that our fine Miss Harriet would one day start up against you?" he demanded of his daughter.

"Papa," replied Vivian, "I don't think we'll suffer the effect of competition from Washington, D.C."

He shook his head direly. "Why don't *you* be the proprietress and let the girl run it for you?"

"No, papa," said Vivian firmly. "People don't work for others with the same will that they work for themselves. They don't have their heart in it. I know this very well. Do you think I'd work so hard for my salon if I didn't own it? No, I've thought it all out and my mind is made up. It must belong to Harriet lock, stock, and barrel. But in return for my help and a loan to get started, she must promise to do things my way—use my Vivian Method and my products." She gave her father the impudent smile that made her look so much younger than twenty-six. "You always wanted to sell more of our lotions, papa. Now is your chance."

Jamie suggested she trademark the words *Vivian Method*. He also filed patent applications for the formulas he had developed for her, and it was his idea that Harriet's salon adopt the distinctive decor of the Philadelphia shop, down to the sheer rose-colored draperies at the window and the single gilt rose painted on the glass.

Grateful for his interest and filled with enthusiasm, Vivian boarded a train for Washington, D.C.

"Don't feel you must hurry back," Jamie said in parting. "Mavis and Rosalie will care for your ladies, and I'll be here at home with Irene. The thing you must do is see Harriet well established. Once that's done, you'll have a fine new source of income coming to you each month without lifting a hand."

Vivian had every intention of accomplishing just this. She wore the self-assured air bequeathed her in double measure by both beauty and success. Her sparkling green eyes now held experience as well as warmth, humor as well as mystery. Her clothes were of the best: a black silk faille suit worn over a black chiffon waist through which gleamed arms and shoulders. Its high, tight collar was constructed of bands of black satin ribbon separated by bands of sheer black net, the whole held in place just under her delicately modeled chin by two velvet-covered stays pointing straight upward to the lobe of either small ear. She carried a large muff of black sealskin, and an enormous black velvet picture hat with a black quill tucked on the underside of its brim was fixed charmingly aslant on her pompadour of burnished red hair.

Her appearance pleased her, but less out of vanity than satisfaction with the total effect she meant to create. This consideration had dictated the hotel at which she would stay—the Hay-Adams, one of Washington's finest—and the chauffeur and motor car that would await her upon her arrival at Union Station. Harriet had gone ahead to arrange these details.

"I've never been in such a fancy place before, ma'am," said this young woman several hours later, standing in the middle of Vivian's hotel room.

"Harriet," said Vivian crisply, "I forbid you to call me ma'am ever again. You are no longer my employee. We are associates. You must call me Mrs. Fitzhugh, and from this moment on I shall address you as Miss Flanagan."

"Nobody ever called me that in my life."

"Well, quite a few will be doing it now. Starting tomorrow morning when we visit Lady Bendel."

Vivian had had no intention of arriving friendless and alone to start a new business in a strange town. In order to establish Harriet quickly and successfully, she needed help, just as she herself had needed help several years ago.

And who was more likely to give it than the satisfied patrons of her own Philadelphia salon? All of these ladies knew and liked "Miss Harriet." Many were the young woman's regular customers, and most of them had two or three well-placed friends in Washington to whom they were more than willing to write little notes of introduction.

Lady Bendel, for instance, was a good friend of Tanis, the Lady Langhorne. In the hushed grandeur of her apartment in the Mayflower Hotel, she said, "My dear Mrs. Fitzhugh, Lady Langhorne has written me all about your wonderful new method. I can't *wait* to begin!"

Vivian smiled serenely. "Miss Flanagan and I," she murmured, "were wondering about a convenient location for the salon. Might you be able to suggest . . ."

"My dear, I haven't the foggiest notion of locations. But wait, now. You must just speak to my friend Mr. Harrison Connover, in the Connover Building. You must be sure to tell him the Lady Bendel sent you. Heavens, he'll find you a spot!"

Each day Vivian and Harriet started off, driven by chauffeured limousine, and everywhere they found that yes, Agnes had written, Josephine had written, Estelle, Louise . . .

"Vivian Method Comes To Town" ran a heading in the pages of *The Tattler*. There followed an interview with Miss Vivian of Philadelphia and Paris, innovator of a highly successful new treatment of the hair. Miss Harriet, exponent of that method, would be opening her salon soon . . .

"I don't mind telling you I'm near frightened out of my wits," said Harriet on the day she signed the lease on an acceptable property.

"Harriet," said Vivian firmly, "I know you're frightened. It wouldn't be human not to be. I was frightened, too, when I started out. But when you get to feeling that way, here is what you do." Taking the lease from Harriet's hand, she opened it. "You look at your name right up here. Harriet Flanagan, it says. It means you're the head of a business. It means you're in command. It means no one can tell you to come here or go there. But it means even more. It means that if I did it, you can, too. And if you can do it, so can Rosalie and Mavis and all my other girls."

She stopped abruptly, startled by her own words. Until this moment the thought hadn't occurred to her; but now she could see her Vivian Method and her lotions spreading all across the land. A tingle coursed through her and she grasped Harriet's arm, peering into the girl's awe-struck face with eyes that glowed. "Yes, Harriet," she whispered, "the future of dozens of young women now rests with you."

48

She hadn't heard about the collapse of a coal mine in West Virginia. She had been too busy in Washington to read the newspapers, too tired at night to do more than bathe and drop into bed. But now she was home, and here was Halls standing just inside the front door saying, "Mr. Fitzhugh, he said he had to get photographs of it, ma'am. He said it's such a disaster, so many lives lost . . ."

"How long has Mr. Fitzhugh been gone?"

"Five days, ma'am."

"And Miss Irene?"

Halls smiled broadly. "Miss Irene, she's fine. She's sound asleep in bed."

Vivian hastened up the stairs, pleasure at being home swept away by the news of her husband's absence. Stepping into her daughter's bedroom, she saw that the child slept peacefully, just as Halls had said. Vivian placed a light kiss on the smooth forehead and quietly departed.

But once she was outside the door, anger seethed through her. Jamie had promised to remain at home and keep an eye on Irene. It mattered to Vivian not a whit that the little girl was perfectly safe and well cared for. Jamie had given his word, and she had relied upon it. She had taken comfort in the thought of his presence in the house, imagined him having supper with Irene, reading her a story at bedtime, seeing her off to school. Instead, he had gone to West Virginia without so much as leaving her a note.

She caught herself up. Or was there a note? Had he left a message? Hurrying down the hall to their bedroom, she snapped on the overhead electric light that drained the dainty wallpaper and comfortable furnishings of their color. No, there was nothing on her embroidered linen bureau scarf, her vanity table. She turned to the brass bed and looked down upon the lace-edged pillows. Such a romantic repository. It was the place Mallory would have chosen to leave a message. But had she really thought to find a *billet doux* from Jamie there?

Annoyed at such foolish expectation, she went downstairs and pulled the bellpull in the parlor. "Did my husband leave a message for me?" she asked when Halls appeared.

"No, ma'am."

"Are you quite sure?"

"Yes, ma'am."

Of course Halls was sure. When had he ever forgotten such things? Fresh resentment filled her, and slipping out from nooks and crannies where for so long they had been denied and hidden came other instances of Jamie's fecklessness.

Each month he counted out ten ten-dollar notes and placed them on her bureau. From the start of their marriage this amount had represented his sole contribution to the household. She knew his earnings were not commensurate with his growing prestige, took into account that his expenses were high, his equipment, his travel—still, he never once had offered a bit extra, and although she could well afford their comfortable living, this rankled.

No man, she silently raged, had so few responsibilities. When, she asked herself, had she ever troubled him with a problem about the servants, about repairs, taxes, any of the other myriad details of housekeeping? The most obvious little chores he passed right by, never once thinking such things should concern him. And she had aided and abetted him in this. Yes, it was her fault as much as his. Small wonder he still jokingly styled himself her star boarder. But, Vivian decided, such humor had worn thin.

Thus it was that one night shortly after Jamie's return,

with Irene in bed and the servants finished with their duties, she set aside the accounts on which she had been working and looked up from her desk.

A small fire burned in the grate against the autumn chill, and Jamie sat reading in his chair, long legs crossed one over the other, the maroon smoking jacket he wore contrasting nicely with his dark hair. He had come to like the clothes Vivian bought for him as gifts from time to time. An expensive tweed jacket and plus fours was a favorite, as was this smoking jacket. His tastes had changed in other ways, as well. He now enjoyed carefully prepared food, fine wines, good cigars.

"May we talk a bit?" she asked.

Polite and well modulated, her voice nevertheless carried an edge of command that instantly brought Jamie's head up. "Certainly, my dear."

"I must tell you," she said, having memorized precisely how she would begin, "that I was most disappointed to return from Washington to find you absent, after you had promised me you would be keeping an eye on Irene."

Placing a marker at his page, Jamie closed his book. "I knew you were out of sorts these past few days," he said amiably. "I thought it was just some little business worry or other. I didn't dream I was to blame. I wish you had told me sooner, Vivvie. It doesn't help to stew over things." He shook his head. "No, Vivvie, that was wrong of you. Here I've been wondering what was the matter all this time."

"Well, now you know."

She hadn't meant to snap. She had intended to be as calm and collected as, no matter how trying the circumstances, she invariably remained at the salon. But somehow her husband's mild reproof invited the reverse of this. "You had given me your word," she continued testily. "I relied upon it. But when I returned . . ." Recalling that eager homecoming, her dashed expectations, her voice rose skittishly. "When I returned, I discovered you had been off in West Virginia for almost a week!"

"And Irene was perfectly safe and sound."

"That's not the point!"

"Of course it's not the point," agreed Jamie. "You feel let down. I can see that now, and I'm sorry. Very sorry. Even though," he added, "it seems to me you are making a mountain out of a molehill. After all, one small girl hardly requires more than a houseful of servants to look after her. I knew perfectly well that Irene would be fine. And I resent . . . Yes, Vivvie, I resent the fact that you can think I would have gone off otherwise. I happen to be fond of Irene."

He was like an eel slipping through a net. "We're not discussing your fondness for Irene," she said sharply. "We're talking about a broken promise."

He looked offended. "Ah, yes, a broken promise. I've just said I appreciate your feelings in the matter. But bear in mind it was a promise I made with the best will in the world and had every intention of keeping."

"But didn't."

"*Couldn't* would be more accurate."

"Please don't tell me you *had* to go to West Virginia."

"I felt I did. I felt I owed it."

"To whom?"

"To Lulu Miller. She sent me a telegram. She begged me to go down there and take pictures."

"And why," demanded Vivian, "would Lulu Miller want you to do that?"

"Because it was her old man's coal mine. Yes, Vivvie," he continued, a touch of righteous triumph to his voice, "her father's coal mine. Pinkerton men had been hired to keep the newspapers out. But being the boss's daughter, Lulu could sneak me inside. We're going to use what I got to help rally public support for the miners. Safety laws must be passed or, by God, this kind of disaster will be repeated again and again.

"I just wish," he said, the vein over one temple beginning to twitch—the pulsing vein that presaged one of his headaches, "I just wish you could have been with me, Vivvie. I wish you could have seen the look on a coal miner's weary, dirt-streaked face when he's lost his buddy. I wish you could have seen a miner's family waiting out beyond the shafts for a man who won't be coming back. But my photos will show you. My photos will expose to the world the inhumanity, the injustice, the conditions . . ."

He went on, growing more excited, talking, explaining, and Vivian nodded dully. Pinkerton men guarding the mines, newspapers kept out, public support needed, the poor miners . . . Such a good cause. She felt defeated, her sword sent spinning from her hand.

* * *

The photographs of the mine disaster possessed the stark poignancy for which Jamie had become famous. They whipped up considerable public outrage.

"Now you can see why I had to go," Jamie told her.

Vivian exclaimed over them, but with a zest she no longer felt. You're jealous of a camera, she scolded herself, and forthrightly turned her attention to her own absorbing life, and to Irene. The little girl apparently was destined to be one of those fortunate ones who does everything well. Especially quick with figures, she also displayed an aptitude for the piano.

"A talent she inherits from your sister, Mary Claire, no doubt," said the Reverend Mother when Vivian visited Irene's school.

Did this tranquil woman, Vivian wondered, know that Mary Claire's talent had led her to become a Ziegfeld Follies showgirl? "My sister," she said, "is married to a gentleman who has a furniture factory in Grand Rapids. She has two little girls."

The Reverend Mother nodded. "How time flies."

But here at the Villa Maria Academy it seemed to stand still. There was the same pleasant fragrance of incense and beeswax that Vivian remembered, the same soft drone of voices from the classrooms; at the open windows, in the mild April breeze, deeply hemmed white lawn curtains still gently rose and fell. It might have been eight years ago, with Mary Claire a scholar here, with Mallory still alive. Mallory . . . She knew now the missing would never end. "Irene's father would have been happy to hear your good opinion of her progress."

"Ah, Mr. Mallory, yes!" exclaimed the nun. "Such a fine man, God rest his soul."

"You remember him?"

"Indeed, yes. A great, strapping, hearty man. A handsome man. And able to get things done. I recall we needed a new slate roof. Such an expense! But he . . ."

Vivian hung on the words, a smile on her lips, bright tears dazzling her eyes. So few people mentioned Mallory's name anymore. Had they forgotten him? More likely they were afraid to cause her pain. But really, it was quite the contrary. She treasured the Reverend Mother's little tale.

* * *

Bunty O'Hare waited for her in a rented carriage under the Villa Maria's imposing porte cochere. Vivian had considered the purchase of a motor car, but Jamie didn't favor the idea. People, he said, became slaves to their autos, forever tinkering with them and doing this or that. He refused to be chained to a machine in such a way. Much simpler to hire a carriage, hail a hansom cab, catch a train.

At one time Vivian would have thought it a disgrace for a woman of means, such as she had become, to depend upon public conveyance. But now she merely smiled in tolerant amusement at the rather disreputable gig Bunty had been able to hire. The Reverend Mother's report on Irene had been good, the spring day was a fine one, and she settled back against the seat to enjoy the sunlight that sparkled and danced on the Schuylkill River, and the fragile beauty of the buttonwood trees coming into hazy leaf along Fairmount Drive.

When they reached the city, newsboys appeared to be everywhere, excitedly hawking their newspapers. Something was afoot, and Bunty drew up to a corner to learn the news.

"It's the *Titanic*," a youngster shouted. "It's gone down."

"Impossible!" gasped Vivian.

Half the world, it seemed, shared this disbelief. The largest, the strongest, the safest ship afloat, it was supposed to be unsinkable. How *could* it go down?

But as the hours passed, it became chillingly clear that the impossible had happened. In Vivian's salon her customers, many of whom had had friends or relatives on board, talked in stunned whispers, and as the missing became known, their names were on everyone's lips. Thus it was that Vivian overheard the name Delacey.

"Delacey!" she exclaimed, breaking her own cardinal rule never to comment. "Max Delacey? Drowned?"

A woman eyed her coolly. "Not Max. His wife."

49

She wrote him a little note of condolence. Tore it up.
Wrote it out again. A civil, impersonal little note, and she
received a civil, impersonal, little thank-you in reply.

Recalling her loss of Mallory, Vivian found Max Delacey's bereavement often on her mind. But such empathy
gave rise to other memories best forgotten if she were to
follow Father Shield's advice and not dwell upon the past.
And there was much in the present that required her attention. Encouraged by the success of Harriet's salon in Washington, both Mavis and Rosalie were eager to start their
own establishments, one in Boston, the other in Chicago.

"There's no reason why you should not," declared
Vivian, and once more followed the procedure that already
had proved so effective: "Rosalie is opening her own salon
in Chicago," she would confide to her Philadelphia patrons. "Mavis is opening a salon in Boston. They'll be using
my Vivian Method, of course, and my own exclusive products. Would you happen to have a friend or two in Boston?
In Chicago?"

And as each new salon opened, with its pink draperies,
its gilt rose, and its young proprietress primed with determination—"If I did it, if Harriet did it, you can do it,
too,"—orders winged back to Philadelphia for those magi-
cal soaps and lotions in what had become the Vivian line.

"You've outgrown the back room of the Tipperary," said
Jamie one day. "You'd better look around for a spot to
build a little chemical plant."

"Jamie, do you think I dare!" she gasped.

Jamie laughed. "You know very well you dare."

Once she had decided to go forward with this suggestion,
Jamie spent hours drawing up plans. Unlike the disinterest
he had shown in renovations on the house, the design for
her chemical plant appeared to engross him. Vivian was de-

lighted. She was learning, she told herself, to accept her husband as he was and not wish for changes.

"Indulge me!" he would cry out in exasperation if, at times, she complained of his cool disengagement from the daily demands of living, his absorption in his career. "I'm not like other men."

And hadn't she known this from the beginning? Hadn't she recognized his quixotic brilliance, his inventiveness, his differentness way back in the days when she had hurried down the alley to Morrissey's blacksmith shop? Wasn't this why she had married him?

But building a chemical plant involved more than dreaming up plans with T square and drawing paper, however fascinating. The myriad details that Jamie brushed aside with such impatience fell to Vivian, who consulted construction companies, compared prices, arranged financing, and spent hours inspecting possible sites.

Clinton Webb came to her assistance in this last, suggesting a half acre of ground out near the Webb woolen mills in East Falls. "You'll find a goodly supply of cheap labor," he told her. "East Falls people are hard workers and dependable. A plant built there will keep them close to home. They'll like that."

Under the deeply fringed silk lampshade that shed its glow over the parlor table, he spread out a map of the city. "You've got the railroad right down here, don't you see?" continued Clinton, tracing a line with a finger. "You'll be able to ship your Vivian products to every city in the country."

Vivian looked up at him inquiringly, the lamplight making a spun gold halo of her hair.

Clinton nodded. "Yes, Vivian, every city in the country. You do realize you have introduced a whole new concept of doing business. You do realize this, don't you?"

"What new concept?"

"Why, the scheme of setting up others in their own establishments, but insisting they use your method, the products you manufacture. That's never been done before."

"But it's so logical."

"Once you think of it. I'm serious, Vivvie. You are an extraordinarily clever woman. And you deserve all the success you've had, all you will have. It's only the beginning."

"Here, here now. She doesn't need all that."

They turned to the doorway to find Jamie lounging

there. He wore his maroon smoking jacket and held in his hand a glass of the wine he would continue to drink all evening.

"Clinton has found us our site," said Vivian, swift to cover the little awkwardness. "Come see."

"Not *our* site, Vivvie dear. *Your* site." He looked at Clinton. "I insist upon having no share in any property belonging to my wife. I am merely,"—He raised his glass— "her star boarder."

Vivian was puzzled. She knew Jamie wasn't feeling his liquor. He could hold gallons without showing it. He was pretending to be tipsy. But why? So he could feel free to be rude?

"Clinton," she continued smoothly, "says there is a goodly supply of cheap labor in the neighborhood. He says the people are hard workers and dependable. He says they'll like having their place of work close to their home."

Jamie sauntered over to the table. "Where is the site?"

"Right here," responded Clinton politely, pointing to a spot on the map. "One half acre."

Jamie turned away. "Not big enough."

"Really?" Clinton looked to Vivian. "I understood the building was to be approximately thirty-six hundred square feet."

"Right you are, Clinton, my boy," sang out Jamie from his chair. "But thirty-six hundred square feet on one floor."

"One floor!"

"That's right, old man. One floor. So people can look out the windows and see trees and grass. So on their lunch hour they can walk out the door and eat at picnic tables. So instead of feeling like mechanical dolls, they feel like human beings." He smiled. "How's that for a concept?"

"I must be going," said Clinton stiffly.

"Oh, what's the rush?" responded Jamie. "Stay a while. Have a drink. Speaking of cheap labor, tell me how you're doing with those slavies in your woolen mills."

"Jamie!" cried Vivian sharply.

Jamie eyed her balefully. "Sorry, my dear, but it *is* slave labor. Hard on the constitution, too. Eagleville Sanitorium is full of former employees of the Webb Woolen Mills. I'm wondering, Mr. Webb, have you ever made a donation to the sanitorium at Eagleville? Ever paid a visit? You should, you know. You'd see a lot of familiar faces there.

Many *pale* faces. That's one reason they call it the White Death."

"Vivvie, forgive me, I must go," said Clinton. "If I can be of any further assistance . . ."

"You *can* be of further assistance, since you ask," drawled Jamie. "You can keep your advice to yourself, and leave my wife alone."

The front door was scarcely closed on Clinton Webb when Vivian, hitching up her skirt, went pounding back up the stairs to the parlor. "And just what," she demanded, eyes snapping, "am I to make of that?"

But if fury blazed within her, Jamie was consumed by it. Leaping from his chair, he flung his wine glass into the fireplace, where it shattered into pieces. "You are to make of it just what I make of it!" he shouted. "Don't tell me you have lived with me all these years and can still put up with that pompous, insufferable philistine prattling along about how cheap you can buy your labor, how hard people will work for you. Oh, yes, and by the way, keep them close to home. If possible, arrange to own their homes so they are in your clutches not only for their jobs but for the roof over their heads. Christ, no wonder they work hard! No wonder they're dependable!"

He flung back his head. "Jesus God in Heaven!" Striding across the room he caught her by the shoulders, his fingers digging into the flesh of her arms, his dark eyes hot with anger, the vein on his temple jumping. "Vivvie, your chemical plant is going to be an example of the finest, the best working conditions known to man. It's going to have big clear windows and plenty of electric light, and stools so people can sit down to their work. And outside it's going to have trees and benches just like a park. And you are going to care about the people who work for you in the plant as you care about your girls in the salon. And there will be no cheap labor. You've got to pay a decent wage. Yes, Vivvie, you've got to remember you aren't a Webb, born with a silver spoon in your mouth and raised in luxury. You've got to remember your beginnings and think back to how hard you worked, how tired you got, how little you earned. You've got to remember, Vivvie. If you don't, who will?"

His rage had spent itself, leaving his face drained of color, stark, anguished. And as it had diminished so had her own passionate fury.

"Jamie, Jamie," she sighed. Reaching up, she gently

smoothed back a lock of hair. "Such a headache you'll be having."

She well understood her husband's sentiments about working people. How could she not? But there could be no excuse for his shocking treatment of Clinton Webb. At a loss as to how to make amends, Vivian decided the next day to be late for work and drop in on Nancy.

Young Clinton was already off to school, and Neil had left for the law office in which he was now a partner.

"Have a cup of coffee, at least," urged Nancy, recovering from her surprise at so early a visit, and ordered a tray brought to the front parlor.

"I just feel so perfectly awful about it," confessed Vivian, upon describing the deplorable little episode.

"Now you mustn't, dear," responded Nancy firmly. "I'm sure Clinton understands. He and papa are coming for luncheon this noon, and I'll make very sure to tell him of your distress."

"Nancy, would you? Really, I'd not blame him if he never spoke to me again."

"Come now!" cried Nancy lightly. "Clinton not speak to you! Why, there's no one of whom he thinks more highly. He's grateful to you, Vivvie. As I am. It's largely thanks to you that we're a family again. Except . . . except for dear mama."

Vivian's eyes traveled over the attractive room with its fine paintings and furnishings. Not relishing his lonely life, Dr. Webb had moved in with Anthea and Clinton, and the Cavendish Square house had been sold to a young couple with two little girls. Vivian could see many pieces from that elegant residence gracing, for a wonder, Neil Randall's parlor.

"Do you think," she asked shyly, "that Mrs. Webb . . . your mother . . . would have minded what has happened?"

Approve was what she meant, and Nancy was quick to grasp it. "She'd be delighted! All things considered, it turns out I've made a fine catch after all. Even papa grudgingly admits it. But who could have imagined Neil representing those wicked old 'interests' he used to rail against? And making sacks full of money doing it."

It *was* surprising. But a faint bitterness had laced Nancy's words. "You're not pleased with Neil's success?"

Nancy sighed. "Oh, he's worked very hard and all. Certainly I'm proud of him, but . . . Well, I could have married any number of young men who are doing just what Neil is doing." Suddenly she leaned toward Vivian, eyes alight. "Vivvie, don't you remember how Neil used to be? How determined to right wrongs? Save the world?" She sank back against the cushions, an exceptionally pretty young matron, dressed in an attractive blue hankerchief linen morning frock, presiding over a handsome sterling silver coffee service, and frowning unhappily.

"I don't know," she continued pensively, shaking her head. "When you start out in life, everything seems so clear, so simple. You know just how things should be, just what you're going to do. But then something happens. You discover there are a lot of things you haven't taken into account.

"I guess Neil still thinks of suffering humanity. But he wants the best for young Clinton—the best kind of school, the best kind of life. I want that too, only . . ." Her eyes fastened upon Vivian. "Your Jamie has stuck to his guns. He's refused to compromise. I've got to admire that."

Vivian forbore to mention that such tenacity was sometimes hard to live with. Her sister-in-law was but one of an increasing number of Jamie's admirers. This celebrity was due to factors over and above his way with a camera. A mystique had attached itself to him, invited by a certain Robin Hood drama in the causes he championed, enhanced by a daredevil quality in his dark eyes, an intensity that invested his long, lean body even in repose. He was noted for being at the spot where things were happening, and was destined to become more so, for with the new rotogravure section in the newspapers, and a world war about to start up, photography was to come into its own.

But war was the farthest thing from anyone's mind that fall of 1913. Philadelphia society returned from summers at Newport and Bar Harbor, and suddenly the Orchestra was in its season, Assembly dances were in full swing, and engraved invitations to art show openings sponsored by the stylish Philadelphia Academy of Fine Arts fluttered through the air. Business prospered, none more satisfactorily than Vivian's, its tooled leather appointment book a perfect barometer of the social climate.

Vivian found herself busier than ever, and happier than she had been in a long time. The need for frequent consultations with Jamie on plans for her cosmetics plant, the excitement of developing with him a new kind of building, fostered a closeness between the two of them that had been absent from their marriage. Theirs had been a marriage of opposites and they never had had much in common. But now they were united in this absorbing new project, and when, early in April, Vivian discovered she was pregnant, it seemed a fitting expression of the new dimension to their lives.

While not exactly jubilant, Jamie was not so opposed to the prospect of a child as Vivian had feared.

"I know you want another," he told her. "And with the money you're making we could support half a dozen, so there's no good reason not. Besides," he added, "maybe I'll like being a papa once he gets here."

Vivian smiled at Jamie's assumption. For her part, she would love the child, boy or girl. And pray that Jamie would, too. How many times had she not thought of little Danny, his son by Connie Mathews? Early in their marriage she had urged him to establish some contact with the child. So easy to pose as a friend of the family, make an occasional visit to be sure all was well with the lad. This suggestion, however, invariably met with such violent rebuff that at last she had given it up. But Danny was often in her thoughts, and always in her prayers.

By May, with frost out of the ground, work on the plant began in earnest. The site was just outside the city, a full acre lot with plenty of room for picnic tables. Three, sometimes four times a week, Jamie would pick Vivian up at the salon and drive her out for an inspection in the Model T he had, at long last, purchased.

It was on one of these trips in late June that they came upon a little group of workmen excitedly talking together. It meant nothing to either of them to learn that an archduke in Austria had been shot and killed.

50

In July, one month after the Archduke Ferdinand was assassinated by a Serbian national, Austria declared war on Serbia. Russia, Serbia's friend and protector, mobilized immediately, and so the Austrian Imperial Council declared war on Russia, too, and on France for good measure. Germany, eager for expansion, joined Austria in these declarations and, breaking its treaty with Belgium, drove through this small country, the better to surprise France. Britain, Belgium's ally, sprang to its defense. By August, all Europe was at war.

"Leave?" said Vivian. "For France? Now?" The incredulous words, addressed to her husband, were insufficient to express her disbelief.

Wearing a lacy negligee, she lay resting on her chaise longue, for her pregnancy had not gone well and, as when she carried Irene, complete bed rest had been prescribed. In the midday heat opaque green shades with fringed tassels and bands of handpainted pink roses had been pulled partway down against the blazing sun, and an electric fan droned. Jamie stood before her, in his hand the letter he had just received in the afternoon mail.

" 'Dear Mr. Fitzhugh,' " he read aloud to her, stumbling over words in his haste and elation. " 'The *New York American* would like you to leave for France immediately to take pictures of the European conflagration, and bring home to the great American public the first photographic documentation ever made of the ravages of war . . .' "

It was here that Vivian had interrupted, and Jamie raised his head to frown at her darkly. " 'It is our hope,' " he continued, " 'that you will accept this historic assignment, for in our considered opinion you are by all odds the first choice for such a mission. So great is our respect for your abilities that we are prepared to agree to any reasonable financial arrangement.

" 'Hoping this will elicit a prompt and affirmative response, I am . . .' "

"May I read it for myself?" asked Vivian.

With almost military bearing Jamie approached the chaise longue and presented the letter. Vivian scanned it, gathering her wits, playing for time. She had no doubt of Jamie's desire to accept the assignment.

"It's a great honor," she said at last. "I only wish you could go."

The bright enthusiasm with which, moments after the postman's ring, Jamie had bounded up the stairs to the master bedroom, was replaced by instant belligerency. "And why can't I?"

"You might get killed."

He laughed, relieved. "I've no intention of rattling around in the front lines, if that's what is worrying you."

How much simpler, she thought, to once again indulge him, send him off with her blessing. It was very likely he would indeed return safely. He wasn't foolhardy. The risks he took were always calculated. But she said firmly, "Then, too, there's the baby."

"Damn the baby!" he exploded. "This is just why I didn't want one!" Flinging himself from her, he clapped a hand to his forehead. "Christ, Vivvie, you make me say things I don't even mean."

Returning to sit on the edge of the chaise longue, he took her hands in his. "The baby will be fine," he assured her, his composure clearly an effort. "You have everyone here to help you when the time comes: Dr. Cassidy, Clarissa and Halls, your parents. What good is a husband at a time like that? Smoke cigars and pace the floor, that's all he can do, poor fellow." He gently cuffed her chin. "It's you who must bring it off. And you will. I know you will, just like a good little soldier. In six or seven weeks it will all be over."

She winced. After this, could anything be the same between them? "I have no doubt I will bring it off," she told him. "But I want you to promise me you will remain here at least until I do so. As you say, six or seven weeks."

"But in six or seven weeks the war may be over! And even if it's not, they want me to leave right away. You saw the letter. It says *immediately*."

His voice had a querulous whine. Strange she had never noticed it. "You must write and explain the circumstances."

"And let them send someone else?" Beside himself, Jamie rose once more to pace the room. "Vivvie, for God's sake be sensible. You must see I can't turn this down. You must see it's the opportunity of a lifetime. I'm not the only photographer in the world. They could have asked Lewis Hine, Stieglitz. But they asked *me*, Vivvie. Your husband. I'd like to think you'd be proud of that."

"I am, Jamie," she replied, ignoring the reproachful tone. "But it's not only the baby. There's also my cosmetics plant."

"As to that, there's no problem at all," responded Jamie, brightening. "All young Jerry Doheny need do is follow my plans. Be sure I'll leave him full instructions."

"And if he doesn't understand about something?"

"Why then he must just come and ask you."

"He is to come to my bedroom?"

Jamie ran a distracted hand through his hair. "He must speak to your father, then."

"To papa? Sure, papa wouldn't know one end of those plans from the other."

"Your cosmetics plant must wait, then!" shouted Jamie at last. "Wait 'til I'm back home again."

"No, Jamie."

Her voice was soft, but so imperious that Jamie cocked his head as though unsure he had heard aright. What wife, he seemed to ask, even with so permissive a husband as himself, dared such defiance? But this slender young woman with the clear implacable eyes, regal as a queen among her satin pillows, was saying yet again, "No. You can't go. I need you here.

"It has nothing to do with the child, really," she continued calmly. "The child will be born. It has nothing to do with my cosmetics plant. The plant will be built. It has to do with me and my need of you when my hour is come."

"You're not the only woman to have a child with her husband away at the wars."

"I don't care about other women!" she suddenly cried. "You've always left me just when I most needed you. Yes, Jamie, and you have!" she insisted in cold fury. "You left me first at Morrissey's blacksmith shop that night you ran out on me. You left me waiting for you at Ma's the night we meant to get engaged. You left me before Mary Claire's wedding, and because you did I . . ."

She stopped, choking back her words, dropping her face into her hands, refusing to flaunt his cuckolding.

Evidently mistaking this for weakness, Jamie smiled. "Well, well. Quite a speech, I must say. But somehow it fails to tug the heartstrings when I think of women who will never see their sweethearts and husbands again, when I think of men with arms and legs blown off—"

"Stop," she cried, refusing to be sucked into the morass of his words once more. "Don't tell me about women losing their sweethearts and husbands! I don't want to hear. Don't tell me about men with their arms and legs blown off. Don't tell me how hard it is for others, for right now it's hard for me as well. And if you won't stay by me, if you won't see I need you, then go! Go! But don't come back again."

That night Clarissa came into the master bedroom and packed a suitcase for him, and he went.

Vivian had known he would. He had left her so often. As she heard the front door close, tears filled her eyes. But not for him. There was nothing new about what was happening. Like her father, Jamie had never been there when she needed him. It was for Mallory that she wept.

51

The headline appeared on the front page. "Fitzhugh Dies."

How few people, thought Vivian, looking at it, are widely recognized by a single name. Jamie, of course, had been well known to readers of the *New York American*, having for the past three months filled its pages with photographs of war-torn Europe. But the Philadelphia newspapers had also used just the single name. Vivian couldn't help thinking how pleased Jamie would be. What a hallmark of the fame he so cherished!

Picking up the scissors, she carefully cut out the news story and placed it in a large pasteboard box on the floor beside her desk. For many evenings now she had occupied herself in this manner after Irene went to bed. She was gathering everything she could lay hands on to paste into scrapbooks for Jamie's small son who, watched over by Mrs. Swan, lay upstairs in his bassinet in the nursery. The scrapbooks, together with an enormous collection of Jamie's photographs, would be the only way Randall Fitzhugh would come to know his father.

Jamie had died not on the battlefield but in a chateau being held by the British in the bitter fighting around Ypres, his death the result of a recurrence of the malaria he had picked up in Panama several years ago. To Vivian's eternal satisfaction, he had received the news of Randall's birth before he took sick. One of the things she was preserving was a sealed letter from him addressed "To Randall, my son."

To her, his letters had been repetitions of things said countless times before. He begged her forgiveness, her indulgence, her understanding. He hoped the photographs appearing in the *New York American* would be his emissaries in pleading his cause.

She wrote to him only once, about the birth of Randall. She didn't say she forgave him.

"That's wrong, girl," said Mamie, shaking her head. "Suppose he's killed over there? We've all got to forgive."

Vivian leveled upon her mother a hard green gaze. "The way you have forgiven the Randall girls?"

Some days later her father said, "Your mother has asked the aunts to dinner."

"High time," Vivian observed.

By the end of January, all expressions of sympathy had been duly acknowledged. Most of the notes were from people she didn't know. But there were a few she especially treasured: a warm little note from her sister, Mary Claire; and notes from Dolly and Tom O'Reilly, Lulu Miller, even Thurman Foy and Morrissey. A card came from Connie Mathews—purple, with a white lily on the front. On the lily Connie had written Danny's name. Seeing it, Vivian felt a pang. Shouldn't there have been another letter "To my son"?

Max Delacey wrote. He had read of Jamie's death in the newspapers. His note was correct, polite. Vivian answered in like manner. Then, as once before, she tore it up and wrote it out again. She added a postscript. Was a postscript ever added to such things? "I hope if you are ever in Philadelphia, you will drop by."

After she mailed it off, she was sorry she had written it.

As always, Vivian found work a solace, and threw herself into it. The interior work on her cosmetics plant would soon be completed. Recognizing her accomplishments, the Chamber of Commerce invited her to become its first woman member, and she immediately accepted. Mavis, Rosalie, and Harriet were doing strikingly well with their salons, and Vivian had plans to open three new ones. Ma Mallory and Gert Barkin vied with one another caring for Irene, and Mrs. Swan was devoted to Randall. Everyone was thoughtful, everyone was helpful, everyone was kind.

And spring was coming. The days were getting longer. Vivian noticed this one Saturday evening toward the end of March as she was locking the front door of the salon. The sun lingered on the plate-glass window, burnishing the gilt rose beside her name. Turning homeward, her attention was caught by a long black Daimler pulled up against the curb. At the sight, she caught her breath and her hand fluttered up to the gray squirrel collar of the black coat she wore. As she stared, the door to the driver's side opened and Max Delacey stepped out.

Vivian wasn't aware of moving across the deserted sidewalk to meet him. It never occurred to her to ask a question or say a word. When he opened the door to the passenger's side, she got into the sumptuous vehicle. Max rounded the back of the car and slid in under the wheel. He turned to her then and smiled, and it was as though she had been sitting beside him forever. She didn't ask where they were going. She didn't care. All she was aware of as they moved smoothly off into traffic was that his hand covered hers.

Epilogue

On September 19, 1915, the following appeared in the gossipy pages of *The Item*.

The glamorous and gorgeously beautiful Vivian Fitzhugh of this city was married quietly yesterday in the rectory of St. Bonaventure's to Max Delacey, wealthy and socially prominent New York businessman.

The bride, we have learned, wore a gown imported from Paris, France. It was cut in the new chemise style and featured tiers of cream tulle, silver, and gold. With this she wore the Delacey pearls.

The new Mrs. Delacey was the widow of Jamie Fitzhugh, world-famous war photographer who died last year while on assignment in France. Before her marriage to Mr. Fitzhugh she was the widow of the late Brian Mallory, remembered as one of Philadelphia's most powerful political leaders.

Mrs. Delacey is famous in her own right as the innovator of the Vivian Method of hairdressing. She is the owner of Vivian's, off posh Cavendish Square, and has franchised salons in many other cities. Lest this not be enough, we hasten to add that she has built a cosmetics factory on the outskirts of our fair city where she will manufacture her Vivian line of hair lotions, and she was recently welcomed as the first female member of our noble Chamber of Commerce.

We have it on good authority that the bride will continue her business activities with the wholehearted support of her husband. Indeed, her next franchise will be assigned to a new salon in the Delacey Arcade on New York City's elegant Fifth Avenue.

Mrs. Delacey has a daughter, Irene, by her first husband, and a son, Randall, by her second. Mr. Delacey has two daughters, Gabriella and Dawn, by his first wife, Nadine Folinsby Delacey, who perished in the *Titanic* disaster.

After a honeymoon at Kimberly, the country estate of Senator and Mrs. Cavendish of this city, the happy pair and their family will take up residence in the home the couple have just purchased on Cavendish Square.

Ballantine's World of Historical Romance...

TA-13